SPRINGWATER
WEDDING

Also by Linda Lael Miller

Linda Lael Miller

Springwater Wedding

BOOKSPAN LARGE PRINT EDITION

POCKET BOOKS
New York   London   Toronto   Sydney   Singapore

POCKET BOOKS, a division of Simon and Schuster, Inc. 1230 Avenue of the Americas, New York, NY 10020

Copyright © 2001 by Linda Lael Miller

ISBN: 0-7394-1740-1

POCKET and colophon are registered trademarks of Simon & Schuster, Inc.

Printed in the U.S.A.

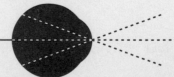

This Large Print Book carries the
Seal of Approval of N.A.V.H.

For my aunties

Marion Bleecker
Kay Paparich
Billie Wiley
Shirley Bleecker Bass
Lillie Kramer
Wanna Bartol
Donna Sly and
Winnie Lael

I love you all.

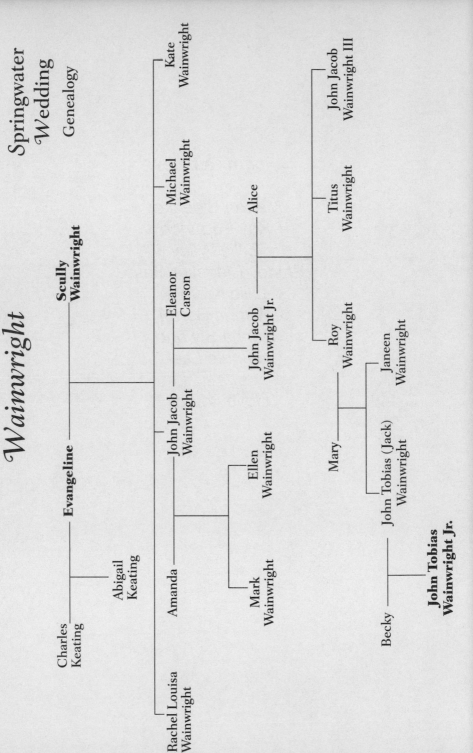

Wainwright

Springwater Wedding
Genealogy

Scully Wainwright

Evangeline

Charles Keating

Abigail Keating

Rachel Louisa Wainwright

Kate Wainwright

Michael Wainwright

Eleanor Carson

John Jacob Wainwright

Amanda

Ellen Wainwright

Mark Wainwright

John Jacob Wainwright Jr.

Alice

Titus Wainwright

John Jacob Wainwright III

Roy Wainwright

Mary

Janeen Wainwright

John Tobias (Jack) Wainwright

Becky

John Tobias Wainwright Jr.

McCaffrey

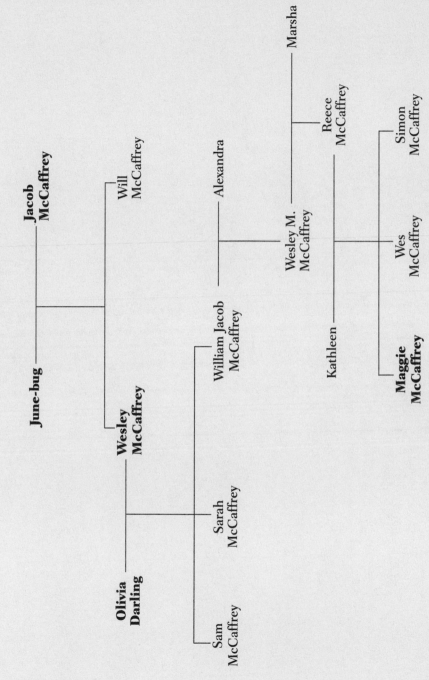

Jacob
McCaffrey

June-bug

Will
McCaffrey

Wesley
McCaffrey

Olivia
Darling

Sarah
McCaffrey

Sam
McCaffrey

William Jacob
McCaffrey

Alexandra

Marsha

Reece
McCaffrey

Wesley M.
McCaffrey

Kathleen

Wes
McCaffrey

Simon
McCaffrey

Maggie
McCaffrey

SPRINGWATER
WEDDING

1

Maggie stuffed the woody stems of a cloud of white lilacs into a gallon jar, and some of the water spilled over onto the counter in the kitchenette of her parents' guest house. "J. T. Wainwright," she said, with typical McCaffrey conviction and a wealth of personal experience to back up her theory, "is a whole new twelve-step program, looking for a place to happen. I'm trying to start a business here. Make a life for myself. I don't need that kind of trouble."

Daphne Hargreaves Evanston, her best friend since Miss Filbert's kindergarten class at the old schoolhouse, now an historical monument, like the Brimstone Saloon across the street from it, watched with a wry and twinkly smile as Maggie took a sponge from the sink to wipe up the over-flow. Married for the past two years, Daphne was glowingly happy and wanted to see all her friends find the same rather irksome bliss. "Oh, come on, Mags," she chided cheerfully. "J.T. was a little wild as a kid, but he became a cop, so he must have straightened out."

Maggie was stubbornly silent, and Daphne, who could be just as stubborn, fixed her with a mock glare.

"He *was* a cop," Maggie allowed in due time, and somewhat grudgingly. She straightened a little. "But since when is join-ing a big-city police force the equivalent of a religious conversion?"

Daphne shook her head and made a tsk-tsk sound. "Methinks thou protests too much, my friend," she said, folding slender arms. "J.T. was shot in the line of duty. He *must* have been committed to his job, to put himself in the path of a bullet."

Maggie hated to think of J.T.—or anyone else, she quickly pointed out to herself—struck down by gunfire, and she shuddered. Images of that lethal confrontation, far away in a New York City warehouse, had disturbed her sleep many a time over the six months since it had happened, although she'd been out of contact with J.T. for much longer.

"It must have been terrible," Daphne reflected somberly, giving voice to her friend's thoughts, as she often did. Sometimes Maggie believed she and Daphne had some kind of psychic connection; they'd been known to go shopping in separate cities, on different days, and come home with duplicate pairs of shoes. "All the pain and the blood, and then his partner being killed, too. Just like his father was. A person can only stand so much violence—it's no wonder he turned in his badge."

Maggie set the flowers in the middle of her grandmother's round oak table, the thump muffled by a lace doily. She was starting to feel sorry for J.T., and that would not do. When her heart softened, she'd discovered, so did her head.

"That's the official story, anyway," she said, with a little sniff. "That he turned in his badge, I mean. There are those who say J.T. only quit to avoid being fired, and you know it as well as I do."

Daphne sighed, plainly exasperated. "You don't really believe that," she said.

"J.T. has a temper," Maggie pointed out, losing ground fast and damned if she'd admit it. "Don't you remember the time he beat his uncle nearly to death with his bare fists? He nearly went to prison for that."

Daphne narrowed her eyes. "Yes," she challenged, "I remember. It was right after Clive Jenson threw his wife—J.T.'s aunt—down the cellar stairs!"

"Violence," Maggie said, fluffing the flowers, "does not justify more violence. You said as much yourself, just a few moments ago."

A brief silence fell. Then, "You're still interested," Daphne accused, delight dancing in her silver-gray eyes. Her face took on a dreamy expression, and she sighed again. "It was so romantic, the way he showed up at your wedding and everything—"

"You need therapy," Maggie said, still fussing with the lilacs. "It wasn't 'romantic,' it was downright awful." She closed her eyes, and the memory of that day a decade before loomed in her mind in three distinct dimensions and glorious Technicolor. She saw herself, clad in a simple white dress, standing beside Connor, her husband-to-be, on the gazebo steps. She smelled the lush, sweet scent of the pink roses in her bridal bouquet. She even heard the minister's voice again, as clearly as if he'd been standing right there in the guest house with her and Daphne:

"If anyone here can show just cause why these two should not be joined together in holy matrimony, let him speak now or forever hold his peace . . ."

Right on cue, J.T. squealed into the driveway behind the wheel of his rusted-out pickup truck, startling everyone, bride, groom, and guests alike. He jumped out of that old wreck, leaving the motor roaring, the door gaping, and the radio blaring a somebody-done-me-wrong song, and vaulted over the picket fence to storm right up the petal-strewn strip of cloth serving as an aisle. His ebony hair glinted in the late-spring sunshine, and he was wearing jeans, scuffed boots, and an old black T-shirt.

Given the fact that he'd been the one to end their stormy relationship more than a year earlier, when they were both in Springwater for Christmas vacation, J.T. was the last person Maggie had expected to see, especially on her wedding day.

Resplendent in lace and satin, Maggie watched, speechless, as J.T. strode up the aisle. Connor stood clench-fisted at her side.

Stunned by J.T.'s rejection the previous Christmas—she'd given him a blue sweater and he'd handed back a broken heart—Maggie had begun dating Connor almost as soon as she got back to college. They had a lot in common—similar tastes in music and art, the same political and religious beliefs—and Connor was handsome and smart, with a brilliant career ahead of him. J.T., on the other hand, was hotheaded and often self-absorbed, with all the earmarks of a lifelong misfit. He'd been in trouble with the law more than once, and there was a vast, dark terrain inside him, a place closed to everyone else on earth—Maggie included. Passion, she suspected, was all she and J.T. had ever really had together. Great, frenzied sex, followed by loud fights or sullen silences.

Previously stunned into horrified immobility, the wedding guests rose of one accord from their rented folding chairs to murmur and stare, and Maggie's brothers, Simon and Wes, edged toward the intruder from either side. Simon, serving his medical residency at the same Chicago hospital where Connor would intern, was dark-haired and powerfully built, while Wes, a junior at Montana State, majoring in elementary education, had fair hair and blue eyes. Reece McCaffrey, the patriarch of the clan, rose to his feet as well, though the expression in his eyes as he gazed at J.T. was one of compassion, not anger.

"You can't do this, Maggie," J.T. rasped, as Simon and Wes closed in, handsome and grim in their tuxedos, each grasping one of his arms. He shook them off fiercely, his gaze a dark, furious fire that seared Maggie's heart and made her nerves leap beneath the surface of her skin. "Damn it, you *know* it's wrong!"

She was unable to speak, for her breath had swirled up into the back of her throat, into an inner storm raging there, and her eyes were glazed with tears.

"J.T.," Wes said quietly, reasonably. Wes, always the cool head, the peacemaker. "Come on, buddy. You don't want to do this."

"Is he drunk?" Connor rasped. He was a few years older than Maggie, with hazel eyes and light brown hair that was already receding a little, and no discernible sense of humor. Of course, she hadn't realized that until much later.

J.T. was stone sober; Maggie could tell by the look in his eyes. He'd changed his mind about her, about them, and she felt a surge of furious sorrow. It was a little late, wasn't it? She'd wept over this man, walked through the fires of rage and a hurt so dizzying she'd feared it would overwhelm her. Where had he been when she needed him, wanted him?

Well, damn it, she'd come to her senses, where J.T. was concerned at least. Gotten over the pain, for the most part, and built a whole new framework for her dreams. Her course was set, her future was mapped out, one, two, three. She was returning to Chicago as Mrs. Connor Bartholomew. She planned to finish her degree at Northwestern, land an interesting job after graduation, and settle into a new life. Once Connor had finished his surgical residency they could buy a little house in the suburbs somewhere and start their family.

Oh, the best laid plans.

Staring at J.T., she shook her head, very slowly, still unable to get a word out.

J.T. shoved a hand through his dark, sleekly rumpled hair. "I made a mistake, Maggie," he said, his voice at once quiet and charged with emotion. "A bad one. Don't compound it by running away from what we were, what we had."

"Get out," Connor growled, red in the neck and along his jawline, and he started down the gazebo steps as if to lunge at J.T. To the manor born, and trained to keep his hands clean at all costs, Connor wouldn't stand a chance against Springwater's bad boy. Maggie caught hold of his arm.

She kept her gaze fixed on J.T. "It's over," she managed to say. Then she turned her back on him, once and for all, and set her face toward the future she truly believed she wanted.

How wrong she'd been.

Daphne wrenched her back to the here and now with a snap of her fingers. "Mags?"

Maggie made a face, but a grin was tugging at the corners of her mouth. She'd missed Daphne, she'd missed Springwater, and though she wasn't ready to admit as much, even to her closest friend—heck, she could barely admit it to *herself*—she'd missed J. T. Wainwright. Which just went to prove that even the most solid people had their weaknesses.

"Sooner or later, you're going to have to face him, you know," Daphne observed, opening the refrigerator and peering inside. She brought out a pitcher of ice tea, jingling with fresh ice cubes, and plundered the cupboards for crystal tumblers. "Springwater is a small town, after all. You won't be able to avoid J.T. forever."

Maggie drew back a chair at the table and sank into it. "Why did he have to come back here?" she asked, not really expecting an answer. A detective with the New York Police Department, J.T. recently had returned to Montana to run the sprawling ranch that had been in his family for well over a century. Beef prices were low, the home place was practically in ruins, and ranchers all over Springwater County were plagued, with greater and greater frequency, by rustlers and various sorts of malicious mischief, but J.T. evidently was undaunted.

That, too, was like him. He didn't make plans or draw up lists or consult experts. He just plunged in, worked hard, and improvised, taking things as they came. To Maggie, goal-oriented to a fault, that was the equivalent of riding a runaway roller coaster.

Daphne came through with a reply, as she filled a glass for herself and then, at Maggie's nod, another. "I guess J.T. came back for the same reason you did," she said. "Springwater is home. His roots are here."

"Home," Maggie echoed, a little wistfully. To her the term covered far more territory than just the big, wonderful old house on the other side of the long gravel driveway where she and her brothers had grown up; it meant Reece and Kathleen McCaffrey, her mom and dad. And after nearly forty years together, after three children and five grandchildren, with another on the way, they were sleeping in separate bedrooms and, when they spoke at all, discussing the division of property.

Maggie was baffled by the rift that had opened between them and, even though she knew it was not only impossible but downright dysfunctional too, she wanted desperately to fix the problem somehow, turn back time, make everything all right again.

Daphne sat down, then reached out to squeeze Maggie's hand. Her fingers were cool and moist from the chilled glasses. "Home," she repeated, with gentle emphasis. "You've still got one, you know, so stop looking so forlorn. Everything's going to be all right. You'll see."

Maggie attempted a smile, took up her ice tea, and clinked her glass against Daphne's. "Thanks," she said, and sipped.

"J.T. looks good," Daphne observed, only moments later, never one to waste time and verbiage bridging one subject with another. *"Really* good. Hot damn, what a body."

Maggie rolled her eyes. "Is that any way for a devoted wife to talk?" she teased. "What would Ben say?" Ben Evanston, Daphne's handsome husband, was a mining engineer. He and Daphne had met when his company had contracted to reopen the old Jupiter and Zeus Silver Mine, which was part of her inheritance, and married soon after. They'd immediately started trying to have a child, so far to no avail.

Daphne ran one perfectly manicured fingertip around the rim of her glass, her gaze lowered. In that quiet, unconsciously elegant pose, with her dark hair upswept, she resembled the portrait of her ancestress Rachel English Hargreaves even more closely than usual. Maggie glimpsed her own gaminelike reflection in the polished glass of the china cabinet against the opposite wall and noted the contrast. She was thirty years old, with short brown hair and large blue eyes, and outside of Springwater, people still asked for ID when she ordered wine with her dinner. She sighed.

When Daphne looked up, she was smiling mischievously. "I can still appreciate a fine specimen of man when I see one," she said.

Maggie laughed. "You're horrible," she replied. It was good to be home again, drinking ice tea with her best friend. She'd moved back to Springwater less than a month before, after selling her condo in Chicago and giving up a lucrative hotel-management job there, having at last made the decision to simplify her life, get off the fast track, and pursue an old and persistent dream of turning the old Springwater stagecoach station into a bed-and-breakfast. The move was long overdue—she'd essentially been treading water emotionally since the

breakup of her marriage two years before—
but she was still getting acclimated to all the
changes. Absorbed in her own plans and
projects, she'd been caught off guard when
J.T. suddenly returned to Springwater.

Daphne glanced down at the doorknob-
sized diamond on her left-hand ring finger
and frowned as it caught the afternoon light.
If someone onboard the *Titanic* had been
wearing that ring, they could have summoned help at the first sign of trouble.
Daphne's expression changed, and she
sighed.

"What is it?" Maggie asked, immediately
worried.

Daphne smiled bravely. "I thought I'd be
pregnant by now, that's all," she confided.

Maggie knew, had always known, how
much Daphne wanted a houseful of children. Even when they were little girls,
Daphne would play only with baby dolls—
no Barbies for her. "Give it time, Daph," she
counseled gently. "You haven't been married all that long."

Daphne perked up, nodded, but a
shadow of sadness still darkened her eyes.
"Right," she said.

"Everything's all right between you and

Ben, isn't it?" Maggie asked. With a failed marriage behind her, and a couple of going nowhere romances on top of that, she wasn't exactly an authority on love, but what she lacked in expertise she made up in concern. Daphne had lost both her parents in a plane crash while she and Maggie were still in college, and Ben was all the family she had. Family was everything to Daphne, and to Maggie, too, for that matter.

"Everything's fine," Daphne finally said, in reply to Maggie's gentle question, but she looked away. Presently, she spoke again. "Do you ever wish you and Connor had had a child?" she asked, perhaps to fill the silence.

Maggie prodded the blooms with one finger, bestirring their luscious scent. Connor and his new wife, Janice, had just had a baby boy, and while Maggie had few regrets about ending her marriage, she *did* feel slightly cheated. During the eight years she'd spent with Connor, her desire to start a family had been consistently shoved to the back burner. According to Connor, there was never enough time, enough money, enough anything. Janice, on the other hand, must have gotten pregnant on the honey-moon.

"It's probably a good thing we didn't," Maggie reflected.

"That isn't what I asked you," Daphne persisted.

Cornered, Maggie shrugged ruefully and hoisted her glass in a second salute. "All right, then," she replied. "Yes, I would love to have a child and no, I don't wish Connor and I had had one together." A part of her, a reckless part she'd never shared with any-one, not even her dear friend, wished some-thing altogether different—that she'd left Connor at the altar that long ago summer day, climbed into that battered old truck be-side J.T., and sped away. Though she couldn't rightly say how such an action would ultimately have affected J.T., there could be little doubt that she and Connor would both have been better off. Their mar-riage had been a mistake from the first, al-though they'd both tried valiantly to pretend otherwise.

"Do you realize that every woman from our graduating class—every last one of them, besides you and me—is a mother?" Although Daphne's tone was light, even humorous, there was a frantic note to it. "Even Virginia Abbott."

"There were only six of us," Maggie pointed out reasonably, but she *was* a little stung by the comparison all the same. O.K., she'd married the wrong man. Instead of kids she had Sadie, a spoiled beagle now snoring on the hooked rug in the living room, with all four feet in the air. In general, though, Maggie had done pretty well in life: good grades in college; a fine job afterward, with profit-sharing and a 401(k) big enough to choke the proverbial horse; the intelligence, enthusiasm, and confidence to get a new business up and running. She was healthy, with a family and lots of friends, and happy, too, though there *were* nights when she lay awake, staring at the ceiling and feeling like a traveler who's just missed the last boat to the land of milk and honey.

"Virginia Abbott," Daphne marveled, sounding mildly disgusted. "Good Lord. A stretch in reform school and the world's worst case of acne, and she *still* ended with a minivan, an adoring husband, and four kids!"

Maggie resigned herself to a lengthy diatribe, settling back in her chair and taking another long sip from her ice tea.

"And Polly Herrick," Daphne went on. "Look at her. President of the P.T.A.!"

Maggie hid a smile.

All of the sudden, Daphne ran out of steam. She flung out her hands and gave a laughing sigh. "Listen to me running on," she said. Then, with a glance at her watch, she got to her feet, rinsed her ice tea glass at the sink, and popped it into the top rack of the dishwasher. "I've got shopping to do. Ben is barbequing steaks tonight, and then we're going to watch *The Best Years of Our Lives* on video. Join us?"

"Oh, right," Maggie scoffed good-naturedly. "That would be cozy. The bride. The groom. The woman from across the street. Shall I bring my dog?"

Daphne laughed, getting to her feet. Now that school was out, she was on hiatus from teaching, and she insisted on helping Maggie with the heavy work over at the Springwater Station. They'd done the worst of the cleaning—the place had been closed up for several years—and for the past few days they'd been sorting through the contents of trunks, crates, and boxes, looking for old linens and other antiques that could be used to lend authenticity. "Tomorrow, then," Daphne said. "We're still going to that estate auction over in Maple Creek, right?"

Maggie nodded. "I'll pick you up at six sharp. We can have breakfast on the way."

Daphne, never an early riser, looked rueful. "Six sharp," she confirmed, with a notable lack of enthusiasm. When she wasn't teaching, she liked sleeping in. "See you then."

With that, she was gone.

Sadie got up off the rug, stretched methodically in all directions, one leg at a time, and ambled into the kitchen area to check out her food bowl, the trunk of her body swaying from side to side as she went, like a sausage suspended on strings. Finding nothing there but half a dog biscuit and the remains of that morning's breakfast, she raised baleful brown eyes to Maggie's face and gave a despondent little whimper of protest.

"Did you know," Maggie said, already headed toward the tiny laundry room at the back of the cottage, where she stored kibble, a fresh dog dish in hand, "that the typical beagle gets way too much to eat on account of 'sad-eyes syndrome'?"

Sadie panted, wagging at warp speed. "Great," she seemed to be saying. "It's working."

Maggie chuckled, shook her head, and gave the dog an early supper. While Sadie dined, Maggie slipped out onto the back step and watched the sun set behind the gazebo. The structure was all but swallowed up in climbing rose vines just beginning to bud, and it was not only innocuous, but beautiful, in a misty, Thomas Kinkaid sort of way. In the ten years since her wedding day she had returned to Springwater many times for holidays and short vacations and, rarely if ever, associated the gazebo with any unhappy memory. Now that Daphne had gone back to house and husband, though, it seemed that she couldn't get J.T. out of her mind, couldn't forget the way he'd looked in the golden light of that spring afternoon long ago—not just angry, but earnest and confounded and, worst of all, betrayed.

"I'm sorry," she told his ghost, and turned to go back into the guest house.

*   *   *

J.T. gestured, in mid stride, toward the barn, with its sagging roof and leaning walls. The whole ranch was a disgrace; Scully and Evangeline, the first of the Springwater Wainwrights, must have rolled over in their graves more than once in the years since he'd turned his back on the land to play homicide cop in the Big Apple. His aunt Janeen had been too sick to run such a demanding enterprise, and her husband, Clive Jenson, had been no damned good. In point of fact, he'd abandoned Janeen, left her to die alone, devoured by cancer.

Sometimes it seemed to J.T. that there was a curse on the Wainwright name, and on all the attendant property.

"Purvis," he said to the older man double-stepping along beside him, "look at this place. I'd like to help you out. I really would. But I don't have *time* to take on another job."

Purvis Digg, a friend and contemporary of J.T.'s late father, Jack Wainwright, had served in Vietnam, and though he apparently didn't suffer from flashbacks or delayed-stress syndrome like many of his fellow veterans, he'd somehow gotten stuck in the sixties just the same. He wore his salt-and-pepper hair long, even though it was thinning on top, and bound back with a leather bootlace. Sometimes he added a headband, Indian style, though J.T. had yet to see a feather. He sported a fringed buckskin jacket bought secondhand during the Johnson administration, combat boots, and thrift-store jeans embellished with everything from star-and-moon-shaped patches and old Boy Scout badges to grease stains.

"But you're a cop," Purvis argued.

Reaching the corral gate, which was falling apart like everything else in J.T.'s life, he stopped, one hand on the rusty latch. "I *was* a cop," he corrected his old friend.

"Once a cop, always a cop," Purvis said.

J.T. thrust splayed fingers through his dark hair. He'd lost his partner to a punk who would probably be back out on the street in another eighteen months, and taken a bullet himself, and while he'd recovered physically, he wasn't sure he'd ever get over the memory of seeing Murphy fall. Then there was the funeral, watched on video in his hospital room: full honors; the brave, baffled face of the dead man's widow; the plaintive wail of sorrow from his teenage daughter. "Look, Purvis—"

"Feel pretty damn sorry for yourself, don't you?" Purvis broke in, reddening a little at the base of his jaw. Like most everybody else in and around Springwater, he knew all about what had happened in that warehouse six months back. "Well, here's a flash for you, Junior: You're not the first guy who ever lost somebody they cared about. Your dad was the best friend I ever had—we joined the service on the buddy plan, and he saved my life in 'Nam—and one fine day somebody shot him right out of the saddle, if you recall."

Grief and exasperation made J.T.'s sigh sound the way it felt: raw. "Damn it, Purvis, that's a low blow. Of course I 'recall'!"

"Then you probably *also* recollect that nobody ever rounded up the shooter."

J.T. clenched and unclenched his left fist. He could not, would not, hit a skinny old man, but the temptation was no less compelling. "I recollect, all right. I still have nightmares about it, on a regular basis." *Alternating with the ones about Murphy,* he added to himself.

Purvis slapped him on the shoulder in an expression of manly commiseration. "Me, too. How old were you when Jack was murdered? Fourteen?"

"Thirteen," J.T. said, averting his eyes for a moment, in order to gather his composure. His father had ridden in from the range that afternoon, on the first hot breath of a summer thunderstorm, so drenched in blood that it was hard to tell where the man stopped and the horse began.

J.T., working in the corral with a two-year-old gelding on a lead line, had vaulted over the fence and run toward his father. Jack had fallen from his paint stallion the same way Murphy had gone down in the warehouse, in an excruciatingly slow, rolling motion. And like Murphy, Jack Wainwright had most likely been dead before he struck the ground. J.T. had still been kneeling in the dirt, rocking Jack's body in his arms, when Purvis, stopping by because someone had reported hearing a shot in the vicinity, had shown up in the squad car and radioed for an ambulance. It had been too late for J.T.'s dad. Too late, in some ways, for J.T. himself.

"I didn't bring that up just for the hell of it," Purvis said, in his gruff way. "And maybe it was a little below the belt. The thing is, J.T., that wasn't an isolated incident. Sure,

we had a lot of relatively trouble-free years
around here, but that's all changed over the
last couple of months. Some of the same
crap that was going on back then is happening again now—the ranchers around
here are losing livestock to theft and poison
same as before. Just last month, somebody
took a shot at Dave Knox while he was out
looking for strays. And I've got me a crazy
feeling that we're dealing with the same
outfit."

J.T.'s next instinct was to grasp Purvis by
the lapels of his campy jacket and wrench
him onto the balls of his feet, but he restrained himself—the tendency to lose his
cool had gotten him into trouble a few
times, early in his career as a cop. A rap on
the knuckles from the department, which included a series of anger-management
classes, had pretty much straightened him
out, but he still had to be careful.

"Are you telling me you think these are
the same people who killed my father?" he
demanded, after taking a long breath.

Purvis swallowed, then nodded. "Yup."

"You got any proof of that?"

"No," Purvis admitted. "Just an ache in
my gut that says history is repeating itself."

He paused. "J.T., this situation ain't gonna go away by itself. I ain't as young as I used to be, and I can't run these bastards down without some help. If I *don't* get them, the ranchers will have my badge, and you know as well as I do that once I'm gone they'll be up in arms like a bunch of yahoos out of some black-and-white western. We'll have the feds crawling all over the valley after that, but not before a few more people get hurt or killed."

"There must be somebody else," J.T. breathed. He was weakening, and Purvis surely knew it. Digg would never be drafted into the Rocket Scientists' Hall of Fame, but he was no rube, either. Law enforcement was not just his job, it was his religion.

"There's nobody else," Purvis insisted. "Oh, I could come up with a pack of hot-headed rednecks, call 'em a posse. But you're the only professional around here, besides me. You're a cop. You can ride and shoot. Besides that, you're a rancher, just like them, and you're Jack Wainwright's son. You've got a stake in this too."

J.T. was silent. Purvis might be a hick lawman from a hick town smack in the middle of no place, but he had the tenacity of a pit bull, and he could argue like a big-city lawyer when it served his purpose.

Purvis came in for the kill. "What do you figure Jack would do, if he were in your place?"

J.T. closed his eyes, opened them again. The first seismic tremors of a headache stirred at the base of his skull. He didn't have to guess what Jack Wainwright would do, or Murphy either. They would have pushed up their sleeves and stepped into the fray. "All right," he said. *"All right."*

Purvis grinned. "Judge Calloway can swear you in tomorrow," he said.

"I'm going to an auction in the morning," J.T. replied. An elderly, widowed rancher had died over at Maple Creek, and the estate was being liquidated. He intended to bid on a couple of quarter horses and maybe a beef or two. Then he'd be able to call this pitiful place a ranch again, with a semistraight face.

The marshal of Springwater could afford to be generous; he'd gotten what he wanted. "All right. We'll have supper together tomorrow night, then, over at the Stagecoach Café. You, me, and the judge. Be there by six."

J.T. gave a rueful chuckle and shook his head. "You got it, Pilgrim."

Purvis laughed, administered another resounding shoulder slap, and turned to head back to his antiquated, mud-splattered police car. Halfway there, he turned. "Say," he added, as a jovial afterthought. "I reckon you know that Maggie McCaffrey's back in town. Going to spit shine the old Springwater Station and make one of them fancy little hotels out of it."

J.T. knew all about Maggie's return to Springwater; uncannily, her homecoming had very nearly coincided with his own, though they'd managed to avoid running into each other so far. He hadn't seen Maggie since the day he'd tried without success to keep her from marrying Connor Bartholomew. He'd made an ass of himself, in more ways than one, and even after all this time he wasn't anxious to face her— and not just because he wasn't good at apologizing. He'd been married, fathered a son, gotten divorced, and dated dozens of women, before and after his ex-wife, Annie, but somewhere down deep he'd always had a thing for Maggie. He'd known it, and so, unfortunately, had Annie.

Murphy had warned him. You're going to blow it all if you're not careful, he'd said. You've got a nice wife and a great kid, but all you think about, all you talk about, is this damn job. What are you saving yourself for? A second chance with your high school sweetheart? Wise up, cowboy. It isn't what could have been that matters. It's what *is.*

"I'll have to stop by and say hello," J.T. said to Purvis, as lightly as he could. "The Station's been sitting empty for a long time. It's good to know somebody is going to re-store it."

Purvis nodded. "A McCaffrey, too," he agreed, pleased. "It'll be almost like the old days, when Jacob and June-bug was runnin' the place."

J.T. might have laughed if he hadn't just been roped into signing on for an indefinite stretch as Purvis's deputy. The way the marshal talked, Jacob and June-bug Mc-Caffrey were just out of town instead of dead and buried for well over a century. "Al-most," he agreed.

Purvis lifted a hand in farewell, climbed into his rig, and started up the engine. J.T. watched until the aging lawman had turned around and headed down the long dirt road leading to the highway.

"Shit," J.T. said aloud. He gave the gate latch a pull, and the whole thing collapsed, clattering to the ground.

He hoped it wasn't an omen.

The sky was pink and gold, with just the faintest rim of blue, when Maggie and Sadie pulled up in front of the old Hargreaves mansion across the street from the Spring-water Station. Resigned to surrendering her shotgun seat, Sadie jumped nimbly into the back.

Maggie gave the horn a tentative tap, and Daphne immediately came out of the house, dressed, as Maggie was, in jeans, sneakers, and a lightweight blouse. Her hair was pulled back into a hasty ponytail, so that she resembled a teenager, and her fresh skin was bare of makeup.

"Coffee," she pleaded. "Now."

Maggie grinned. "Hang on, my friend," she said. "McDonald's is probably open."

Daphne made an event of fastening her seatbelt, greeted Sadie, and yawned. "Even Ben is still asleep," she said. An avowed workaholic, her husband was notorious for getting up early. Before long he'd be out at the mine, directing crews and equipment.

Once they'd pulled out of the McDonald's drive-through, Daphne became more voluble. "Don't forget," she said, sipping. "You promised us breakfast." She looked back over the seat. "Didn't she, Sadie?"

Sadie, lying on the seat with her muzzle resting on her paws, gave a cheerful whine.

"I'm a woman of my word," Maggie assured them both.

Half an hour later they were in Maple Creek, just over the county line, waiting for a seat at Flo's Diner. Because of the auction, which was to take place only a few miles away, the place was crowded.

"Look!" Daphne said, nudging Maggie. Flo was doing a brisk trade that morning, and it looked as though they might be standing for a while. "There's J.T."

Maggie followed her friend's gaze to the dark-haired, dark-eyed man in the rear booth. In a decade, he'd changed, of course, but only for the better. The planes and angles of his face gave him a rugged look, and he was thicker through the shoulders and the chest. At Daphne's exuberant wave, he grinned in that lazy, lopsided way

Maggie had never been able to forget, and stood. With an easy gesture, he indicated the seats opposite his own.

"Come on," Daphne said, and before Maggie could balk, her friend had linked arms with her and started toward J.T.'s table.

Maggie felt her face catch fire; she might have been sixteen instead of thirty. Her heart shinnied up into her throat and got itself stuck there, just like old times.

"Hi, J.T. What great luck, running into you," Daphne chimed.

J.T.'s gaze lingered on Maggie, wry and all too knowledgeable. He obviously knew she would have preferred to be practically anywhere else besides Flo's Diner, face-to-face with the first and only man she'd ever truly loved.

"Hello, Maggie," he said, with a nod.

Maggie nodded back. "J.T."

"Well," said Daphne, "that was easy." She sat down cheerfully, sliding to the inside of the booth and reaching for a menu.

J.T. put out a hand in silent invitation, and Maggie took a seat beside Daphne. Only then did J.T. sit down again.

"We're here for the auction," Daphne

said, when the conversation didn't take off right away. "What about you, J.T.?"

"Same thing," he said. His gaze was still fixed on Maggie's face. "Thought I'd pick up a couple of horses. Maybe some cattle."

Maybe some cattle, Maggie thought. Same old J.T. He either didn't realize, or didn't care, that ranching was a risky proposition these days, with so many people cutting back on red meat.

Daphne nudged Maggie hard with one elbow, though she did not look up from her menu. The message was clear enough: "Say something."

"I'm—I'm looking for antiques—quilts, old linens, things like that," Maggie explained, with awkward goodwill. "I'm reopening the Springwater Station as a bed-and-breakfast."

J.T.'s eyes burned into hers. "I'm surprised," he said. "That you came back to Springwater to live, I mean. I had you figured for a city girl." His tone was affable enough, but the remark was meant as a jibe, and Maggie knew it. Even before their breakup, there had been fundamental differences between them; she'd thought he was rash and impetuous, and he'd accused her of being too careful. Even rigid.

Her cheeks ached with the effort to smile. Damn if she would let him get to her right off the bat like that. "People change," she said.

"Not usually," he replied, with flat certainty.

"Did you learn that on the mean streets of New York?" She kept her voice neutral.

"No," he answered. "I learned it on the mean streets of Springwater."

Daphne closed her menu with a snap. "What's good here?" she asked, as Flo herself, a plump redhead in a pink uniform, trundled toward them. J.T. had already ordered, and Flo brought him a wide smile, along with his plate of bacon, eggs, and hash brown potatoes, fried crisp.

"What'll it be, honey?" the older woman asked good-naturedly, turning to Maggie.

"I'll have oatmeal," Maggie said, for the sake of appearances. She'd been hungry a few minutes before, but now she wasn't sure she could get so much as a bite down.

Daphne sighed, eyeing J.T.'s breakfast with longing. "Me, too," she said, resigned.

"Don't let your food get cold," Maggie said, when J.T. hesitated to pick up his fork.

"By all means, eat," Daphne added.

"That's two oatmeals?" Flo asked. "Want any toast? Coffee?"

"Coffee, please," Maggie said, with an agreeable nod, and Flo made a note on her pad and hurried away. The diner was jumping.

"What about Sadie?" Daphne asked.

"Sadie?" J.T. asked, leaning forward a little. He'd begun to eat, but with mannerly reluctance.

"My dog," Maggie said.

"Ah," he said, as though it explained a great deal, her having a dog. "No husband? No kids?"

Was he rubbing it in? Everybody in Springwater knew what every other Springwater native was doing, whether they still lived in town or not. He would have heard about her divorce, not to mention any children she'd had. Maggie smiled sweetly. "Just Sadie," she said. "What about you?"

An expression of genuine sadness flickered in J.T.'s eyes, if only for an instant. "A son, Quinn. He's six."

Maggie had known about the little boy, of course, but hearing the words from J.T.'s own lips had an effect on her emotions all the same. She found herself strangely stricken, unable to contribute much to the conversation after that, and left Daphne in charge of chatting.

The coffee arrived, then the oatmeal. Maggie ordered a side of sausage links to go, for Sadie. She and Daphne settled up their bills, and J.T. attended to his.

She thought she was going to make a clean getaway, but while Daphne was using the rest room, J.T. followed Maggie out to her car and stood nearby while she fed an eager Sadie from a foam take-out box.

"Maggie," he said, low, when she tried to ignore him.

She looked up at him, questioning.

"I think we have a few things to say to each other, don't you?"

2

Maggie stared up at J.T. for a long moment, there in the parking lot of Flo's Diner, trying to make sense of a perfectly simple sentence. *I think we have a few things to say to each other, don't you?*

It should have been easy to respond; instead, she felt as if she'd just tumbled headlong into the eye of a whirlwind, and thereby lost all faculty for language. Awkwardly, she rummaged for Sadie's leash and affixed it to the dog's collar. The beagle, having already gobbled down her breakfast, jumped eagerly to the ground, ready to do other business.

J.T. took the leash. "Maggie," he insisted, his voice deep and grave.

Maggie plundered her jacket pocket for a packet containing an antibacterial wipe and a small plastic capsule with a blue plastic bag inside. "For do-do," she explained stupidly, and wished, in the next moment, that she could vanish in the cool morning air, like the mingling vapors of their breaths.

J.T. grinned. "Relax, McCaffrey," he said. "This is no big deal. I just want to apologize, that's all."

She blinked, amazed. She'd known J.T. Wainwright for most of her life, though after his parents were divorced, when he was in fifth grade, he hadn't been around as much, dividing his time between the ranch at Springwater and his mother's new home in Las Vegas. J.T. had never shown a propensity for saying he was sorry—about anything. "Apologize?"

He leaned in close and whispered his answer. "I'd define the word for you, McCaffrey, but I'm afraid you'd feel compelled to explain the meaning of 'do-do' in retaliation."

She laughed, in spite of her dazed state, and punched him lightly in the chest with the knuckles of her right hand, the way she'd done when they were kids, arguing over a play on the softball field, or who got to use what fishing pole. "It would serve you right if I did."

Sadie pulled J.T. across the parking lot toward a clump of shrubbery, and Maggie followed. "Probably," J.T. agreed, averting his gaze, with a wry expression, when Sadie squatted, tail pointed straight up like a flagpole. "I'm sorry, McCaffrey," he said. "For everything."

Maggie snapped open the blue bag, a responsible dog owner attending to her duties. "Spoiling my wedding, you mean?" *Not to mention dumping me at Christmas before that, and taking the heart right out of me.*

"Did I spoil it?"

"Yes," Maggie said, but she couldn't quite make herself meet his eyes. "Well," she amended, when the silence lengthened, "it shouldn't have happened in the first place. But *if* it had been the right thing to do, you would have a lot to be sorry for, buster."

J.T. laughed, though there was a note of sorrow in the sound. Maggie stooped, used the bag, tied it neatly, and made for the nearest trash bin, trailed by dog and man.

After disposing of the evidence, she opened the packet and wiped her hands with the little square of moist paper inside. "I acted like an idiot," he said.

"True," she replied, tossing the wipe into the garbage after the poop bag. "At least twice."

"Twice?" He looked genuinely puzzled.

"Have you forgotten what happened over Christmas vacation, J.T.?" Odd, even after all that time, how much it hurt just to remember. They'd made so many plans together, dreamed so many dreams, and J.T. had dashed them all, just like that, on some kind of whim. "You said we'd grown apart, that we ought to see other people. I believe you were dating a cocktail waitress in Vegas at the time—or was it a showgirl?"

J.T. thrust out a long sigh. "I thought I was doing the noble thing," he said. "I figured you deserved better than me, and I was probably right about that. Problem was, I couldn't forget you, even when we were both married to other people."

"None of this matters now, anyway," Maggie said, trying to sound nonchalant. As if saying it made it so.

His expression darkened a little, but only

briefly. "The hell it doesn't," he said. "We had something together, McCaffrey. Something good. Something *important.*"

They had returned to Maggie's Pathfinder, and Sadie jumped obediently into the area behind the rear seat. J.T. ruffled the dog's velvety ears before lowering the hatch. Inside, Sadie yelped and pushed her nose against the window, making smudges on the glass.

Daphne was taking her time crossing the parking lot toward them, and Maggie was glad to see her, though she knew her friend wouldn't arrive in time to save her from having to answer J.T.'s mild challenge.

"Sex," Maggie insisted, in a fierce whisper. "That was what we had going for us, J.T. Sex, and nothing more." *Liar,* accused a voice hidden in the shadows of her heart. *You loved him as much as any woman has ever loved a man. Maybe that's the whole problem—you never stopped.*

J.T. glanced toward Daphne, who was practically dragging her feet. He rested his strong rancher's hands on his hips. "The sex didn't start until the summer after we graduated high school," he argued quietly.

"But we—you and me, Maggie—*we* go back a lot further than that."

Maggie couldn't deny his assertion. She'd fallen for J.T. almost as soon as she'd known the difference between boys and girls—in some ways, it was as if she'd *always* loved him, throughout time and eternity—and every time she thought she was over him, he came back to Springwater and Maggie found herself right back at square one. He'd changed, of course, after his father was murdered, when he was just thirteen—who wouldn't have?—but Maggie's feelings for him had grown rather than diminished. So had her misgivings, however, especially after he put his uncle in the hospital one sultry summer evening. While it was true that Jenson had seriously injured his wife, J.T.'s aunt, in a drunken rage earlier in the evening, that didn't justify J.T.'s using his fists the way he had.

To everyone's amazement, Janeen had stayed with her husband, and together they'd taken over the ranch after Jack Wainwright died. Despite his history with Clive Jenson, J.T. had still come to visit whenever he could, but of course he and Clive were at permanent odds after that falling-out. By the time Maggie went off to college at Northwestern, J.T. had a countywide repu-tation for fighting, among other things, and poor Janeen was at her wit's end. After Maggie's marriage to Connor, J.T. had re-turned to Las Vegas and enrolled in junior college. Everyone in the old hometown had marveled at the irony when news filtered back that he was majoring in criminal jus-tice, and when he went to work for the NYPD as a rookie, after two years of school and more training at the police academy, there was rampant amazement back in Montana. Just last year, his Aunt Janeen had passed away, following a long bout with breast cancer and, according to Maggie's mother, Clive had not been seen more than a few times since around the time the initial diagnosis was made.

"O.K.," Maggie said, having stalled as long as she could "you're right. We go way back."

"You *could* explain," he suggested mildly.

She swallowed.

"I was scared. Are you satisfied? You were wild, always in some kind of scrape. You had a terrible temper, and a lot of people thought you were either going to get killed or wind up behind bars someplace—"

He looked as though she'd struck him. "Surely you didn't think I'd ever hit you," he murmured.

Maggie sighed gustily. "Of course I didn't think you'd hit me," she said. *I could never have loved you, if I'd believed that for an instant.* She made a new start. "Connor, if you will recall, had just finished medical school. He had a future, a plan for his life. *You* figure it out."

J.T.'s eyes shot fire, and though the expression on his mouth resembled a smile, it fell short of full wattage. "So you married him." It wasn't a question, it was a statement, brimming with quiet scorn. "Because he was predictable. Because he was *boring.*"

"There are worse things," Maggie snapped, "than being boring!"

He folded his arms, rocked back on his heels, looked cocky. "Not many," he said.

She stubbornly refused to take the bait.

"It didn't last," he said, more gently. As if she didn't know.

"No," she said, on a long sigh. It was still an enormous disappointment to her that she hadn't been able to make the marriage work. Emotionally, she'd been somewhat adrift ever since the divorce.

J.T. responded with a sigh of his own. "I'm sorry about that, Maggie. I know you wanted a home and family, like the one you grew up in."

For a moment, she was choked up. She swallowed hard and blinked. Then she managed a game little smile and an offhand shrug. "The world didn't end," she heard herself say.

J.T. frowned pensively, as though troubled. "Didn't it?" he asked, so quietly that she wondered, even a second later, if she'd only imagined his words.

Daphne, unable to delay her progress any longer, had arrived finally. She stood nervously near the passenger door grinning foolishly and wringing her hands a little.

J.T., always the first to recover in any awkward situation, smiled, touched his hat brim to acknowledge her, then spoke once more to Maggie. "I think it's great that you're restoring the Station," he said, as though they were casual acquaintances, with no history beyond the simplest hellos, how-are-yous, and good-byes. "I'd like to stop by and see it one of these days."

Maggie found herself caught up in yet another storm of emotion. "O.K.," she said lamely, almost croaking the word.

"See you," J.T. replied. Then, turning, he walked away, got into a blue late-model pickup truck, and drove off toward the auction.

After a few moments of collecting herself Maggie climbed into the Pathfinder alongside Daphne, started the ignition, and sat there, trembling.

"Mags?"

"What?"

"Do you want me to drive? You seem a little—well—shaky."

If she'd been alone, Maggie would have rested her forehead against the steering wheel and taken deep breaths until she felt more composed. J.T. had rattled her, just by being J.T., and a lot of old emotions, ones she'd thought had been long since laid to permanent rest, were rising to the surface. "I'm perfectly fine," she lied.

"Right," Daphne agreed, and shook her head in affectionate amazement.

At the sale, held on a rundown ranch a

few miles out of town, Maggie tried to concentrate on household goods, but her gaze kept straying to J.T., who was leaning against a corral fence a hundred yards away, apparently oblivious to her presence, bidding on livestock. He'd bought at least five head of cattle before Maggie stopped trying to keep count.

"Your father," Kathleen McCaffrey said briskly, the next day, arranging a bouquet of pink peonies in a crockery pitcher, "has lost his mind. I do believe he's having one of those middle-of-the-fence crises people talk about."

Maggie was on her way to the Station, the back of her vehicle loaded with tissue-wrapped sheets, tablecloths, and the like, bought at the previous day's sale. She'd stopped by the big house to invite her mother to join her for lunch around noon; they'd have sandwiches and salads and admire the elegant old linens together. Both of them loved antiques of any kind, especially ones from the era when Springwater was first settled.

She sighed. "Mom, Dad's a lot of things, but he's not crazy."

"Isn't he?" Kathleen asked, in arch tones. She was a tall woman, still beautiful, with a perfect complexion and rich Maureen O'Hara–red hair. Her eyes were a vivid shade of green, and they flashed with the heat of her legendary Irish temper. "He's been threatening to buy one of those motor homes and take to the road."

Maggie felt the pit of her stomach drop a centimeter or two. Her parents had been on the warpath for some time, that was nothing new, but if one of them picked up stakes and left, they might never resolve their differences. Of course, they'd shown no signs of doing that anyway. "When did he decide this?"

Kathleen fluffed the peonies, even though they didn't require fluffing. They were perfect, pretty enough to grace the cover of one of Martha Stewart's mail order catalogs. "I believe he's been mulling over the idea since before he sold the lumberyard and retired," she said, with a little sniff. Obviously, Reece McCaffrey had not troubled to mention these longtime ruminations to his wife until very recently. "He showed me a sales flyer. Maggie, the thing is as long as a boxcar, and better suited to one of those

rock-and-roll bands—the Graceful Dead, or
somebody like that." Kathleen pursed her
full lips in disdain, though there was a
bruised look in her eyes. "He was never a
very good driver, you know. He's bound to
kill himself, just trying to merge with the traffic on some freeway!"

So Kathleen *did* still care for her husband.
Maggie couldn't help being pleased, despite the unpleasant image of her father
wiping out himself and three lanes of traffic
after barreling up an on-ramp at his usual
rate of travel, at roughly the speed of email.
"I see," she said carefully.

"The old fool," Kathleen said.

There seemed to be no point in defending
Reece, in reminding Kathleen that he had
worked hard all his life running the lumberyard, putting three children through college
and one, Simon, through medical school as
well. He'd always yearned to travel, Reece
had; Maggie knew that and so did everyone
else in the family. He'd just never had the
time, the spare funds, or the opportunity.
"Why don't you go along with him?" Maggie
ventured to ask. "It would be good for both
of you to get away."

Kathleen sighed as deeply as if Maggie

had suggested she join a convent in India or make a long pilgrimage in bare feet. "I've just sold another painting on eBay," she said. "It was the last one I had. I can't leave now."

Kathleen, a self-trained folk artist, painted in colorful acrylics, sometimes on canvas, sometimes on wood panels or heavy paper. Some of her offerings were the size of postage stamps, while others were so big they had to be hauled away in trucks. All of them, without fail, followed the same theme: pears.

"Couldn't you paint on the road?" Maggie asked. *A pear,* she thought, *is a pear, whether you paint it in Springwater or Timbuktu.*

"I'd have to leave my computer!"

"Nonsense," Maggie said. "You could buy a laptop and keep track of your on-line auctions that way."

Kathleen glared at Maggie. "I love Springwater. It's my home, and it inspires me. Besides, you've just come home, after being away all these years, and Wes and Franny are about to have another baby—"

Maggie suppressed a sigh. If ever there'd been a futile argument, this was it. "How about lunch?" she asked. "Are you coming over or not?"

Kathleen relaxed a little. "I *would* like to see what progress you've made fixing up the Station," she admitted. "What time? I usually finish painting around one."

"I was thinking of twelve-thirty," Maggie said, "but I can hold out till one. Can't speak for Sadie, though."

Kathleen smiled. Although the beagle had numerous unredeeming qualities, such as digging in flower beds and howling at every-thing from butterflies to dust bunnies, Kath-leen was a fan. "I'll bring her an oatmeal cookie to make up for the delay."

Maggie wished her mother would make an overture toward Reece, even one as modest as that, but didn't dare say so. "O.K.," she answered, and left it at that.

Kathleen's thoughts had strayed; a thoughtful frown creased her forehead. "You know, I think I might be glutting the market with pears," she mused. "Do you suppose I ought to branch out into artichokes?"

Maggie bit the inside of her lip, as she al-ways did when she felt like smiling and thought it imprudent to do so. "Good idea," she said.

Kathleen beamed. "I'll get some at the supermarket this afternoon. Artichokes, I mean. I really do think I'm ready to move up."

Maggie made for the front door, waggling her fingers in temporary farewell. "See you around one," she chimed.

"Good-bye, dear," Kathleen replied, already bustling off in the direction of the screened sunporch, which she had fitted out as a studio a few years before, when the passion to paint had struck her anew. Kathleen had sketched even as a child, Maggie knew, and had dabbled in watercolors and oils as a young adult, but she'd given up her art, calling it "a little hobby," when she married. No doubt the demands of keeping a house, helping out at the mill office, and mothering three children left little time for such pursuits.

"Artichokes," Maggie confided, with a smile, to Sadie, who was waiting in the passenger seat of the Pathfinder. "She's going to paint artichokes." The trouble between her parents notwithstanding, and for all that Kathleen's choice of subjects amused her, she was glad her mother was painting again.

Sadie whimpered, as if in protest.

Maggie started the engine and put the transmission into drive. "It's true," she insisted, and grinned. "Artichokes."

Less than two minutes later they pulled up in front of the ancient stagecoach station. Even though it looked pretty rundown, most of Maggie and Daphne's efforts having been focused on the interior, the sight of it still filled Maggie with quiet, nostalgic pride. She had workmen coming the next day to begin restoring the outside, patching the chinks between the logs, rebuilding the fireplace chimney, shoring up the sagging porch and its overhanging roof. The windows would get new frames and glass, too.

Maggie supposed she was like her mom in a lot of ways, a small-town girl at heart, and a natural stay-at-home. Although she'd been anxious to leave Springwater and get a look at the big, wide, sophisticated world when she'd gone away to college, she'd yearned for home almost from the moment she'd left it. She loved the simpler way of life, the sense of family and of community, being surrounded by people and places she'd known from childhood.

Maggie had barely gotten inside and unfastened Sadie's leash when a horn sounded out front. She went to one of the old, bubbled-glass windows and peered out. "Speak of the devil," she murmured, watching as her dark-haired, broad-shouldered father, normally a somber fellow, sprang down from the cab of the longest recreational vehicle Maggie had ever seen. The thing gleamed in the sun, freshly waxed no doubt, and lacking only a satellite dish to qualify as a rolling monument to conspicuous consumption.

She went outside grinning, and Sadie bounded alongside her, unfettered and dizzy with the joy of even that limited amount of freedom. "Wow," Maggie said, enjoying the frank delight shining in Reece's brown eyes as she took in the long vehicle.

Reece bent to pet the dog for a few moments. "Pretty impressive, isn't it?" he asked, straightening to his full height of well over six feet and gesturing to indicate the RV, as though Maggie could have mistaken his meaning. He'd always been a handsome man and, judging by the portrait of the first McCaffreys hanging in a place of honor over the dining room fireplace at home, he bore an uncanny resemblance to old Jacob.

Maggie's heart melted in the face of the childlike pleasure he took in this new toy of his.

"That it is," Maggie agreed, approaching the gleaming monstrosity. "Does it have a hot tub?"

Reece chuckled. "No," he said, "but it's got two bedrooms and a good kitchen, and the bathroom's pretty fancy." He hurried to open the door for her and bow slightly. "Have a look."

She stepped inside and was immediately wonder struck. There was a wet bar opposite the kitchenette, for heaven's sake, with a mirror behind it, and a long leather couch graced one wall. The bathroom was done up in faux marble, pink and black, and it was every bit as big as the one in Maggie's condo back in Chicago. The master bedroom would have done Elvis proud, with its mirrors and leopard-skin comforter, and the second, smaller, one was a study in econ-omy of space. It included a built-in des and was obviously wired for computers an other sophisticated electronic equipment.

"I thought this one might do as an offi for your mother," Reece offered grave with a sort of sad and hopeful pride. ")

know, for her Internet stuff. Like as not, though, she'll be so mad when she finds out how much I spent for this rig, she'll show me the road awhile before I'm ready to leave."

Maggie's stomach clenched at the mere thought of her parents breaking up, never mind the reality. She was a grown woman, thirty years old and certainly self-support- ing, and still the idea made her feel like an orphan lost in a snowstorm.

She summoned up a cheerful smile and patted her dad on one shoulder. "It's spec- tacular," she said. She was sorely tempted to ask if he'd blown a serious chunk of their retirement money on the purchase, but it was basically none of her business, so she kept that particular concern to herself. "Where did you get it?"

Reece's still powerful chest seemed to swell with pride. "Bought it off ol' Jim Young, out at Young Motors. You can hardly tell it's had any use."

Maggie thought of her parents sleeping under a leopard-print comforter surrounded by mirrors, and had to chuckle at the image, despite everything. "That's true," she said, linking her arm with her dad's. "Come on in-

side and have a peek at the Station—it's coming along so well, a person almost expects to look up and see June-bug McCaffrey herself cooking at the stove or sitting in that old rocking chair by the hearth, piecing a quilt."

Reece smiled and they left the RV, single file, then proceeded up the overgrown stone walkway, each with an arm around the other. Sadie, having long since lost interest in the Elvis mobile, was sniffing around in the overgrown grass of the Station's yard. Maggie closed the gate carefully and left her dog to cheerful exploration.

Reece whistled through his front teeth when he entered the old log building—Maggie had always coveted his ability to whistle like that—taking in the time-mellowed plank floors, the natural rock fireplace where so many of Springwater's early citizens had been married, with Jacob McCaffrey himself officiating, the highly polished and very ancient wood cookstove where June-bug had made meals for weary stagecoach travelers as well as a continuous stream of family and friends. Even the trestle tables were authentic; Maggie had spent long hours sanding them down to their original finish, with lots of help from Daphne, and she'd found several inscriptions carved into the wood—"Toby McCaffrey + Emma Hargreaves," in one place, and "Joshua Kildare" in another.

Surprisingly, Reece's eyes glittered fiercely for a moment; Maggie thought he might actually weep. "It's like stepping back in time," he said, in a low and wondering voice.

He couldn't have offered higher praise, and Maggie hugged him impulsively. "There's still a lot to do, but I'll have Jacob and June-bug's old room ready to occupy in a few days. Then I plan to move in."

The fierce gaze turned luminous as Reece looked down into his daughter's face. "Now, honey, don't you be in too big a hurry to move out. We aren't using that guest house anyway, and it's a pleasure to have you close by."

Maggie let her head rest against his upper arm for a moment. "I know, Dad. I know. But I'll be right down the road. Besides, you're planning to hightail it out of here in that palace on wheels, aren't you?"

He sighed, and his great shoulders stooped a little. "I'd sure like to see the redwoods and Yellowstone Park, and some of those places with road signs that say things like, 'See the Two-headed Serpent, 5 miles ahead,' but it wouldn't be much fun alone."

Maggie stood on tiptoe and kissed his cleft chin. "Hang in there," she said softly. "Things will turn around." Hadn't Wes and Simon, her brothers, been swearing up and down that everything would be all right between their parents?

"I hope you're right, honey," Reece said, and hugged her once again. He'd barely gotten the words out when the door of the Station creaked open and Kathleen stood in the chasm, looking as if the locks of her hair might turn into snakes, Sadie panting at her side, curious as usual.

"Reece   McCaffrey,"   Kathleen   said, cheeks apricot, eyes blazing, "did you buy that—that *thing* out there?" She pointed dramatically.

"Yes, woman," Reece replied, "I did."

"Oh, boy," Maggie murmured, and stepped back, hopefully out of range. Her parents rarely fought—at least, it used to be that way—but lately they'd raised the art of matrimonial combat to new levels.

"You take it back, right this instant," Kathleen commanded. "That Jim Young—I always *knew* he couldn't be trusted!"

"He thinks right highly of you," Reece said regretfully.

Maggie took another step back as her mother began to fulminate. Oh, but she was in her Irish glory, was Kathleen O'Shaunessey McCaffrey, all flash, fury, and fire. "Mom, Dad," Maggie began lamely, "don't scare the dog."

Neither Reece nor Kathleen so much as glanced in Maggie's direction. Sadie crawled under the restored cookstove, rested her muzzle on her paws, and yipped once, disconsolately.

Kathleen was shaking one index finger under Reece's nose. "Have you lost your *mind?*" she demanded, and Maggie thought she detected the hint of a brogue in the meter of her mother's words, even though she'd never lived on the old sod. "If you think I'm going to be one of those women who give up their house to wander from pillar to post like a gypsy, Mr. McCaffrey, you're sadly mistaken!"

Reece's nose was a fraction of an inch from Kathleen's, and a muscle was leaping in his jawline. "Nobody's asking you to give anything up!" he thundered. "I'm offering you the world—well, the United States and Canada, anyway—I'm offering you New England in October, damn it!"

Furious tears stood in Kathleen's emerald eyes. "Have you gone deaf, now? I'm happy *right here* in Springwater!"

"Well, nobody would ever guess it after passing five minutes under *our* roof!"

"Mom?" Maggie dipped a toe into turbulent conversational waters. "Dad?"

A third voice interceded from the doorway just then. "Am I gonna have to run the two of you in for disorderly conduct?"

Maggie, Reece, and Kathleen all turned as one to find Purvis Digg, the town marshal, standing on the threshold, squinting as his eyes adjusted to the dimness of the room. Sadie trotted over to sniff at his boots.

"I'm willing to press charges," Maggie said, under her breath.

"You just stay out of this, Purvis Digg," Kathleen said. "I'm having a discussion with my husband! That's not against any law, is it?"

Purvis nodded to Maggie, with a half grin, and swept off his beat-up western hat. "No, ma'am," he said. "But you're havin' it sort of loud like."

Reece was chuckling by then, and that only made Kathleen angrier. "Don't you come home," she told Reece, shaking that familiar finger again, "until you've taken that foolish *bus* back to Jim Young's car lot, where it belongs."

Reece set his jaw, and his eyes snapped. He could be at least as stubborn as Kathleen when he got his back up, and he wasn't a man who favored ultimatums. "So that's the way of it?" he drawled.

"That," Kathleen said, chin high, cheeks bright, "is the way of it."

"I don't reckon I'll be home straightaway, then. I wrote Jim a check for that rig, and if I know him, he's already taken it to the bank. There'll be no going back on the deal now."

Kathleen looked as though she might lift off like a rocket, trailing smoke and flames. Then, with hard-won dignity, she turned to address Maggie in a surprisingly cool voice, given the state of her temper. "I'll take a rain check on lunch, dear," she said. At Maggie's speechless nod, she turned her attention on Purvis, like a beam of strong light. "Do say hello to your mother, Purvis. Tell Tillie we've missed her at quilting club meetings."

Purvis nodded appreciatively, and with respect. "I'll do that," he said. "I reckon she'll be back there stitching with the rest of you, soon enough. Her arthritis is a lot better than it was over the winter."

"Good," Kathleen said. After that, having visibly dismissed her husband from the universe, she stooped, gave Sadie a brief pat on the head, and then left.

"That went well," Maggie said, resigned.

Reece ignored her and stormed out. She heard the engine of his motor home start up with a roar and chortle away, flinging gravel.

"He's going to force me to write him a ticket," Purvis lamented good-naturedly, "speeding like that."

Maggie sighed. "I'll tell you what I think you ought to do," she said. "Arrest the pair of them. Throw them into the same cell and let them fight it out." The first Springwater jailhouse had burned to the ground in 1957, but the town council had erected a replacement of brick and mortar with the insurance money. The place boasted three cells, one computer, a fax machine, and not much else. "On second thought, you'd better not.

My mother could never tolerate any room where the toilet sits right out in the open."

Purvis laughed. "Guess I'll just let them slip through my fingers, then," he joked. "They're a pair, ain't they?"

"That they are," Maggie agreed. She knew her eyes were twinkling. "So you didn't *really* come by to run my folks in for disturbing the peace, now did you?"

"No, ma'am," he grinned. "I saw J.T.'s truck around the corner, and thought he might be here."

Maggie stiffened a little, looked around, as though expecting to see J.T. lurking somewhere nearby, having gone unnoticed in all the commotion. "Why would you think that?" she asked, aware that she was being unnecessarily touchy and quite unable to help it. "He could be any one of several places. The post office, for instance. Or the feed store."

"If he'd gone to the feed store," Purvis pointed out, ever the lawman, though his color seemed a bit high, "he'd surely have parked in their lot, so's he could load grain sacks and the like into his truck."

Maggie spread her hands. "I haven't seen him," she said.

"If you do, let him know I'm lookin' for him, if you will," Purvis said.

"Sure," Maggie promised, with a nod.

Purvis was about to take his leave when a young girl appeared in the doorway. "Hello, Cindy," he said, touching his hat in passing.

Cindy, a truly beautiful, delicate-looking creature, no older than seventeen and enormously pregnant, crept shyly into the room. She was wearing a worn smock and old jeans, probably agape at the waistline. Her blonde hair was pulled back into a pony-tail, and her blue eyes were wide and wary. She put out a slightly tremulous hand to Maggie. "Hi," she said.

Maggie warmed to the girl instantly, and smiled. "Hello," she replied. "Can I help you?"

Cindy ran her tongue nervously over her lips and then straightened her spine with touching determination. "I need a job," she said. "I thought you might be hiring, with a new business and all. I can make beds and cook, and I've had lots of experience cleaning up after folks."

Maggie considered the girl, her head tilted to one side. "How old are you, Cindy?"

She held Maggie's gaze, though not without some skittishness. "I'll be eighteen in March," she said.

"Ah," Maggie said. It was early June, which meant that March wouldn't be rolling around for a while, of course. "Are you looking for a live-in position?"

Hope flared in Cindy's eyes, and Maggie's tender heart climbed up into the back of her throat. "No," she said, shaking her head. "Billy Raynor and me, we're married now. He just went to work for J.T. Wainwright, as a ranch hand, mending fences and the like, and we're going to live in a trailer he's got out there."

Maggie wanted to put her arms around Cindy and hold her like the child she was, but she sensed that the girl's grasp on her dignity was a fragile one and she didn't want to undermine it any further. "When's your baby due?" she asked, very gently. She ushered the girl toward one of the tables and urged her to be seated.

Cindy sat, somewhat nervously. She had the air of a person who expected to be declared a fraud and chased out at any moment. "I'm seven and a half months along," she said. "Sometimes I think I've got twins in here."

Maggie headed for the kitchen. The chrome trim on the antique cookstove gleamed, thanks to a lot of elbow grease. "Can I get you something? A cup of herbal tea, maybe, or some water?"

Cindy nearly smiled, though not quite. "Do you have any diet cola?"

Maggie went to the refrigerator, which probably dated back to the fifties, and pulled out a can of cola. "I'm afraid there isn't any ice," she said, after checking the trays in the temperamental old freezer.

"That's all right," Cindy said gravely. Her eyes were fastened on the cola as Maggie brought it to the table and set it down in front of her. "Thanks," she added, opening the can and taking a long, thirsty drink.

Maggie sat across the table, hands folded. "You're welcome."

"About the job—"

Maggie had not intended to hire anyone until she actually opened her doors for business, but that didn't seem practical, considering all she had to do if she wanted to accept paying guests by Founders' Day, just a month away. Cindy wasn't up to any sort of heavy work, but she could probably manage a lot of other tasks, such as running errands and making beds. "It would be part-time at first," Maggie heard herself say.

Eagerness flickered in Cindy's haunted eyes. "That's O.K.," she said quickly. "I've got to look after the trailer and everything anyhow."

"What about school?"

Cindy lowered her gaze. "I had to quit," she said miserably. She looked at Maggie squarely then, and there was pride in her face. "But I'm smart. No matter what my dad says, I'm real smart."

Maggie nodded. "Of course you are," she said. "Do you know how to use a computer?"

For the first time, Cindy smiled full out. It was dazzling. "I took some classes at school," she said.

"Good," Maggie said, smiling. She'd brought her personal system with her from Chicago and set it up in the tiny office off the Station kitchen, once a bedroom. "Maybe you can show me a thing or two. Can you start right away?"

Cindy looked as though she might surge

to her feet on a swell of delight. "Tomorrow? Eight o'clock?"

"Nine will be early enough," Maggie said. "It's minimum wage at first—"

"I'll be here before nine," Cindy promised, with spirit. "And thank you." She rushed over to Maggie on an impulse, took both her hands, and squeezed them hard. "Oh, thank you. You won't be sorry for hiring me, I promise."

Maggie smiled. "I'm sure I won't," she said. "See you tomorrow."

Cindy nodded and dashed out, as though she couldn't wait to start getting ready.

Fifteen minutes later, when Maggie had set Sadie on one of the trestle tables to brush her teeth, a task she regularly undertook, J.T. startled her with a light rap at the open door and a low chuckle.

"Must be hell to floss," he observed.

Maggie's face burned. What was it about J. T. Wainwright that made her feel as though she'd regressed to preadolescence in the space of a heartbeat? "What do you want?" she demanded, and instantly regretted the sharpness of her tone.

He took his hat off, hung it on one of the pegs next to the door, as many, many men had done before him. "I hope that isn't your official greeting," he said. "You'll be out of business in a week if it is."

Maggie's response cost her dearly. "I'm sorry," she said. He'd said he'd like to see the Station, hadn't he? And now here he was. Mustn't read too much into it.

"I guess brushing a dog's teeth takes a toll on a person," J.T. allowed, his dark eyes twinkling.

Maggie laughed, put aside the special toothbrush and poultry-flavored paste, and went to the sink to wash her hands. "You came for the nickel tour," she said.

He inclined his magnificent head, and his slow, lingering gaze pulled sweetly at all of Maggie's nerve endings. "That's one reason," he answered.

3

"You've got mail!" exulted a familiar electronic voice from somewhere behind Purvis Digg's computer screen. He set aside the long list of reports he'd been going over for the past few hours: cattle stolen, a few here and a few there, all around Springwater, chemicals poured into the Kilpatricks' well, tires slashed on trucks and tractors, a minor but nonetheless disturbing burglary over at the high school.

Seated at his desk in his lonely office, Purvis was glad to take a break. He rubbed his hands together, took a slurp of instant coffee from a mug he'd bought at a garage sale sometime in the seventies, and

reached for the mouse to click on the mailbox icon. The usual string of junk messages
arose, and Purvis scrolled down, deleting as
he went, until—hallelujah, there it was—he
came to "Cowgirl243–Hey, Lawman."

Beaming, he opened the attached message. "Ok, ok, you've convinced me. I'll
meet you for coffee Thursday night. I get out
of my meeting at 8:30. Is that too late? Flo's
Diner is just across the street. Ever been
there? Keep smilin', Cowgirl."

Purvis flexed the fingers of both hands.
"I'll see you at Flo's, 8:35, on Thursday. I'll
be the guy standing on the sidewalk, wearing the badge. Don't stand me up. Lawman." He hit "send" and was logging off
when J.T. came through the doorway,
framed by a halo of early-morning sunlight.
He wasn't wearing the badge Judge Calloway had given him, but with the stubborn
types like J.T. you had to be grateful for
every concession, however small. He'd
taken the oath, albeit reluctantly, and he
was here.

That, for the moment, was good enough
for Purvis.

"Morning," J.T. said. He was dressed for
the range in old jeans, a western shirt that

might have come from the bottom of a rag bag, and one of Jack Wainwright's hats. Purvis recognized it right off and felt a pang of nostalgia. A day never passed that he didn't miss his good friend.

"There's some coffee over there," Purvis said, indicating the small, cluttered table where he kept the makings of java.

J.T. shook his head, grinning. "Thanks," he said, "but no thanks." He hung his hat on the peg, next to Purvis's own. He nodded toward the computer. "You surfing the Internet on company time, old buddy?"

Purvis felt a flush climb his neck; he knew J.T. was only ribbing him, but he took his responsibilities seriously and worked hard at his job. Fact was, there was a lot of waiting around involved, and not being much of a reader, Purvis liked to pass the time either playing computer games or checking out various law enforcement Web sites. The FBI, now, they had a dandy. "For me," he said, "company time is twenty-four-seven. You ready to dabble in some police work?"

J.T. dragged up a chair and sat down facing Purvis's desk. He shoved a hand through his hair and sighed. "God knows, I've got nothing better to do," he drawled, hoisting his right foot up to rest on his left knee. He looked like the genuine article, Purvis thought, a real cowboy lawman, right out of Springwater's colorful history.

"Heard you hired yourself a ranch hand," Purvis said, settling back, his hands cupped behind his head. "Look out. Pretty soon, you're going to have a real cow outfit going out there again. Might raise some ghosts."

"Ghosts" was a poor choice of words, Purvis realized, when he saw a muscle bunch along J.T.'s jawline. He hadn't meant to remind him of Jack's death, but then, it was probably never far from his mind anyway. It had to bother him even more than it did Purvis that they'd never found the son-of-a-bitch who'd gunned Jack Wainwright down in cold blood.

J.T. said nothing.

Purvis smiled, just to lighten the mood a bit. It was the least he could do, he figured, since he'd been the one to bring up the unfortunate topic in the first place. "You made a good choice, picking that Raynor kid for the job. He's a hard worker and keeps his nose clean. Hasn't been easy, I'm sure, coming from a background like his."

J.T. heaved a sigh. It was plain enough

that he'd rather be digging post holes, mucking out stalls, or nailing shingles on a barn roof, which just went to show that he really did have an aversion to police work. Purvis reckoned a few years pulling homicide detail in a place like New York City would do that to just about anybody, but at the same time, he was desperate enough to hold J.T. to his promise.

"Where do you suggest we start this investigation?" J.T. asked.

"That's the hell of it," Purvis replied. "Until they make a move, we're pretty much stuck, far as I can see."

"We could set a trap," J.T. said thoughtfully. "Bait it with cattle."

"Where we gonna get beef?" Purvis asked. The ranchers around Springwater were pretty desperate to put an end to the rustling and all the rest, but he doubted they'd be inclined to lend out the seventy to a hundred head of stock they'd need to draw the outlaws' interest.

"I was thinking of the auction over in Kalispell," J.T. replied.

"There ain't enough money in the town treasury for a shopping spree like that, I'll tell you right now," Purvis pointed out. His gaze wandered to the computer screen; try though he might to concentrate, half his mind was on Cowgirl243. *Hey, Lawman.*

"Stay with me, here, Purvis," J.T. said, snapping him back to attention just like that. "I'm talking about stocking my own range. I've already bought several head of cattle as it is, a couple of horses, too. I need more."

Purvis let out a long breath. "You're willing to put your own animals at risk for the sake of an investigation?"

J.T. shrugged. "There's always an element of chance," he said. "Even without rustlers, a rancher has wolves and coyotes to think about. Not to mention fire, blizzards, droughts, and low prices."

It was enough to make Purvis wonder why anybody would want to run a ranch, with all those things working against them. There was only one answer: It was in their blood, the way the law was in his. He leaned forward, hands folded on the surface of his desk, and spoke quietly. "If these are the same people behind your dad's shooting—"

J.T. smiled grimly, and the look in his eyes turned flint hard. "They might be inclined to come after me, too," he finished, when

Purvis's words fell away. "So much the better."

Purvis wanted to bring in the bad guys, but something in J.T.'s manner worried him mightily. "Maybe this isn't such a good idea after all. Everybody around here knows you've been deputized. They're gonna guess what you're up to right off, and if they had anything to do with Jack's killing, they might be gunning for you, too."

"Maybe," J.T. agreed. "They might also see it as a challenge, like I do. With me, it's both professional and personal—professional if they're just a bunch of ordinary thieves. Personal if one of them killed my father."

Purvis shifted in his chair. If anything happened to J.T., he'd have to take an ample share of the blame. On the other hand, they weren't going to beat these rustlers out of the brush and into the open by playing it safe, and something sure as hell had to be done before matters went from bad to worse. "Fair enough," he allowed. "You need any help getting ready?"

J.T. grinned. "You know how to string barbwire?" he asked.

* * *

Maggie stood on a stepladder, soapy sponge in hand, washing the log wall of the room she would be occupying as soon as the last spiderweb was gone and the antique lace curtains were hung. The bedstead, a mahogany, intricately carved four-poster, had come down to Maggie as a teenager, along with some of June-bug McCaffrey's modest jewelry and a few musty remembrance books. It had been in her parents' guest house since Maggie left for college, and Wes and Reece were bringing it over later, in the back of a borrowed truck.

". . . and then he said, 'That's one reason,' " she told a blue-jeaned Daphne, who was just handing up a fresh bucket of water.

Daphne's mouth formed a perfect O. "That's all? He didn't elaborate? He just left you hanging there?"

Maggie dunked her sponge with a vengeance, wrung it out, and slapped it against the wall. She'd been unsettled ever since her encounter with J.T. at the Station the day before, when he'd hinted that there was more to his visit than a simple desire to see what she was doing with the old place and then never said another word about it.

"That's right," she said, scrubbing. "That's his specialty. Leaving people hanging."

Daphne laughed, resting her hands on her slender hips and looking up at Maggie with sparkling eyes. "He really got under your skin," she observed, sounding thrilled with the possibility.

"He did not," Maggie lied. "I couldn't possibly care less what J. T. Wainwright says or does not say."

"Right," Daphne said.

Maggie decided it was high time to change the subject. "What do you think of Cindy?" she asked. She'd sent her new employee to the post office a few minutes before, to buy postage for the meter and rent a mailbox under the name Springwater Station.

"Poor kid," Daphne answered, on a wistful note. "Her father is Odell Hough. Do you remember him?"

Maggie bit her lower lip. There were dozens of Houghs in and around Springwater; some of them were solid citizens, and others were rumored to brew moonshine, live in camper shells with no plumbing, and sleep on bare mattresses. "Not specifically," she admitted.

Daphne glanced toward the doorway and lowered her voice, even though Cindy couldn't possibly have stepped into the corridor without raising a noisy greeting from Sadie. "He's a real creep," Daphne said. "After his wife died, there were some reports that he was neglecting the children, if not outright abusing them, and the county tried to take them away. He fought it and won, but believe me, I had both those kids in my class and they would have been better off in foster homes."

Maggie was stricken. "No wonder," she murmured, thinking of Cindy's pregnancy and the fact that she'd dropped out of school to get married.

Daphne nodded, and it soon became apparent that her thoughts were taking a similar track. "She wanted to get out of the house. After that shack of Odell's, that old trailer on the Wainwright place probably looks like a palace."

Maggie remembered the trailer well enough; it was an ancient one-bedroom thing, the size of a breadbox, and it rattled in every brisk wind. She'd lost her virginity to J.T. there, one spring night when they were seventeen.

It seemed there was no escaping thoughts of J.T., no matter which direction the conversation took.

Daphne said something, peering suspiciously up at her, though Maggie didn't catch what it was.

The first time was supposed to be painful, Maggie had heard, but when J.T. made love to her that night, so tenderly, so awkwardly, she'd liked it so much that it scared her—

"Mags?" Daphne persisted.

Maggie snapped out of it. The memories had left her with a hot, achy feeling deep between her hip bones. "What?" she countered.

"You were way off in the distance. What were you thinking?"

"None of your business," Maggie answered sweetly. "By the way, are you here to wash windows or quiz me about my love life?"

Daphne folded her arms and grinned. "Would you 'fess up to anything, if I did?"

Maggie sighed and tried to look stern.

Undaunted, Daphne patted Maggie's sneakered foot. "Just tell me this, then," she persisted. "Why don't you stop pretending and go after that man? It's obvious you're crazy about J.T."

"All right!" Maggie fretted. "There might be a *smidgeon* of truth in that—I do find J.T.—well—attractive. But he's still as reckless as he ever was." She paused, took a breath. "I need structure in my life. I need stability—"

Daphne rolled her eyes. "Where did 'structure and stability' get you with Connor?" she reasoned, plainly out of patience. "Take a chance for once, Mags. Live on the edge!"

"I don't think I know how," Maggie mused.

"You just close your eyes and leap!"

Maggie grimaced. "Or not."

Daphne sighed. "What a shame. You and J.T. practically throw sparks just being in the same room. You're perfect for each other."

"No," Maggie said, resigned, *"you and Ben* are perfect for each other. J.T. and I are old news. His motto is 'Damn the Torpedoes, Full Speed Ahead!' and mine is 'Better Safe Than Sorry.' Don't you see, Daph? We're just too different."

"Oh, Mags," Daphne whispered. "What

happened to you? Did Connor hurt you so badly—?"

"Connor didn't hurt me," Maggie said quietly. "J.T. did."

"But—"

Maggie pulled in a deep breath, let it out slowly. "I'm not in the market for a relationship, Daphne," she said. "Maybe I will be, later, when the Station is up and running. Maybe I'll meet somebody—somebody I have things in common with—but right now, I just want to play it safe."

"That can get to be a habit," Daphne warned. "A bad habit."

Maggie got down from the ladder, smiled, and hugged her best friend. "Stop worrying about me, O.K.?" she said. "A woman doesn't need a man to be happy."

Daphne sighed. "No," she agreed thoughtfully, "but it certainly helps."

Before Maggie had to answer, Sadie erupted into a chorus of cheerful barking, and Cindy stepped into the room, back from the post office.

The girl was smiling. "I could do that," she said, nodding toward the ladder, bucket, and sponge. "Wash the walls, I mean."

Maggie shook her head. "No ladders, and

no reaching over your head," she said firmly. "It isn't good for you."

Cindy was far too young to become a mother, but pregnancy looked good on her nonetheless. She was glowing, and her eyes twinkled. "You sound just like Billy. He's always telling me to take it easy. I'm not supposed to lift things, or help feed the horses, or anything."

"Good for Billy," Daphne said. "Listen to your husband, Cindy."

Cindy rolled her eyes. "I don't have much choice. That trailer of ours is so little, we don't even have to talk. We can hear each other thinking."

Both Daphne and Maggie laughed, then Daphne consulted her watch and whistled. "Look at the time. I'm supposed to meet Ben after work." She waggled her eyebrows comically. "I'm ovulating," she added, in a confidential tone. Daphne never missed a viable opportunity to conceive, and she wasn't particularly secretive about the fact.

Maggie shook her head, smiling. "Don't let us keep you," she teased.

Daphne grinned. "Not a chance," she said, and vanished.

"Is it all right if I use the telephone? To

make a personal call, I mean?" Cindy asked a few minutes later, as Maggie stood in the middle of the room assessing the clean walls. "Billy's over at his mom's, helping Travis move the freezer out to the garage. If I catch him I can let him know I'm through working for the day, and he'll pick me up." Cindy had been working steadily since she arrived, running various errands and familiarizing herself with Maggie's computer, and for the time being there wasn't much else for her to do.

"Of course," Maggie said, tossing her sponge into the bucket with a sense of real satisfaction. The Station had been empty for years, after serving as a makeshift library and, before that, as the town hall. If she just hung in there, putting one foot in front of the other, plugging away at her list of tasks and goals, it would soon be restored to its former glory.

"You going to knock off for the day?" Cindy asked.

Maggie shoved her hands into the hip pockets of her jeans and assessed her accomplishment once more. "Sort of. My dad and brother ought to be showing up soon with my bed. I think I'll sleep here tonight."

"Won't you be scared? To be all alone, I mean?"

"I won't be alone," Maggie said. "Sadie will be with me."

Cindy shivered a little, looked up at the bare rafters that had supported the sturdy roof through decades of Montana wind, snow, rain, and summer heat. "Travis says a lot of people have probably gotten old and died here. He says there must be a *bunch* of spooks."

"Travis?" Maggie asked. She'd never heard of the guy and already she tended to dislike him. "Who's that?"

Cindy blushed and averted her eyes. "He's Billy's half-brother," she answered.

"I see," Maggie said, troubled by something in the girl's manner. "Well, you needn't worry about any ghosts that might be haunting this old place," she said. "If they're here—and that's doubtful—they're good, solid citizens."

Cindy still looked nervous, but she managed a smile. "Well, I'd better hurry up and call Billy before he heads back out to the ranch."

Maggie nodded and went to empty the bucket to rinse out the sponge. When she headed back to take down the ladder and put it away, Cindy was sitting at one of the trestle tables, her chin in her hands, looking downcast.

"I missed Billy," she said. "Doris said he left half an hour ago." A moment later, she burst into tears.

Sadie whimpered and curled up close to Cindy's feet, the better to lend whatever canine comfort might be necessary. Maggie laid a hand on the young woman's thin, heaving shoulder.

"What's the matter, honey?" she asked gently.

Cindy seemed to melt under the least bit of tenderness. Had simple caring been so rare in her life as that? No doubt it had, considering what Daphne had said earlier about the girl's childhood.

She snuffled ingloriously. "Nothing," she said.

Maggie sat down on the bench beside her. "Come on, now. Nobody cries like that over 'nothing'." But maybe they did, she thought. While she'd never had the experience herself, she knew pregnant women were often emotional. Cindy's hormones were probably running amok.

The young woman wiped her face with both hands, and the gesture was so child-like, so guileless, that Maggie wanted to break down and weep herself. "It's just that Doris doesn't like me."

"Doris?"

"Billy's mom."

"Oh," Maggie said.

"She thinks I was trying to trap Travis."

Maggie was confused. "Travis?"

Cindy blushed again. "I mean Billy," she said.

The confusion didn't abate. "O.K.," Maggie responded, in what she hoped was a cheerful tone of voice. Then she patted Cindy lightly on the forearm. "Sadie and I will give you a ride home. I'll just leave the door open for Dad and Wes."

Cindy hesitated, as though afraid she would be overstepping by taking Maggie up on the offer, then nodded. "Thanks, Maggie."

Maggie stood, and so did Sadie, who had a sixth sense when it came to prospective car rides. "Come on," she said to the eager dog. "You can keep us company."

Fifteen minutes later they passed the Wainwright ranch house, a rambling log structure on a high rise overlooking the valley, and Maggie marveled at how the place had fallen apart since she'd last seen it. Once one of the finest spreads in the county, it had been neglected for a long while, and it showed. If Scully and Evangeline Wainwright, the original owners of the property, weren't rattling chains in the night out of sheer protest, their great-grandson, Jack, surely was.

There were new, unpainted rails in the corral fences, though, and stacks of lumber, sawhorses, and other signs of industry stood around the overgrown yard.

A kind of sweet shudder went up Maggie's spine.

The trailer stood some hundred yards behind the main house, tucked in behind an old grape arbor, long since out of control. Smaller even than Maggie remembered it being, the pink-and-white mobile home was no longer mobile, but set up on cement blocks. Somebody had made a real effort to spruce the place up: The aged pink-and-white metal walls gleamed in the sun, and the grass had been tamed into something vaguely resembling a lawn.

"Come in," Cindy said, half pleading. "I've got some ice tea brewed."

Maggie didn't have the heart to refuse, even though she wanted to get back to the Station while her dad and Wes were still there. "Sure," she said.

Sadie bounded out on the driver's side after Maggie, spotted a blue, black, and gold butterfly, and went in fearless pursuit. Cindy led the way into the trailer, leaving the door ajar in case the beagle decided to join them.

The inside of Billy and Cindy's modest home was as well cared for as the outside, and Maggie knew then, if she hadn't before, that Cindy would make an exemplary employee, not to mention a good wife and mother.

"Billy does most of the work," the girl said shyly, following Maggie's gaze.

Maggie smiled. She didn't know Billy Raynor—he might be a paragon—but she wasn't willing to give him all the credit. Cindy was surely being too modest.

"Have a seat," Cindy said, heading for the refrigerator. She could nearly have reached it from the couch, the place was so small.

Maggie sat. Through the open doorway she could see Sadie, still cavorting in the yard. Cindy had said she was seven and a half months along. "Your baby is due in August?" she asked, to make conversation.

"First week in September," Cindy said shyly, busy pouring tea from a plastic pitcher. "Travis says, wouldn't it be funny if the kid came on Labor Day?"

Travis again, Maggie thought, but she offered no comment. Sometimes she just couldn't help interfering, but she mostly confined her efforts to Reece and Kathleen and, of course, Daphne. "Funny," she agreed.

Just then, Sadie began to bark, not out of alarm, but in gleeful greeting. Cindy handed Maggie her glass of tea and went to the door.

"Hi, beautiful," Maggie heard a male voice say.

"Hi, Billy," Cindy responded, and though there was warmth in the way she spoke, Maggie heard a note of something tentative as well, and wondered if Billy didn't hear it, too. "My boss is here. Maggie McCaffrey, this is my husband, Billy Raynor."

"Hello, Billy," Maggie said.

Billy was only a few inches taller than Cindy, and he looked, as Reece would have said, as if he might blow away in a high wind. He had earnest blue eyes and light hair razed to a buzz cut, and everything about him said "cowboy."

"Howdy," he said, with a polite nod, holding his straw hat in both hands.

"I tried to call you and let you know I needed a ride," Cindy said, making for the fridge again. Billy accepted a can of bargain cola with a beatific look of appreciation; she might have given him manna from heaven or, at least, ambrosia. "Doris said you'd already left, so Maggie brought me out here."

"That was kind of you, ma'am," Billy said. He'd seated himself at the tiny fold-down table just inside the door, laying his hat aside with the elaborate ease of a much older man. "We're obliged."

Maggie felt uncomfortable, as though she were intruding on a honeymoon, and finished her tea quickly. "I'd better be getting back to town," she said, rising.

Cindy took her empty glass. "I'll see you tomorrow," she said, and the statement sounded almost like a question. She looked fearful, as though expecting to be fired on the spot.

"Bright and early," Maggie confirmed.

She collected Sadie, got behind the wheel of the Pathfinder, and started back over the rutted dirt road. Distracted, she was looking into the rearview mirror, remembering the night she and J.T. had made love in the trailer's berthlike double bed, when she heard the shout, accompanied by Sadie's warning bark.

"Hey!" The voice startled her back to reality.

Maggie slammed on the brakes, practically throwing Sadie through the windshield, and nearly strangled when she saw J.T. right in front of her, struggling to calm the terrified black-and-white paint gelding he was riding.

Maggie jumped out of the Pathfinder. "Are you hurt?" she cried.

"No," J.T. answered, still working with the frantic horse, "but I have to give you credit. You sure as hell tried!"

Maggie, never inclined toward a temper, barely kept herself from thumping the hood of her own vehicle with one knotted fist. "Nonsense," she argued. "It was an accident."

Finally, the gelding settled down a little, though its ears were tucked back and its nostrils were flared. J.T. swung out of the saddle to face her. "You could have killed this horse, not to mention me."

Full of terror and chagrin, Maggie started to cry. "Don't you think I know that?" she blubbered.

J.T.'s stern look softened into a lopsided grin, and he pulled her loosely into his arms, patting her back awkwardly. "Hey, McCaffrey," he said, "take it easy. I shouldn't have yelled at you like that. I'm sorry."

Maggie smelled fresh hay on his shirt, and another, more subtle scent she remembered from years before. She took one stumbling step backward, shaking. Sadie had moved to the driver's seat and watched them with panting interest over the top of the steering wheel. "I think I'm going to throw up," Maggie said.

J.T. cupped her chin in one hand and lifted. "Take a couple of deep breaths. You're all right, I'm all right, and the horse is all right." He grinned, glancing over the top of her head toward Sadie. "And the dog looks like she might be planning to drive off without you."

Maggie, still weeping, began to laugh, almost hysterically.

"Still going to throw up?" J.T. inquired.

Maggie shook her head, and promptly began to hiccup.

"You really are in bad shape, aren't you?" He looked and sounded amused.

"No, damn it," Maggie managed to argue, hiccupping again. "I am just fine. I just—I just need to get home."

J.T. nodded, stepped aside. "Do you remember?" he asked quietly, before Maggie could turn away.

She knew what he meant, though she wished she could have misunderstood. He was gazing in the direction of the trailer, now occupied by another pair of young lovers. "Yes," she said, barely breathing the word. She couldn't look at him because she was sure to see a reflection of her own memories in his eyes.

"Hey, Maggie?"

She bit her lower lip.

"Look at me, will you?"

She forced herself to meet his gaze. "All right," she said. "I'm looking at you."

He chuckled. "Have supper with me."

Her heart picked up speed. "I can't," she replied, with some relief. "My dad and Wes are delivering a bed to the Station right about now. If I don't keep an eye on them, they'll put it anywhere but where I want it."

"Ummm," he said, with a sage nod. "How about tomorrow, then?"

There was no graceful way out. She wasn't even sure why she *wanted* one, graceful or otherwise, but the truth was, she was scared stiff. Her inner child, if there was such a thing, wanted to bolt and scramble down the hill, run all the way home, leaving dog, car, horse, and man behind. "Tomorrow," she repeated.

"It'll be here when the sun comes up in the morning," he teased.

"All right," she said.

"All right?"

"I'll have dinner with you. I'll *make* dinner, at the Station."

"Even better," J.T. said.

"Good."

He grinned at her discomfiture. "What time?"

"Seven," Maggie answered, sounding a lot more sure of herself than she actually felt. Why was she so scared of this man, she wondered frantically. The answer came on the heels of the question; J. T. Wainwright scared her because she knew there was fury in him, even darkness, but it was more than that. He stirred some vague wildness inside her and scattered her well-ordered emotions every which way.

"Shall I bring anything? Wine, maybe?"

She managed a smile, hoped it looked casual. "Sure. Sure, that would be great." She turned, started back toward the gaping driver's door of the Pathfinder. Her knees were wobbly, and her head felt light. "I'll see you then."

"If not before," he said.

Get a grip, McCaffrey, Maggie scolded herself, *you're not a teenager.* She pretended not to hear, waved cheerfully, and got behind the wheel. J.T. mounted the paint gelding, touched the brim of his hat in the old-fashioned way, and rode out of her way.

She didn't dare look into the rearview mirror again until the gates of the Wainwright place were far behind her.

"Maggie seemed like a real nice lady," Billy said, his eyes lighting up with appreciation when Cindy placed a plate of macaroni and cheese in front of him. If she cooked the least little thing for him, he acted like it was the blue-plate special from a fancy restaurant in Missoula or some-where, instead of some goop out of a box. "She work you real hard?"

Cindy filled a plate for herself, sat down across from Billy, and looked at the food with resignation. She'd eat, because she didn't want her baby doing without, but she didn't have to like it. "No," she answered, at last. "She hardly expects me to work at all." Cindy brightened a little, just thinking about her job. "I get to use the computer, though. I'm learning a lot of new stuff."

Billy's smile was wide. "That's good." He hesitated, chewed, and swallowed a hefty bite of mac and cheese. " 'Course, you'll want to quit and stay home when the baby comes."

Cindy barely suppressed a sigh. "Maybe," she said. Billy had had a hard life, just like her, but there was a stubborn inno-cence about him. He liked to pretend every-thing was perfect, but he wasn't the one with the guilty conscience. "We need what-ever extra money we can get our hands on, especially now."

Billy finished his macaroni and put his plate in the sink. He was still hungry, she knew that, but he was going to pretend about that, too. A lump formed in her throat; she wouldn't be able to swallow another bite. A hardworking man like Billy ought to have meat for supper every night, but there was no money for such luxuries, and the marketing would have to wait until one of them got a paycheck. For the time being they were living on donations from Doris's kitchen cupboards, and every boxed dinner and can of beans came equipped with one of the woman's long-suffering sighs.

Sometimes Cindy heard Doris's voice even in her dreams. *If it weren't for you, Miss Priss . . .*

"Here," Cindy said, and pushed her plate across the table to Billy. "I'm feeling a little sick."

Billy looked genuinely worried. God bless him, he truly cared for her; he'd proven that over and over again, through the years. He'd fought her battles, given her valentines, told her she was pretty and smart, believed in her no matter what. He deserved so much better than the likes of her.

"You need to eat, honey," Billy said.

Tears brimmed in her eyes, and she shook her head. Her throat was so tight, it hurt. "I can't," she said. "I told you—I feel sick."

Billy took the plate and finished her share of the macaroni and cheese slowly. "Things are gonna get better," he told her. "I promise."

Cindy sniffled, then smiled. "That's one thing about you, Billy Raynor. Your word is as good as gold." At least, she thought, *one* of them had some integrity, and some faith in the future.

"So's yours," Billy assured her. "You just need to start believin' in yourself a little more, that's all."

Cindy looked away. A year ago, she and Billy had been going steady, and she'd still been in school, getting O.K. grades. Then they'd had a silly fight over something Billy's mother Doris had said, and Cindy had stormed out of the Raynor house, angry and crying. It should have been Billy who came after her, but instead it was Travis. Travis, who had somehow conned her—to this day she wasn't sure how he'd managed it—into breaking up with Billy and being his girl instead. The relationship hadn't lasted long— Cindy had known it was a mistake, for all the good that did—but the damage was done.

Cindy had been a virgin when she left Billy, but by the time Travis was through with her, she was expecting a baby. Although Billy had cried when she told him she was pregnant—except for the night her mother died, that was the worst thing she'd ever been through—he'd sworn he loved her just the same, and he'd vowed to raise his niece or nephew as his own child. She knew he meant it, too. When Billy Raynor made you a promise, you could take it to the bank.

He'd long since forgiven her, but the question was, would she ever be able to forgive herself?

4

"Please tell me you like that bed right where it is," Maggie's younger brother, Wes, said, with a winsome grin. A colleague of Daphne's at Springwater Elementary, he was a charmer, always had been, and one of the most popular teachers in the school district into the bargain. He and Reece had lugged the enormous antique into the Station while Maggie was out, and had set it up between the two long, narrow windows in Jacob and June-bug's old room. Reece stood by, looking hopeful and a little wan; strong as he was, the problems between him and Kathleen were taking a visible toll.

Maggie gave her brother a one-armed

squeeze and smiled. "It's perfect," she said. She could hardly wait to add crisp cotton sheets, one of June-bug's own quilts, retrieved from a chest at her parents' house, and the crocheted ecru pillow shams she'd purchased at the estate auction she'd attended with Daphne. Everything was back from the cleaners and ready to use; in the morning she would make up the beds in the guest rooms. "Thank you." She kissed her dad's cheek. "Both of you."

"You're welcome," Reece said, in his deep, somber voice. "I'd better be headin' out, though. There's a meeting of the Founder's Day committee tonight, down at the Brimstone."

The Brimstone Saloon, opened in Springwater's early days by Trey Hargreaves, an ancestor of Daphne's, was one of the oldest continuously operated bars in Montana, and only minor changes had been made in the intervening century. The plank floors, an admitted improvement over the previous sawdust, had been put in at the turn of the twentieth century, and the bar, mirror, and many of the tables were original. The back room had been the gathering place for various community groups from the beginning.

Wes, fair-haired and blue-eyed, a born heartbreaker who was madly in love with his wife, Franny, and dedicated to their two small children, chuckled and gave his father a mock slug to the shoulder. "You'd better not have anything stronger than coffee," he teased, "or Mom will hang your hide on the barn door."

Reece's answering smile was wistful and fleeting. "Fortunately," he said, "we don't have a barn." The look in his eyes said *Your mother doesn't care what I do.*

Maggie was eager to change the subject. "How about you?" she asked Wes, giving him a nudge. "Can you stay and have supper with me?"

Wes looked regretful. "Can't do it, sis," he said. "Franny's 'morning sickness' has been lasting most of the day lately. I've got to get home and help with the kids."

Maggie smiled at the thought of Wes and Franny's three-year-old twins, Jodi and Loren. They were beautiful, healthy children, a girl and a boy, respectively, and Maggie adored them, as she did Simon's kids. "I'd be glad to keep them once in a while, Wes. Just call when you need a babysitter. And tell Franny I'll be by to see her when she feels up to a visit."

Wes nodded, already headed toward the door. As a kid he'd been something of a handful, and Reece and Kathleen had attributed many a gray hair to him. As a man, he was an amazing teacher, husband, and father. Although Maggie certainly loved Simon, she was closer to her younger brother. "She's been wanting to see what you're doing with the Station," he said in parting. "I'm sure she'll drop by once she feels better."

Maggie smiled and waved and watched her brother disappear through the open door. Then she turned to Reece. "Things are pretty rocky between you and Mom, I take it," she said softly.

Reece shrugged those powerful McCaffrey shoulders. "I reckon you could say that," he allowed, then bent to kiss Maggie's forehead. "Don't be worrying about your mother and me, now. We haven't quite given up yet."

Maggie embraced him. "Good," she said, and the word came out on a raspy breath, sounding a little like a sob.

Reece kissed her forehead once more, and then took his leave. Since the McCaffrey house was right around the corner, and the Brimstone stood just a block down the street, he was on foot. Maggie watched him from the Station's porch, then called Sadie inside. After making up the bed, she and the dog crossed the old, tumbledown corral area and entered Reece and Kathleen's yard through a creaky back gate. Maggie intended to make a light supper for herself and Sadie, pack a few things, and head back for her first night in her new home.

Kathleen was near the gazebo, watering fat pink-and-white peonies with a hose, and Maggie stopped to admire her. Kathleen was tall and slender, and her auburn hair gleamed in the late afternoon sunlight like that of some mythic Celtic goddess. Maggie might have stood there for a long time, just watching her, if Sadie hadn't yipped a greeting and given away their presence.

Kathleen smiled, the water from her hose gleaming like an arch of diamonds. "Hello, darling," she said to Maggie, and at the same time, bent to ruffle Sadie's ears with her free hand.

Maggie drew in the fragrances of old-fashioned roses and fresh-cut grass and clean, rural air, drew in also the still comforting presence of her mother. "Hi," she said, and kissed Kathleen's apricot-and-cream cheek. "Your garden looks great, Mom. Just like always."

"Thank you," Kathleen replied, with quiet warmth. "I've made a lovely salad for supper. Would you like to join me?" Her proud chin wobbled, almost imperceptibly, and she fixed her fierce green gaze on the peonies, her favorite flowers of all time. "I believe your father is otherwise occupied."

"He's at the Founder's Day meeting," Maggie said, and then felt silly. Her parents were grown-ups, even if they didn't always behave accordingly, and perfectly capable of managing their private lives without her nudging things along.

"Hmmph," Kathleen said. Maggie had no idea what she meant and didn't try to find out.

"Salad sounds good," she said. "Is it your famous feta cheese and tomato concoction?"

Kathleen beamed. "Yes," she said. "I know that's your favorite. There's garlic bread, too." She carried the hose over to the wall and turned off the faucet. "How about you, Sadie?" she asked, as the dog bounced around her in beagle celebration. "Would you like some salad, too, or would you prefer leftover meatloaf?"

Sadie yowled with delight and streaked toward the backdoor of the house, leaving both Kathleen and Maggie laughing.

"Simon called today," Kathleen said lightly a few minutes later, as Maggie set the table and she put out the salad and bread. "He and Penny have decided to take the boys to Europe on vacation this year, instead of coming to Springwater. I do hope they don't run into some terrorist over there."

Maggie thought it imprudent to mention that terrorists could turn up anywhere, even in places like Springwater. "They'll be okay, Mom," she said. "Maybe they'll come here for Christmas."

Kathleen sighed. "It won't be the same," she said, and stared off through the window above the sink for a long moment. "Without your father, I mean."

Maggie didn't know what to say, and so held her tongue. In fact, she went still, feeling stricken.

Kathleen mustered up one of her brave, dazzling smiles, and while it faltered a little, she managed to hold it up. "I'm sorry, darling," she said. "There I go again, getting ahead of myself, dreading things before they happen."

Maggie crossed the gleaming linoleum floor to face her mother and laid her hands on those proud, straight shoulders. "Is it really so bad, Mom?" she asked, very softly. "Surely the two of you can compromise—"

Tears sprang to Kathleen's eyes; she blinked them away. "I know you think it's about my painting pears, and that wretched *trailer* your father bought, but it's more complicated than that."

"But you've been so close for so long—"

Kathleen stroked Maggie's hair once, with a light pass of her right hand—the hand that had tested Maggie's, Simon's, and Wes's foreheads for a thousand potential fevers, signed their report cards, directed the placement of Christmas trees. "Sweetheart, people change. You know that."

Maggie had to look away. She thought of Connor, of J.T., of herself. "Yes," she agreed. "And they also stay the same."

Kathleen hugged her. "Let's have our supper," she said gently and, after dishing up cold meatloaf for an ecstatic Sadie, she took her customary place at the round table in the breakfast nook. Maggie joined her.

"I saw Daphne at the post office this afternoon," Kathleen said, "and she told me you'd hired Odell Hough's girl. Isn't she expecting a baby?"

"Yes," Maggie replied thoughtfully. "That's her. Tell me: What does the local rumor mill have to say about Billy and Cindy Raynor?"

Gossip was alive and well in Springwater, as in most small towns, though Kathleen generally didn't have a taste for it. She sighed. "Where do I begin?"

Purvis was on his way to Flo's, all spiffed up in the new jeans and western shirt he'd bought special at the Maple Creek Walmart store, before he realized he didn't know his date's first name. He'd always called her by her screen name, Cowgirl, and she'd known him as Lawman.

As he parked his mother's 1992 Escort in front of the diner, he let out a long sigh. Since he drove Springwater's one and only police car most of the time, he'd never seen the need to get a rig of his own. His mom lived just a few blocks from his place, and she stayed home most Thursday nights to watch her programs on TV. Besides, she was getting past the age when she ought to be driving, though he hadn't figured out how to tell her so just yet.

He glanced at his watch. It was 8:15, and across the street, in the First Presbyterian Church, the basement lights were on. He wondered what kind of meeting Cowgirl was attending, and decided it was probably one of those reading groups where women got together to talk about some Oprah book.

Purvis sat, arms folded, motor running, drawing deep, slow breaths. A part of him wanted to slam that Ford right into reverse and scream out of there, headed straight for the relative safety of Springwater, but he was determined to give this first encounter with Cowgirl a fair chance. They'd been talking on-line for just over a week, and he knew the important stuff, even if he hadn't a clue what her name was. She liked fireplaces, old movies, rainy days, pizza with pineapple and ham. She believed in God, voted, enjoyed going to garage sales and potluck dinners, and loved horses, which was probably why she called herself "Cowgirl." She'd grown up in California and moved to Maple Creek a few months before, looking to start fresh, live a simpler, quieter life.

The pit of Purvis's stomach began to twitch a little as his mind turned inevitably to his own situation. He'd never been married—never had more than a few dates, in fact, in all his life. He just wasn't the type women gravitated to, though he didn't reckon he was repulsive or anything like that; more like invisible. Fact was, the ladies didn't seem to notice him at all.

Somebody rapped at the window of Purvis's borrowed Escort and startled him half out of his hide. He jumped high enough to squash the crown of his hat against the roof, and probably would have, too, if it hadn't been made of hard straw. He turned and saw Odell Hough looming on the other side of the glass.

Unsmiling, Purvis rolled down the window. "Hello, Odell," he said, mostly because he didn't have any choice. He couldn't pretend he hadn't seen the guy, after all.

Odell was a big bugger, usually dressed like an old-time railroad man, in overalls that resembled mattress ticking and one of those silly beanie caps put out by chewing-tobacco companies. He had been good-looking once, Odell had, but years of low living had left him loose-fleshed and red-eyed. His teeth, once as good as any movie star's, had gone to hell, and most of his hair had fallen out. Purvis figured that was why he always wore the hat. "Well, now, *Purvis,*" Odell boomed, in exuberant greeting. "What brings you to Maple Creek?"

Purvis was damned if he was going to tell Odell Hough, of all people, about his Internet flirtation with a woman called Cowgirl. Hell, he hadn't even said anything to his mother, and he was close to her. "Just out takin' the air," he lied. "What about you?"

Odell was chewing on a toothpick—Purvis hated that habit almost as much as smoking—and Hough's little pig eyes narrowed as he assessed his captive audience. His breath made Purvis wish he'd brought along the oxygen tank he carried in the squad car. "Hear J. T. Wainwright's joined the force," he said, ignoring Purvis's question and lending a mocking note to the word "force." "What's that all about?"

"Everybody needs time off once in a

while," Purvis said lightly. "I been running the show by myself for a long time."

Odell weighed that reply and, from his expression, found it wanting. "It ain't like Springwater is a hotbed of crime," he said.

Purvis sighed. "It's getting that way, what with all that's been going on lately."

"That so," Odell responded. It wasn't a question; everybody knew there had been some rustling and other trouble around Springwater the last few months. "He'll go back to New York soon enough," Hough added, chewing away. That toothpick of his must have been mere wood pulp by then. "Wainwright, I mean. Not much left of the old family place."

Purvis scraped up a smile and hoped it looked cordial. "J.T.'s planning to stay on," he said. "Says he's going to make that ranch pay again."

Odell made a skeptical, huffing sound. Like he was some kind of authority on running any kind of profitable operation. Except for the occasional stint pulling green chain at Reece McCaffrey's lumber mill whenever the commodity cheese, beans, and wieners ran out, he'd never held down a real job in his life. "City boy," he scoffed.

Purvis was offended on J.T.'s behalf. "That's a load of sheep dip," he said, glancing up at the rearview mirror. He saw, to his alarm, that Cowgirl's meeting was letting out across the street; everybody in the group was carrying the same book, a thick paperback. Quickly, he shifted his gaze back to Odell. "J.T. was born in Springwater County, and his great-great-granddaddy was one of the first settlers."

Odell scoffed again, but then he straightened up to go. "Got to get down to the Grange Hall and hook up with my boy Randy," he said. "He has to go to them AA meetin's for ninety days straight, thanks to you."

Purvis's grin was steady. He'd arrested Randy Hough for drunken driving two weeks before and brought him to Maple Creek to turn him over to the sheriff's department. Apparently the judge had sent the kid to AA, as well as giving him thirty days suspended and jerking his license. "Well now, Odell," he said, and glanced at the rearview mirror again, wondering which one of the women crossing the road was Cowgirl, "I know you're grateful, but it was my job. All I can say is, you're welcome."

Odell's coarse face went crimson, and his mouth twisted into an ugly grimace. For a moment Purvis thought he was going to swallow the toothpick. Instead, he muttered a four-letter word, thrust himself away from the car door upon which he'd been leaning, and ambled off down the lumpy sidewalk in the direction of the Grange Hall.

Purvis stayed in the car until he saw Odell turn the corner. Then, with a resolute sigh, he set his hat aside on the passenger side, opened the door of the Escort, and got out. When he turned toward the road, he found Nelly Underwood standing right there, looking up at him. *I'll be the one wearing the badge,* he recalled writing, in his most recent email message.

"Purvis?" she asked. She had a disbelieving look on her face. Nelly might live in Maple Creek, but she worked at the library in Springwater. Purvis had met her at a church get-together a few weeks back, put on especially for singles. He'd liked her, too. She was a peppery little critter, though way too young for him, with lots of freckles and brown hair that fell to her chin in a spill of curls. Her dark eyes were large with uncertainty and surprise.

"Evening, Nelly," he said, and looked over her shoulder toward the Presbyterian Church. The lights were out and most everybody was gone. Maybe his cyber friend had decided to take a hike after getting a look at him. Either that, or Odell had scared her off.

Nelly held the book against her scrawny chest. She was wearing old jeans and a white tank top that had seen its share of washings, plus a few extra. "Lawman?" she persisted softly, as if dreading the answer.

Purvis felt his eyes go wide, and he swallowed so hard he thought he'd be digesting his Adam's apple in short order. "Cowgirl?" he countered.

Nelly's smile was sudden and bright, and it fair knocked Purvis back on his heels. She began to laugh. "I should have known," she said, between gasps.

Purvis flushed red, torn between running like a rabbit and flat-out loosing his temper. One thing was for sure—he was not amused. "Damn it, why didn't you tell me you were Nelly Underwood?" he asked.

She put one hand on a narrow hip, holding the book in the curve of her other arm, schoolgirl style. Her eyes, laughing a moment before, were snapping with temper. "Why didn't you tell me *you* were Purvis Digg?" she shot back.

He heaved a big sigh and made a motion like he was going to run his fingers through his hair before he remembered that he couldn't because it was skinned down tight against his head and bound back with the usual bootlace. "You didn't ask me," he pointed out.

She stomped one small foot. She was wearing scuffed cowboy boots. "Well, *you* didn't ask *me,* either. I thought you were a state patrolman or maybe a sheriff's deputy."

Purvis sighed. "Well, I ain't." He realized, too late, that his response came out sounding more angry than any of the hundred other emotions he was feeling just them.

She turned on one heel, ready to stride away, leaving a trail of dust behind her. Purvis caught hold of her elbow, just gently, and stopped her.

"Wait a second," he said, knowing he ought to just let her go. "Wait."

She looked up at him, blinking, and he realized, to his horror, that she was trying not to break down and cry. "What?"

He heaved a sigh. "We agreed to have coffee together, if I recall correctly," he said. "Come on. I'll buy you a jolt of caffeine and a piece of pie." Flo built a good pie, and as far as he was concerned, Nelly Underwood could stand a few extra calories.

She hesitated, then smiled, and Purvis felt his heart quiver a little. "O.K., Lawman," she said, linking her arm with his and nodding once toward the neon-lit window of the diner. "Let's go."

Maggie took the long way around to the Station, a small suitcase in hand, Sadie springing along at her side. The stars were out, beaming down out of a black sky, and despite her personal concerns, Maggie was happy. Happy to be back in Springwater, among people she knew and loved, doing something that connected her to the several generations of McCaffrey women who had preceded her. While she'd enjoyed her job in Chicago, running a chain of small boutique-style hotels, the original owners had sold out to a major corporation a few years before and upper management had been intent on removing all semblance of beauty, grace, and personality from the inns ever since. Maggie's life had become a grind. When her mother had written that there was talk of tearing down the old Springwater Station and replacing it with a small strip mall—Reece, who owned the property, had received a sound offer from some huge company with a dot-com after its name— Maggie had made a series of quick but hardly impulsive decisions. She'd insisted on matching the outsider's price, sold her condo, transferred her stocks and bonds to a money market account, hired movers, packed her personal belongings and her dog into the Pathfinder, and headed for Montana. She hadn't once regretted the decision, though there had been a few surprises: J. T. Wainwright, for one.

She stood in front of the Station for a few moments, looking over at the Hargreaves mansion where Daphne lived with her relatively new husband. She liked Ben; he was a good man, smart and funny, and he obviously adored Daphne. All points in his favor, especially the last.

As if conjured by Maggie's thoughts of her, Daphne stepped out onto her porch, waving. "Hey, Maggie!" she called. "Come on over and have a cup of tea with me.

Ben's locked away in the study with his computer."

Maggie was pleased by the prospect of a chat with her friend. Though she had been looking forward to a quiet night in the Station, sleeping in that beloved old bed, she'd missed Daphne very much during the years in Chicago, and it seemed that they still had a million things to catch up on, no matter how much time they spent together. "Sounds great," she replied. "I'll be there in just a second." She carried her suitcase inside, then headed across the road, Sadie trotting along behind her.

Daphne was waiting on the step, elbows on her knees, chin cupped in her palms, just as Maggie had seen her a thousand times before. There was a mischievous glint in her eyes, and Maggie remembered her friend's announcement earlier that she was ovulating and had to hurry home to meet Ben, in hopes of conceiving. She smiled to herself and shook her head.

"Hi," Daphne said, reaching out to ruffle Sadie's ears.

"Hi, yourself," Maggie answered.

Daphne stood, grinning. "It's so good to have you back in Springwater," she said, beaming at Maggie. "Now, come inside, and let's have that tea. I have something to tell you."

"What?" Maggie asked, following Daphne into the grand entrance hall. The house was elegantly appointed inside, and contained many antiques that had been in the family since soon after Trey and Rachel Hargreaves were married.

Before Daphne could answer, Ben stepped out of the study, smiling. He was tall, with rich chestnut hair and warm eyes. "How've you been, Maggie?" he asked.

"Fine," Maggie said, smiling back. "How about you?"

"Busy," Ben said. Then he sighed. "I guess I'd better get back to my report," he told her. "If I don't buckle down, I'll still be working at midnight."

"You'd better not be," Daphne said.

Ben chuckled and retreated back into the study.

"You said you had something to tell me," Maggie reminded her friend, once they were alone in the kitchen. Sadie, that shameless flirt, had stayed behind, kissing up to Ben.

Daphne busied herself filling the teakettle, setting it on the stove to heat, getting out mugs and spoons. "I'm going to be a mother," she said, almost breezily. "Well, sort of."

Maggie frowned a little. "How can you 'sort of' be a mother?"

"Ben and I have decided to become foster parents," Daphne answered. A shadow flickered in her eyes, was quickly gone. "At least *I've* decided—Ben is dragging his feet a little, but I know he'll come around. I'm going to pick up the application papers tomorrow, over at the courthouse in Maple Creek."

Maggie didn't know what to say. On the one hand, she thought it was a wonderful idea; Daphne certainly had a great deal to offer a child, even taking Ben's reluctance into account. On the other, she knew such arrangements were usually temporary, and Daphne was bound to become deeply attached. How would she react when the baby either was returned to its birth family or moved on to another foster home? Daphne was bound to be devastated, and she'd already had more than enough sorrow in her life, losing her parents the way she had.

"Maggie?" Daphne prompted, when Maggie didn't speak right away.

She swallowed, rummaged up a shaky smile. "That's—that's great."

"Then why do I get the feeling that you want to talk me out of this?"

Maggie sighed. "It isn't that," she said gently.

"Lots of these children come up for adoption, you know," Daphne put in.

"And lots of them don't," Maggie said.

The teakettle whistled, and Daphne filled the mugs and carried them to the table, small tags dangling over the rims. "This isn't just about Ben and me," she said. "It's about a child in need of a home and family."

Maggie reached out, touched her friend's hand. "I know," she said. "It's just—"

"That you want me to be careful?"

Maggie hesitated, then nodded.

Daphne's eyes filled with tears of emotion, though she was smiling. "Some things are worth taking a chance on, Mags," she said.

They sipped their tea in companionable silence for a minute or so, and Maggie decided it was time to change the subject.

"J.T. is coming to my place for supper to-morrow night," she said.

Daphne's whole face lit up with pleasure, in the space of an instant. "Really?"

Maggie nodded. "He sort of invited him-self."

"Heck, who cares?" Daphne replied, wav-ing one hand. Then she paused. "Is he com-ing to the guest house, or the Station?"

"The Station," Maggie said.

Daphne cheered. "Yes!" she whooped, punching the air with one fist.

Maggie just gazed at her, confused.

"Well," Daphne enlarged, "he wouldn't make a move on you in your parents' guest house, now would he?"

"He'd better not make a move on me at all," Maggie said primly.

"Whatever," Daphne replied, with a note of friendly skepticism.

Maggie rolled her eyes. "You," she told her friend, "are an incurable romantic."

Daphne laughed, and it was a wonderful, reassuring sound. Surely everything would be all right.

"Life," Maggie mused, after another brief lapse in the conversation, "is way too com-plicated."

Daphne nodded, cupping her hands around her teacup and smiling. "Indeed it is," she agreed.

Maggie glanced at the clock on the kitchen mantel and sighed. "I'd better get out of here," she said. "I've been trying to balance my checkbook all afternoon, and if I don't find the error, I'll lay awake all night staring at the ceiling."

Daphne walked her to the front door, and Sadie padded out of the study, tags jingling cheerfully, to join her mistress.

"Good night," Maggie smiled.

Daphne kissed her lightly on the cheek. "Thank you," she said.

"For what?"

"Being my friend."

"That's the easy part," Maggie replied, and then she and Sadie started for home.

After an hour spent grappling with her checkbook, Maggie locked up the Station and retreated to the fairly modern bathroom adjoining her private quarters, where she showered, put on a nightgown, and brushed her teeth. Sadie, normally a dog who took liberties, seemed to know that beagles and antique quilts don't mix, and curled up with a tired sigh on the hooked rug beside the bed.

Maggie had just crawled beneath the covers, book in hand, reading glasses perched on the end of her nose, when the telephone rang. She reached for the receiver, spoke quickly, and maybe a little breathlessly. "Hello?"

J.T.'s chuckle wove its way through the wires and around her heart. "Sorry if I startled you, McCaffrey. I didn't mean to do that."

Maggie glanced at the windup clock on her nightstand. Eight-thirty. Not an unreasonable time to call. She was getting jumpy in her old age. "You didn't," she said, fudging a little. "I wasn't expecting anybody to call me here, that's all." She waited, and the silence lengthened. "J.T.?"

"Umm?"

"You dialed *my* number, remember?"

He laughed. "Yeah," he said. "I remember."

She caught herself smiling and stopped. "If you can't make dinner tomorrow night, I'll understand," she said, suddenly unable to think of any other reason why he might have called.

"Nice try," he replied, "but I'll be there."

"J.T.—"

"What?"

"What's going on? You didn't call to hear my voice."

He sighed heavily. He was lonely and so, Maggie realized, was she. All the more reason to be careful. "Maybe I did," he said. "Maggie, what happened? Between you and the doc, I mean?"

It was none of his business, but he'd asked so quietly, so sincerely, that Maggie lowered her defenses a little. Temporarily, at least. "Connor and I just couldn't make things work. We tried, but you know how it is."

"I'm sorry."

"It's old news, J.T. What about you? How did you happen to wind up a divorced father?"

There was a lazy and rather rueful smile in his voice. "I became a father in the usual way. As for the divorce, well, Annie couldn't take being married to a cop. Especially a homicide cop." He paused, and Maggie knew he was running a hand through that thick, dark hair of his. He'd always done that when he was thinking, even as a little boy. "It wasn't her fault; I was a lousy husband, never home, always focused on the job. We finally decided to go our separate ways."

"But you were still together when you were shot, right?"

She could almost see him shaking his head. "No, Annie was already remarried by then."

"You faced an ordeal like that alone?"

"I had pals on the force. My mother even put in a brief appearance, between husbands."

Maggie, raised in the heart of a loving family, with a large network of friends and acquaintances, was appalled. "Oh, J.T."

"I'm not asking for sympathy here, McCaffrey."

"What *are* you asking for, then?"

Once again, he sighed. His laugh was broken, rusty sounding. "God, I wish I knew. I really wish I knew."

She made a soft sound.

"What?" J.T. prompted.

"I was thinking of that time we went skinny-dipping out at the springs," she said.

He chuckled. "Purvis caught us and

threatened to lock us up for indecent exposure. How old were we?"

"Eighteen," Maggie replied, somewhat
wistfully. A tear trickled down her cheek and
dropped off into space. When, she wondered, had she started to cry? "I was just
back from my first year at Northwestern."

"Yeah," J.T. reflected. "I wonder if Purvis
could have made the charges stick? I can't
speak for myself, but there was nothing indecent about the way you looked that night,
McCaffrey. You were a prime example of
really *righteous* exposure."

She dried her cheeks on the sleeve of her
nightgown, still laughing, still crying.

"What happened, McCaffrey?" J.T. asked
seriously. "Where did we mess up?"

She squeezed her eyes shut, literally unable to answer.

"Are you crying?" His voice was low. Tender.

"No," Maggie sobbed.

He sighed eloquently.

"All right," she said. "So maybe I am, just
a little."

"Why?"

"Because things might have been so different," she answered. She squeezed her

eyes tightly shut as a wave of pain and regret swept over her. She felt impossibly lonely, as though she had slipped into some inner void and become lost in her own heart.

"It's not like we're old and gray, McCaffrey. We could start over, you know."

How could they start over? They were still as different from each other as two people could be, and as unsuited. "What do you suggest?" she asked stiffly, stalling.

She should have seen it coming.

"We could start by skinny-dipping," he said.

5

"Mags!" Daphne called from somewhere in the furthest reaches of the Station. "Come and see what we found!"

Maggie, seated at her computer in the small office off the kitchen and public area, tugged off her reading glasses and pushed back her chair to stand up and stretch. "What?" she called back, smiling at the note of pleasure she'd heard in Daphne's voice and glad at the prospect of a break. She'd spent most of the morning making minor adjustments to the new Springwater Station Web site, designed for her by a friend in Chicago, and although the bed-and-breakfast wasn't quite ready to open, several on-line reservations had already come in. All the guest rooms would be full during the weeklong celebration centered around Founder's Day. Daphne had gone to Maple Creek as planned, and met with a social worker, and she'd been in high spirits ever since she'd returned.

Cindy appeared in the doorway of the office, all twinkling eyes and sunny smiles. The girl's new best friend, the feckless Sadie, was at her heels. "Daphne says you'll have to come and see for yourself," she said.

A part of Maggie urged her to stay at the computer, finish the job, but she resisted. In Chicago, she'd worked twelve- and fifteen-hour days, taking only the rare weekend off, but this was Springwater. She was determined to shift gears and slow down—even if it killed her.

She followed Cindy and the dog back to the storeroom, which had been added onto the Station around 1925 or so. Maggie had been thinking of converting the space into a small museum, displaying some of the community's rich history, such as June-bug's old recipe books—"receipts," she'd called them—and Jacob's careful accounts of income and expenditures. There were a number of other treasures, too, rescued from the ancient stables out back before they finally collapsed a few years ago: harnesses, saddles and other tack, cooking implements, old tools, and the like. Reece and Kathleen had a small collection of photographs from Springwater's heyday as well, and were willing to lend them for the project.

Daphne was kneeling in front of a tattered storage trunk, the kind with thumb latches, and the lid was raised, revealing a lining of carefully pasted bits of ephemera, including letters, newspaper clippings, and the like. Her eyes were shining as she turned and met Maggie's curious gaze. "Look," she said, almost reverently and, as carefully as if she were uncovering a sleeping infant, she folded back several layers of old cloth to reveal what appeared to be a wedding dress, an exquisitely made Victorian concoction of silk and lace and seed pearls.

Maggie's breath caught. She took one step forward, then another, spellbound.

"It's almost perfectly preserved," Daphne mused, running a hand across the pearl-studded bodice. "Who do you suppose it belonged to?"

Maggie didn't need to speculate; she knew. She'd seen the dress in more than one of the photographs in the McCaffrey collection—it had belonged, originally, to Olivia and Will McCaffrey's daughter, Sarah, and stitched, according to the notes in the family album, by the regular attendees of the Springwater quilting bee, who had presented the gown as a wedding gift. Junebug had been among those industrious women, as had Olivia, Rachel Hargreaves, Jessica Calloway, Savannah Parrish, Miranda Kildare, and Evangeline Wainwright. Two of Sarah's daughters had worn the dress eventually, and so had Maggie's paternal grandmother and two of her aunts. Then, mysteriously, it had been lost; Maggie had been deeply disappointed that she couldn't wear the gown when she married Connor.

"In a way," Maggie breathed, kneeling beside Daphne to touch the delicate dress with fingertips that trembled a little, "it belongs to all of us." She explained what she knew of the gown's history, and there were tears of wonder in Daphne's eyes long before the brief tale ended.

"Amazing," she said.

"Totally awesome," Cindy added.

Sadie trotted over to give the dress a sniff, immediately lost interest, and went off to pursue personal objectives.

"It's a pity there's no one to wear it," Maggie reflected.

"What we need is a bride," Daphne agreed. Slowly, she got to her feet, and so did Maggie. They stood side by side, the glorious creation suspended before them, Maggie holding one shoulder of the garment, Daphne the other. "Isn't it magnificent?" Daphne breathed. "I almost feel as though one of us could put it on and go back in time."

Cindy stared raptly at the gown, then extended one slightly tremulous hand to touch the antique fabric. "I used to look at dresses like that in the Spiegel catalog, over at the library," she murmured. "I actually thought I'd get to wear one someday." She made a rueful, self-deprecating sound, meant, Maggie was sure, as a nonchalant little laugh. "Me, Odell Hough's daughter." Her voice broke, and she turned and hurried out of the storeroom, leaving Maggie and Daphne looking after her.

"That poor kid," Daphne said quietly, her eyes luminous with sympathy.

Maggie simply shook her head, saddened to think of a little girl huddled in the library poring over unattainable wedding dresses.

Bouncing back, Daphne held the lacy marvel up to her chest and looked down at its flowing folds. There had to be ten yards of silk in the skirts alone; she and Maggie might have been kids again, playing dress-up in somebody's attic. "Those women were awfully small."

"It could be altered," Maggie responded, assessing the garment.

"I think you should try it on."

Maggie laughed. "Don't be silly. Suppose I tore the fabric?"

"It looks pretty strong to me," Daphne said, tugging gently at one of the bodice seams. "Come on, Mags. Put it on."

A lot of old dreams rose up in Maggie's heart and swelled into her throat, aching there, and she couldn't speak. Tears brimmed in her eyes and, once again, she shook her head. "I can't."

Daphne put one arm around her shoulders and gave her a brief squeeze. "Sure you can," she said.

Maggie swallowed, took the dress in her arms, and sat down on the lid of a second trunk to admire it. For just a few moments, she allowed herself to dream, to imagine herself being married in the lovely gown like so many Springwater brides before her.

Daphne sighed. "It's like an omen," she said.

"It does seem to have an almost magical element," Maggie managed. Then she looked up at Daphne and smiled. "I suppose I could assemble a display for the museum."

"You're kidding," Daphne accused. "That dress is an heirloom, Mags. If you're not going to wear it, then it should be preserved for a niece or a cousin or someone."

Maggie found herself hugging the gown, oddly unwilling to let it go, then or ever. "Yes," she agreed, meaning, *no.*

A few moments later, they agreed that the wedding dress ought to be taken down the street to the dry cleaners for special laundering. Daphne packed it carefully in tissue paper and set out on that errand, and Maggie went back to the computer, but as absorbing as they'd been earlier, it was hard to keep her mind on the tasks at hand. She kept thinking about the gossamer gown, envisioning herself wearing it, along with a flowing veil, walking down the aisle of Springwater's tiny church. Waiting for her, in the groom's traditional place, was J. T. Wainwright.

The thought filled her with a reckless sense of happiness, the sort of crazy, dangerous emotion only J.T. could have inspired.

Gradually, she became aware of furious whispers coming from the main room, where Cindy was folding colorful brochures advertising the Springwater Station as a bed-and-breakfast. They would be sent out to addresses from a rented mailing list, as well as prominently placed at the counters of other businesses in town.

Maggie got up, concerned, and went to the doorway.

Cindy was working determinedly, while a good-looking young man, probably in his mid-twenties, stood over her, a cocky grin slanting his mouth. He had dark hair and deep blue eyes and, though lean, he was powerfully built, reminding Maggie a little of J.T. when he was around that age. "I told you, Travis," Cindy hissed, almost desperately, "I can't afford to lose this job. Unless you're here to book a room, you'd better run along."

Travis. Maggie was still absorbing the implications of the boy's identity when, standing across the table from where Cindy sat with her back to the office, he leaned over, hands braced against the table's edge, his face only an inch or two from Cindy's, and drawled, "If I did rent a room, would you share it with me?"

Maggie slipped back, out of sight, but not before Cindy slammed the palms of both hands down onto the tabletop and cried hoarsely, "For God's sake, Travis, leave me be! I'm a married woman."

"Married to my wimp of a little brother."

Maggie hadn't planned to eavesdrop, but the situation was too disturbing to ignore. She wasn't entirely sure Cindy was safe, given the tone and general drift of the conversation.

"Billy is more of a man than you ever thought of being, Travis DuPres. This might be your baby I'm carrying, but Billy's the real father. Now go, before you get me fired!"

Maggie let her forehead rest against the inside of the doorjamb, feeling heartsick even though Cindy's announcement was hardly news. According to Kathleen, the facts surrounding the baby's conception were common knowledge in Springwater.

Travis murmured something in response to Cindy's remarks, and by that time Maggie was fairly certain she could speak and still retain her composure.

"Cindy? Are you out there? If you are, could you bring me one of the brochures, please? I want to scan it into the computer for that email campaign we've been planning."

Travis swore audibly, and Maggie heard his footsteps as he stormed across the old plank floorboards. The main door slammed in the distance.

"Y-Yes," Cindy replied, at some length, "I'm here. I'll be right in—I-I just need to use the bathroom first."

A full five minutes passed before Cindy came into the office, her red, swollen eyes giving her away even though she tried to put up a confident front. "You heard," she said.

Maggie merely nodded, and gestured for Cindy to sit down in the chair next to her desk.

Cindy sank into the seat. "Are you going to fire me?"

Maggie sighed. "Of course not. You've been doing a good job."

Cindy remembered the brochure clutched in one hand, and thrust it across the desk at Maggie. "Thanks," she muttered.

Maggie set it aside. It was too crumpled to scan and, besides, the request had been a ruse. The email customer list was Cindy's project; she could manage the whole job on her own. "If you ever need my help," Maggie told the girl softly, "I expect you to tell me."

Cindy's eyes widened a little. "Travis won't come here again. I'll sic Billy on him if he does, or my brother Randy."

From what Maggie had seen of Travis DuPres, Billy wouldn't stand a chance against him. As for Randy Hough, well, he was a thug, according to Daphne. He and Travis were probably buddies. "There's no need for that," Maggie said quietly. "If Travis causes any problems around here, I'll take care of the matter myself."

Cindy looked fearful, not for herself, it seemed, but for her employer. "You don't want to mess with him, Maggie." She paused. "I mean—"

"I know what you meant," Maggie said. "I'm not afraid of Travis DuPres or anybody else. If he bothers you again, you come to me."

Cindy lowered her eyes, swallowed visibly. "You don't think any less of me?"

"Why would I?"

"You must know," Cindy said miserably. "Everybody does. I was Billy's girlfriend, and we broke up over something stupid, and I got involved with Travis. Just long enough to get pregnant. But then, what can you expect from a Hough?"

"Things happen, Cindy," she said quietly. "People make mistakes, no matter what their last name happens to be."

Cindy was weeping again when she looked up. "I love Billy," she confessed, in a miserable whisper. "I love him so much, sometimes I don't think I can stand it. But he's only standing by me because of the baby. I know it kills him inside, remembering what I did."

Maggie sat back in her chair, fingers linked in front of her, and might have giggled at her own unconscious assumption of a

classic shrink's pose if the situation hadn't
been so very sad. "Maybe he really has forgiven you," she ventured. "Billy, I mean.
Maybe you're the one doing all the remembering."

Cindy looked grateful just to have somebody listen to her. God knew, the kid probably didn't have a lot of people to turn to
with her problems. Her shoulders, rigid before, sloped now, with disgrace and sorrow.
"My dad said he'd kill me if I didn't 'take
care of the problem.' I couldn't do what he
wanted. Billy and I talked things over, and
he offered to marry me and tell everyone the
baby was his. The whole town of Springwater knows different, of course. It hurts me so
much, knowing how Billy must feel."

Billy Raynor went up another notch in
Maggie's estimation; he was kind to Cindy,
Maggie had seen that when she visited their
trailer. In fact, Billy had looked at his young
wife with what could only have been adora-
tion, as though she were a madonna blos-
soming with a holy child. "I wonder if any of
us can ever really know how somebody else
feels," Maggie speculated.

Cindy nodded, dashing at her tears. "He's

so good to me," she cried, "and I feel just terrible about it."

"Listen to yourself," Maggie said, calling upon all the psychological training she'd garnered watching late-night reruns of *Oprah.* "You feel terrible because someone is being *good* to you?"

"I know," Cindy sniffled, making a wan attempt at a smile. "That's pretty screwed up, isn't it?"

"Yes," Maggie replied, but kindly. "Cindy, you need some counseling."

Cindy looked as though she'd been slapped. "You think I'm crazy?"

"Of course not. Everybody has rough times, things they need help sorting through."

"I can't afford no—any—doctor."

"You can go to the county mental health people, over in Maple Creek," Maggie replied, quietly but firmly. "They'll charge little or nothing."

"How would I get there? Billy's got an old truck, but he needs it for work."

"I'll drive you to the first appointment myself," Maggie said. "After that, you can take my car." She was silent for a few moments, watching Cindy's reaction. "You are getting prenatal care, aren't you?"

Cindy nodded. "Doris took me to the welfare people, and I got medical coupons," she said, plainly ashamed. "We didn't know what else to do. It was just Billy working, and—"

"Cindy," Maggie interrupted.

"Wh-what?"

Maggie picked up the telephone receiver and handed it across the desk. "Here. I'll dial information, and you ask for the mental health office. I'll go look through the rest of the things in that trunk while you're making an appointment."

Briefly, Cindy looked as though she might balk. Then an expression of grateful acceptance, even relief, came over her face. "How come you're being so nice to me? Is it because you feel sorry for me?"

"I don't feel one bit sorry for you," Maggie lied, for the sake of the girl's dignity. "I'm your employer and your friend, that's all. I care what happens to you, to Billy, and especially to that baby you're carrying. It isn't good for you to be so stressed out. Dr. Parrish must have told you that."

Ellen Parrish, also a member of an old

Springwater family, was the only M.D. in town, so it was a safe bet that she was Cindy's attending physician.

Cindy nodded. "She did," she confessed, in a small voice.

Maggie tapped out three numerals on the telephone dial and left Cindy to make her counseling arrangements in private.

Purvis went over the list of complaints he'd received from various ranchers, regarding severed fence lines and stolen cattle, but his mind wasn't on his work. He kept remembering his get-together with Nelly—aka Cowgirl—the night before, at Flo's Diner.

At first, the conversation had been awkward. She hadn't really wanted to be there, and neither had he, but after the waitress brought them coffee and they each ordered a piece of Flo's legendary peach pie, things had begun to flow like creek water over smooth stones.

Purvis braced one elbow on the surface of his desk, dropped his chin into it, and let himself travel back, unrestricted, to that rear booth, with its red vinyl seats, glowing jukebox, and push-in napkin holder . . .

"I wouldn't have figured you for the type to use a computer, except maybe for solving crimes," Nelly said. For a little thing, she sure knew how to tuck into a piece of peach pie.

Purvis felt himself flush. "I'm a little on the different side, when compared with most folks," he said, "but I'm not stupid. I keep up with the times."

Nelly's brown eyes sparkled as she looked him over. That expression of mischief made her look extra pretty, especially when one corner of her mouth tipped upward. "Touchy, touchy," she said. "Nobody said you were stupid, Purvis. Old-fashioned, maybe, but not stupid."

A humiliating sense of relief rushed through him. "Tell me about your book club," he blurted, and immediately went red again.

She smiled. "It's not a book club," she said. "It's a support group."

Purvis started to ask what kind of support group, and stopped himself just in time, for all the good it did. He could see that Nelly knew what he'd been going to say.

She held up the book. *Starting Over When You've Lost Everything,* it was called.

That stymied him completely; his desire to know what had happened to Nelly was exceeded only by his fear that she might come right out and tell him. If she'd lost her whole family in an accident or something really terrible like that, he wasn't sure he'd be able to stand it. So he just sat there, scared to say a thing.

She spoke softly, fiddling with a packet of pink sugar all the while, but her gaze was direct. "I had a house, a business, and a husband. I was going to have a baby, too, but I miscarried. Right after that, my husband, Allen, just up and vanished—owing the government a lot of money in back taxes. They took the house and the business—the IRS, I mean. I was left with my clothes, a few books, and my car. End of story."

Purvis sagged back in the vinyl seat, both relieved and stricken. "Why didn't you say any of that when we were emailing each other?"

Her smile was small and sad. "I was afraid you wouldn't want to swap messages anymore," she said. "Some people are scared bad luck will rub off if they get too close."

He reached out, took her hand,

squeezed. "You've been through the mill," he said. "I'm sorry."

She hesitated a few moments, then pulled back her hand. Purvis could have kicked himself for grabbing her that way. "It's okay," she said, looking through her own reflection on the diner window.

"What brought you up here to Montana?" he asked.

She grinned, and a light shone in her eyes. "I always wanted to be a cowgirl," she said.

Purvis was amazed, though he supposed he shouldn't have been. After all, her screen name was "Cowgirl." "You didn't know anybody up here, or anything like that?"

She shook her head. "That seemed like a plus at the time," she said.

"Wow," Purvis muttered. It wouldn't have occurred to him to make such an impulsive move. He'd been to Vietnam, and that was travel enough for him.

She laughed, and the sound was cheery, like Christmas music on a snowy afternoon. "I just opened up an atlas to the western states one day, right before I left L.A.," she confided, leaning forward, "and I jabbed down my finger and when I opened my eyes, there was Springwater, Montana. I got a job there right away, but I couldn't find an apartment, so I rented a little place here in Maple Creek." She paused again. "What about you, Purvis? For all our chitchat over the Internet, you didn't really tell me much about yourself, either."

He was baffled. What was there to tell? He was a small-town cop, none too popular with his constituency at the moment, and a bachelor. He was lonely.

"Have you ever been married?" she asked.

"No," he admitted. He'd paid his taxes right along, and he owned the house he lived in outright, such as it was. He had money in the bank, too. And for all of that, he still felt as though he'd missed the boat, because he'd never had what he wanted most in the world: a wife and kids. A family all his own.

She cocked her head to one side, eyes dancing. "What? No deep, dark secret? No skeletons in your closet?"

Except for some videos he'd accidentally ordered off a sleazy Web site one time, and sent back unwatched in a fit of chagrin, he couldn't think of anything. He sure as hell wasn't going to mention that, so he just shrugged.

"Maybe you *are* an innocent man," Nelly surmised, narrowing those lively eyes speculatively. "Like the one in that Sherrie Austin song."

Purvis blushed all over again. He'd heard the tune, all about boarding up windows and pulling down blinds and lying down with an innocent man. "I was in Vietnam," he said then. Maybe God knew why he'd brought that up, but *he* sure didn't.

"My dad went to Vietnam," Nelly said. "He never came back."

Her dad. Well, that about summed up the matter. What was he doing having coffee with a woman young enough to be his daughter? He ought to be horsewhipped.

"I'm sorry," he said, and he meant it. He might have known Nelly's father; he'd left a lot of friends behind in that God-forsaken place. One day, if he got the chance, he hoped to visit Washington, D.C., and find all their names on the Wall.

"I was a baby then," Nelly said, as though that made everything all right. "My mom and I lived with my grandparents." She studied him. "Were you ever in love?"

He shook his head. "Nope," he said, and grinned. "Not unless you count Ann-Margaret."

"Who?"

That really made him feel old. She'd probably never heard of Joplin, or the Stones, or Bob Dylan, either. He debated just paying the check, excusing himself, and leaving, but decided that would be the coward's way out. Flo came over, refilled both their cups, and left, humming.

"So you've basically had a perfect life," she prompted, letting the subject of Ann-Margaret slide.

"I was a little messed up when I got home from 'Nam," he confessed. "Spent some time in and out of VA hospitals. When I finally got my head together, all the good women had either left town or married off." He grinned, to lighten the mood a little, and Nelly grinned back.

"I got married right out of high school," she said. "Dumbest thing I ever did."

"You're pretty hard on yourself."

"Maybe," Nelly confessed. She turned her head again, gazing at the darkening window beside their table again, as though she expected to find something important written there. "I'd like to have babies some-day," she said.

Purvis was surprised by the little splash in the center of his heart, like a trout jumping for a bug. It wasn't as if she was offering to bear his children, was it, and millions of women wanted kids. Still, it did something profound to Purvis, her confiding such a private dream. "You will."

"You really think so?"

He leaned forward. "Yes," he said. "You're young and you're pretty and you're smart. Some smart fellow's bound to come along and want to tie the knot."

Some of the starch went out of her. "It isn't that easy, Purvis. I want somebody special. Somebody who thinks *I'm* special."

He smiled. "You'll find him."

She looked up, searched his face, her eyes full of hope and dreams and doubt. "Maybe," she repeated. "I'm a good cook, Purvis. Do you like spaghetti?"

A sweet shiver went through Purvis; he'd never felt quite like he did just at that moment, all off balance and hot under the collar. She expected to see him again. "Yep," he said, well aware that he was blushing and mortified because of it.

"You're a nice man, Purvis Digg," she said.

"Thanks," he replied, practically strangling on the word.

She laughed. "You're supposed to say I'm nice, too."

He was perplexed. He'd never dreamed there was a script for these sorts of things, but then, where women were concerned, there was a hell of a lot he didn't know. "I am?"

She made that sound again, that throaty giggle that brought Christmas and glittering fields of snow to mind. "Not if you don't think so," she said, when she got her breath. Her cheeks were pink, and her eyes sparkled with merriment. Damn, Purvis thought, if she wasn't every bit as pretty as Ann-Margaret.

"I don't reckon you'd want to see a movie with me tomorrow night?" Purvis heard himself ask. He felt as though he'd been thrown off a horse blindfolded; the wind was knocked clean out of him and he was surrounded by a haze. There was a buzzing sound in his ears.

"I've got a class at the high school, over in Springwater," she said. "It's a college extension program. Computer stuff. We could get together afterward, though, if you don't mind waiting. Have some spaghetti before the show."

He sat there like a lump, for what seemed like forever, trying to take it all in. He had a real date, and nobody had fixed him up. "Okay," he said.

"Good," she replied, reaching for her purse and that *Starting Over* book of hers. It seemed well-thumbed, and he knew without looking that there'd be notes in the margins, and places highlighted in colored ink. "Now, I guess I'd better get home. Work tomorrow. We're getting in a whole bunch of new books from the district office."

"You want me to drive you home?"

"I have my car, Purvis," she said reasonably. "I only live a few blocks from here anyway."

"I could follow you, then. Make sure you get there safe." Fine. Now she was going to think he was a pest, maybe even a stalker.

She smiled. "That would be nice," she answered, and Purvis felt something soar inside him, like he'd just opened his front door and found the prize patrol standing on the porch, complete with TV cameras and a big cardboard check. "I live on Sycamore Street, in a garage apartment. It's the Dooley place."

Purvis had known Mrs. Dooley all his life; she and his mother were friends, and he'd mowed her lawn every week for a full year after he'd gotten home from 'Nam. Her son, Zeb, had been in his unit, killed in an ambush one hot summer night, and even after all this time it was still hard for him to face the old lady. He'd always thought there should have been something he could have done to help when it would have counted.

He laid a ten-dollar bill on the table for Flo and stood. "What time does your class let out tomorrow night?" he asked.

"Not until eight," she said. "Shall I meet you somewhere afterward?"

"I'll pick you up at the school," he answered. They walked outside together; he meant to stand by until she was safely inside her car. With the likes of Randy and Odell Hough and God knew who else around, a person couldn't be too careful.

"It's okay," she confirmed, with a slight smile. "Good night, Lawman."

He laughed. "Good night, Cowgirl," he said.

She got into her battered red VW, cranked up the engine, and put the bug in reverse. She waved, with a flutter of fingers, and backed out of her parking space, heading toward Sycamore Street. . . .

The reverie ended right there, and it ended abruptly. Somebody snapped their fingers in front of Purvis's face, loud as a gunshot, and he sat there, blinking and disoriented.

"Yo, Purvis."

Purvis focused on J.T., who was leaning over the desk, looking at him curiously, as though he'd never seen a specimen quite like him. "J.T.," he said, as a greeting, and his voice sounded as rusty as an old plow left out in the field through a series of bad winters.

J.T. grinned and plunked into the visitor's chair. "Just stopped in to ask if you could go to the auction with me on Saturday. You know, for the cattle."

"I remember," Purvis said, still disgruntled.

"You look weird," J.T. said. "What's the matter?"

"So do you," Purvis shot back. "I figure the reason is your own business."

J.T. laughed. "Fair enough," he said. "Well? Are you coming to the auction with me or not?"

"Sure," Purvis said, subsiding a little. He wanted to tell J.T. all about Cowgirl— Nelly—but it all seemed sort of fragile. Talking about her so soon would be like breathing too hard on a dandelion's ghost before making a wish. "What time?"

"Bright and early. I'll pick you up at your place around six."

Purvis groaned. "Six it is," he said. It finally registered then, just what was different about J.T. He was wearing new jeans and a white shirt, open at the throat. Purvis leaned around the desk to peer at his feet. New boots, too. "Them your big-city detective clothes?" he jibed.

J.T. waggled his eyebrows. "No. They're my supper-with-Maggie-McCaffrey clothes," he said.

"You don't say," Purvis replied. "Well, you behave yourself, hear? Maggie's folks are good friends of mine, and I'd hate to have to deck my own deputy for stepping out of line with their daughter."

"Me, out of line? Why, Purvis, I'm insulted by the mere suggestion."

"You're full of crap, is what you are," Purvis retorted, grinning. "Maybe I came of age in the sixties, boy, but I never lost my memory."

J.T. laughed, gave a loose, smart-ass salute, and left Purvis to his lonely pursuit of truth, justice, and the American way. He sighed. God, what he wouldn't have given to be that young again.

He looked good, damn it. Real good.

Maggie slipped back from the Station's front window, hoping J.T. hadn't seen her watching him come up the walk. He moved with a confident swagger that would have galled her in anyone else. On him, that cocky strut worked only too well.

Maybe, she decided, frowning, he thought he was going to score with her. If so, he was in for a major disappointment. Probably.

She went to the door and wrenched it open.

J.T., catching sight of her expression, leaped back as though he'd just come face to face with Medusa herself, though his

eyes were shining with amusement, and
Maggie realized, to her private embarrassment, that she'd greeted him with a glare.

She relaxed, even smiled. For some reason she thought of the wedding dress, and
put it out of her mind by force. "Hi," she
said.

"Is this the wrong night?" he teased, pretending chagrin.

"With you, Wainwright," Maggie retorted
wryly, "any night would be the wrong night."

He stepped up onto the porch and pretended to be wrenching an arrow from his
chest. He held a bottle of wine under his
other arm. "Hey, what do you say we have
supper down at the Stagecoach Café?" he
said. "That way, I can be fairly sure there's
no poison in the food."

She laughed and stepped back to let him
enter her domain. "Too late," she said. "I've
already cooked, so you'll just have to risk
the strychnine."

He came over the threshold, bent to greet
Sadie, who wanted to go home with him
and be his dog from that day forward, judging by the effusive way she greeted him.

"She likes me," J.T. said, a little smugly.

"She likes the UPS man, too," Maggie said.

J.T. sighed deeply. "Alas. Another devious woman."

Maggie gestured toward the window on the opposite wall, overlooking June-bug's garden, now sadly overgrown, but still charming, especially at twilight. She'd set up a small table out there, with wineglasses.

"Shall we go outside and sit down?" she asked. Meant as an invitation, the question came out sounding a little like a command.

J.T. did another of his comical recoils. Then his expression turned soft, and his dark eyes gleamed with a sort of smoldering amusement that made her nerves jump. He took in her pale blue silk blouse and beige slacks. "You look great, Maggie."

He usually called her McCaffrey; even when they were younger, and madly in love, J.T. had used her last name. Hearing him say "Maggie" had a strange effect on her, in a multitude of scandalous ways and places.

"Thanks," she said.

He drew her easily into his arms, as though to begin a waltz. He smiled down at her. "Remember, Maggie? How we used to hide in that old rose arbor outside and neck like crazy?"

She managed a nod. In that moment, it seemed that the memory was impressed into her very cells. He led her through the Station, outside, and around to the place where the table stood. Then he bent his head and tasted her lips, and when he drew back, she could still feel the warmth of his breath on her mouth. In fact, she could still feel his kiss.

"Let's do it all again," he said. "Maybe we can get it right this time."

She didn't have to ask what he meant.

6

"Forget it," Maggie said, looking up into J.T.'s familiar, craggy face. She wondered if he knew she was bluffing, if he could possibly imagine how difficult it would be for her to resist any further advances he might choose to make. She certainly hoped not. "Last time I handed you my heart, you gave it back on a skewer. I'd prefer not to go through that again."

His brow knitted. He was still holding her loosely, his hands grasping her hips in a way that made her heartbeat skitter. "I've paid for that mistake, in more ways than one. How about another chance?"

The idea took her breath away. She

averted her gaze, would have stepped out of his embrace, except that J.T. caught her chin in his hand, gently turned her back to face him. "Whatever happens, McCaffrey, I'm sorry I hurt you, ever. If we can't be lovers, let's at least be friends."

She hadn't realized she was holding her breath until she released a quivering sigh. She smiled a wobbly little smile. "You've always been a smooth talker," she said.

He laughed, kissed her lightly on the nose. She was all too aware of the hardness and heat of his body, excruciatingly close to her own. Then, suddenly, he stepped back, eyes twinkling, and thrust out his hand. "Hello," he said heartily. "My name is J. T. Wainwright. The 'J.T.' stands for John Tobias."

She stared at him, puzzled for a moment, and then smiled again and took the offered hand. "Maggie McCaffrey," she said. " 'Maggie' is short for 'Margaret Corrine.' "

"Good to meet you, Ms. McCaffrey," he replied.

She felt her heart swell to overflowing, then burst wide open. Happy tears smarted in her eyes. "Mr. Wainwright," she responded.

"Call me J.T."

"And I'm Maggie."

He thrust out a great, comical sigh. "Oh, yes," he said. "Indeed you are."

And they danced again, there in the yard of the Springwater Station, in the fading light of early evening, accompanied by the sort of music that is heard only by the heart.

"J.T.?" Maggie hated to spoil the mood. One thing about J.T., he was a romantic devil.

His dark eyes were dreamy, and a little bit bad. His voice was a low, hoarse growl. "What?"

"Sadie is licking my ankles."

He looked at her in astonishment for a moment, glanced down, and then laughed. "Now, there's an idea," he said.

Maggie gave Sadie a gentle shove with the side of one foot. "Stop it," she said to the dog. "I get the message. It's supper time."

"I'd rather lick your ankles," J.T. observed dryly, his eyes alight.

The shove she gave him was a little *less* gentle than the one she'd administered to the dog, though she was smiling. "I wasn't talking to you," she said primly. "Anyway, you'll have to settle for my world-class salmon mousse pastries. One of the items I'll be serving when the bed-and-breakfast opens."

"You cook?" he asked, feigning surprise.

"Not as well as you do," she said, remembering his specialty, chicken enchiladas, from their youth. "But yes, I can cook. I took classes from a chef we hired for one of the hotels I managed in Chicago."

He followed her back inside, into the kitchen area, examined June-bug's carefully restored cookstove with interest while she dished up a bowl of kibble for Sadie. "This thing actually works?" he asked. He touched the shimmering handle on the oven and drew his hand back with an audible release of breath.

"Watch out," Maggie said. "It's hot."

"Smart ass," J.T. replied.

She grabbed two pot holders and elbowed him graciously aside so she could open the oven and remove the pastries inside. The luscious aroma rose around them in a steamy mist.

Sadie immediately lost interest in the kibble she'd just been given and tried to lick Maggie's ankles again.

"Allow me," J.T. said, apparently volunteering to carry the food out to the table in the garden. The alternative didn't bear considering.

Maggie considered it all the same, and a rush of heat went through her, leaving her a little dizzy. "Thanks," she said, somewhat lamely, and headed for the refrigerator, as much to duck his gaze as to fetch the salad she'd made earlier. Between them, they managed to carry all the food outside in one trip.

"It's going to be great, seeing this place up and running," he said, somewhat wistfully, tilting back his head to assess the Station in the gathering summer dusk.

Maggie shared the vision, seeing in her mind all that the old building had been, and would be again. "Yes," she said. "That's been a secret dream of mine for a long, long time." The tablecloth rippled in a gentle breeze, and a candle, inside a copper lantern, waited to be lighted. The first of June-bug's treasured roses were just beginning to bloom. She was relieved when he didn't ask if she'd had *other* secret dreams.

J.T. poured what looked like a rich cabernet into the waiting wineglasses. Although

Maggie saw the memories of the times they'd made out in that arbor smoldering in his eyes, he had the good grace not to mention them aloud. "When do you think you'll be ready to open for business?"

"A week or two," Maggie answered, watching as he set the wine bottle aside. He'd rolled up the sleeves of his well-pressed white cotton shirt, and his forearms were muscular and brown from the sun.

He caught her staring and grinned. "McCaffrey," he said. "Stop looking like you're about to scamper into the underbrush. I'm not planning to bite you." He allowed his gaze to slide over her, at leisure. "Not so it would hurt, anyhow."

Maggie felt a hot flush surge through her system and turned away quickly, nearly tripping over Sadie. "All right, that's it," she told the dog sternly. "Time out. You've been underfoot long enough. Go inside."

Sadie gave a small whimper and let her usually perky ears droop, but she skulked off, following Maggie's pointed finger and eventually disappearing around the side of the Station. No doubt she'd head straight for the bowl of kibble Maggie had placed near the kitchen sink.

When Maggie turned back, J.T. was standing with his arms folded, a crooked grin tilting his mouth. "Shall we?" he asked, and drew back her chair. The motion stirred the carpet of grass beneath their feet, and the scent was as delicious to Maggie as that wafting up from the food.

She sat, flustered. As a younger man, J.T. had been a rascal and a rogue, and he still was, she didn't doubt that, but somewhere along the line he'd acquired some halfway decent manners. Or maybe he'd just gotten better at seduction. Scary thought, given that he had considerable natural talent in that area as it was.

Not for the first time, Maggie wondered about his ex-wife, Annie. Maybe she'd been the one to smooth away some of J.T.'s rough edges.

He took a chair across from her, ducked his head a little, his expression questioning and still luminous with some private and barely contained amusement. "What are you thinking? I can see the gears moving." He placed his linen napkin in his lap, his eyes never leaving hers. Crickets chirped around them, in chorus, and a few birds, not yet bedded down in their nests for the night, chimed in.

"That you've changed."

"Haven't you?"

She considered the question. "Not really," she said thoughtfully. "Most people don't, you know."

He lifted his glass, waiting for her to do the same, and when she did, the edges clinked musically. "To things that never change," he said.

Maggie smiled. "Such as?"

"Such as the Big Sky, the timber on the mountainsides, the best things about Springwater." He settled back in his chair. "God, I missed this place. I should never have left."

Maggie opened the little door in the copper lantern, picked up the butane firelighter, set the wick aflame. The romantic glow added to the ambience. "Did you like living in New York?"

J.T. considered the question as Maggie indicated the salmon pastries on the platter between them with a nod. "There's no place quite like it," he said, with typical ambiguity, serving himself and extending the platter to Maggie.

"Which means—?"

He smiled. "The city's great, in terms of food and culture and all that. On the other hand, a homicide detective sees any place from a different perspective. The truth is, I got so caught up in my job that just about everything else in my life went by the wayside."

"Including your wife and son?" she asked cautiously.

He looked rueful. "Yeah," he said. "Including my wife and son. Murphy—my partner—used to lecture me about that all the time." J.T. assumed another personality, another voice, imitating his late friend. " 'You think you've got forever,' he'd say. 'You know what's important in this life, Cowboy? Family, that's what.' " He paused, sighed. "When it came to relationships, Murphy knew what he was talking about. He and Doreen were truly happy together."

She couldn't speak for a moment; her throat had closed, drawn tight by some indefinable, bittersweet emotion. She busied herself with the salad tongs, serving J.T. and then herself. During that brief interval, the only sounds were those of the last birds of the day, and the crickets.

J.T. assessed her with warm, discerning eyes. Took a sip of his wine, still regarding her over the rim. "I didn't mean to make you sad," he said.

She swallowed. Smiled. "I was just thinking that I've been fortunate," she said, "where family is concerned. I had the usual fights with my brothers, but we're all close, even now. Mom and Dad made sure of that."

He nodded. "It was a little different for me, as you know. The irony is, I wanted to give Quinn everything I never had. I sure screwed up there."

She said nothing, just ate slowly and listened.

"Why did you come back here?" he asked, finally.

She speared a bite of salad. She hoped her slight, one-shoulder shrug seemed nonchalant. "I guess I'm just a small-town girl at heart," she said. "I didn't always know that about myself, of course." Without warning, the old image sprang into her mind, vivid as ever, of J.T. vaulting over her parents' back fence and interrupting her wedding. She could have strangled him at the time, but there had been other emotions, too, conflicting ones. Even after all these years, she still felt a perverse little thrill at the memory.

"Maybe you needed the time you spent away from Springwater. Maybe we both did," he said.

As simple as that observation was, it touched a nerve. Or maybe it was the recollection of her wedding day. "How's your mother?" Maggie asked.

J.T.'s expression was rueful, though his eyes danced. Obviously, the abrupt change of subject wasn't lost on him. "Same as ever," he said. "She still lives in Las Vegas. Divorced another husband last year."

Maggie watched as he refilled both their wineglasses. Reminded of her own parents' problems, she had to avert her eyes and blink a couple of times. The last thing she dared do was cry—J.T. would most likely try to comfort her if she did, and it was no mystery where *that* might lead. She wasn't ready—with all she was trying to do, start a business, make some kind of life for herself, she simply didn't have the personal resources to go through some grand, ill-fated passion with her childhood sweetheart. Her heart was still too bruised.

"I can't imagine growing up in Las Vegas," she mused, thinking of J.T.'s childhood again.

He flashed one of those lethal grins, the type Maggie had always thought should be registered as a threat to women everywhere. "It was interesting, to say the least," he said. "Having a showgirl for a mother, I mean. Poor Becky. I made her life miserable after she left my dad and dragged me to Nevada; she's probably glad I'm grown up and gone."

"Were you really so bad?" She couldn't think why she'd asked the question; she knew he had been hard to handle as a kid, especially after his father was killed. When he visited Springwater he invariably got into trouble with his uncle, who probably would rather not have had to deal with him at all.

His eyes glowed liquid brown. "Yes," he said. "Don't you remember?"

Another veiled reference to their lovemaking. Maggie felt her face go hot. "No fair," she said. "We just met. We have no history."

"I forgot," he said.

She laughed.

He got up from his chair, went into the arbor, came out with a pink rosebud, barely open. Drawing Maggie to her feet, he brushed the underside of her chin with the flower, and she caught its scent, felt its velvety beginnings. "I've missed you," he said, and this time he spoke seriously.

She let her forehead rest against his shoulder, just for a moment. "And I've missed you," she admitted.

He tipped her chin upward and kissed her.

A shudder of desire went through her, and he must have felt it, because his embrace tightened a little, just before he let her go and stepped back.

"Sorry," he said. "Let's talk about something—well—normal."

She was at once grateful and disappointed. She began clearing the table, and he helped, and as they carried things inside she gave him an account of her day, ending with the scene between Cindy and Travis DuPres.

"Travis is basically no good," J.T. said when she'd finished. They were both in the kitchen then, Maggie folding the tablecloth, J.T. setting the copper lantern on the mantel, the candle still alight. "He and Billy were raised the way I was, pretty much, except neither one of them had a father like mine.

Doris isn't a bad woman—that's their mother—but she's led a rough life. Couple of loser husbands, one of them in the pen. Drives around town in an old Pontiac, held together mostly by duct tape and four-letter words, plays bingo five nights a week, that kind of thing."

"Cindy wants her approval in the worst way," Maggie said, putting on an apron.

"She told you that?"

"Not in so many words, but I can tell."

He sighed. "Far as I'm concerned, Billy Raynor ought to be a candidate for sainthood. He works twice as hard as any other man I could have hired for a trailer and starvation wages, and he's determined to give Cindy what she's never had, a real home and a family."

"The whole situation breaks my heart," Maggie admitted. "I wish there was something I could do."

"There is," J.T. said, his gaze warm and solemn, both at once. "Be a friend to her. Try to steer her in the right direction."

"She's signed up for counseling over at mental health," Maggie replied. "Her first appointment is Monday afternoon. I said I'd take her, to get the ball rolling, and after that, she can use the Pathfinder whenever she has an appointment."

J.T.'s smile was slow and it permeated Maggie's system like a shot of warm brandy. "That," he said, "was more than decent."

"Maybe Billy should be encouraged to go with her."

J.T. sighed. "Billy's probably sounder, emotionally speaking, than the average shrink. He knows the whole situation, and he's prepared to deal with it."

"He must love Cindy very much."

"He does," J.T. replied. "I just hope she realizes what she's got. Billy will make one hell of a husband and father. Travis, on the other hand, will probably be in the big house, sharing a cell with dear old dad before he's thirty."

"You seem pretty sure of that."

"I was a detective. Before that, I walked a beat and dealt with every kind of sewer rat there is. Travis is the type probation officers describe as incorrigible."

A shudder moved down Maggie's spine. "Is he dangerous?"

"He could be," J.T. said. He ought to

know, she figured, given his experience in law enforcement.

"My God," Maggie breathed. "You don't suppose he's involved in the trouble the ranchers have been having lately?"

"Wouldn't surprise me," he answered, off-hand. "Time will tell." In the next moment he went from casual to completely focused. He narrowed his eyes and leaned forward slightly; she felt the impact of his intellect full force. "Did he threaten you in any way?"

She was flustered. "No—oh, no—it wasn't—I didn't even meet him."

J.T. eased off. "Sorry," he said, and thrust a hand through his hair, leaving it delectably rumpled. "I guess I overreacted a little."

"Instinct, I suppose," she replied, with a smile. "You must have been a very good detective." J.T. had always been good at everything he tried, with the apparent exception of falling in love.

He said nothing, but simply gazed out the window at June-bug's garden, where they'd taken their supper, a place awash in purple shadows and magic, his wineglass in hand.

"What made you give up law enforcement?" she heard herself ask. "Was it the shooting?"

He turned his head, met her eyes. His expression was unreadable, especially in the fading light. "That helped," he said.

Maggie crossed the room, reached out, closed her hand around his, and he set aside his glass, his expression solemn. She started to speak, then stopped.

"My partner was killed," he told her, though she hadn't asked, and he was well aware that she already knew. He seemed to be looking past her, through her, into another time and place. No doubt he was doing just that. "We were heading into a warehouse—we'd trailed a suspect there—and Murphy was in front. It was dark, and before my eyes adjusted, there were shots. Three of them. Murphy took two and went down. I don't think I even felt the one that hit me."

Maggie waited, stricken. Mesmerized, as though she were actually witnessing the scene, not just hearing about it.

"It was Murphy's twentieth wedding anniversary. There was a big party scheduled for that night, at his all-time favorite restaurant, a funky pizza place in Queens." He paused, and she saw his lips twitch, trying for a smile and falling short. "He and his wife were leaving on a cruise the next day. Four days and three nights. Bahamas. They got a deal on the tickets—two for one."

Maggie felt tears prickle the backs of her eyes. Still, she didn't speak.

J.T. ran his tongue over his lips. "Murphy was more than my partner. He was my best friend. After Annie and I were divorced, I spent a couple of Thanksgivings and Christmases at his place, with his family. Hell, he and Doreen and their daughter, Katie, they *were* my family."

"They sound like wonderful people."

J.T. nodded grimly. "Even after what happened, Doreen came to the hospital and tried to cheer me up. I missed the funeral. One of the guys brought me a video, but it wasn't the same as paying my respects in person."

Maggie realized she was still touching his hand, and squeezed lightly.

He pulled away then, stood, went to find the nearest light switch. An electric glow spilled through the room, scattering ghosts and shadows. "I'm sorry, Maggie. I didn't mean to dump all that on you."

She welcomed the light, but she also missed the special intimacy the gathering darkness had afforded. She turned, headed toward the kitchen, where the dirty dishes waited. "We've had our moments, you and I," she said quietly, "but I'd like to think we're friends. Friends listen to each other."

Once inside, he edged her aside from the sink, pushed up his sleeves, turned on the tap. At her glance, he grinned wanly. "I was a busboy in college," he said. "For about a week, anyway. I left to park cars for one of the casinos." He chuckled, shook his head. "I had to take a big cut in pay when I became a cop."

She laughed. "I'm impressed. That you do dishes, I mean."

"I'm a man of infinite talent and scope."

"Good," she replied. "You wash, and I'll dry."

He looked around even as he squirted soap into the sink. "No big commercial machine?"

"This is a restored stagecoach station," Maggie pointed out sweetly. "No big commercial machine."

He smiled. "Know what, McCaffrey?" he asked. "This is nice."

Maggie smiled back. "It is," she agreed.

*   *   *

Purvis was wearing his new Walmart duds again. He was even thinking about getting his hair cut. Watching with a smile as Nelly came out of Springwater High School, carrying her textbook and looking like a teenager, he opened the passenger door of the police car and waited for her to climb in.

"We're going to the movies in this?" she asked.

"My mom's using her Escort tonight," he answered.

Nelly sat down and automatically fastened her seat belt. When Purvis was behind the wheel and starting the engine, she ventured, "Isn't this some kind of violation?"

Purvis checked the rearview mirror, flipped on the headlights, and pulled out onto Springwater's main street. "Nope," he said. "Technically, I'm always on duty. That means I can drive this car anytime."

"What if something happens?" she asked, and she sounded a little titillated at the thought. "Suppose you have to chase a speeder or apprehend a bank robber?"

He grinned. "Well, there's no bank in Springwater, so we can probably rule out the probability of a heist. In the case of a speeder, I guess I'd just ask you to hold on and put your head down if any shooting broke out."

"Do you like this job, Purvis?"

He glanced her way. The lights of Springwater's few neon-equipped businesses passed over her face as they progressed down the street toward the drive-in at the other end of town, and Purvis got a strangely reverent feeling, as though both of them were bathed in the glow of stained-glass windows.

"It's all I know," he said. "Do you enjoy working at the library?"

She nodded. "I'd like to get my degree in library science," she said.

"You could do that," he said, wanting to be supportive. Of course, she'd have to leave Springwater, and he hated that idea.

"Purvis, there isn't a four-year college within a hundred miles of here."

"I've taken a couple of courses in criminology by correspondence."

She looked at him with new interest. "That's impressive," she said.

He shrugged, feeling wildly humble.

"Are you looking to advance?" she asked.

He laughed. "I'm as high as I'm ever going to go, in a one-man police department," he said. "I just figured the more I knew about my job, the better. Do you want to get something to eat before we go to the movies?"

"I was going to serve you supper, remember?" she asked, smiling. "I made a great spaghetti sauce. It's waiting in my refrigerator—all we need is the pasta."

Just then, the radio crackled. "Purvis, you there? Over."

He reached for the microphone with a sigh, and pressed the button with his thumb. "Yo, Rosie. How's tricks? Over."

"I'm doin' real good, Purvis, now that I'm on that new medicine for my palpitations. How about you? Over."

"I'm good. Over."

"Your mother? How's she? Over."

"Mom's fine. What can I do for you, Rosie? Over."

"Well, I just had a phone call from Pete Doubletree, out at Stonecreek Ranch. He said somebody poisoned a bunch of his cattle. Not fifty feet from his windmill. Can you believe it, Purvis? I don't know what this world is coming to. Over."

Purvis felt his jawline harden, and consciously relaxed it again.

Nelly sat up a little straighter in the seat, eyes wide.

"I'll head out there right now," he said. "Call J.T. for me, will you? Tell him to meet me at Pete's place. He's at the stagecoach station having dinner. Over."

"I already did that, Purvis," Rosie said, apparently unfazed by the note of benign irritation in his tone. "Saw him head to the Station a little while back. He and Maggie McCaffrey ate dinner right out in the side yard, next to the rose arbor. They used to neck there. Over."

Purvis rolled his eyes and expelled a breath. "Thanks," he said, flipping on the flashing lights and the siren. "Over and out, Rosie." The squad car shot from a moderate pace to a streak, and he flung a sidelong glance in Nelly's direction. They were already a considerable distance from the high school, and she'd ridden to class that night with a friend, because of their date. "You mind coming along? I don't have time to take you back to Maple Creek."

Nelly raised her voice to be heard over the screaming siren. "I'd rather go with you," she said, even though she looked nervous. "I'll stay out of the way, I promise."

Purvis floored the accelerator, and Nelly gripped the edges of the seat and held on for dear life.

The dead cattle were scattered hulks in the headlights of the various vehicles gathered around the scene. J.T. walked from one to another, feeling sick to his stomach. Right then, he'd have given just about anything to be back at the Station again, washing dishes with Maggie and sneaking scraps to the dog, but from his current perspective, the earlier part of the evening didn't even seem real. He might have imagined it all.

Purvis arrived with a screech and bounded out of the car before the engine stopped ticking. There was someone with him, a woman, but whoever she was, she stayed put. "What the hell—?"

Pete Doubletree was beside himself, and understandably so. He met Purvis halfway and grabbed him by the lapels of his jacket. "When's this going to stop, Purvis?" he shouted. "When?"

"Take it easy," Purvis said, with gruff gentleness, and removed the rancher's hands from his clothing. "We'll find whoever did this. I give you my word on that."

"This is the third time something like this has happened in the last year!" Pete yelled. "You know what your word is worth to me?"

J.T. stepped in. "Better get somebody from the sheriff's office out here," he told Purvis grimly. "We're going to need some technical help."

Purvis managed to shake Pete off and strode over to the nearest cow carcass. "Sweet God," he breathed. At the same time, he pulled a cell phone from the inside pocket of his fringed jacket and punched in a number. "Purvis Digg, over at Springwater," he barked, when someone answered. "Put me through to the sheriff." He paused, and J.T. saw a vein stand out in the other man's neck. "I don't care *what* he's doing. I expect him to call me back within five minutes!" He rattled off a number and disconnected, dropping the phone back in his pocket.

"How many are there?" he asked, running one hand over his face, as if trying to wake up from a bad dream.

"I counted seventeen," J.T. answered. "Probably strychnine."

"God almighty," Purvis said.

"Yeah," J.T. agreed. He glanced around at the glare of headlights coming from seven or eight pickup trucks. "These ranchers," he said, "are on the edge."

Purvis nodded. "Half of them are hotheads. They're likely to pick out a suspect for themselves if we don't come up with one soon, and they won't be overly concerned with little things like due process."

"We'd better think of some way to calm them down. And quick."

Again, Purvis nodded. Then he turned to face the gathering mob. He was, J.T. thought, with no little admiration, a brave man.

"Enough's enough," growled an older rancher, a tall guy J.T. vaguely recollected from the Cattleman's Association meetings he'd attended with his dad. Fists knotted at his sides, the cowman stormed toward Purvis.

J.T. moved in a little closer, but he kept his hands in his pockets. He wasn't armed, and neither was Purvis, but every one of the ranchers was either carrying a rifle or sporting a gun belt with a pistol in the holster. It might have been a scene from an old movie, J.T. reflected, but it was all too real.

"Now, Ed," Purvis said to the other man, "you just hold your horses now. J.T. and me, we want to find the bastards who did this just as bad as you do. Last thing we need is a bunch of vigilantes getting in the way."

Ed looked like he might have a stroke on the spot. Before he could blow his top, though, Purvis's cell phone rang. Evidently, it was the sheriff calling back.

Purvis answered a bunch of questions, then flipped the phone shut again. "They're sending some forensics people out, along with a few deputies."

"Good," one of the ranchers yelled, out of the engine-thrumming glare. "Maybe we'll get some action!"

Ed was shaking his finger under Purvis's nose. "You listen to me," he ranted. "Don't you go thinkin' the Cattleman's Association can't ask for your badge and get it, because we can. And we will, damn it. We will, if you don't put a stop to this yesterday!"

Again, J.T. admired Purvis's restraint. He'd have been tempted to pop the guy one himself, just to get his attention, which only went to show that he really wasn't cut out to be a cop. Maybe he never had been.

Purvis held both hands out, palms forward. "We've got to work together on this, Ed," he said. "We can't accomplish much of anything by fighting among ourselves."

J.T. thought of Maggie again, standing beside him at the sink. Their hips had touched a couple of times, purely by accident, of course. At least, it had probably been an accident on Maggie's part. J.T. was a take-charge kind of a guy, especially in situations like that one.

"Just exactly *what* are you proposin' to do?" demanded yet another rancher. "So far, we've seen plenty of nothin'!"

This raised derisive cheers from the crowd. J.T. kept his mouth shut, though it wasn't easy. This was still Purvis's show.

"I want all of you to go on home, back to your own ranches," Purvis called out. "For the time being, you'd better put whatever spare men you have to watchin' your herds."

"You're goin' to have to do better than that," Ed challenged, shaking his fist.

"Go on home, Ed," Purvis said patiently. "It's late, and we got work to do."

Pete Doubletree spoke up. "We're calling a special meeting of the Cattleman's Association," he said, shouting so the whole crowd could hear. "Tomorrow night, six o'clock, in the back room at the Brimstone!"

There was another rallying cry, but one by one the ranchers got back into their trucks and drove off, with a lot of tire-spinning and gear-grinding.

"We're on your side," J.T. said, when it looked as if Doubletree was going to tie into Purvis again.

The rancher, younger than most of his colleagues, subsided a little. "This is going to ruin me," he said. Then he turned and walked over to crouch beside one of his lost cattle.

"See anything that might give us a clue who did this?" Purvis asked, out of the corner of his mouth.

J.T. shook his head. "If there were any tracks," he said, "they're gone now. Nothing like half a dozen pickups to tear up a crime scene."

"Son-of-a-bitch," Purvis breathed.

"At least one," J.T. agreed. It was going to be a long night, and he felt about twenty

years older than he had when he left Maggie behind at the Station.

Purvis sighed, glanced toward the car.
The woman got out, came toward them,
hugging herself, picking her way through
mud, grass, and cow manure.

"It'll be awhile until I can take you home,"
Purvis said to her.

She nodded, glanced at J.T., nodded
again, this time in greeting.

"Nelly Underwood," Purvis said. "This is
my friend and deputy, J. T. Wainwright."

"Hello," J.T. said. Interesting, he reflected.
He hadn't known Purvis was dating, and the
thought cheered him considerably. It would
seem that, after all these years, Purvis Digg
was having a near-life experience.

7

It was 3:47 in the morning when J.T. got home from Stonecreek Ranch and immediately fell into bed, wondering how the hell he was going to get through a full day on a little better than an hour and a half of sleep. Then the matter was taken out of his hands—the telephone rang.

Muttering, he raised himself up onto one elbow and fumbled for the light switch. He squinted at the caller I.D. readout, recognized the number as Annie's, and snatched up the receiver on the third ring. "Hello?" he rasped. His life as a big-city cop had made him more than a little paranoid, particularly where his son Quinn was concerned. A call

at that hour, made from his ex-wife's number in Atlanta, almost certainly meant trouble.

"Dad?" Quinn's voice was small, quavery.

J.T. closed his eyes for a moment, dazed
with relief that it wasn't Annie calling to say
Quinn was sick, hurt, missing, or any of the
thousand and one other bad things that
could happen to someone you loved when
you weren't around to protect them, and
sometimes even if you were. He willed his
heart and respiration rates to slow down to
normal, and when he figured he could strike
the right note, he spoke. "Hiya, buddy," he
said. "How are you?"

Quinn was six, and he'd been the main
reason J.T. had held on to life immediately
after he'd been shot. Every time he'd
wanted to just give up and go under, to let
the pain swallow him, he'd seen Quinn's
face, heard his voice, the way he was hearing it now. Remembered that a boy needed
a father, even the long-distance variety.
"Mostly I'm all right," the kid answered. He
sounded the way J.T. felt—close to tears. It
was hard, living so far from his only child,
but he'd had some time to get used to it.
When Annie's second husband, Brad, an

engineer, had accepted a major construction project based in Atlanta, well before the
shooting, J.T. had agreed that Quinn should
go along. Annie was an exceptional mother,
if a little on the fussy side.

J.T. wound the phone cord around an index finger and worked up a smile, hoping
the kid would hear it in his voice and be reassured somehow. "What's up?"

"They're fighting."

"Who?" J.T. asked, though of course he
knew.

"Brad and my mom. I think they might get
divorced."

"Hey," J.T. said gruffly, "people disagree
sometimes. You know that. Wait and see—
they'll kiss and make up tomorrow."

Quinn's voice wobbled. "You and Mom
used to fight. And *you* got divorced."

"Yeah," J.T. said, shoving a hand through
his hair, "but that was different."

"Why?"

J.T. paused for a beat. "It just was. You're
going to have to trust me on that one, Bud,
at least until you're a little older."

"She said she wasn't about to drag a little kid all the way to South America," Quinn
confided, lowering his voice in case of

spies. "And *he* said the two of us can damn well stay here, then, for all he cares, but it's a big promotion and he's going. Then he went out and slammed the door. He drove away really fast."

J.T. took a few slow, measured breaths. Brad was a good guy, a solid nine-to-five type and a decent stepfather, and J.T. didn't really care what went on between him and Annie, but when Quinn got caught in the cross fire, that was something else. "It's gonna be all right, buddy," he said finally. Then, carefully, he added, "Why don't you go find your mom? I'd like to talk to her."

"I can't. She's sleeping now. She cried a lot, Dad. I heard her."

"O.K.," J.T. said. He sat up, put his feet on the floor, and resigned himself to getting no sleep at all. "How about if I give her a ring later on this morning?"

Quinn didn't hesitate. "She'll be glad if you call."

"Right," J.T. said, rubbing his eyes with a thumb and forefinger.

"I want to come out there and live with you. If Mom goes to South America with Brad, I mean."

J.T.'s heart cracked and then split right

down the middle, like a block of seasoned wood struck with a sharp ax. "No promises, pal," he said. "Not before your mother and I talk, anyway."

"You'll call her for real? First thing?"

J.T. smiled. "First thing," he confirmed. "In the meantime, we'll have to hang tough, you and I. You got your pajamas on?"

"Yes," Quinn said, in the tone of voice usually accompanied by an eye roll. "It's only six o'clock in the morning here, and I don't have school because it's summer."

"Well, then, since you're dressed for sleeping, why don't you go back to bed for a while?"

Quinn sighed. "I can't do that, Dad," he explained. "It's light outside."

J.T. glanced at the darkened window opposite his bed and smiled again, ruefully this time. Holding the receiver to his ear with one hand, he scrounged on the floor for last night's clothes. He'd feed the horses after he'd finished talking with Quinn, then come back inside, shower, put on clean jeans and a fresh shirt, if he had any, nuke himself a frozen breakfast sandwich, and go rouse Purvis. Getting to the auction early would mean extra time to look over the livestock.

"So how do you like the new neighbor-hood? Made any friends yet?"

"I don't want any friends here," Quinn said. He could be stubborn as hell, and he came by it honestly. Annie's skull was every bit as thick as J.T.'s own, so genetically, the kid had never had a chance. "They're all geeks."

"Nah," J.T. answered, stepping into his jeans, pulling them up, and buttoning the fly. He'd learned to dress quickly, while doing four other things, early in his law enforce-ment career. "You just don't know them yet, that's all. And they don't know you. Give them a chance, Q."

"They're scuzz-head-robo-zoids."

J.T. shrugged into his shirt, grinning. "Quinn."

"Well," Quinn insisted, with growing spirit, "they *are.*"

How to win friends and influence people, J.T. thought. "You think we don't have scuzz-head-robo-zoids out here in Mon-tana?"

"I wouldn't care. I'd be with you."

The words jabbed into J.T.'s throat and stuck there, hurting. "Remember what I said, Q. Nothing is settled until your mother and I have talked this through. Got that?"

"Got it," Quinn said. "Dad?"

J.T.'s voice went hoarse again. "What?"

"I love you."

J.T. squeezed his eyes shut, hard. Opened them again. Cleared his throat. "I love you, too, pal. Don't forget that, O.K.?"

"O.K."

"Look, I'll pick up a cell phone today and call you right away with the number. Then, whether you get to come out here to the ranch or not, you'll be able to get in touch with me twenty-four-seven. That work for you?"

"It works."

"Good. Now, go back to bed."

There was a grin in his son's voice. "Dad."

"O.K., then just stay out of trouble till your mom's on her feet and able to defend herself."

"Don't forget to call me with your cell number."

"I won't forget, bud. I promise."

"O.K. Bye."

"Bye, Q."

The line went dead. J.T. fumbled, hanging up the phone, and it took a couple of attempts just to set the receiver in place. In those moments he missed his son with such acute desperation that the emotion all but blinded him. He staggered into the bathroom, bent over the old-fashioned pedestal sink, and splashed his face with cold water until he'd at least partially regained his senses. Then he brushed his teeth, ran a brush through his hair, and headed for the back stairs. In the kitchen, he flipped on the lights, pushed the start button on the coffee-maker, and went to the barn.

A slow shiver spilled down his spine as he crossed the backyard; it was the kind of chill he used to get in the city sometimes, when something was about to go down. He ascribed it to imagination and a lack of sleep and kept walking, but the hairs on the nape of his neck stood on end for a long time afterward.

"They found us a baby!" Daphne blurted, bursting into Maggie's office at the Station, later that morning, her eyes big.

"Already?" Maggie asked, laying aside her glasses.

"There's an urgent need for foster

homes," Daphne said, pushing the office door closed behind her and leaning back against it. Her face was glowing, as if she'd given spontaneous birth only minutes before. "We're getting a little girl, Mags. Her name is Tiffany, and they think she's about two. The social worker is bringing her over from Maple Creek this afternoon."

Maggie stood, crossed the room, hugged her friend. " 'They think' she's two?" she asked.

"Nobody knows for certain," Daphne confided, looking solemn for a moment.

Maggie raised her eyebrows, waited for further explanation.

Daphne seemed charged with energy again, almost manic with excitement. "I've got to go shopping," she said. "We don't have a crib or the right kinds of food or clothes or toys—"

Maggie was nothing if not a realist, and she knew that foster children were often shunted from Point A to Point B, and then back again, for a variety of bureaucratic reasons. It seemed that her friend had become attached to this little one already, even before meeting her, and that kind of emotional vulnerability was a dangerous thing. She didn't want to see Daphne get hurt.

"Daph," she began carefully, and then stopped, not knowing how to go on.

Daphne knew her well and guessed at her misgivings. "Stop worrying," she said softly. "I'm taking in a baby who needs a home, temporary or otherwise, not crossing a minefield."

Maggie nodded. She might have pointed out that there were other kinds of minefields besides the physical ones, but Daphne was a grown woman, intelligent and well-educated. She didn't need Maggie to tell her that this was a major emotional risk. "Go," she said. "Cindy and I can hold down the fort alone for the rest of the day."

Daphne's eyes were shining. "I'll call Ben. Maybe he can take a couple of hours off."

"Good idea," Maggie answered, indicating her office phone with a gesture. Daphne hurried in and snatched up the receiver.

Cindy, who had gone out on an errand, returned just as Daphne was coming out of the office, quelling an expression of disappointment as she approached. "Ben's tied up," she said, seeing that she hadn't been quick enough. Maggie had seen the look on her friend's face, and she was troubled. "Well, I guess that's to be expected. He's in the middle of a workday. See you later."

"Where's she going?" Cindy asked conversationally, laying a roll of stamps, a bag of office supplies, and a cash register receipt on Maggie's desk.

"Shopping," Maggie said. "She and Ben are getting a foster child this afternoon."

"Oh," Cindy said, and seemed to sag a little.

"Sit down," Maggie told her, gesturing toward the chair in front of her desk.

Cindy sat, with a heavy sigh. She looked overwrought and very tired. Perhaps the job was proving to be too much for her.

"Are you all right?" Maggie asked.

"Yeah," Cindy said, attempting a smile and falling a little short. "I just feel kind of sad all of the sudden, that's all. You know, to think about that baby's mom and how she must feel, having to let somebody else step in and take over."

It wasn't difficult to see why the concept would trouble a pregnant young girl, especially one who had been married such a short time, and under less than idyllic circumstances. "It must be very hard," she said, feeling sympathy not only for Tiffany's unknown mother and father, but for Cindy and Billy, too.

Cindy nodded, hands resting on her protruding belly, unconsciously shielding her child, but her face brightened slightly. "I'm starved. What if I make us some lunch?"

Maggie smiled, feeling more cheerful herself. "Good idea," she said. "You'll find the makings of sandwiches in the refrigerator."

"I'm on it," Cindy said.

Maggie went back to her work at the computer. The Springwater Station Web site was already generating inquiries about the B & B, and even a few reservations, and she needed to tend to business. Cindy brought her a tuna sandwich and some diet cola a few minutes later.

Hours later she was alone, still working at her desk, having progressed to a preliminary financial report by then, when she raised her eyes and saw J.T. standing in the doorway, leaning with one shoulder braced against the door frame. He was wearing jeans, a work shirt, boots, and a denim jacket, and his hair was rumpled, as if he'd been combing it with his fingers. A 5 o'clock shadow darkened his jaw and there was a hollow look in his eyes that suggested serious sleep deprivation.

"You look like five miles of bad road," she said, not unkindly, assessing him over the rims of her reading glasses.

He chuckled. "Golly gee, ma'am. Is that any way to talk to a hardworkin' cowboy and peace officer like myself?"

Maggie suppressed a smile as she set her glasses aside and pushed back her chair to stand and stretch. "I trust you wiped your feet before you walked on my clean floor?"

He rolled his eyes. "Sorry," he said. "I was raised in a barn, you know. Literally." He looked around. "Where's the guard dog?"

Maggie had to laugh at the thought of Sadie protecting her from anything more threatening than a stray dust mote or a renegade grasshopper. "She's keeping my mother company this afternoon. Mom's painting a new artichoke series, and I guess she needed canine support."

"Ah," J.T. said, not even pretending to understand. Just then, his shirt pocket rang. "Wainwright," he said, holding up one hand in a just-a-moment gesture and grinning at her. His expression changed to one of solemn concentration. "Hi, Annie. Yeah, I know you called back as soon as you could." He paused, stepping out of the doorway to let Maggie pass. "Listen, we need to talk about Quinn."

Maggie headed for the kitchen to make coffee and, at the same time, afford J.T. some privacy. She hoped everything was O.K. with his little boy.

Ten minutes later J.T. joined her in the kitchen area, took a mug from the shelf, and poured himself a cup of coffee. She was seated at one of June-bug's trestle tables, flipping through a magazine.

He stood on the other side of the table, looking even more haggard than he had when he came in. "May I?"

She gestured for him to sit down. "Be my guest. Everything all right?"

He took a seat, heaved a long sigh. "My son, Quinn, is coming out here to stay with me for a while."

"That's good, isn't it?"

He shoved a hand through his hair. "For me, it's great. For Quinn, well, I'm not so sure."

"Why's that?"

"He's only six," he said, "and he's never

really been away from Annie. Besides, I'm not used to looking after little kids, and I live on a ranch. Suppose he gets hurt?"

Maggie smiled, touched by the obvious depth of his love for his child. "You'll do just fine. He'll love the ranch and, I hate to point this out, but he could be hurt anywhere."

J.T.'s responding smile was tentative, and brief. "There's trouble brewing around here," he said. "And I'm bound to be right in the middle of it, now that Purvis has stuck me with a badge. Do I need to remind you what happened to *my* dad? Suppose it happened again, Maggie? I don't want Quinn to see what I saw, go through what I went through."

Maggie winced. She considered the grim fact that a number of Pete Doubletree's cattle were dead, and all that that might mean, not just for Pete and his family, but for the whole community. "Maybe your dad's killing was random, or even an accident."

J.T. shook his head. "It was neither," he said.

She let out a long breath. "And you're afraid history will repeat itself?"

"Yeah," J.T. admitted. "Maybe I am. Something is wrong, McCaffrey. Something was wrong back then, and it's still wrong now."

She closed her eyes for a moment, quietly terrified. She couldn't refute his words, although she knew he had no proof. J.T. had been a cop for a long time; no doubt his instincts were sharp where such things were concerned.

A long silence fell. Then he assessed her thoughtfully. "What about you, McCaffrey?" he asked.

"What about me?"

His jawline softened, and his eyes glinted with a sort of beleaguered mischief. "Are *you* afraid history will repeat itself?"

She knew he wasn't referring to his father's murder now, but to their star-crossed love affair, back in the days of their reckless youth. "Maybe," she said.

He sighed again and simply waited.

"I don't want to be hurt again," she admitted.

"When did you turn into a coward?"

Her temper flared, despite everything. "I'm *not* a coward. I'm just careful, that's all. Sensible."

He pondered her remarks calmly, a sad smile lingering in his eyes, while the ghost of a grin haunted his mouth. "Maybe you're right," he said, after another silent interlude. "This is a dangerous world. A person is never more aware of that than when they have a child."

Maggie had no doubt that he was remembering things he'd seen during his career as a homicide detective, and she couldn't blame him for being scared. His concept of childhood had to be very different from her own, and not just because of his experiences with the police force. Although they'd both been raised in and around Springwater, in some ways they might as well have grown up on different planets. "I'll bet you miss Quinn. It'll be good for both of you to spend some time together."

J.T. relaxed a little, grinned. "He's a terrific kid. Smart. Funny."

"I believe it," she smiled.

J.T. took a thoughtful sip of his coffee. "For better or for worse," he said, "he'll be here in a few days. Annie's bringing him out from Atlanta herself. She leaves for South America sometime next week."

"South America," Maggie marveled.

J.T.'s mouth tilted up on one side.

"Brad—that's the new husband—has evidently been appointed to head up some construction job down there. Sounds like a very big deal—more money, lots of prestige."

He spoke of his ex-wife's second marriage without bitterness, and Maggie found that comforting, though she wouldn't have wanted to explain why. She and J.T. were water under the bridge; his feelings, or lack of them, for the mother of his child were none of her concern. "Will this mean they have to leave Atlanta?"

J.T. shook his head, and for a moment his expression was almost somber. "No idea," he said.

She sat up a little straighter. They'd had a good time together, she and J.T., the night before, until he was called away to help Purvis investigate the incident out at Stonecreek Ranch. When he left, she'd watched him go with mixed emotions, disappointment and relief in equal measures. "What brought you here today, J.T.?" she asked quietly.

"I was going to ask you to go riding with me."

"And now you've changed your mind?"

He shook his head, grinning again, though a certain sadness lingered in his eyes. "Nope," he said, and hesitated. He heaved a sigh, mussed his hair with the splayed fingers of one hand. "But I guess I should have called first. It was an impulsive decision to drop in."

She wanted to reach out, touch his hand, but she didn't. It seemed to her, though he was making light of things, that he was still caught in a backlash of emotion following the call from his ex-wife. "We can go riding another time," she said. "Let me get you some more coffee." She stood, crossed the room, and returned with the glass carafe moments later to refill J.T.'s cup. "You look like you've had a long day."

His mouth—that mouth Maggie spent an inordinate time trying not to think about—crooked upwards at one side. "It just so happens that I *have* had a long day. I was out late, and it was early when Quinn called. Purvis and I spent hours at the livestock auction over in Maple Creek, though we made a side trip to get this phone." He tapped his shirt pocket, where the device languished once more. "Last night was nice, McCaffrey." His gaze caressed her, flowed over her nerve endings like scented oil, warm and soothing and, at the same time, setting her on fire.

"It was," she agreed, treading carefully. "I could whip up a couple of omelettes, if you'd like some dinner." Food seemed like a safe topic.

"It's my turn to cook," he pointed out, and grinned. "Let's go to the Stagecoach Café."

Maggie, who had dined in some of the finest restaurants in the world, was ridiculously pleased at the prospect of a down-home supper in a place with linoleum floors, vinyl booths, and a vintage Coca-Cola machine, and not a little relieved that the tension had been broken. An otherwise sensible woman, she could not be trusted where J. T. Wainwright was concerned.

"You're on," she said.

They walked down the street to the Stagecoach Café. The place was brightly lit, the worn floors gleamed with fresh wax, and as they entered, an old country tune was playing on the jukebox. She and J.T. had danced to that song, cheek to cheek, at the high school prom.

She slid automatically into "their" booth in the back corner, opposite the kitchen, and then found it hard to meet J.T.'s gaze. She knew she'd see memories in his eyes, the same bittersweet ones that had so often haunted her over the past ten years.

"McCaffrey," he said, with mock sternness.

She looked up. It was the bravest thing she'd done in days. "What?" she asked.

His mouth slanted in a saucy grin. "They're playing our song."

She laughed and rolled her eyes.

"I've always wanted to say that," he said.

Rosie, the same aging waitress who had served them burgers and shakes a thousand times, approached the table, pad and pencil in hand. Rosie's bright red lipstick flared around her mouth, trapped in the cracks surrounding her lips, but her blue eyes were kind and the circles of rouge on her cheeks gave her a merry look. "Well, now," she said. "I was wondering when the two of you would wander in here together."

J.T. favored Rosie with a charming grin. "When you turned me down, Rosie," he teased, "I turned to McCaffrey for comfort. You've got nobody to blame but yourself."

Rosie laughed and pretended to swat at J.T. with her order pad. "Smart-aleck," she said. Her sweet gaze swung to Maggie. "What can I get you, sweetie? The chicken fried steak is good tonight." She leaned down slightly, and spoke in a confidential whisper. "I'd stay away from the meatloaf, though."

Maggie grinned. "Chicken fried steak, then," she said. "The low fat version, please."

Rosie rolled her eyes. "Like we've got low-fat *anything* in this place," she said. "And like you'd have to worry about it either way."

"You're going to get a big tip," Maggie said.

"Good," Rosie replied briskly, busily writing down the order with her stub of a pencil. Then she turned back to J.T. "All right, hotshot. What'll it be?" Her eyes twinkled, and her mouth was pursed. "I don't have all night, so spit it out."

"Whenever I miss New York," J.T. drawled, looking over the top of his menu at Maggie, "all I have to do is come in here and see you, Rosie. I'll have a double cheeseburger, extra tomato, hold the onion, and an order of curly fries. And a chocolate shake. Make it the high-fat version."

"Hmmph," scoffed Rosie, but she scribbled the pertinent information. "Come back in ten years, Mr. I-Can-Eat-Anything, and we'll see what you order *then.*"

"Only if you promise to wait on me personally," J.T. replied.

She laughed, patted his shoulder, and turned to hurry toward the kitchen. "Hey, Fred!" she yelled, to the owner and fry cook. "Look who's in here having chicken fried steak and cheeseburgers!"

Maggie shook her head, smiling. "She never changes."

"Thank God," J.T. answered. "I love that woman."

The jukebox stopped playing, and it seemed to Maggie that every other sound receded except for that of her own heartbeat. J.T. studied her solemnly for a long moment, then got up, crossed the otherwise empty restaurant, dropped some coins into a slot, punched a few buttons.

Their song started to play again, and Maggie felt her heart climb into her throat as she watched J.T. turn and walk back toward her. He put out his hand, and she took it, and then, though it wasn't the least bit sensible of them, they were dancing, cheek to cheek, in the middle of the Stagecoach Café.

Billy Raynor was sitting on the top step out in front of the house, the glow of the porch light catching halolike in the ridge left by his hat. The kid was a hard worker—he'd helped unload the seven head of cattle J.T. had bought at auction that morning, as the start of his herd—and he'd still been at the barn, feeding the horses, when J.T. had gone into town to buy supplies at the feed store.

"Hey, Bill," he said, getting out of the truck in the gravel driveway and starting up the walk. "Everything all right?" The new cattle, yearlings mostly, were still in the corral, and therefore safe, or so he'd supposed. Maybe he'd been wrong.

Billy nodded, got awkwardly to his feet. He was something of a paradox to J.T., youthful, with his thin chest and shoulders and gangly wrists, but more of a man than a lot of people twice his age and size. "I just figured I'd hang around a while, see if there was anything I could do to help you and Purvis track down those crooks that killed Pete's cattle."

The last thing J.T. wanted was Billy playing detective, but the kid's pride mattered,
so he was careful with his response.
"You've got your work cut out for you right
here," he said. "Between feeding livestock,
mending fences, and keeping a sharp eye
out for any kind of trouble, you'll have about
all you can do."

Billy managed another nod, and J.T. wondered what was really troubling him. He
hadn't waited on the porch just to commis-
erate about the rustling or to exchange idle
chitchat with the boss. "I'll say good night,
then," he said, hat in hand. "I reckon tomorrow morning will come around early."
Through the trees behind the house, J.T.
glimpsed the lights from the trailer Billy and
his bride were sharing, and it gave him a
lonely feeling. He never so much as
glimpsed the place without remembering
his first time with Maggie. Holding her in his
arms this evening as they danced had
brought back a lot of happy times. Talking
with her, hearing her laugh as they ate and
swapped stories, had been even better.
Leaving her chastely at the door of the
Springwater Station, with just a kiss on the
cheek, had been harder than ever.

Fatigue saturated every cell of J.T.'s body, and he was all but stumbling with it, but the kid had something on his mind and he felt compelled to find out what it was. "Got time to come in for a while?" he asked.

Billy hesitated, then nodded. Even in the dark J.T. saw the color rise up the youth's neck and throb along his jawline. He swallowed visibly and stepped aside so J.T. could pass and open the front door. Followed him in.

The emptiness of the place seemed to echo around them.

"I always liked this house," Billy said, as he trailed J.T. across the large front room, with its towering rock fireplace and beamed ceilings. "I used to imagine what it must have been like all them years ago, when Scully and the missus lived here."

They crossed the dining area, with its floor-to-ceiling windows, and headed on into the kitchen. J.T. had left a light burning over the sink when he went out that morning, he'd been in such a rush to meet up with Purvis and get on with his day. Struggling against all that open-country gloom, the bulb made a thin showing. "I guess it must have been pretty noisy, for one thing,"

J.T. observed. "They had a lot of kids, according to family stories. Can I get you a Coke or a beer or something?"

Billy shook his head and stood poised in the kitchen doorway, as if to turn and bolt back the way he'd come. "No, thanks. I shouldn't have bothered you."

J.T. gestured toward the round wooden table, where Scully and Evangeline Wainwright and their children had gathered, season after season, year after year. The clan had finally boiled down to just him and Quinn, he thought, and felt another brush of sadness. "Sit down," he said.

He got a cup from the shelf, dropped in a tea bag, added water, and shoved the whole works into the microwave, smiling a little. Tea. The herbal variety, no less. After the shooting, he'd discovered that he liked the stuff. His partner would have given him a hard time about that; whiskey had been Murphy's tonic of choice.

Billy sat, scraping the chair legs against the ancient linoleum as he did so. Out of the corner of his eye, J.T. saw the ranch hand flush again. "I reckon you know Cindy and I haven't been married long," he said.

J.T. didn't look at Billy; in fact, he sensed

that the kid was praying he wouldn't. "You told me," he answered, busying himself at the counter while he waited for the microwave. "The wedding was five or six months ago, right?"

"Six," Billy said.

J.T. continued to wait while the oven whirred. Through the glass door, he saw the water bubble over out of the mug, tea-colored, and stabbed at the stop button with one fingertip.

"She didn't have an easy time of it, growing up with no mother and Odell for a dad," Billy went on.

J.T. turned to face Billy, the cup momentarily forgotten in the oven. "No," he said. "I don't suppose she did." Then, carefully, "You two have a fight or something?"

Billy sighed, cleared his throat. "I don't know as you'd call it that. Cindy's mad at herself, more than anybody. And she gets pretty emotional these days, because of the baby."

Leaning back against the edge of the counter, arms folded, J.T. didn't comment. Obviously, Billy needed to talk, and tired as he was, J.T. meant to listen. It was about all he could do.

Billy blinked rapidly, but he didn't look away. "I love Cindy," he said. "I want her to be happy. But it doesn't seem like she knows how. To be happy, I mean. To let somebody love her and take care of her."

J.T. kept quiet. In point of fact, he was a little choked up himself. Annie had often accused him of a similar problem—she'd said he was constitutionally incapable of letting anyone really care for him. He only loved from a safe distance, she'd claimed, and he couldn't deny that he had a long history of insulating himself from any intense emotion. Some guys drank too much, or did drugs. Some chased after all the wrong women. J.T., well, he simply stepped back, retreated, lost himself in his work. He might not have gone through the grieving process, after Murphy died, if he hadn't been stuck in a hospital with no way to escape his own feelings.

"She says it was a mistake, our getting married," Billy went on. "She claims I deserve better than her. But that isn't the way I see it, J.T. I think I'm the luckiest guy there is."

J.T. ached for both of them. They were just a pair of kids themselves, and here they were, starting a family. "Cindy's pretty lucky, too, it seems to me," he observed. He remembered the tea then, reached for it, and promptly burned his hand. Stifling a curse, he sat down across from Billy, the cup cooling in front of him. He deliberately focused his mind on what the boy was saying; it wouldn't do to fall face first onto the table, all thought washed from his brain by a flash flood of exhaustion.

Billy looked hopeful. "I guess I just need to hang in there," he said.

J.T. didn't like presenting himself as an expert, especially where women were concerned. He'd lost Maggie, thrown her away, in fact, and he'd let Annie go without a fight. She'd pleaded with him to leave the NYPD, saying the job was eating him alive, accusing him of using it as an emotional hideout, and he'd refused, over and over again, each time more adamantly than the last. Ironic, he reflected, that he'd ended up resigning after all, long after she'd met Brad and remarried.

"Sounds to me like you have a pretty good handle on the situation," he said.

Billy looked shyly grateful. "Maybe I

ought to bring her some flowers or something."

J.T. nodded. "That's a fine idea," he told the boy, and got out his wallet. Billy hadn't had a paycheck yet, and he was probably broke. He tossed several twenties onto the table—neutral ground—so that the kid would feel he had a choice about accepting them. "Here. A little advance on your pay."

Billy hesitated, then smiled and picked up the money, folding the bills and tucking them into his shirt pocket. "Thanks, J.T.," he said. "Cindy's been craving Rocky Road ice cream. I guess I'll drive into town and pick some up. The Safeway's still open."

J.T. was touched. Doris Raynor had a lot to answer for, when it came to mothering, but she'd done something right with this younger son of hers. "Sounds like a good plan," he agreed.

"I'll feed the horses first thing in the morning," Billy said hastily, on his way to the backdoor.

J.T. nodded again. "After that, we'll turn the cattle out to graze."

"What about branding and doctoring them up and the like?" Billy asked, one hand on the doorknob.

"That can wait," J.T. said. "Fetch that ice cream for your wife and then get some sleep. Like you said, morning will be here before you know it."

Billy grinned, opened the door, and went out.

J.T. sat alone with his tea for several minutes, even though he was damn near too tired to lift the cup. *Young love,* he thought, with a bittersweet ache in his heart.

He took his time before heading upstairs, rinsing out his cup, scanning the inside of the refrigerator for the makings of breakfast, switching off lights. When he was sure Billy wasn't going to come back with one more innocent sorrow to share, he climbed the steps.

After a hot, restorative shower and the usual ablutions, J.T. dropped into his bed, still unmade from the day before, and kept right on falling, settling at long last into the abject and murky depths of slumber.

The dream ambushed him sometime later, cornered him in a shadowy, sleep-logged part of his mind. This time, instead of Murphy, the ghost was his father.

He was a kid again, just thirteen, working in the corral as he had been that day long ago. Jack Wainwright appeared, on cue, drenched in crimson, as was the horse he rode. J.T. felt the same sick horror he'd felt then; only too aware that he was in the grip of a nightmare, he wondered if it was possible to die in just this way, sound asleep, facing a specter he knew was imaginary.

He'd had the dream before, of course, but not for a long time, and not in such vivid detail. Usually, he relived Murphy's death. As he stared at his father, a shout caught like a ball of rusted barbwire in his throat, and the scene took on a new element. Jack Wainwright locked gazes with his son, tried to speak. Just as he'd tried to speak the day he died.

J.T. sat bolt upright in bed, gasping, his bare skin prickly with a cold sweat. He leaped out of bed and went to the window, sure he would see a dead man there, mounted on a bloody horse. For that reason, when he made out the shadow of a rider, traced in darkness and moonlight, it was a moment before the implications sunk in.

When they did, he grappled into his jeans and raced downstairs, nearly killing himself on the steps, and wrenched open the kitchen door. The rider was gone.

J.T. went back for his boots, rummaged in the pantry for a flashlight, and hurried outside. He found the hoofprints right where they should have been, and couldn't decide whether he was relieved by the discovery that he hadn't been hallucinating, or scared shitless. Both, he concluded, there at the edge of the backyard, in roughly the same place where his father had fallen all those years ago.

His strongest impulse was to saddle up and give chase, but he knew it would be useless in the dark. At sunrise he'd find the trail and follow it as far as he could.

He glanced toward the trailer, saw that the lights were out. What he needed, he decided, was an old-fashioned alarm system. A dog.

The image of Maggie's beagle came to mind, and he found himself grinning. Maybe something a little meaner, he thought. Sadie probably would have left with the night rider, of her own free will.

Upstairs, he took another shower, rinsing off the dream sweat, then went back to bed.

Lying there, with his hands cupped behind his head, he assessed his situation.

The source of the nightmare was no great mystery: he'd lost his father in a very violent way, as a young boy. Now his son was coming to stay on the ranch, and Springwater, for all its charm, was not a safe place. Not for him, and not for Quinn.

It's your imagination, his reason argued, but a cold fist seemed to grip his gut. Old ghosts were stirring. He'd just seen one.

The pounding on his front door brought Purvis surging up out of a deep sleep; grumbling, he groped for his pants. "Hold your horses!" he yelled, and yelped again when he struck his big toe on the leg of the console stereo as he passed it. The hammering only intensified.

Purvis's irritation gave way to alarm. Simultaneously, he pulled open the front door and flipped on the porch light. A local kid, one of the high school crowd, stood in the glow, his face white with some residual horror.

Oh, Lord, Purvis thought, *here we go.* "What is it?"

"There's a man dead," the youth replied,

his voice shaking. He'd shoved both hands into the pockets of his jacket, maybe in an effort to steady them.

"What?" Purvis demanded. He shuffled through a mental file, located the kid's name. Jimmy. Jimmy Kendrick. His dad owned the dry cleaners.

"He must have fallen off the water tower, you know, near the entrance to the old Jupiter and Zeus? Some of us were out there—just hanging around and stuff—and we found him laying there."

"Who is he, do you know?" Purvis rasped, leaving the door agape while he went back into the dark house for his boots, a shirt, and his lawman gear. Jimmy waited on the porch, though it was obvious that he wanted to bolt.

"I d-don't know. There's—there was *a lot* of blood—"

Purvis heard a retching sound, and fig-ured the boy was puking over the porch rail, into the flower bed. He passed Jimmy's hunched figure at a high lope and headed for the squad car. "I'll have some questions for you later," he warned.

"Y-Yes, sir," Jimmy said.

Behind the wheel, Purvis started the motor and fumbled for his cell phone, which was plugged into the cigarette lighter, and dialed J.T.'s number with quick, stabbing motions of his thumb.

8

The defunct water tower, which once served the needs of the Jupiter and Zeus Silver Mine, was almost fifteen miles from J.T.'s ranch. By the time he arrived the sheriff's people were already there, taking pictures, measuring distances, stringing the familiar yellow crime-scene tape from pillar to post.

J.T. came through the crowd without slowing his pace, the nickel badge Judge Calloway had given to him displayed in the upraised palm of one hand. He found Purvis crouching beside the body, which was awash in blood, limbs sprawled at a variety of impossible angles. Although J.T. had seen worse, many times, violent death wasn't something he had ever gotten used to; acid chafed the back of his throat, and he swore. It didn't help that this was someone he recognized.

Purvis looked up at him, his face illuminated by the glare of several portable floodlights. "Throat's been cut," he said.

J.T. hunkered down to get a better look at what remained of his uncle-by-marriage, Clive Jenson. He glanced up at the dark bulk of the water tower, wondering why anybody would take the trouble to open a man's jugular *and* launch him off a platform fifty feet in the air.

"Some kids found him," said one of the sheriff's deputies, a woman in jeans and a flannel shirt, with her hair caught up in some kind of plastic clip.

"They see it happen?" J.T. asked automatically, though he already suspected Clive had taken his swan dive without an audience, unless you counted the killers. From the looks of things, he'd been lying here for a while, bones splintered, bleeding into the dirt.

"Not as far as I know," Purvis said. "Jimmy Kendrick made the report. He and some other kids were out here, probably necking and drinking beer, and they stumbled across the body."

"Shit," J.T. breathed, through his teeth. He'd never liked the man, and there was no use pretending he had, but he wouldn't have wished a fate like this on anybody, not even Clive. The kids who had found the body would probably never get the image of it out of their minds, and the burden of such a gruesome memory could be a heavy one to carry. Nobody knew that better than he did.

The techs finished with the crime scene fairly quickly, which was good, because a light, steady rain had begun to fall, and Purvis took J.T. aside while the coroner's assistants were zipping the body bag and loading it into the back of a county ambulance. "I gotta ask you this, J.T.," Purvis whispered hoarsely, raising his collar against the drizzle and hunching a little, "even though I know you ain't gonna like it. Where were you tonight?"

J.T. sighed, thrust a hand through his hair. He thought of the rider he'd glimpsed in the side yard at the ranch, and the tracks he'd meant to follow when the sun came up. Tracks that would probably be washed away long before he could get back to them. "I was with Maggie McCaffrey until about nine o'clock, over at the Stagecoach Café," he answered. Although Purvis's question was routine, there were bound to be people who remembered the enmity between Clive and J.T., and were thus inclined to speculate on the power of old grudges. "After that, I went home, did some chores, set up my computer, and went to bed."

Purvis waited.

"Alone," J.T. clarified. "Billy was here for a few minutes."

"And you haven't seen him around town recently? Clive, I mean? Maybe he called or stopped by the ranch, and you talked to him?"

"No," J.T. said. There was an edge to the word.

"No need to get testy," Purvis responded. "I'm not saying you killed him."

"God knows," J.T. rasped, half to himself, "I wanted to a few times."

Purvis heaved a great sigh. He probably hadn't had any more sleep than J.T. had, and like as not, he wouldn't be getting a whole lot of shut-eye in the near future, either. Once word got out that Springwater's

crime wave had escalated to include murder, poor old Purvis would be dancing bare-
foot on a hot griddle.

"Clive leave any kin that you know of?
Anybody we ought to notify?"

"He had a son by a previous marriage,"
J.T. recalled, after some thought. "His name
escapes me. I never met the guy—I don't
think he and the old man were all that
close."

"You got any of his or Janeen's papers
around the house?"

J.T. nodded, watching as the ambulance
trundled away with what was left of his late
aunt's husband. "There's some stuff stored
in an old file cabinet," he said. "I'll see what
I can find."

Purvis rubbed the back of his neck with
one hand. "Thanks," he said. They walked
together toward the town's one and only
police car and J.T.'s truck, parked behind it.
"I'll admit, I wish you'd spent more of last
night with Maggie."

J.T. knew his grin was brittle. "So do I," he
said. His reasons were a little different, of
course. The rain hadn't slackened; J.T.
wished he'd thought to wear a hat, but he'd
left the house in a hurry after Purvis's call.

"Who hated Clive Jenson?" Purvis muttered, in a distracted tone, musing aloud.

"Just about everybody," J.T. answered.

"Enough to kill him," Purvis stipulated.

J.T. sighed. That specification certainly
narrowed the field, though he was sure several viable candidates still remained. "Let's
find out," he said, with resignation. "We can
start by going over to your office and running a few background checks."

Maggie stared at J.T., the next morning at
the Station, after he told her about Clive
Jenson, looking for any sign of grief, but all
she saw was a sort of jaded weariness that
made her soul ache. Homicide, in all its
manifestations, was old news to J.T. More-
over, she sensed that he was already re-
treating into the investigation; he wasn't the
same man she'd danced with, laughed with,
at the Stagecoach Café only the night before.

"Clive and I weren't close," J.T. said, and
she saw a veil drop behind his eyes, effectively shutting her out. "There's no sense
pretending otherwise."

"I can't believe this is happening," Maggie said, taking an emotional step back her-

self. "This is *Springwater.*" The very air seemed to sparkle after the night's rain, and the sun was shining brightly, making the whole idea of murder seem impossible.

"Believe it," J.T. replied. He finished the coffee she'd given him, carried the mug to the kitchen, and set it in the sink. "Purvis is going to ask if you spent time with me last night. The sheriff's detectives might, too."

Maggie's eyes widened. "They don't think—?" She couldn't bring herself to finish the sentence.

"It's routine," J.T. said briskly.

She sank onto one of the benches, absently petting Sadie, who had immediately lain her muzzle on Maggie's knee. "Still," she said.

"McCaffrey," J.T. drawled, rounding the table and leaning forward, hands braced against the edges, to look down into her face. "I didn't like Clive, but I didn't kill him, either."

She felt an indignant flush climb into her face and throb there. "Well, I *know* that," she said, and she thought she saw relief flash in his eyes.

"Good," he said. "Now, I'd better get over to Purvis's office. We've got more reports to fill out, even though we were at it half the night, and one of us will have to contact next of kin."

Maggie nodded, still feeling weak. She couldn't get over it. She couldn't get *past* it. Murder. *In Springwater?*

"Later," J.T. told her, and then he was gone.

Daphne showed up only a few minutes after he left, carrying a little girl in her arms. The child was beautiful, with fair hair and bright brown eyes, and she clung shyly to her foster mother while studying first Sadie, then Maggie, with sober interest.

Maggie smiled and got to her feet. "This must be Tiffany," she said.

"Isn't she precious?" Daphne beamed.

"Yes," Maggie said, putting out an index finger. Tiffany assessed the digit thoughtfully, then clasped it in her moist little hand and squeezed. "Hi," Maggie greeted her.

Tiffany buried her face in Daphne's neck.

"Ben says there was a M-U-R-D-E-R up by the Jupiter and Zeus," Daphne reported, looking serious now.

Maggie nodded, no longer smiling. "Clive Jenson," she said.

"J.T.'s uncle?"

"Yes," Maggie said, and shuddered.

Daphne set Tiffany on her feet and squatted beside her while she and Sadie eyed each other. Sadie made a tentative, friendly lap at Tiffany's face, and Tiffany gave a gurgling, joyous laugh.

"I thought dear old Clive was long gone," Daphne said, at some length, still supervising as Sadie and Tiffany made each other's acquaintances.

Maggie frowned. "My mother mentioned that he'd been back in town a few times since his wife died. He wasn't tremendously popular, given the way he had deserted Janeen."

Daphne winced. "Can you imagine leaving a person you supposedly loved to face something like cancer all alone?"

Maggie shook her head, watching with growing affection as Tiffany and Sadie made friends. "Tell me about Tiffany," she said, glad of the happy distraction the child's presence provided.

Daphne lowered her voice, although it was doubtful a two-year-old child could have understood much of any adult conversation. Including one about M-U-R-D-E-R.

"She was abandoned at a rest stop," she said. "Late last week."

Maggie was incredulous. "No," she protested.

But Daphne nodded. "A retired couple were passing through in an RV, and they found her wandering around on her own when they stopped to stretch their legs. They brought her to the sheriff's office in Maple Creek." She paused. "Nobody seems to have any idea who left her or why."

"Then how did they know her name? Does she talk?"

Daphne shook her head, her silvery eyes filling with sadness as she watched Tiffany awkwardly stroking one of the dog's petal-soft ears. "She says "mama," and "no." That's about it, as far as anyone can tell. But somebody had printed 'This is Tiffany' on the back of her hand. I saw a photograph— the letters were awkward. Childlike."

Maggie blinked, overcome by the image of a toddler abandoned at a rest stop, with only a few scrawled words to identify her. "What's going to happen now?"

Daphne's shrug was deliberately casual.

"She'll be a ward of the court while an investigation is conducted. At some point, adoption may become a possibility. In the meantime, Tiffany will be staying with Ben and me."

"And you and Ben want to adopt her?" Maggie ventured softly.

Daphne nodded. Her spine stiffened slightly, and there was a defiant glint in her eyes, as though she expected an argument. "Yes," she answered. "But I—we—understand that it might not happen, and we're okay with that."

Maggie wasn't sure she believed that last part—Daphne obviously had bonded with Tiffany after less than twenty-four hours, even though it seemed Ben wasn't as eager to proceed with an adoption—but she kept her misgivings to herself. Daphne was her best friend, and whatever happened, good, bad, or indifferent, she would be there for her. She prayed that Daphne wouldn't be hurt and summoned up a smile. "A celebration is in order," she announced, turning toward June-bug's kitchen. "And in my family, that means homemade cookies. Want to help out?"

*   *   *

It had been one hell of a night, and the day that followed was a long one. J.T. checked the area where he'd seen the rider—sure enough, the tracks were gone—then did ranch work most of the day. He spent the late afternoon and part of the evening going through the ancient file cabinets in the storeroom off his study and, eventually, his efforts were rewarded. He found a dusty old address book, the entries inside neatly penned in his aunt's hand. Feeling a variety of emotions—he'd loved his father's sister, after all, and he hadn't been around when she needed him most—he flipped to the Js.

His eye went immediately to *Jenson, Steve.* The address that followed was the federal penitentiary over in Walla Walla, Washington. J.T. sighed. He hadn't remembered the name when he and Purvis discussed Clive's next of kin, but he knew this was the man they were looking for.

He reached for the telephone, realized it was past closing time for most federal offices, including that of the warden at Walla Walla, and headed for his computer, instead. In five minutes he had all the information he expected to find. Steve Jenson had been released a year before, after serving seven-to-ten for a string of armed robberies in Spokane and Seattle. He'd skipped out on his parole right away, and a warrant for rearrest had been issued, but never served. No sense in trying to contact Jenson regarding his father's death, since he was still on the run.

J.T. made a few notes, including the name and number of the parole officer assigned to the case, and put in a call to Purvis. No answer at the office, at home, or on the cell phone. Frowning, J.T. printed out Steve Jenson's mug shot, fuzzy as it was, got up from his desk to find the truck keys, and set out for town. He'd show the picture to Purvis, when he found him, and to some of the boys who hung out down at the Brimstone Saloon.

He found Purvis at the Stagecoach Café, having dinner with Nelly Underwood, the woman who'd been with him the night he and J.T. met at Pete Doubletree's ranch, after the cattle were poisoned. Although they invited him to sit down, J.T. declined, figuring he'd interrupted enough as it was.

He proceeded to the Brimstone Saloon, where the usual crowd of pool-playing beer

drinkers had gathered to pass a construc-
tive evening. After coming up dry with every
one of them, J.T. headed for the bar. He
vaguely remembered the bartender and,
fortunately, the man was wearing a plastic
name tag.

"Evening, Charlie," he said.

Charlie nodded and even smiled, though
his eyes looked a little squinty. "J.T.," he
replied. Apparently, his memory was better
than J.T.'s own. "What'll you have?"

J.T. ordered a beer, since technically he
wasn't on duty. "This your usual crew?" he
asked, indicating the clientele with a slight
nod of his head.

"Pretty much," Charlie said, sighing.
Maybe he aspired to better things than
swabbing the bar in Springwater's historic
saloon, old Charlie. And maybe not. "Randy
Hough and Travis DuPres usually stop in.
Haven't seen them tonight." The bartender
eyed J.T. narrowly again. "Not that Randy
drinks anything but soda when he's in here."

J.T. let the comment pass. He laid the
printout on the bar. "You seen this guy
lately?"

To his credit, Charlie really studied the

mug shot. "No," he said, at considerable length.

J.T. enjoyed a sip of his beer. "Ever?"

Charlie cleared his throat. "Maybe. There's something familiar about him. But you've got to admit, J.T.—it's hard to identify somebody from a picture like this."

"Yeah," J.T. admitted. He wasn't sure he'd recognize himself from a bad mug shot, let alone some yahoo he didn't know. And this one was fuzzy, old, and somewhat generic, like so many of its type.

"Why?" Charlie prompted, when J.T. didn't volunteer anything.

"Why what?"

"Why are you looking for him?"

"You probably heard that Clive was killed last night. This is his son. Somebody has to let him know what happened."

"Oh," Charlie said. A tiny muscle twitched under his left eye.

"Name's Steve," J.T. supplied. "Steve Jenson. He might be calling himself something else these days, though."

"If I see him," Charlie said, with a swallow, "I'll let you know."

You're a bad liar, Charlie, J.T. thought, but he made sure his smile was cordial. "I'd appreciate that." He laid his money on the bar and turned to leave. He'd run a check on the bartender, too, just for the heck of it.

Purvis flagged him down as he was driving past the Stagecoach Café. "What you got?" he asked, peering through the open truck window. For the first time it dawned on J.T. that Purvis Digg was a new man. He'd had his famous ponytail cut off, and he was wearing a uniform with the dry cleaning creases still in it. There was no sign of Nelly.

J.T. told him about coming across Steve Jenson's name in an old address book of his aunt's, running a make on the 'net, and finding out that Clive's next of kin had a prison record.

"Good work," Purvis said, grinning. "You reckon he's around here someplace?"

J.T. sighed. "No telling. I didn't get much out of that crowd over at the Brimstone. I'd bet anything the bartender's at least seen him, though."

Purvis looked rueful. "Charlie? He'd rather climb the tallest tree to tell a lie than stand flat-footed on the ground and tell the truth. Let me have another look at that paper."

J.T. handed it over, and Purvis studied it

with the aid of the interior light J.T. flipped on for his benefit.

"I've seen him someplace," Purvis said with conviction, extending the picture.

"Keep it," J.T. said. He grinned. "Where's your girl?"

Purvis actually blushed. "You mean Nelly?"

J.T. chuckled. "No," he joked. "I meant Margaret Thatcher. Of *course* Nelly."

Purvis looked sheepish and smug, both at once. "I know what you're thinking."

"Oh, yeah? What's that?"

"That she's a little young for me."

"Never crossed my mind."

Purvis glanced from side to side, as though he thought somebody might be listening. "I like her," he confided.

J.T. smiled. "Does she like you back?"

"I think so," Purvis admitted, almost in a whisper. He sounded awed.

"Good," J.T. answered. "Then go for it."

"You want to come over to the office for a while? Brainstorm a little?"

"Sure," J.T. said, wondering if he would ever sleep again. "I'll meet you there."

They drank coffee, went through old posters and bulletins, and pitched theories at each other until it was nearly 11 o'clock. Then, with a full day's work awaiting him on the ranch the next day, J.T. decided he'd better head for home.

The lights were on at Springwater Station, and he wanted to stop in and see Maggie, but he couldn't bring himself to do it. He felt too raw, too exposed. Besides, he rationalized, by now, she'd be getting ready for bed, and he didn't dare pursue that line of thought, not if he wanted to get any rest at all.

He was playing the radio and whistling along when he rounded the first bend in his long driveway and saw the fire looming crimson against the night sky. His gut lurched painfully, and he shoved the gas pedal to the floor, swearing even as he fumbled to open his cell phone and dialed 911. The barn was ablaze, and maybe the house, too; from that distance, he couldn't tell.

He thought first of Billy and Cindy Raynor, perhaps roasting in their cracker box of a trailer, and then of the horses. He shouted into the phone, then flung it onto the seat and sped toward the homestead, leaping out of the truck when he reached the barnyard, leaving the motor running and the door agape.

The house and trailer were untouched, as yet, but the barn was an inferno. J.T. bolted toward the stable doors, concentrating on getting the horses out. He'd groomed the pair and fed them earlier, and shut them up in their stalls personally. Now, they were trapped. A wall of heat and fire nearly knocked him down when he hit the threshold; he put one forearm across his eyes and started inside.

"J.T., wait!" somebody shouted, and looking back through the blistering smoke he saw Billy running across the yard. "The horses are safe—they're down by the creek, with the cattle!"

J.T. backed away from the barn just as the roof caved in, sending a spray of sparks and flaming brands sky-high. Billy grabbed J.T. by the arm—or was it the other way around?—and they ran. Both of them were burned in the rain of fire, though it would be much later before either of them were aware of the damage.

J.T. grabbed a garden hose, hooked it up to a spigot in the yard, and drenched Billy, then himself, before starting to wet down the roof and walls of the house.

"What the hell happened?" he yelled, not really expecting an answer.

"I don't know exactly!" Billy shouted back. "I heard a rig—that's what woke me up—and I came running. I saw two men get into a truck and tear out of here."

J.T. hadn't met anybody on the road out of town; even though he'd been mulling over Steve Jenson's whereabouts, Clive's murder, and what little he knew of either man's past, he would have noticed. He was used to thinking along three or four different tracks at once. "Nobody you recognized?"

"I was worried about getting to the horses," Billy replied. "And it was dark."

J.T. nodded grimly. His aunt Janeen always had said that bad things happened in threes. First there was the poisoning out at Stonecreek Ranch, then Clive's swan dive off the rusted water tower on the grounds of the old Jupiter and Zeus Silver Mine, and now this. It was hard not to turn superstitious.

Glancing in the direction of the kids' place, J.T.'s reeling brain kicked into gear. "Go get your wife, now!" he yelled to the boy, over the roar of the blaze. In the distance, he heard a fire siren. "If the propane tank catches a spark that trailer will go into orbit!"

Billy's eyes widened in his sooty face; he hesitated only a moment, then turned and sprinted toward the tin can where his young, pregnant wife was waiting, probably scared out of her skin.

J.T.'s words proved prophetic. No sooner had Billy and Cindy fishtailed away in Billy's truck, maybe ten minutes later, than the trailer exploded in four directions, and with a roar that left J.T.'s eardrums throbbing. The fire truck arrived from town, spilling volunteers while he was still staring at the wreckage. He might have been sick about then, if he'd had a moment to spare.

The sun was coming up over the eastern hills, spilling pink and gold light into the valley, when they finally had the fire out for good. J.T. surveyed the ruins of his barn and the trailer, and the scorched side of his house, and shook his head as if to clear his vision of something he had only imagined. His eyes felt gritty with smoke and soot, his throat was parched, and his head swam.

Billy had long since returned from taking

Cindy to his mother's house in town, and he stood at J.T.'s elbow, in the misty chill of early morning, looking as though he might break down and cry. "This is God awful," he said.

"Hey," J.T. answered, working up a smile and slapping him lightly on the back. "We needed a new barn anyway."

Purvis, who had arrived a few minutes after the volunteers and fought the fire along with everyone else, crossed the yard to join Billy and J.T. He was looking pretty drawn by that time, and little wonder. He'd been through the wringer over Pete Doubletree's dead cattle and the murder of Clive Jenson, and now there was a clear case of arson to contend with. "I promise you, J.T.," he said, "I will find the son-of-a-bitch who did this."

J.T.'s take on the matter was simple. This was a case of malicious mischief that had gotten seriously out of hand. The men had meant to destroy the barn, all right, but he was pretty sure the trailer catching fire was an accident, and if the culprits had wanted to do him any real harm, they'd have set the house ablaze, too. With him in it.

Billy told Purvis about the truck he'd glimpsed, and the two men. "They was just shadows, really," he said. "I didn't figure I could go after them and leave the stock to burn to death."

J.T. laid a hand on the kid's shoulder. He was grateful that both the newlyweds were still alive, let alone the horses. "I appreciate what you did," he said. "You're a brave man, Billy. By the same token, if you ever take another risk like that on my account, I'll personally skin you alive."

Even through all that grime, Billy's face seemed to glow with embarrassed pleasure. "I was just doing my job," he said modestly, in his own defense. Then he gazed sadly in the direction of the trailer, now twisted and blistered, its frame curled in upon itself like some strange and futuristic creature that had died in agony. A powerful shudder moved through the younger man as the full reality of what might have happened struck home at last.

"You and Cindy can use the downstairs guest room for the time being," J.T. said quietly. Purvis offered no comment, but he looked mighty sympathetic.

Billy nodded, plainly distraught. "Thanks. Cindy's at my mom's place right now. I guess I'd better head for town after I bring the animals back up from the creek. Mom and Cindy will be worried if I don't show up pretty soon."

"I'll get the horses," J.T. said. It was his place, after all, and his problem. "You go back to Springwater and get some rest."

Billy obeyed, and J.T. started toward the path leading down to the creek. Purvis came along, matching him stride for stride.

"Is it just me, or is this whole damn county going to hell all of the sudden?" the older man asked.

J.T. managed a bitter grin. "You've sure been earning your pay lately," he responded. He didn't mention his suspicion that the worst was yet to come; Purvis probably shared it.

"I reckon you ought to go in and see Doc Parrish about those burns," the lawman said.

For the first time J.T. was aware of small, fierce patches of pain, sprinkled liberally over his back, shoulders, and arms. "I'm all right," he said.

"Stubborn, is what you are," Purvis answered.

"That too," J.T. agreed, and grinned. He saw to the horses, found his way back to the house and up the stairs, and collapsed into bed without even bothering to undress. He slept a full fourteen hours.

Kathleen McCaffrey stood back from her canvas, a large rendering of a misshapen artichoke lying on its side, and frowned as she wiped her hands on a paint rag. The screened sunporch was bright with the glow of a fragrant summer morning, and Maggie's dog was curled on a rug near the outer door, eyes raised in wary speculation.

"That's pretty good, Mom."

Kathleen waved a scornful but loving hand in her son's direction. "It's a horror, Wesley, and you know it. I guess I'm not ready to graduate from pears."

Wes grinned. Although his coloring was fair, he resembled his father in many ways. All three of her children did, in fact—not a redhead in the bunch, although her youngest grandchildren, Jodi and Loren, had her green eyes and blaze of hair. Wes was leaning one shoulder against the doorjamb, arms loosely folded. "What was it you always told me? 'It takes *time* to master new things, Wesley.' Wasn't that it?"

She waved him away again, though she

didn't really want him to go, and she was smiling. "How are Franny and the kids?"

He grimaced. "Franny is probably on her knees in front of the toilet. I wouldn't have left her this morning if her mother hadn't been there. Jodi wants to start ballet, and Loren is learning to swear."

"Poor Franny! Have you spoken to Ellen Parrish?"

Wes nodded. "She put her on medication for the morning sickness, but there isn't much else she can do. Franny had the same problem with the twins, remember? And everything was all right."

Kathleen had forgotten her lopsided artichoke; she wiped her hands again and set the rag aside, frowning. Once she'd taken that everything's-bound-to-be-all-right approach to life herself, but lately she'd learned that the very earth itself could turn to vapor beneath a person's feet and leave her tumbling through space. "All the same," she said, "I think you should call your brother and get his opinion."

Wes grinned in that lazy, lethal way peculiar to McCaffrey men. Kathleen had often wondered what she'd unleashed on the world, turning out a new generation of the

rascals. She loved both her sons without re-
serve, and God knew she was proud of
them, though she kept a special place in her
heart for Maggie because she was the only
girl. "All right," he agreed. "I'll give him a
ring and see what Simon says."

Kathleen rolled her eyes.

"Is there any coffee?" Wesley asked, and
that was when she realized he hadn't simply
stopped by. He was on some kind of mission.

"Of course," she answered, worried.
"What is it, Wesley?" She passed him,
heading into the spacious, sun-filled
kitchen, and he followed.

"There's been some more excitement
around Springwater," he said.

Kathleen turned to face him. "Yes," she
said. "I heard about that terrible murder."
She didn't add that she didn't consider
Clive to be any great loss. It wouldn't do to
speak ill of the dead.

"There's more, I'm afraid."

"More?" Kathleen braced herself. She
wondered what Springwater was coming to.
It had always been such a peaceful little
town. But then, there *had* been incidents,
hadn't there? Jack Wainwright had been

shot dead on his own land years before, and no one had ever been arrested for the crime. She sank into a chair, one hand over her mouth.

Wes drew up a chair of his own and sat. "Somebody set J.T.'s barn on fire last night. It burned to the ground, and though they got out in time, Billy and Cindy Raynor's trailer was blown to bits."

Kathleen couldn't speak.

Wesley got up and brought back a glass of water, which she accepted gratefully.

"This is dreadful," she managed. She drew several shaky breaths and then stood, setting the glass aside. She needed to be doing something, whether it was necessary or not. Her eyes stung with empathetic tears as she spooned freshly ground coffee into the old-fashioned electric percolator she'd been using for thirty years. "Was anyone hurt?"

Wes shook his head.

She felt a dizzying rush of relief, and a need to prattle. "The ladies aid will want to take up some kind of collection for those poor children, I'm sure. They could certainly stay in our guest house for as long as they needed—"

Wesley grinned at her. "I love you, Mom," he said. He gave the endearment a few moments to sink in. "I suppose they'll live with J.T., though. He's been rattling around in that big old house all by himself anyway, and Billy will want to be close to his job." Wes paused, glanced toward the open backdoor. "Is Dad around? Like as not, there'll be a barn-raising soon, and I expect he'll want to donate some of the materials." Although Reece had sold the family milling operation, he'd kept back a sizable inventory of lumber and other supplies. No doubt that made him feel as though he was still a part of things, where the business was concerned.

"I'm sure your father will be happy to help," she said, a little stiffly. It seemed that Reece was eager to grant everyone's wishes lately—except for hers, of course. She was expected to turn her back on everyone and everything she knew—family, friends, house, garden, the very warp and woof of her existence—to simply uproot herself from a life more than forty years in the making and take to the road like some gypsy.

"Is he here?" Wesley asked again, carefully.

Kathleen got out two large ceramic mugs, made during her pottery-and-ceramics phase, and set them on the counter. "As far as I know," she said coolly, "yes."

Wesley sighed audibly, but before he could formulate a reply, Reece himself breezed in from the backyard, accompanied by the whooshing sound of the sprinklers and the scent of new-mown grass, looking cheerful as you please. Clean-shaven and spit-shined, as a matter of fact. Kathleen's blood simmered, and she tightened her lips. Her worst suspicions were proving to be true, she thought, as something collapsed inside her. Reece McCaffrey had taken up with another woman.

"Mornin'," Reece said.

Wesley nodded cordially at his father. Men. They were all alike, and no better than they should be. "You're out and about early, Dad," he remarked.

"No earlier than you are," Reece answered lightly. He caught Kathleen staring, and she looked away, flushed, but not before she saw him grin that McCaffrey grin. Well, if he wanted coffee, he could just get

out his own cup and pour the stuff for himself, she fumed.

"I guess you've probably heard about
J.T.'s fire," Wesley said.

Reece nodded. "Things are buzzing down
at the Stagecoach Café," he said. "Murder
and arson, in one week. Poor Purvis is probably in way over his head this time."

Before anyone responded to that observation, Maggie's dog tottered in from the
sunporch, and Kathleen dished up a bowl of
kibble, then leaned down to set it on the
floor.

When she straightened again, her gaze
collided with Reece's, and she realized, by
the twinkle in his eyes, that he'd been admiring her backside while she was bent
over. She might have slapped him right
across that handsome kisser of his, if they'd
been alone. Or not.

He chuckled, and Wesley looked away
and cleared his throat.

Kathleen glared at Reece and stormed
back to the counter, where there was nothing whatsoever to do except wait for the
coffee to brew. It was percolating nicely, filling the kitchen with a fragrance that evoked
earlier, better times. Tears sprang to Kath-

leen's eyes, despite the formidable opposition of her will.

Behind her she heard quiet words pass between her son and husband, then the screen door opened and closed again, with a dearly familiar creaking sound.

Strong hands came to rest on Kathleen's shoulders, hands she knew so well.

"Kathy," Reece said. He was the only one in all the world who called her by that name; it was a private intimacy, theirs alone.

She sobbed, overcome by heartbreak.

"What is it, darlin'?" Reece asked. "How can I help you?" He turned her around and took her into his arms and she allowed it only because she didn't have the strength to resist.

"You—were—out all—*night*—" she wailed.

He chuckled into her hair, a deep, rumbling, comforting sound. "That I was, Kathy," he said, teasing her with his version of the brogue. In the past, it had always made her laugh. It was, she thought, like hearing John Wayne say, *Tennis, anyone?* "I slept in the RV."

She looked up at him. "Alone?"

He scowled indignantly. "Of course I was alone," he said.

She wanted to believe him, wanted it with all her heart, but there was no sense in kidding herself. Where there was smoke, there was fire, and Reece McCaffrey was definitely up to something. Why, until he'd bought that silly motor home of his, he'd spent most of his time on the computer in the family room, surfing the Internet, and when Kathleen looked back on that lull before the storm, she realized he'd been downright furtive about it, too. When Helen Bisbee's husband ran off with a woman he'd met via email six weeks back, Kathleen had of course been outraged on poor Helen's behalf. Reece had said it served Helen right, the way she'd gotten so caught up in playing bingo every night of the week. It wasn't hard to make the link between Helen's admittedly compulsive bingo-playing and Kathleen's own foray into the worlds of folk art and e-commerce.

She stepped back, out of her husband's embrace, and looked away. Let him take his silly RV and *whoever* he might be chatting up, on-line or in person, and hit the road. She meant to stay put, in the house where they'd raised three children, and she'd hold her head up if it killed her. Which she thought it just might.

"Kathy? You don't really think—?" He couldn't even say the words, it seemed. But then, he'd always been a smooth talker.

It still affected her, though, his being so close, and after all these years. "J.T. will be needing some lumber," she said.

Reece was still for a long while. Then, with a sigh, his workingman's hands at his sides, he stopped trying. "Yes," he ground out, looking grim. "I'd better see to that, hadn't I?"

He walked away from her, paused at the screen door. The hinges squeaked as he pushed it open. "Kathy," he said again, more firmly this time.

She made herself meet his gaze, calling upon all the pride and defiance she possessed. A thousand times she'd worked up the nerve to challenge him, to demand to know what was going on, but she'd always backed down, afraid of the answer.

"I was telling the truth when I said I spent the night alone in the RV," he said. And then he went out, quietly closing the door behind him.

Kathleen put a hand to her mouth and

closed her eyes tightly, but tears came anyway. She wanted so much to believe him, to find her place in his heart again, but it seemed to her that they'd set out on divergent paths, and maybe there was no going back. She wanted to stay in Springwater and paint, and he wanted to travel all over the United States and Canada for the rest of their lives. Neither was inclined to compromise.

She looked down at the dog. "Oh, Sadie," she said, "what shall I do?"

Sadie collapsed onto the rug in front of the sink and heaved a despondent, snuffling sigh of her own. Plainly, she would be of no significant assistance.

9

Maggie felt dazed, standing in J.T.'s driveway, as though she'd awakened suddenly while sleepwalking to find herself there, surveying the gnarled and blackened skeleton of his barn. J.T. came out of the house by the backdoor, moving slowly, even reluctantly. Damn him, she thought, he's drawn to me, and he knows I'm drawn to him, and even now he's walling himself off. Doing his best not to care.

She watched him, her throat thick with sorrow and confusion and with the stench of charred wood aching in her sinuses. She couldn't speak for a moment, she was so shaken, her mind flooded with horrific images of what might have happened to J.T., to Cindy and Billy, if the fire hadn't been contained in time.

J.T. sighed. Freshly showered and wearing jeans, boots, and a white T-shirt, he was damnably attractive. Maggie was torn by conflicting desires; on the one hand, she wanted to embrace him and weep with relief. On the other, she knew that would only complicate matters further.

"Scully Wainwright built that barn with his own hands," she said, falling back on history, the safest topic that came to mind.

J.T. nodded, surveyed the wreckage, folded his arms.

"It was arson?" she asked. She needed confirmation of what she'd already heard in town just to believe her own eyes. A prompt denial would have been preferable to the truth, if only temporarily, but J.T. was his usual blunt self.

"That's the verdict," he said, without apparent emotion. "The insurance company has looked it over already. They found a gas can and some other evidence that it was deliberate."

"What about the animals?"

J.T. smiled gently at her concern, and the

usual tension undulated between them, as elemental as their heartbeats and the currents in the atmosphere itself. "All of them are safe. A little edgy, maybe—like the rest of us."

Through the trees separating the main house from where Billy and Cindy had lived, Maggie glimpsed the ruins of the trailer, twisted and blistered. Her stomach did a slow roll—dear God, what if they'd been sleeping?—and her knees went weak. For a moment, it was as if she'd lost them all— J.T., Cindy, and Billy—and she was overwhelmed.

J.T. was standing directly in front of her when she opened her eyes. He took her upper arms in a firm but painless grasp and held her steady. A grin tilted his mouth sideways. "Take a deep breath, McCaffrey," he said. "Everything and everybody is *all right.*"

She knew that wasn't true. J.T. himself was a casualty of things that had happened on this ranch, not only last night, but in the distant past, and so, indirectly, was she. Still, she swallowed hard and nodded. Tried to smile.

"Come on," he said, tugging her toward the door, which still stood ajar in the bright light of that summer morning. "I'll buy you a cup of coffee. You look like you need reviving."

She allowed him to take her loosely by the elbow, usher her toward the house, up the back steps. In the kitchen she sank into a chair at the table, assaulted by memories of earlier, happier times, while J.T. got a mug down from the cupboard and poured the promised coffee. "What happens now?" she asked, as he took a chair across from her and leaned forward, bracing his muscular forearms against the table top.

He shrugged. "I build a new barn."

Emotionally swamped, she still wanted to bolt, but she made herself sit, and spoke in a mild, almost nonchalant tone of voice. "What about your uncle?"

J.T. sighed again, shoved the splayed fingers of his right hand through his hair. "There's an ongoing investigation, for all the good it seems to be doing. The body's being held at the country morgue until further notice."

Maggie was quiet for a long time, sorting through her feelings. Then, turning her half-filled mug slowly on its base, she added, "That's all you've got to say?"

J.T.'s gaze smoldered. "Are you looking for sentiment, McCaffrey? Clive used to beat the hell out of me about every other day, once my dad was gone. He knocked my aunt around, too, though I only caught him at it once." He drew a ragged breath, thrust it out again. "You'll pardon me, I hope, if I don't cry at the funeral."

"Why did you spend so much time here, if things were so bad? Why didn't you stay in Las Vegas, with your mother?"

J.T.'s jawline hardened, and his eyes flashed. "Because you—" He stopped, looked away, looked back, fiercely. "Because, damn it, right or wrong, for better or for worse, this ranch is my legacy. My home."

Maggie felt another dizzying upsurge of that strange jumble of jubilation and despair that J.T. so often aroused in her. He had started to say, *Because you were here,* she knew that as well as she knew the streets and houses of Springwater, but no power in heaven or on earth would ever make him admit as much. Which only went to prove what she'd suspected all along: No matter how attracted she and J.T. were to each other, no matter how deep their love or how strong their passion, the barriers between them were insurmountable. She would accept nothing less than his whole heart, and he simply wasn't able to open up that much.

Tears sprang to her eyes.

J.T. groaned. "McCaffrey, don't cry. *Please,* don't cry."

"I can't help it," she said angrily.

He folded his arms, leaned back in his chair. "I'll say it again—I didn't kill Clive Jenson."

"What brought that on?" she demanded furiously, crying harder and not even trying to stop. "Did I say I thought you did?"

"You wouldn't be the only one."

She bit her lower lip. "You must have some idea who—" She fell silent at the look on his face.

"Like I have some idea who killed my dad?" he interrupted with quiet fury.

She sighed. "Look, J.T., I'm on your side. Stop treating me like a hostile witness."

"I'm sorry," he said tightly. He didn't seem all that contrite to Maggie, but then, with J.T., it was hard to tell.

"What are you going to do?" she asked evenly.

He paused for a long time before answering. "The usual. Go over the scene again. And again. Read the coroner's report until my eyes cross. Ask a lot of questions." He paused. "And pray this doesn't attract the press. Things are getting pretty weird around here, and Purvis and I have our hands full as it is, without a bunch of reporters underfoot."

"Do you think it's all connected—the poisoning incidents and the fire and—and what happened to your uncle?"

"No telling," J.T. said, calmer now. "If I had to venture a guess, I'd say yes. Springwater is a small community, after all. There can't be that many big-league criminals around here."

Maggie agreed, feeling glum. "Let me know if there's anything I can do to help," she said, a little stiffly, finishing her coffee. "Billy and Cindy are welcome to use my folks' guest house if they need it."

"They'll be bunking in here for a while," J.T. said. "I'm planning to build a small house for them to live in, where the trailer was. One of those prefabs."

She watched him. "So you're staying?"

He frowned. "Why wouldn't I stay, McCaffrey?"

She swallowed so hard it hurt. "You're obviously a target of some kind—" Until then, she didn't think she'd consciously acknowledged that fact, or how much it frightened her. When she'd first heard about his shooting, while she was living in Chicago and he was still with the NYPD, she'd been physically ill. Dear God, If something were to happen to J.T.— He reached across the table, cupped a hand, callused from ranch work, under her chin. "I'm back," he said. "And I'm here to stay." He grinned that lethal grin, the one she had no defenses against. "Get that straight, all right?"

She pulled back slowly, stood, and crossed the room to set her cup in the sink, pretending he hadn't complicated everything by touching her that way, just when she thought she had him all figured out. "There's Quinn," she fretted. "Will he be safe here?"

J.T.'s expression was instantly serious. "I'll see to it," he said.

Maggie believed him. Anyone who wanted to harm the boy would have to go through J.T. first. She nodded, reassured. "I'd better head back to town," she said with brisk resignation. "I've got a business to run, you know."

J.T. rose from his chair, and his presence seemed to fill the kitchen, to thrum in the very air itself, like the reverberations of some silent but completely cataclysmic explosion. Maggie wondered if he was aware of the power and prowess he exuded, and decided he had to be. J.T. was many things, but stupid wasn't one of them. "Thanks for stopping by, McCaffrey," he said, in a low drawl. "Given what a coward you are, it must have taken a lot of courage."

Heat surged into her face, an aching fever, and anger pinched the pit of her stomach. His nerve was colossal. *"What?"* she marveled.

"You heard me," he said, obviously enjoying her outrage. "When it comes to the two of us, as in you and me, you're *chicken,* McCaffrey."

"Of all the nerve!" Maggie stormed. *"You,* of *all* people—"

He stood watching her, damnably unruffled, and if she'd been the violent type, she surely would have doubled up her fist and socked him one. "Okay," he said reasonably, "if you're not scared, prove it. Let's go to bed."

Her mouth fell open. She couldn't believe he'd actually said that. Nor could she believe how much she wanted to accept the outrageous invitation. *"Go to hell!"* she managed, after strangling on a couple of attempts to speak, and then she stomped out.

He followed her all the way to the driveway, where her Pathfinder was parked. "About that date to go riding—"

"We don't have a date!" Maggie raged. "You can take that horse of yours and—"

He started to laugh. "Chicken," he said.

She slammed the car door, ground the key in the ignition. "We're not kids anymore, J.T. We can't sleep together on a dare!"

"Why not?" he asked.

Completely stumped for an answer, she turned the Pathfinder around and sped down the driveway without looking back.

Just as J.T. had feared, reporters began arriving the following evening, drawn to Springwater by the dramatic death of Clive Jenson. Apparently it was a slow news week elsewhere in the world. Perhaps war,

famine, and political scandal finally had become too commonplace to be of interest.

Maggie's reactions to this latest development were mixed. Like sharks scenting
blood in the water, the self-proclaimed jour-
nalists hounded poor Purvis for answers he
couldn't give and stirred up the already agitated populace with none too subtle hints
that the marshal ought to step down and let
J.T. Wainwright take over his job. On the
other hand, all of Maggie's rooms were
filled—she'd had to hustle to open ahead of
schedule—and the local merchants, usually
forced to scramble for a living, were doing a
brisk business as well.

Late in the afternoon, the day after the
tabloid people came to town, J.T.'s ex-wife
arrived at the Station, with her young son in
tow. She was slender and delicate-looking,
with flyaway blonde hair and anxious green
eyes. The dark-haired, dark-eyed boy at her
side so resembled J.T. that Maggie's heart
did a slow somersault at the sight of him,
and then tumbled into the pit of her stomach, bouncing there like a fallen acrobat in a
net. *Quinn,* she thought, with a sense of bittersweet wonder. This was Quinn, the child
who might have been her own—and wasn't.

"I'm Annie Wilcox," Quinn's mother said, putting out a hand. The dining room at the Station was noisy, packed with the overflow from the Stagecoach Café down the street. Although Maggie still served only breakfast at the B & B—she was planning to expand to lunch and supper when profits justified hiring a cook—her guests kept the coffeemaker going nonstop. "This is the Springwater Station, isn't it?"

Maggie shook Annie's hand. "Yes," she said kindly, liking the other woman instantly, just as she'd always known she would. "I'm Maggie McCaffrey."

Annie smiled in response. "J.T.'s told me a lot about you," she said. "I was wondering if we could—if we could talk?" In one quick, rather harried glance, she took in the reporters lining several of the trestle tables, some engaged in spirited conversations, some tapping steadily at laptop computers, others scribbling away on pads of paper.

Maggie indicated the open doorway of her office with a nod. Quinn, meanwhile, had spotted Sadie, who was eyeing him from the seat of a rocking chair on the other side of the dining room, and he immediately headed in that direction. Seeing a shadow of worry fall across Annie's face, she said quietly, "She's friendly."

Annie braced her spine, then nodded. "Both J.T. and Brad say I'm too protective of Quinn," she admitted. "It's just that—well—he isn't used to animals and neither am I."

"If you'd rather he joined us here in the office—"

Annie shook her head resolutely. "I have to learn to let go, don't I?" she asked, and Maggie assumed the question was rhetorical. "I mean, Brad and I will be in Venezuela for at least six weeks, and Quinn will be living on the ranch with J.T."

Maggie touched the other woman's arm. "He'll be fine," she said, and then wondered if she was being presumptuous, offering blithe assurances. After all, someone had burned down J.T.'s barn and blown the Raynors' trailer sky-high, and there had been a brutal murder as well. Springwater was no longer a picture-postcard town, idyllic and peaceful.

Inside the office, Maggie offered Annie a chair, and the other woman accepted readily. She looked wan, even a little frantic, and Maggie felt her heart go out to her visitor.

Perhaps Annie didn't want to leave her son and travel to South America but felt, for some private reason, that she had no choice.

Now you're dramatizing, Maggie scolded herself. "Are you sure you wouldn't like some tea?" she asked.

Annie's smile was tentative, and she shook her head. "No, thanks," she said.

Maggie took a seat behind her desk, folded her hands on the blotter because she knew she'd fidget if she didn't. "How can I help you?"

Annie sighed. "What seemed like a good idea on the plane and on the drive here from Missoula seems sort of silly now," she murmured. "I thought I wanted to tell you that there's nothing between J.T. and me—that we're friends, and that's all—but now that I'm actually here, I realize my objective wasn't quite that noble. I wanted to see the woman J.T. has been thinking about all these years."

Maggie didn't know what to say, so she held her tongue.

Annie squirmed a little and smiled again, effectively breaking the tension. "Now I really feel like a fool," she said. "I should have stuck with my original story."

Maggie laughed. "Go on," she said.

Suddenly, though, there were tears in Annie's eyes. "I'm sorry," she said quickly, reaching for a tissue from the box Maggie automatically pushed toward her. "I've been under a lot of stress lately. It's so hard to leave Quinn, even though I know J.T. loves him very much."

Maggie nodded. "I can understand why you'd feel that way," she said.

Annie sniffled, then chuckled. "Do you have to be so nice?" she asked.

Maggie laughed again. "I can't help it. I'm just an all-around decent kind of a gal."

After a few moments, Annie turned pensive once more. Although she spoke without rancor, her words struck Maggie to the soul. "You broke J.T.'s heart," she said. "You knew that, didn't you?"

Being completely human, Maggie's first impulse was to deny the charge, to point out that actually J.T. had been the one to initiate their breakup, but she knew that wasn't the whole truth. She also felt that Annie deserved an honest answer. "Yes," she said, though she knew that was an oversim-

plification of a very complex matter. "I suppose I did. Not on purpose, of course."

Annie drew a deep breath, let it out
slowly. "Do any of us set out to break
another person's heart?" she reflected. "He
never stopped loving you, you know."

Maggie thought of her last encounter with
J.T., when he'd challenged her to sleep with
him, but instead of anger, she felt sadness.
It had been an outrageous thing for him to
say, of course, but maybe he'd been at least
partially right in calling her a coward. No
one had the power to hurt her that he did.
"I'm not sure J.T. knows how to love," she
murmured, and immediately wished she
hadn't made the observation aloud.

Annie merely smiled, though she, like
Maggie, was obviously sad. "I don't agree,"
she said. "He loves Quinn. He loved his
father."

Maggie didn't speak.

"And I'm fairly certain he's never loved
any woman but you," Annie finished.

Maggie bit her upper lip. Tears smarted
behind her eyes. She opened her mouth,
closed it again.

"It's all right," Annie insisted gently. "I
adored J.T., once. We had a child together.

But we were never meant to be, and I'm truly happy with Brad. I guess what I want now, more than just about anything else, is for J.T. to find what I've found. And I think that can only happen with you."

Maggie helped herself to a tissue and dabbed at her eyes, furious with herself for breaking down in front of a virtual stranger. "It seems impossible," she said.

Annie leaned forward, touched Maggie's hand. "Don't give up too quickly," she replied. Before she could say more, a small voice spoke from the doorway.

"Mom?" Quinn asked, Sadie wagging and panting at his side. Once more, his resemblance to J.T. struck Maggie with an almost physical impact, sending up another flare of bittersweet emotions. "When can I see my dad?"

Annie glanced at her watch. "I guess we should call before we drive out there," she said.

"I've got his cell number," Quinn announced importantly. "I can reach him twenty-four-seven. He said so."

Maggie and Annie exchanged slight smiles, then Annie nodded her O.K.

"You can use my telephone if you'd like,"

Maggie told the boy, indicating the one on her desk.

"Thanks," Quinn said. All business, he pulled a well-worn scrap of paper out of his pocket and unfolded it, smoothing the page carefully. Before he could dial the first digit, however, there was a mild stir in the public area of the Station, and then J.T. himself loomed in the doorway, as though conjured by the mere mention of his name.

He had known Annie and Quinn were on their way to Springwater, of course, but from the expression on his face Maggie concluded that he most certainly hadn't expected to find them waiting in her office.

He linked gazes with Maggie for a moment—again she felt the connection with poignant force, quite against her will and better judgment—then nodded to Annie. "Hello," he said, and turned, beaming, to Quinn. "Hey, buddy," he said, and his voice sounded a little husky to Maggie. She was touched by the expression in his eyes as he watched his son, even though she'd been sorely tempted to strangle the man just twenty-four hours before.

Quinn gave a whoop of pure joy. "Dad!" he yelled, and hurled himself into J.T.'s arms. "I was going to call you on your cell phone just now."

J.T. ruffled the boy's hair. "And here I am," he said.

"They're quite a pair, aren't they?" Annie asked quietly, her eyes shining with pride and affection as she watched J.T. and Quinn.

Maggie nodded, blinked. "Yes," she said, startled to realize that somehow the very landscape of her heart had been altered, in that short interval since J.T. had arrived, in ways she could never have anticipated, let alone defined. "Yes, they are."

The next few minutes passed in a happy, noisy blur; J.T. spoke to Maggie, said something about calling her later, but his exact words didn't register. Annie thanked her for her hospitality and then left with Quinn and J.T., the three of them looking very much like a family.

Maggie straightened her spine and lifted her chin as she stood in the doorway of the Station, watching them move down the walk toward the gate. Okay, so maybe she felt a little lonely and left out. No one had ever died from feelings like that—had they?

*   *   *

J.T. had never brought Annie to Springwater, and the significance of that struck
him as he drove up the long driveway toward his house, Quinn safely belted in the
passenger seat while his mother followed in
the rental car. J.T. had always thought his
job was the main impediment to making his
and Annie's marriage work but, in retro-
spect, he had to admit, at least to himself,
that Springwater itself, as well as the ranch,
had been a factor, too. It was all sacred
ground to him; Springwater meant home,
and home meant—

Maggie.

He glanced up at the rearview mirror and
silently apologized to his ex-wife for all the
times he'd unwittingly hurt her.

"Do you have horses?" Quinn asked,
barely able to contain his excitement. If he
hadn't been confined by a seat belt, it
seemed to J.T., the boy might have been
floating in midair. "Do you have dogs?
Chickens? Cows? I'd really like to get a
dog—"

J.T. chuckled. "There are a couple of
horses," he said, stemming the flow. "No
chickens yet, but we could get some. That

would be a good job for you, herding hens
and roosters. No dogs, though. Sorry."

Quinn's eyes widened when he sighted
the ruins of the barn etched in stark strokes
of charcoal against the broad blue Montana
sky. "Wow!" he enthused. "What happened?"

"There was a fire," J.T. said.

Quinn's brow furrowed with concentration. "Was somebody smoking?"

J.T. smiled a little grimly, and shook his
head. "No, Q. It was arson. Do you know
what that is?"

The boy looked stricken. "It means that
somebody did that on purpose," he
breathed.

"Right," J.T. said.

"Why?"

J.T. shrugged. "I'm not sure."

"Are you going to find whoever did it and
arrest them?"

"If it's the last thing I ever do," J.T. vowed.

"Wow," Quinn repeated. Evidently, he
found the idea of the bad guys being
brought to justice reassuring, because he'd
perked up again.

J.T. brought the truck to a stop in the
driveway, and Annie pulled up behind him,

shut off the rental car, and got out. Her face was pale. "Good Lord," she said, gesturing toward the blackened remains of the barn. "When did *this* happen?"

J.T. let out a long breath, afraid that Annie would refuse to leave Quinn with him once she knew the truth. "It's recent," he said.

"They did it on purpose," Quinn put in. "Dad's going to arrest them."

J.T. and Annie looked at each other for a long moment, over the boy's head. "Oh, really?" Annie asked, in even tones. He hadn't told her about the badge Judge Calloway had given him; after all, it was a temporary job.

J.T. pulled the boy easily to his side, ruffled his hair again. "I'll look after him, Annie," he said.

"You'd better," she replied. She hesitated, as though thinking about snatching up their son, getting back into the car, and fleeing, but finally she nodded. "Okay," she decided aloud. "Okay." She fumbled with the keys, opened the trunk of the car, and surveyed the luggage as if at a loss. There was something fragile about her, and J.T. sympathized, even though he knew the problem, whatever it was, wasn't his to solve.

J.T. nudged her gently aside, took a suitcase in both hands. "Come on," he said.
"Let's get you settled in."

Annie smiled and, in that instant, they
moved out of their old and awkward es-
trangement and took a step toward genuine
friendship. "This is a beautiful place," she
said, apparently seeing past all the years of
neglect and tragedy that had left their mark
on the people and the buildings, if not the
land itself.

J.T. nodded. "That it is," he said.

Inside, he showed Annie and Quinn to adjoining rooms, glad that Billy and Cindy
were staying in town temporarily with Doris,
so the place wouldn't seem crowded. Then
he and Quinn went downstairs to the
kitchen to rustle up a light supper while Annie showered and changed.

She looked a little less frazzled when she
joined them half an hour later, having re-
placed her skirt and blouse with worn jeans
and a lightweight sweater.

"Hungry?" J.T. asked.

"Ravenous," she replied, smiling.

"Sit down," J.T. said, and left the table,
where he'd been sitting with Quinn, to fire

up the stove again and put another cheese sandwich on the grill. "Want some coffee?"

She shook her head. "It's getting late, and I'll never sleep if I have caffeine now," she said, scraping back a chair and sitting down. "I've got to get up early—my plane leaves Missoula around one."

"Mom's going to South America," Quinn put in, from his place at the table. He'd eaten a full sandwich on his own and gulped down a glass of milk in the bargain. J.T. figured the boy was running on nervous energy; the moment his head touched the pillow that night, he'd be zonked out.

"I know," J.T. said, glancing at Annie.

She sighed. "I don't leave for a few more days. I'm going back to Atlanta first, to tie up a few loose ends, then I'll join Brad in Caracas."

J.T. simply nodded. He didn't have an opinion on the matter; Annie's business was Annie's business. Quinn, on the other hand, was definitely his concern, as much as hers. He was about all they had in common, J.T. realized.

"It's a big promotion for Brad," she said.

J.T. nodded again. He'd gotten to know Annie's husband in the process of picking

Quinn up for visits back in New York and dropping him off again, and he liked the guy well enough. The job must be an important one, if Annie was willing to be separated from her child for six long weeks. "You don't need to explain," he told her.

"Can I go out and look at the horses?" Quinn piped up.

"They're not here, Q.," J.T. answered. "A neighbor is keeping them for me until I can get the barn rebuilt."

Quinn looked disappointed. "I wish you had a dog, at least." Some ranch this is, he might have added.

J.T. grinned. "Maybe we can do something about that. The dog shortage, I mean."

The boy's face lit up. "You mean it? We can get a dog?"

J.T. and Annie exchanged glances again.

"Sure," J.T. said, when Annie didn't raise an immediate objection. She was afraid of animals, and in her desire to protect Quinn, she'd never allowed him to have anything bigger than a hamster. Although it probably wasn't easy for her, she kept her doubts to herself, respecting the fact that the rules

were different at J.T.'s place. He appreciated that.

Quinn erupted with cheers, and J.T.
thought he saw tears glittering in Annie's
eyes. She was smiling.

"Can I go outside and look around?"
Quinn begged his mother, when he'd settled
down a little. "Please, please, *pleeeeeze?*"

Annie glanced at J.T., then sat up a bit
straighter in her chair and looked Quinn in
the eye,. "Yes," she said. "Just use good
sense."

J.T. threw in his own two bits, mussing
the boy's gleaming hair. "Stay clear of the
barn," he ordered. "I mean it, bud."

Quinn nodded in anxious, impatient
agreement, and dashed out, banging the
door shut behind him. It reminded J.T. of his
own childhood, before his parents' divorce,
before Jack Wainwright's death, when this
ranch was the whole world to him, and a
magical one at that.

Annie shivered delicately, no doubt thinking of all the hazards that might befall her
only child out there—rusty nails, spiders,
snakes, people who set barns on fire for the
hell of it.

J.T. grinned at her. "That was pretty

gutsy," he said. He knew it had taken a lot
for shy, city-bred Annie to set a flock of pet
fears aside the way she had, and if there
was one thing J.T. admired in another person, it was backbone.

"Thanks," she said, sounding a little surprised at his praise.

He turned his chair around, next to the
table, and sat astraddle of the seat, his
arms resting across the high back. "You
gonna be O.K.?" he asked.

She smiled. "Yeah."

"Good," he said.

There was a short, benevolent silence,
then Annie spoke again. "I like Maggie."

"Me, too," he admitted.

"A lot, I think."

He laughed. "What is this?"

She shrugged. "What do you think?" she
countered. "Don't blow this, J.T. If you have
an opportunity to be happy, for God's sake,
grab it. Second chances don't come along
all that often."

He rested his chin on one forearm, regarding her seriously. "No," he agreed quietly. "I guess they don't." There didn't seem
to be any point in explaining that he and
McCaffrey were on the outs. He had nobody

to blame for that but himself, he thought. He'd deliberately baited Maggie, right there in that kitchen, saying the words he knew would drive her away, at least temporarily. He meant to apologize, because that was the right thing to do, but he had no illusions that saying he was sorry would change anything between them.

She stood up, went to the sink, and gazed out the window. J.T. knew she was looking for Quinn. "You promise you'll keep him safe?" she whispered. "I couldn't bear it if anything happened to him."

"I promise," J.T. replied quietly.

She didn't turn around, and the silence lengthened before she spoke again. "I was pregnant last year," she said. "We lost the baby."

"I'm sorry," he told her.

She sniffled, wiped at her face with the back of one wrist, nodded. "Thanks," she murmured. It seemed that there was nothing much left to say after that; they'd said it all, a long time ago, in another life.

10

Purvis figured the ranchers were about to string him from a tree branch—or call in the feds because he hadn't turned up any evidence yet, which would be *worse* than being lynched, in his estimation. The sheriff wasn't inclined to be helpful—he had problems of his own, over Maple Creek way, what with the election coming up in November—and the county's forensics people hadn't been able to tell Purvis, J.T., or the cattlemen anything they hadn't figured out on their own using plain old horse sense. Pete Doubletree's cattle had been poisoned with strychnine. It was a malicious act, quite apart from simple thieving, an indication that somebody out there really had a hair crosswise about something.

Then there was Clive Jenson's death. Jenson hadn't slit his own throat and jumped from the catwalk on the old water tower; he'd been carved up and then thrown. Purvis sighed to himself, left with the question of motive. Plenty of people had disliked Clive Jenson, especially after he abandoned poor Janeen, to face her last illness on her own, but that didn't mean they'd murder him. Did it?

Somebody had sure as hell done him in.

Then there was J.T.'s barn and the little trailer house. Purvis shuddered just to imagine what would have happened if young Billy Raynor and his bride hadn't gotten out before the thing blew.

Reflecting on these things, and more, the marshal of Springwater strode into the town library with his head slightly lowered. He'd taken to wearing a uniform lately, instead of his regular clothes, and he'd even gotten his hair cut, causing a real stir down at the Hair House. He wasn't sure whether the local crime wave had inspired these changes, or Nelly.

She was hard at work, checking out a

stack of books for old Mrs. Meyers, and she favored him with a brief, tilted smile as he came in, chased by the first drops of summer rainstorm. The last thing he wanted to do was to bring Nelly to any kind of grief by taking up her time when she was on the clock, so he nodded a greeting to both women and headed for the shelves.

He felt Mrs. Meyers's gaze on him as he walked away and reckoned she'd guessed he wasn't there to do any reading. She'd been his eighth grade teacher, way back when, and knew his limitations in that area and a few others. She was a good-natured gossip, and by now she would have picked up on his attraction to Nelly and started threading her way toward the truth. Maybe he ought to deputize Mildred Meyers, he thought, with a rueful smile, and let *her* unravel all these mysteries.

"I trust you've met Purvis," he heard Mrs. Meyers say to Nelly, as he hurried away.

Nelly said something about email, and Purvis dodged behind a shelf of reference books.

There were a few other people in the library—a couple of giggling teenage girls there to chase boys, Purvis suspected, should any happen to show up. They were working real hard not to seem as if they were on the lookout, and that made him smile. There were one or two older folks, too, poring over magazines, and Sylvia Anderson slipped in by the front way, fresh from the beauty parlor herself, he reckoned from the stiff curls in her blue hair, anxious to get out of the rain.

Mrs. Meyers immediately beckoned to Sylvia and, once again, Purvis caught the word "email." He rolled his eyes and took a book down from the shelf, choosing one with a red cover, partly because that was what came to hand and partly because he'd always liked that color. He perused the title pensively, as though considering it as a choice—in truth, he didn't even have a library card—and felt heat pricking the back of his neck. The book was called *How to Drive a Woman Mad With Passion* and Purvis shoved it back into place with such haste and force that he nearly snapped the spine in two.

He glanced back in Nelly's direction, through a gap in the stacks, and was ruefully relieved to note that she was busy chatting with Sylvia and Mrs. Meyers. Thank the Lord, the teenagers were paying him no mind at all, and the magazine crowd was intent on its own pursuits. He eased around into another aisle, but all he found there were instruction books on knitting and fancy sewing and making snow villages out of something called plastic canvas, things of that sort. He wished Nelly would finish for the day so they could drive over to Maple Creek to the Walmart store. His mother's birthday was just a few days off, and Nelly had offered to help him find a present. After that, they were going to have supper at Flo's Diner.

He supposed the outing could be called a date.

He grinned, pleased at the prospect of an evening with his cowgirl, and thinking how surprised his mom would be when he didn't give her a bathrobe again this year. Ever since he got home from 'Nam, he'd given Tillie the same gifts on every occasion, a robe for her birthday, eau de perfume on Mother's Day, and slippers every Christmas. She always acted like she was thrilled, ripping open her package and gasping, "Oh, Purvis, bump chenille!" as if that was the same as mink. Well, this time, she wouldn't

have to pretend. She really would be surprised.

He sighed. Next year, though, he'd probably be out of work, due to the rise of crime
in Springwater County and his apparent in-
ability to get to the bottom of things, and
thus unable to afford to give her a present at
all. Why, if the Cattleman's Association had
its way, he'd already be history jobwise, re-
duced to sleeping in his mother's sewing
room and flipping burgers down at McDonald's to cover his portion of the grocery bill.
He meant to make this gift count.

A few minutes later, Nelly joined him in
the aisle. Mildred Meyers and Sylvia Anderson went out together, sharing an umbrella
and, no doubt, an opinion or two.

"Hello, Purvis," Nelly said quietly.

"Hello, Nelly," he answered. He was a
smooth talker, that was for sure. A silver-
tongued devil. Yes, sir, there was always a
snappy comeback waiting on the tip of
Purvis Digg's tongue.

She chuckled, and it was a warm, friendly
sound, with a faint crackle to it, like a fire on
a rainy day. "You didn't forget that we're going to Walmart, did you?" she asked, taking
in his uniform.

He shook his head, and she glanced at the book he was holding in both hands. Her brows rose. *"The Pastas of Tuscany?"* she asked, her eyes smiling.

He looked down at it glumly. "I've always thought there must be something to reading, the way folks seem to take to it. I reckon I just don't know where to start."

Her eyes lit up. "Let me help you, then. It's what I do, after all."

"I think I'm past that point," he said with regret. "Where I can be helped, I mean."

She laughed. "Nonsense," she said, walking purposefully to the back wall, assessing the lineup on the shelves, and taking down a thin book that looked as though it had been bound in saddle leather. On closer inspection, it turned out to be plastic. "Try this one."

He glanced down at the volume. Louis L'Amour. A Frenchman. "This isn't about decorating and gluing seashells on things and the like, is it?"

Her mouth made that funny little crooking motion again, the one that made him want to kiss her. "No," she said, with a shake of her head. "Mr. L'Amour wrote westerns, and he was a master storyteller."

" 'Was'? You mean, he's dead?" Purvis was a little jumpy, due to frustration and lack of sleep. He had a lot on his mind these days, after all, and the planned outing to Walmart and Flo's was the first free time he'd had in a couple of days. He glanced down at the book as though it might bite him before realizing he was acting like a fool.

Nelly made an easy gesture with one hand, taking in all the hundreds and hundreds of books on the shelves rising all around them. They might have been in a little city, Purvis thought fancifully, a place where all the buildings were made of multi-colored bricks set on end instead of horizontally. It was a nice place, he decided, and nobody lived there but him and Nelly. "A lot of these books were written by people who are dead," she said reasonably.

"That's downright depressing," Purvis said.

She smiled. "Not really," she answered. "In a way, they're still with us, because they left stories behind." She nodded toward the book in his hand. "Try that one. If you don't like it, you won't have lost anything but a little time."

Purvis looked both ways, like a little kid about to cross a busy street. "I don't have a card," he confessed, in a whisper.

Nelly's eyes glowed with warmth as she leaned toward him and whispered back, "Then I guess I'll have to issue you one."

He liked the idea of having his own library card. There was nothing in his wallet now but a driver's license, one Visa card with a puny five-hundred-dollar limit, and his official police ID. This seemed more personal-like, almost as good as carrying around a picture of a pretty woman or some little kids. "Okay," he said, and had to clear his throat.

When he got to the front desk, where Nelly made out his card and laminated it with one of those slick little machines, the other patrons had all gone, and the two of them had the library to themselves.

While Nelly closed the place down for the night Purvis admired his new library card and waited patiently. Soon, he and Nelly were in the borrowed Escort, rolling along toward Maple Creek. The rain had let up a little, but the highway was still slick, and Purvis drove carefully.

"I heard J. T. Wainwright is going to run

for sheriff, come election time," Nelly said, out of the blue. Sooner or later, Purvis reckoned, she'd hear just about everything, working in a place most of the town frequented on a pretty regular basis. Only the Brimstone Saloon enjoyed more foot traffic.

"I reckon Sheriff Robertson will put up a fight," Purvis said, feeling a little stung because J.T. hadn't mentioned the plan to him. Wearing the sheriff's badge was one of his secret dreams, right up there with meeting Johnny Cash in person and owning a Hummer, and just about as likely to happen.

"I think you ought to run," Nelly said.

Purvis stared at her, not sure he'd heard right. The mere suggestion that she thought so highly of his chances made him feel almost euphoric. "You're kidding," he accused.

She turned slightly in the car seat in order to face him. She didn't look like she was kidding. "I'm perfectly serious," she said.

He sighed. "Well, thank you," he managed, concentrating extra hard on the road ahead, "but right now, I don't think I could get elected to shovel horsesh— manure."

She smiled. "You're much too modest, Purvis," she said. "You've been marshal here for a long time, and you've done a good job. You ought to blow your own horn once in a while."

Tell that to the ranchers screaming for my badge, Purvis thought.

"You *have* done a good job," Nelly insisted, as if she'd been looking right into his brain. It was real nice to have somebody cheering for his team besides his mother, although Purvis figured he'd have as many doubts about his competency as a peace officer as the cattlemen did if he'd been in their place.

It seemed like a good time to change the subject, especially since there was a stubborn slant to Nelly's jaw just then. Damned if she wasn't all ready to argue his case to all comers, he thought, in despairing jubilation. "You ever played miniature golf?" he asked, because that was the first thing that came to mind.

Turned out she loved the game. One more reason to be crazy about her.

They reached the Walmart store twenty minutes later and, as always, the parking lot was jammed with cars from all over the county. Purvis parked the Escort, got out, and walked around to open Nelly's door with a flourish.

Annie left for Missoula just after breakfast the next morning, taking a long time to say good-bye to Quinn before she got into the rental car and drove away, and the boy stood watching until she was out of sight.

J.T. ached for the kid. He knew what it was like, being torn between two parents, and he'd always sworn he'd never do that to a child of his. Famous last words.

When Quinn turned and looked up at J.T., there were tears on his face. He sniffled bravely, squared his little shoulders, and wiped his eyes with one already grubby forearm. "Venezuela is really, really far, isn't it?" he asked.

J.T. swallowed once. Nodded. "Yeah," he said, finally. "It's pretty far."

Quinn gnawed at his lower lip, watching the space where his mother and her compact car had vanished around a bend. "She promised to write me letters and email and call on the phone," he said staunchly.

"She'll keep her word," J.T. offered.

"And she'll be back before I know it."

"Most definitely," J.T. replied, approaching his son and laying a hand on one small shoulder. "Your mom loves you, Q. Nothing could keep her away for very long."

It was a piss-poor promise, by J.T.'s standards; lots of things could go wrong, that was the reality. Nothing was truly simple; life was many-layered and often complex—like his relationship with Maggie—but Quinn was a child and he needed reassuring. He played along readily, though J.T. suspected the kid wasn't fooled. "Okay," he said.

"Okay," J.T. confirmed.

"Can we go get a dog now?"

J.T. laughed, remembering yesterday's conversation in the kitchen and his subsequent promise. "Yeah," he said. "We can get a dog."

"Where?"

"We could check out the pound, over in Maple Creek."

Quinn could barely contain his excitement. "Let's go!"

Ah, J.T. thought, the resilience of youth. "I've got a few things to do around here first," he said.

"Can we invite Maggie McCaffrey to go with us?"

J.T. was caught off guard, to say the

least. Quinn had met Maggie exactly once, and he hadn't had time to form a lasting opinion. But then, kids depended on instinct where such things were concerned; they hadn't learned not to trust themselves. "She's probably busy," he said.

Quinn's expression was solemn. "She likes dogs," he confided. "She has one, you know."

"Yeah, I know," he said, as an image of the ankle-licking beagle came into his mind. "But she's got her hands full, what with all those people staying at the Station."

"We could ask her, though, couldn't we?"

J.T. didn't have the heart to refuse—nor did he really want to—but he crouched so he could look directly into his son's eyes. "We'll ask," he said, "but you have to be prepared for the fact that she might say no. I don't want you getting your hopes up and then being disappointed, all right?"

Quinn sighed, as though he found adults incredibly obtuse at such times as this. "All right," he answered. Then he beamed. "But she won't say no. She likes me, and she likes you, too. Mom said so."

Somewhat to J.T.'s amazement, given the recent strain between him and McCaffrey, it turned out that Quinn was right, at least in his prediction that Maggie would agree to the expedition. Daphne and Billy's wife, Cindy, were at the Station helping out, and once they'd introduced J.T. to the new arrival, a little girl Social Services had put in Daphne and her husband's care, they practically shoved Maggie out the front door.

She looked a little surprised to find herself in the front seat of J.T.'s truck, with Quinn buckled in between them, but there was a glow of excitement in her eyes, and her cheeks pulsed with healthy color. She was wearing blue jeans and a long-sleeved T-shirt with a block print of a fish skeleton on the front, and her short dark brown hair shimmered in the sunlight.

"Looks like you're doing a brisk business these days," J.T. commented, indicating the several extra cars parked nearby.

She gave a good-natured grimace. No doubt she'd been plied with questions about Purvis's competence as a police officer, not to mention Clive's death and the barn burning. "They're mostly tabloid stringers," she said. "The more lurid a story is, the better they like it."

J.T. smiled and, at the same time, consciously resisted an urge to reach out and caress the nape of her neck with one hand, the way he used to do when they were kids going out on a date. He wanted very much to touch her, but he refrained, mostly because of Quinn, but for other reasons, too. McCaffrey might be speaking to him again, but he was surely still on thin ice with her. "I imagine they have expense accounts, however modest," he observed, referring to the reporters.

She laughed. "Yes," she allowed, and they pulled away onto Springwater's newly crowded main street, headed toward Maple Creek and the county dog pound.

Quinn was peering over the dashboard, every cell and fiber on alert. The unspoken but classic question emanated from him: *Are we there yet?*

J.T. was struck by how good it felt, how right, just to be driving along with his two favorite people next to him.

"What kind of dog are we looking for?" Maggie asked, addressing the question to Quinn and giving it proper philosophical weight.

Quinn turned his head to look up at her, and though J.T. couldn't see his son's face, he saw his smile reflected on Maggie's. "I'll know him when I see him," Quinn said.

"I'm sure you will," Maggie agreed.

The conversation lapsed for a few moments, and J.T., who valued both silence and solitude in their places, was ambushed by a need to fill the void. "I don't think I've ever seen Daphne looking so happy," he said. "Is it the kid?"

Maggie's smile was gentle, and he saw reservations in her eyes. "I think so," she said.

"So what's worrying you?"

Maggie sighed. "Tiffany is a foster child, not an orphan up for adoption, and someone could come along and claim her any time. Daphne would have to surrender her."

"On the other hand, McCaffrey, everything could work out fine."

She bit her lower lip, looked away.

He reached across Quinn to squeeze her shoulder lightly. "When did you stop believing in happy endings?" he asked, in a quiet voice.

She turned her gaze on him but didn't speak.

Mercifully, they soon arrived at the animal shelter in Maple Creek. It was a square cinder-block building on the edge of the town. Quinn might have scrambled over Maggie in his eagerness to get inside and make his choice if J.T. hadn't slowed him down a little by taking a loose hold on the back of his shirt.

"Easy," he said.

Once out of the truck Quinn bolted for the front door, while Maggie and J.T. walked slowly, taking the opportunity to talk.

"How are the investigations going?"

"Basically, they're going nowhere. We have a few candidates in mind—Randy Hough and Travis DuPres among them—but nothing solid to go on. Sheriff Robertson is all over Purvis, threatening to send for the feds, and the worst part is that everybody seems to think I ought to be able to step in and wrap the thing up in one fell swoop, just because I was once a homicide cop. And the keyword here is 'once.' "

Maggie walked with her hands pushed backward into the rear pockets of her jeans. "That's pretty much what they expect, all right. At the least."

"At the least?" J.T. echoed, as frustrated by the persistent rumors as he'd ever been by anything, and more troubled still to learn that there were other speculations going around.

She looked up at him, studied his face. If the eyes are windows to the soul, then she was peering in and seeing more than J.T. was comfortable revealing. "I've heard you plan to run against Sheriff Robertson this fall."

J.T. was aghast. "What?"

They'd reached the door of the shelter; J.T. reached past Maggie automatically to hold it open for her. She brushed against him as she passed, quite by accident he was sure, and sucked all his nerve endings to the outside of his skin.

She gave him a meaningful look. Quinn was at the counter chattering to the receptionist. "So it isn't true?"

"It never crossed my mind," J.T. said honestly. "I want to be a rancher, that's all."

She sighed. "Good," she answered, and then they had to let the subject drop for the time being, because Quinn was ready to choose a dog. He stood with one small hand raised to shoulder level to indicate the size he wanted—Extra-large, it would seem. J.T. felt another of those echoing tugs, way back in some hidden corridor of his heart.

Maggie was watching him, and it was plain from her expression that she understood what he was thinking and feeling, perhaps better than he did, though, bless her, she didn't comment.

The teenage girl manning the reception counter led the three of them back into the kennel area, an antiseptically clean if depressingly utilitarian place. The walls were lined with what could only be described as cages, and each one held a mutt of some kind, butt ugly right down to their toenails. J.T. knew that if *he* wanted to adopt the whole crew, which he did, Quinn must be ready to pull a cattle truck up to the backdoor and take them all home.

"This is a *jail!*" the little boy cried, horrified, turning to look up at J.T. and Maggie.

The receptionist waggled her fingers in a sort of Valley-girl farewell and hurried out. She didn't want to deal with Quinn's appraisal of the setup, and J.T. didn't blame her. As the boy's father, he didn't have a choice; there'd be no sidestepping this one.

"It's a shelter," he said, crouching to look into Quinn's eyes, which were glittering with tears. "These guys are the lucky ones, Q. They've got food, water, medicine, and a clean, warm place to sleep. Not a bad deal, in a world where a lot of *people* do without the basics."

"It's *still* a jail!" Quinn insisted.

J.T. might have embraced Quinn if he hadn't been fairly sure it would embarrass the kid to have Maggie for an eyewitness. He settled for ruffling the boy's hair. "They're not being punished, Q.," he said patiently. "This place is kind of like a dog-and-cat hotel." He paused, smiled. "Even has room service."

Quinn cast a desperate glance at Maggie, then fastened his gaze to J.T.'s face again, imploring, skeptical. Even a little accusing. "We've got to take them all home with us, Dad," he said. "They'll ufennize them all if we don't. I saw a story about that on the news once!"

Now it was J.T. who looked up at Maggie, though he wasn't sure why. He sighed and faced his son again, still sitting on his haunches there in the center of the animal shelter, with dogs barking out a chorus of "choose me" all around. There were cats, too, but they looked on in silence. The place was a furry tribunal, and J.T. felt like Pontius Pilate.

"Bud," he said, "we can take two dogs. That's the best I can do."

Quinn's lower lip wobbled.

"More people will be coming in right along," Maggie interjected, leaning down, hands on her thighs, "to adopt other dogs."

Quinn looked around. "Like who?" he asked, despairing. They were still the only three human beings on that cell block.

"Like me," Maggie said. "I can use another dog. Somebody to keep Sadie company."

Confounded, J.T. tossed her a look.

"You mean it?" Quinn asked.

Maggie nodded. "I mean it," she said, and raised one hand, like a witness taking the oath in a court of law.

Quinn's gaze flickered back and forth between Maggie and J.T. for a few moments, then he turned, in stalwart resignation, to the task of choosing.

"You don't have to do this," J.T. pointed out to Maggie, rising to his full height again. He kept his voice low and watched as Quinn knelt at the far end of the aisle to commune with a mass of gray-and-white fur.

"Yes, I do," Maggie said, zeroing in on an

animal that might have been part cocker spaniel, with generous portions of just about every other breed in the universe stirred into the mix. "I like this one."

Half an hour later, they left the pound with three dogs: Maggie's multinational, a black Lab imaginatively named "Blackie," and a mid-sized gray-and-white creature J.T. privately thought of as the "missing link." Once they'd paid the fees, which covered the shots, neutering, and spaying that had already been done, they headed back toward the truck. It was, J.T. reflected, a little like driving a herd.

J.T. hoisted the two larger dogs into the back of the truck, one by one.

"Will they be all right back there?" Maggie asked, with a little frown of concern.

J.T. smiled. "They'll be fine," he said. "They're ranch dogs now. They need to get used to riding in trucks."

"Can I ride with them?" Quinn asked.

"No way," J.T. replied, without hesitation.

Maggie was carrying her own, smaller dog. "Here," she said to Quinn, "you can hold my puppy until we get back to Springwater. Did you come up with another name yet? Besides Blackie's, I mean?"

"Winston," Quinn said.

"Winston?" J.T. echoed.

Quinn, in the meanwhile, scrambled eagerly into the truck, fastened his seat belt, and held out his arms. He laughed when Maggie handed him the dog, and the sound had a purity, an element of joy, that made J.T.'s throat tighten. "Mom read me a book about Winston Churchill," he explained. "He was prime minister of England."

J.T. was impressed. There was no getting around it; his kid was gifted.

Maggie climbed in beside Quinn, eyes twinkling. "I propose that we all go back to the Springwater Station and celebrate," she said. "Chicken livers all around." She laughed at the expression on Quinn's face. "For the dogs, that is. We'll have something else, I promise."

J.T. grinned. "Let's eat at the ranch," he said. "You've always liked my cooking, remember?"

She was looking straight ahead. "I remember," she said, very softly.

At home he threw together a batch of chicken enchiladas, while Maggie leaned against a counter, arms folded, watching him cook. Quinn fed the dogs and then led them, like a piper, into the study.

"Remember," J.T. called after him, chopping lettuce a few feet from Maggie, "use your own screen name and don't get into any of my email."

Maggie smiled. "He could do that?" she asked.

J.T. considered the point. "Yes," he answered, unequivocally.

"Is there something I can do to help?" She meant with the food, he figured, not the kid. Still, it made J.T. feel wary. He was used to doing things for himself, and he took great care not to lean on others, even in small ways. It was safer that way.

"Yes," he said a little stiffly. "You can work up a good appetite."

She smiled again, though he knew she'd caught something in his tone. "No problem there," she said heartily, perhaps for Quinn's sake. "Hey, if you get tired of ranching and dabbling in law enforcement, you can come to work at the Station. I could use a good cook."

"Don't tempt me," he said.

She opened cupboards until she found plates and glasses, and began setting the table. So much for not helping. McCaffrey had never been very good at taking direction. She liked to lead, not follow, and if he wasn't careful, she'd have him dancing to whatever tune she wanted to play.

Before J.T. could think of something to say—as well as he knew Maggie, as much as they'd been through together, he still had a tendency to get tongue-tied around her— a whoop of joy sounded from the study.

"What?" J.T. called, grinning. Quinn's presence kept things from getting too heavy.

"Just a sec," Quinn yelled back. After a couple of minutes, he appeared in the kitchen doorway, beaming. "I got an email from Mom. She's back in Atlanta. And she said she loves me."

J.T. and Maggie exchanged glances. Maggie was smiling. "Yup," J.T. said, and Quinn raced back to the computer again.

"I like Annie," Maggie said. Her expression had turned a mite wistful.

"Me too," said J.T., opening a can of sauce and pouring half of it into the bottom of a casserole dish.

She got out silverware, rustled up paper napkins. She was going to be through setting the table long before the food was ready. "She said—" she broke off, looked away, looked back at him. "Oh, hell."

"What?" J.T. prompted.

"Did I truly break your heart?"

"Yes," he replied, without hesitation.

Maggie frowned thoughtfully. He saw bruises lurking in the blue depths of her eyes. "I remember it a little differently."

He kept working on the enchiladas; he could have made them in his sleep. "Really?" he asked innocently, and waited.

She narrowed her eyes at him. *"You* broke up with *me,"* she said. *"I* was the one with the broken heart."

He poured the remaining sauce over the chicken-and-cheese mixture he'd just wrapped in corn tortillas, and then began to grate more cheddar to sprinkle over the top. "You were already seeing the doctor by then," he said evenly.

Color pulsed in her cheeks. "I wasn't," she said.

J.T. did his best to look casual when he shrugged. "That isn't what I heard," he replied.

"Well, precisely what did you hear?" she asked, lowering her voice.

"You weren't the only kid from Springwater to get into Northwestern right out of high school, you know," he said. "Your big brother Simon made a point of telling me you were dating his buddy, Young Doctor Bartholomew, and wasn't that a fine thing. He'd be able to offer you everything you were used to, everything I couldn't."

Her mouth dropped open, closed again. "Simon said that? Of all the—"

He raised his eyebrows. "You deny that you went to football games with the doc, and a few frat parties?"

"A whole bunch of us went to the games and parties," she said, indignant. "I wasn't paired off with Connor. Damn it, J.T.—*damn* it. Why didn't you just ask me instead of taking my big brother's word for it?"

It had all happened so long ago, but J.T. was surprised to realize that the wounds were still raw. "I guess I was ready to believe that nothing as good as you could ever happen to me," he said.

She began to cry, and J.T. felt patently helpless and, at the same time, his hopes soared. He was at once jubilant and scared stiff; he wanted another chance with Maggie, and he wanted to run from all the things she made him feel.

"McCaffrey," he rasped, took a step toward her.

She shook her head. "Don't, J.T. Just—don't."

11

J.T. stood looking down at the simple head-stone, feeling the loss of his father anew. He rarely set foot in the little churchyard ceme-tery, though generations of his family had been laid to rest here—as he would be as well, sooner or later. Other people found solace, a sense of continuity, making such pilgrimages, but it was different for J.T. The experience invariably stirred the embers of his grief back to full flame, reminded him in no uncertain terms of a fact he tended to sublimate—until Jack Wainwright's killer or killers were found, there could be no lasting peace, no real closure. Not for him.

Quinn, standing at J.T.'s side, scuffled his

feet and slipped a small, rather grubby hand into J.T.'s. "Dad?"

J.T. closed his eyes tightly for a moment, swallowed. "What is it, partner?" he asked, when he felt sure the words would come out right. He imagined himself introducing one generation to the other. *This is your grandson, Dad. I'm so proud of him. Quinn, meet your grandfather, the finest man I ever knew.*

"Do you have any pictures of my granddad?" The small, freckled face was a study in concentration. "I don't think I know what he looked like."

The words took J.T. off guard. Surely he'd shown Quinn photographs of Jack Wainwright, told him stories of hunting trips and horseback rides, Christmases and birthdays—hadn't he? When it came right down to it, he couldn't recall a single instance. After Jack died, he and Janeen, in a frenzy of fierce but silent mourning, had packed everything away, from picture albums to personal belongings to memories. J.T.'s mother, Becky, though hardly a family type, kept in fairly regular contact with Quinn, and they knew each other quite well. In fact, J.T. had no doubt that his son was closer to Becky than he himself had ever been.

"Sure," he said hoarsely. "There are pictures. We'll rustle some up tonight, after the chores are done."

Quinn nodded, surveying the neglected grave as though he might somehow form an image of Jack by measuring the plot with his eyes. "Mom told me Granddad was a cowboy. She said he traveled with the rodeo for a while, riding bucking broncos and Brahma bulls, before he married Nana and they had you."

"That's true," he said, oddly choked up, and he shoved his hands into the pockets of his lightweight denim jacket. Just then it seemed as though their roles in life were reversed; Quinn was the man, and he the boy. "He was a cowboy, all right. The genuine article."

Quinn's brow was crumpled. "What happened to him?" Not surprisingly, Annie had spared their son that part of the story. Little wonder, gruesome as it was.

J.T. crouched, in order to be at eye level with his son. He wouldn't have volunteered the information, but because Quinn had asked him outright, he figured the kid was ready to know the truth. "He was shot, Q."

Quinn's voice was small. "Like you were?"

Vivid images flooded J.T.'s mind, crimson with blood—his own shooting, Murphy's, his father's, all mixed up into one mind-numbing tragedy—and he thrust out a ragged sigh. A child Quinn's age shouldn't have to deal with such grisly realities. Hell, a grown man shouldn't, either. "Yes," he answered. *Except that he didn't make it, and I did, and after all this time, I'm still not sure how I feel about that.*

Quinn made the obvious leap. "You could be dead now, too. Real easy."

Help me out, here, J.T. prayed. He wasn't sure who he was petitioning; he'd all but stopped believing in a benevolent god when his dad died, and Murphy's killing had undone whatever fragile faith he might have had left. "But I'm not, Q.," he said, at some length. "I'm still around, and I will be for a long time."

Maybe, countered a voice in J.T.'s head, the one that always played devil's advocate. During his career as a homicide cop, he'd come to respect that contrary part of his nature, if not actually like it.

Quinn gazed straight into his eyes, his expression wary. He was smarter than a six-year-old ought to be when it came to the vagaries of life, death, and fate, and he obviously wasn't in the market for pat answers. "You can't promise that. Nobody can."

"You're right," J.T. ground out. His haunches were beginning to ache; he longed to stand upright, stretch his legs, but he didn't want to break the delicate connection with Quinn. "Anybody can die, at any time, including me. But if you go through life worrying about everything, being afraid of what *might* happen, you'll miss all the best stuff. The only choice any of us have, partner, is to show up for every day and make the best of things as they come." He wished he could convince Maggie of that. Convince himself.

Quinn pondered J.T.'s words in silence.

J.T. ruffled the boy's hair. "You all right?"

Quinn nodded, and J.T. stood, heard his knees crack as he rose. Hell, he thought, his fortieth birthday was almost a decade away, and he was already getting old. Turn around, and he'd be another Purvis.

He smiled at the thought; there were
worse fates, he guessed. "We'd better get
over to the feed store," he said. "See if we
can find you some chickens to ride herd
on."

Quinn beamed up at him. Then, in a gesture that touched J.T. in some deep, private
place that he'd always kept hidden, even
from himself, the boy squatted, patted the
gravestone that bore his grandfather's
name. "We'll come back, Granddad," he
said. "We'll do some weeding and maybe
bring you some flowers. And I'll tell you all
about my chickens."

J.T. chuckled and squeezed the boy's
shoulder lightly. It was true that the grave
had been neglected, like so many other
landmarks of his life, tangible and intangi-
ble. "Let's go, buddy," he said.

Together, father and son turned to leave,
walking slowly past the much older markers
of Scully and Evangeline Wainwright, and
those of their children and their children's
children. He thought of what Springwater
and the ranch had meant to all of them, and
a sense of reverence came over him. He
would rebuild the place, make it pay again.
For Quinn. For himself. And for them.

J.T.'s truck was parked just outside the churchyard gate. Thoughtfully, he opened the passenger door and hoisted Quinn inside. Then he got behind the wheel, started the engine, and pulled away from the curb.

"Do dead people know when people visit their graves?" Quinn asked.

J.T. felt a rush of love for the boy buckled into the other seat. "Could be," he said. "The truth is, I don't have any idea."

Quinn pondered, his brow scrunched. "Probably nobody does," he concluded.

J.T. took a right turn into the parking lot of the feed-and-grain. "Maybe, when we stop by and pay our respects, it's meant to do us some good, rather than the person buried there."

Quinn's expression said he'd have to work on that concept for a while. He peered over the dashboard at the sprawling feed store. The place had been in business since the 1940s, if J.T. remembered correctly. Before that it had been the site of a livery stable and blacksmith's shop. "Is this where we buy hay for the cows?"

"Yup," J.T. answered. "Next year, we'll grow our own."

A wide grin spread across Quinn's face.
" 'We'? You mean I get to help?"

J.T. remembered how he'd bitched about
working in the hay fields as a kid, plowing
and planting in the early spring, harvesting
in late August. His muscles remembered the
rigors of bucking bales onto the bed of a
truck only too well. "Yeah," he said. "You
get to help."

Quinn gave a whoop of delight. No doubt
his opinion would change by the time he
was sixteen or so.

Inside, they stocked up on grain and oats
for the livestock, and J.T. ordered a ton of
hay to be delivered. That done, he and
Quinn selected half a dozen young hens
from a wire pen in the back of the store.
George Pickering, the proprietor, a round-
faced man with bright blue eyes, caught the
squawking birds by their spindly chicken
legs and tossed them unceremoniously into
a cardboard carrier with air holes. Although
they carried on something fierce, they
weren't hurt, just ruffled.

"Good to see you back here where you
belong, J.T.," George remarked, tucking his
thumbs under the straps of his cobbler's

apron and rocking on his heels. He grinned. "I hear you're courting Maggie McCaffrey. 'Bout time you two got together."

J.T. grinned and shook his head. He'd forgotten the gossipy nature of small towns. "Sounds like you know more about my life than I do," he said easily.

"What's courting?" Quinn asked.

"Never mind," J.T. said.

George blushed, more from consternation, J.T. figured, than embarrassment. "Well, if you ain't makin' time with that woman, you ought to be," he grumbled.

J.T. laughed. "I'll keep that in mind."

"What's making time?" Quinn wanted to know.

J.T. pretended not to hear. "I'll need some feed for these chickens," he said, and reached for his wallet.

George nodded and named a price, and J.T. paid. George hoisted a fifty-pound bag of dried corn onto one shoulder without apparent strain and lugged it outside to the truck.

"You got a plan drawn up for that new barn?" George asked, dusting his hands together after tossing the chicken feed in with their other purchases.

J.T. knew the community was planning an old-fashioned barn raising, since he'd had calls from half the people in town, volunteering everything from nails to free labor to food for the workers. "I'm waiting to hear from the insurance company," he said.

George seemed reluctant to let them go. "Shame about Clive."

"Yeah," J.T. agreed. A real shame.

"Is Clive the guy who was murdered?" Quinn asked, when they were back in the rig and pointed toward home.

J.T. glanced at his son, frowning. "How did you know that?"

Quinn shrugged as off-handedly as if he ran across murders all the time. Maybe he did, J.T. thought ruefully. It was a hell of a world. "I heard those newspaper guys talking, when Mom and I were at the Springwater Station."

J.T. absorbed that. Then said, "That's him." Maybe it was the tone of his voice, maybe it was something in his manner— whatever the reason, Quinn didn't press for more information, not then at least.

When they got back to the ranch, J.T. and Quinn fed the dogs, rigged up a temporary coop for the chickens with wire, a few nails, and some plywood, then headed out to feed the cattle, which were still pastured down by the creek. Billy was there ahead of them, pitching hay out of the back of his own truck. He grinned and waved.

"Well, now," Billy said to Quinn, "if it ain't the foreman himself."

Quinn was delighted. "We bought some chickens in town," he said. "Alive ones, not the kind that are cut up and wrapped in plastic. Dad and I made them a house."

"That's good," Billy said. Though he spoke to Quinn, he was looking at J.T., and his expression was solemn. It was clear that he wanted to say something more, but he refrained because of the boy.

"Me and Cindy are fixing to move into that spare room of yours, if the offer's still good," Billy said.

J.T. nodded. "Anytime you're ready," he answered.

That night, after supper, the Raynors took up residence in the downstairs bedroom in back of the kitchen. The whole process took only a few minutes, since they'd lost practically everything they owned in the fire. The community had given them clothes, blankets, books, towels, and other household goods, and they had a small color television set, too. The room was good-sized, with its own bathroom, and offered about as much privacy as anyone could hope for while living in somebody else's house.

"I could take over the cooking," Cindy offered, appearing in the kitchen. She wore black sweats and sneakers, and her hair was up, held in place by one of those plastic clips. She looked way too young to be a wife, let alone a mother-to-be.

J.T. set down his coffee mug. Under protest, Quinn had gone upstairs to take a bath, both dogs in attendance, and J.T. was feeling a little dazed. He was used to living by himself. "Thanks," he said. "I don't mind whipping up a meal now and then, though. Fact is, I like it."

Cindy's smile was shy. In the few weeks since Billy had come to work as his hired hand, he realized, he and Cindy hadn't exchanged more than a word or two. He was essentially a stranger to her, and she to him. Now that they were all going to be knocking around under the same roof, J.T. figured he'd better come up with some polite small talk.

"Billy cooks sometimes, too," she said proudly. "Fish sticks and pizza and stuff like that. I think it's a fine thing for a man to be comfortable working in a kitchen. My dad takes on like he's being killed if you ask him to open a can of soup."

J.T. smiled to himself and stood, setting aside the albums he'd gotten from a closet in the study a few minutes before. He wasn't sure he was ready to look into the faces of his father and other long-departed relatives, but later on, when he'd corralled Quinn, the two of them would go back in time, at least for a little while.

After laying the dusty volumes on the antique sideboard, he went to the sink, wet a sponge under the faucet, and wiped the red-and-white-checkered oilcloth covering the surface of the table. "My mother always told me that any man who won't cook doesn't deserve to eat," he said. Bless her, Becky had taught him most of what he knew about self-reliance. He'd learned to cook, wash, clean, and generally fend for himself at an early age. He was wryly grateful for the lessons she'd taught him, but he had to admit that he was something of a control freak because of it, and he had a hard time letting down his guard or accepting help.

A stomping sound on the back porch announced Billy's arrival as J.T. was pouring himself a cup of coffee and, a moment later, he opened the door and stepped inside. Young Raynor looked worn out and more than a little distracted as he crossed the kitchen and kissed his child bride lightly on the forehead.

"You're all done in," he scolded tenderly, resting awkward hands on Cindy's shoulders. "What you ought to do is have yourself a warm bath and get to bed. Maybe take in some TV. You must be hungry, too— you didn't eat hardly anything at Mom's tonight."

J.T. looked away, aware that the exchange was an intimate one, for all its mundane innocence. He wished he were in the barn, or at least another room, where he wouldn't see. Wouldn't hear. Something about their innocent closeness made him ache with a sort of longing he didn't care to examine too closely, and while he was coming to grips with that, McCaffrey sneaked into his mind. He imagined her living in this house, touching him gently, letting him touch her . . .

"I'm fine," Cindy insisted. "Are you coming to bed?"

Billy sighed. "Yes," he said, and propelled her gently in the direction of their part of the house. "I need to have a few words with J.T. first, then I'll be along."

She murmured a good night to J.T. and left the kitchen. Her footsteps sounded heavy and slow for someone so young. A door closed in the near distance.

"Coffee?" J.T. said to Billy, still standing near the counter.

Billy shook his head. He looked serious again; a man with something weighing on his mind. "I have an idea it was Randy Hough and my brother Travis who set your barn on fire," he said bluntly.

J.T. had his own suspicions on that score—he clearly recalled that neither Hough nor DuPres had been in the Brimstone Saloon when he took in the printout of Steve Jenson's mug shot, just before the fire started, though it was general knowledge that the pair spent most of their free time there, playing pool—but with no proof, he'd kept his theories to himself. Travis and Randy were regulars at Springwater's favorite watering hole, it was true, but there were certainly other places they could have been. "What makes you say that?" he asked.

Billy's slim shoulders were stooped, as though he'd been carrying the burdens of a much larger, much older man; life had probably never been easy for Billy. "They've got too much money these days, both of them. Somebody's paying them for *something,* and I don't think it's pulling green chain over at the sawmill."

"Did either one of them actually admit anything to you?"

Billy shook his head. "Not yet. I'm working on it, though. Hanging out with them as much as I can, and all like that."

J.T. heard Quinn upstairs, running a foot race with the dogs, from the sounds of it. Quinn was laughing, while Winston and Blackie barked their heads off. So much for peace and quiet. "I don't want you playing hero," J.T. told Billy, keeping his voice down. "Leave this to Purvis and me."

Billy's jawline tightened slightly. He glanced toward the hallway behind him. Cindy was running water in the bathroom and singing a popular country-and-western song in a high, pretty vibrato. "Travis and Randy won't tell you or Purvis anything much," he said. "They may not be real bright, but they know enough to cover their asses."

J.T. thrust a hand through his hair. "This is a dangerous situation," he reiterated. "Just leave it alone, Billy."

Color flared in the younger man's face, but before he could reply, Quinn and the dogs burst into the kitchen from the enclosed stairway and brought happy chaos with them. Quinn was wearing flannel pajama bottoms, and his hair, just washed, was standing out all over his head. "Hi, Billy," he crowed.

Winston and Blackie raised an exuberant canine chorus behind him.

"Settle down a little," J.T. said, addressing both the boy and the dogs.

Billy grinned at Quinn, and then greeted

each of the hounds with a vigorous ear rubbing. "Howdy, Quinn," he said. "How are
you?"

"I'm good," Quinn said, with manly im-
portance.

"How come these dogs are wet?" J.T. inquired.

Quinn pretended not to hear. "Did you
see my chickens?" he asked Billy.

"Sure did," Billy answered. "That's some
fine-looking poultry you got there."

Quinn looked up at J.T. "Can I email
Mom?"

"Sure," J.T. said, shaking his head. He
wasn't used to his son's quicksilver subject
changes and often felt as if he'd gotten off
the conversational train a few stops too
early.

The boy said a hasty good night to Billy,
then dashed into the study, followed closely
by Blackie and Winston, who were game for
any adventure.

"I meant what I said, Billy," J.T. said, when
Quinn was out of earshot. "Purvis and I will
handle the police work."

Billy just looked at him for a long moment,
then turned on his heel and disappeared
into the darkness of the corridor.

J.T. sighed, feeling about a hundred years old all of a sudden, then opened the refrigerator and started gathering the ingredients for an omelette. Quinn and the dogs returned to the kitchen just as he was about to summon them.

"Wash your hands," J.T. said, without glancing at his son.

"You sound like Mom," Quinn replied, but he washed. The dogs collapsed onto the rug by the backdoor with huffing sighs, closed their eyes, and began to snore. J.T. smiled to himself. It was no easy task keeping up with a six-year-old, for man or dog.

"Did you get any email?"

"Yeah," Quinn said, scraping back a chair and sitting. His chin nearly touched the table edge. "Mom's leaving for South America tomorrow."

"You okay with that?" J.T. asked carefully, glancing at his son.

Quinn nodded, then sighed in a way that pinched J.T.'s heart. His eyes looked huge, and his freckles stood out. He was tired, though he would probably fall asleep standing up before admitting that. "I guess." A lengthy pause followed. "What if they don't come back, though?"

J.T. brought the omelette to the table on a platter, along with some buttered toast. "They will," he said.

Quinn looked stubborn. "But sometimes people go away and they don't come back," he insisted.

J.T. answered quietly. "If that happened— and it won't, Quinn—then you would stay here with me and somehow we'd deal with it."

Quinn bit down on his lower lip for a moment, then asked in a small voice, "Am I too big to sit on your lap?"

"Nope," J.T. said, and held out his arms. Quinn scrambled into J.T.'s embrace, and they sat together like that for a while, saying nothing at all, and it felt good.

"I'm hungry," Quinn said, after a few moments had passed.

J.T. chuckled and set him on his feet. He peered at the omelette cooling in the middle of the table. "That's breakfast food, isn't it?"

J.T. grinned and nodded for Quinn to sit down. "Not if you have it for supper," he said reasonably.

"Can we look at those pictures you were telling me about before?"

"Sure," J.T. said. "Let's just finish eating first, though."

Quinn did justice to his dinner, then pushed his plate away and watched while J.T. had seconds. Ranch life sharpened his appetite the way police work never had—maybe it was the fresh air, or the relative lack of dead bodies.

"Mom and Brad tried to have more kids," Quinn confided, out of the blue. "Mom went to the hospital, too, but when she came back, she didn't bring a baby."

Annie had stood at the sink, with her back to him, and told him about the miscarriage. J.T. sensed, not for the first time, that Annie's joining Brad in Caracas, without Quinn, had more to do with shoring up the marriage than she wanted anyone to suspect. "How did you feel about that?" he asked cautiously.

"I'd like to have a little brother," Quinn allowed.

J.T. watched his son, waited, knowing there was more.

Quinn ruminated a while before getting to the heart of the matter. "I probably wouldn't be so special to Mom if she had another kid, though."

J.T. set down his fork and made a game-show buzzer sound. "Wrong," he said, relieved when Quinn grinned broadly. "No matter how many other kids come along, Q., your mom and I will go right on loving you. So will Brad."

"Do you think you'll get more kids?"

J.T. loved kids, especially the one sitting across from him, of course, but he hadn't thought about starting a new family. For the last several years, he'd pretty much been concentrating on survival.

"Maybe," he allowed. "Maybe not. I'd need a wife first, for one thing."

"But if you and Maggie got married and made some babies together—"

J.T. had to clear his throat. "That's a big if," he said. "Nobody said anything about Maggie and me getting married, Q." He couldn't help imagining it, though. Him and McCaffrey as man and wife, making love, laughing together, sharing worries and arguing. Something ground painfully, deep within him.

"But it *could* happen—couldn't it?"

"I suppose," he said, careful to keep his tone even. "Right now, what's important is your knowing that nobody—and I mean *nobody*—could ever take your place with me."

Quinn looked relieved. "It might not be too bad, having a brother," he reflected, at some length, a lot more relaxed, "but a sister—"

J.T. thought back to his own childhood; he would have given plenty to have a whole posse of siblings. Even a sister or two. "Whatever happens, Quinn," he said, "you'll be O.K."

The kid was appeased, at least for the time being. "Hurry up and finish, Dad," he urged, with a nod at J.T.'s plate. "I want to see some more old pictures and stuff."

Half on hour later, with Quinn settled into bed, J.T. perched on the mattress edge with a boot-box full of memorabilia in his lap. One photo, enclosed in a cardboard studio folder, was of a very young Jack Wainwright wearing an army uniform and a G.I. haircut. Although he was smiling, the haunted look in his eyes indicated that the portrait had been made after Vietnam, not before. He wished he'd asked more questions when his father was still around, but it had always seemed they had time.

Other pictures, all of them black-and-white, with zigzag edges and lots of double exposures and splashes of stray light, showed Jack and Becky dressed for a dance. Jack and Becky on horses. Jack and Becky, newly married, standing on the steps of Springwater's one and only church. There were letters, too, and old dance cards from proms at Springwater High.

Quinn pressed a fingertip to the image of a sturdy, solemn-eyed baby sitting under a Christmas tree, surrounded by packages. "Is that you?"

J.T. nodded. Look at that puss, he thought. Even then I was a cynic.

By the time they'd gone through a number of newspaper clippings, report cards, elementary school artwork, and the like, Quinn was yawning.

"Time to snooze, buddy," J.T. said. By then Winston had curled up on the foot of Quinn's bed and gone comatose, while Blackie lay on the floor, muzzle on paws, one bleary eye open and watchful.

Quinn threw both arms around J.T.'s neck and squeezed. " 'Night, Dad," he said.

J.T. swallowed, kissed the boy's forehead. " 'Night," he replied.

He switched off the bedside lamp and left the room, leaving the door ajar and the hallway light on, the way Quinn liked. Downstairs, he got himself another cup of coffee and sat down at the kitchen table to take a closer look at the stuff in the box.

His attention kept going back to one particular photo, a group shot of a bunch of teenagers on some kind of picnic, right there on the Wainwright ranch, he would have bet. Somewhere in the hills, back of the house. They were all grinning and cocky, these kids, a really retro bunch in their hip-hugger pants, granny dresses, and tie-dyed T-shirts—except for his dad, that is. Jack was pure, timeless cowboy, clad in scuffed boots, jeans, and a chambray shirt, western cut. The expression in his eyes said he knew full well that he was different from the others, and that he thrived on the knowledge. His arm was draped loosely over Becky's shoulders, and she was looking up at him like he was made out of ice cream. He recognized other people, too, ones with familiar names like Hargreaves and McCaffrey, Kildare and Parrish.

He squinted at the picture; behind the group loomed the timber framework to support some kind of drilling apparatus. "What the hell?" he murmured, trying to remember if a well had been dug on that part of the ranch.

He turned the picture over, let his gaze slide through the names penned in his mother's handwriting. Not surprisingly, there was no reference to the work site in the background.

The Wainwrights always knew what had been done to their land, and when, and J.T. regarded himself as no exception to the rule. It bugged him that he couldn't recall this particular place.

A feeling of nostalgia swept over him; he missed his dad, missed the woman his mother had only sometimes been. He sighed and glanced toward the phone on the wall, near the door to the dining room, then at the clock on the stove. By Vegas standards, he decided, it wasn't all that late. Anyway, Becky was a night owl.

He crossed to the telephone, lifted the receiver, and punched in the number he rarely called. "Hi, Becky," he said, when she answered . . .

She drew in her breath, probably bracing herself for some new confrontation. "J.T.?" she asked cautiously.

He smiled. "The same," he said.

"Is something the matter?"

"No," he lied. "I just called to see how you're doing."

"Fancy that," said Becky, who had rewritten history to suit herself, in her mind at least, and therefore regarded herself as a dedicated mother, wrongly accused of neglect and a host of other sins.

"Mom," he said, cajoling her a little.

He felt her relax slightly. "I'm just fine," she allowed. "How about you?" How was it, he wondered, that a mother and son could have so little to say to each other?

Well, he imagined himself saying, somebody burned down my barn and blew up the trailer house—that was after Clive bought the farm out at the water tower, mind you—and Maggie McCaffrey is driving me crazy. Except for those things, Mother, I'm just fine.

"I'm O.K.," he said, and he didn't have the vaguest idea what to say next.

Her voice turned girlish. "I'm in love," she confided breathlessly, as though this had never happened before, to her or any other woman.

Now there was a flash. "That's great, Mom," he said.

"I understand Quinn is there with you."

"Yes," J.T. replied. "It's temporary."

"Well, of course it is," she responded. "Annie's his mother. A child belongs—"

J.T. closed his eyes. If there was one thing he could live without, it was a discourse on parenting from Becky. She seemed to sense his reaction and stopped midsentence.

"What was it you wanted, J.T.?" she asked, with a sort of stabbing brightness meant to convey that she was willing to pretend her only son cared about her, whether it was true or not.

J.T. went to the length of the phone cord to grasp a chair from next to the table, drag it across the linoleum, and drop into it. He didn't know what he wanted, but whatever it was, Becky couldn't give it to him. "Just to say hello." He sounded lame, even to himself.

"I was thinking I might bring Buck to meet you," she said.

"Sure," J.T. said, but it took him too long.

"Well, I guess I'd better say good night," Becky said, with a false note of cheer meant to gloss over the fact that even though they each had a telephone receiver in their hand, the lines between them had been cut a long time before.

"Right," he agreed, feeling that old, familiar sorrow.

"I'll talk to you soon," Becky promised, then hung up.

He stared at the receiver for a long moment, then put it back in its cradle with a slight click. Still wondering what he'd hoped to accomplish by making the call in the first place, he locked the doors, shut off the lights, and headed upstairs to get ready for bed.

Hands resting on her hips, Maggie contemplated the new addition to her household, a mass of brown-and-white fur with eyes. Sadie sat in a spill of sunlight from the window, head tilted to one side, ears cocked in perplexity. "What shall we call her, Sadie?" Maggie asked, not expecting an answer, of course. "She needs a name."

"How about Ethel?" piped a familiar voice from the front doorway of the Station, standing open to a fresh breeze. Kathleen McCaffrey came in. "Where is everybody?"

"Ethel?" Maggie echoed, a beat behind. Then, catching up, she spread her arms to take in the empty tables surrounding them. "The reporters have moved on to bigger and better things. Cindy's ankles were swollen and she felt sick to her stomach, so Daphne drove her out to the ranch."

"I do hope you can make this old place pay," Kathleen said. "Maybe you should put in a gift shop."

So that's where I got it, Maggie thought. *This need of mine to have all my ducks in a row, at all times.* It gave her an insight into her mother's reluctance to leave Springwater and go traveling in the RV with Reece, too.

Kathleen went right on chatting, turning the subject back to the dog. "Ethel was my favorite aunt's name. Positively hated it. She called herself Isadora instead, after the dancer."

Maggie chuckled and shook her head. A person could get whiplash trying to hold onto a thread of Kathleen's conversation. "I guess Ethel is as good a name as any."

Kathleen crossed the room and dropped gracefully to one knee to gaze into the dog's liquid brown eyes. "Yes," she said, "I believe it suits. Just the other night, I saw a program on PBS, all about how keeping a pet can lower a person's blood pressure—"

"How would you like to adopt a dog?" Maggie asked, inspired.

Kathleen's face reflected a wide range of emotions, all in the space of a few moments: resistance, solemn contemplation, happy decision. "Why not?" she asked. "I've always wanted a dog of my very own."

"Why not indeed?" Maggie agreed. As children, she and her brothers had kept a progression of pets, everything from hamsters, rabbits, and kittens to a sweet-tempered St. Bernard called Harriet, but each one had belonged to one of them specifically. Kathleen had always been on the fringes.

Now woman and dog were clearly bonding, and the sight cheered Maggie, though she felt a pang, realizing how very many little things she didn't know about her mother. "Aren't you a homely thing?" Kathleen asked Ethel, with boundless affection.

Ethel gave a compliant little whimper, and Kathleen patted her reassuringly before turning her attention back to Maggie again. "Of course," Kathleen said, "I didn't come here to take a stray off your hands, Margaret Corrine."

Maggie smiled. "Whatever your reasons, I'm glad to see you, and so is Ethel. Can I get you a cup of tea?"

Kathleen shook her head. "No, thanks, dear. I'm in something of a hurry. I just wanted to talk to you about the barn raising at J.T.'s ranch. Everybody's gathering there a week from Saturday morning, dressed to work. I'm in charge of arranging for the food supply. There's going to be a barbeque in the evening, and a dance after that. Sort of an unofficial kickoff to Founder's Day."

Maggie waited.

"I'll understand if you can't leave the Station," Kathleen rushed on. "I know you're busy getting the business up and running— but I hope you'll contribute something—you know, fried chicken, pie, potato salad."

Maggie was relieved to see her mother caught up in something besides the problems at home. "Put me down for a bucket of take-out chicken," she said.

Kathleen smiled, nodded.

"How's the painting going?" Maggie prompted, not wanting the conversation to end too quickly. Since the strain had developed between her parents, they'd both become somewhat inaccessible, and she'd missed them very much. Even the most ordinary exchange was welcome.

Kathleen sighed. "I just can't seem to get the hang of artichokes. I guess I'm not ready." Laughter lit her eyes and played on her generous mouth. "It would seem that I am still in my Pear Period."

Maggie grinned. "Do not despair," she said. "I'm sure you'll move on to bigger and better vegetables and fruits in good time."

"Yes," Kathleen said, looking thoughtful again. She'd taken a seat on one of the benches, despite her earlier insistence that she was in a hurry, her back to the trestle table. Distractedly, she stroked Ethel's head, now resting trustingly in her lap.

Maggie sat down beside her. "What is it,

Mom?" she asked, very softly, and against her better judgment.

Kathleen sighed. "There are some things, Margaret Corrine, that a mother finds difficult to discuss—especially with her daughter."

"Okay," Maggie said, but she took her mother's hand, and squeezed it lightly. "Just remember that I'm here, and I love you and Dad with all my heart. I'll help in any way I can."

Kathleen started to speak, thought better of the idea, and averted her eyes for a long moment. "Thank you, dear," she said softly, meeting Maggie's gaze again. Then she stood, surveying the dog, newly christened Ethel, with rueful delight. "How *did* I let you talk me into this, Margaret?" she asked.

Maggie grinned. "Too late," she said. Then she slipped into her office and came out with a leash, which she clipped to Ethel's collar. "She's all yours."

Kathleen shook her head, but she was smiling. She took the leash and held it firmly. "You'll be attending the barn raising, then?"

"I suppose," Maggie answered, with a nonchalance she didn't really feel. The gathering would be held at the Wainwright place, of course, and that meant she would see J.T. She felt an almost reckless thrill of excitement at the prospect, though she was determined to keep her wits about her. Not an easy task, when J.T. was around.

Kathleen sighed, and a dreamy expression came into her eyes. "I met your father at a barn dance, you know," she reflected. Ethel, evidently anxious to begin her new life in the McCaffrey household, was tugging at her end of the leash, easing toward the door.

Maggie knew the story, but she liked hearing it, so she waited.

"It was after a roundup out at the Kildare place," Kathleen went on. "There was a huge harvest moon, orange as a pumpkin—" She stopped, flushed a little. "But of course I've told you about that night a thousand times already."

Kathleen had just moved to Springwater with her parents and, although she'd attended secretarial school in Missoula and gotten good grades, there were few office jobs to be had. She'd waited tables at the Stagecoach Café and quickly made friends with Janeen Wainwright, J.T.'s aunt. Janeen had persuaded her to attend the dance. There she'd met Reece McCaffrey, who had just taken over the family milling and lumber business, and immediately fallen in love with him. A year later, they married, and soon after their second anniversary, Kathleen had given birth to Simon. Maggie had come along a few years later, soon to be followed by Wes.

Maggie kissed her mother's cheek. "Tell me again," she said gently. It was a romantic story, and she loved it.

But a look of sadness came over Kathleen's lovely face. "That was all so long ago," she said. "So much has changed between your father and I."

Maggie sat still, afraid to speak, vastly uncomfortable in the silence.

"You know, of course, that Helen Bisbee's husband ran off with someone he met on the Internet," Kathleen said, staring straight ahead, at some inner vista that obviously caused her intense pain. "And your father's been exchanging emails with a woman over in Missoula. Her name is Abigail."

Maggie felt as though she'd been punched. Her next reaction was disbelief.

"There must be some mistake. Did you read the messages? Did you ask Dad about them?"

Kathleen's face stiffened slightly, and her backbone went rigid. "I do not read other people's mail," she said, "electronic or otherwise. But there's no mistake. He's been communicating with this woman for over a year."

"And," Maggie insisted, "you've asked him for an explanation?"

"Once or twice," Kathleen admitted. "He said she was a retired travel agent. They talk about 'faraway places with strange sounding names,' as he put it."

"Then maybe—"

"I have reason to believe he's been seeing her. In person, I mean."

"What reason?" Maggie asked, even though she really, truly did not want to know.

"She sent him a card for his birthday, by way of the post office, and he didn't even try to hide the thing. Left it right on his desk in the study. She wrote, 'Looking forward to our next visit. Love, Abigail.' "

Maggie swallowed. Not Dad, she thought. But at the same time, she knew that Reece McCaffrey was a man, nothing more, nothing less, with a man's weaknesses. "Talk to him," she urged.

Kathleen glanced at her watch, worked up a brave smile, and neatly disposed of the conversation they'd just had by consigning it to the dimension of denial. "I'll put you down for chicken," she said, and Maggie had to scramble to recall that she was referring to the community meal to be served at J.T.'s barn raising. With that, she and Ethel were gone.

12

Odell Hough woke himself with a snort from the depths of his sinus passages and sat bolt upright on the bare mattress ticking, blinking and murmuring. He ran a hand down his face and blinked in an effort to clear his vision. It was midafternoon and hot, and the rank smells of sweat and mold and stale beer rose with his stirring. He grumbled a curse, groped for the flask on his night table, and tilted his head back for a snort.

"I don't know how you and Randy stand this hole," remarked a familiar voice from the bedroom doorway, causing him to choke on the whiskey. He nearly jumped right out of his hide, too. "When was the last time you hosed the place out?"

Odell damn near dropped the flask, which pissed him off royal. It was one thing to scare a man half to death in his own house and another to endanger his dwindling supply of firewater. He ignored the question, counting it rude. "Damn it," he snarled, "at least I got the manners not to walk in on a man without so much as a knock at the door. You could get yourself shot, doing that."

The visitor laughed. "Hell, I could hear you in here snoring like a pig from all the way out on the porch," he said. "If I'd waited for a come-in from you, old buddy, I'd have been standing out there all day." He looked around at the room Odell's wife, Mary Lee, God rest her soul, had once kept so neat and tidy. "I don't see a gun, either. Not that you could hit the side of a billboard if you were standing on a scaffold beside it."

It would be a waste of breath to go on arguing with this particular hombre; Odell had figured that out some time back. "What do you want, anyhow?" he demanded, still feeling testy. He lumbered to his feet and headed toward his uninvited caller, who didn't step out of the way until Odell was practically on top of him.

"Now what kind of greeting is that?" the man asked. He liked to be called Boss, and though Odell knew his right name, he didn't dare use it. That privilege was reserved for fancier folks than him. "Maybe I just dropped by for a friendly chat."

Odell gave a gruff hoot of laughter and proceeded down the hallway to the bathroom, where he relieved himself in the rust-rimmed bowl. Since Cindy had gotten herself knocked up and left him and Randy to fend for themselves, just as if they weren't any say-so of hers, he didn't bother much with closing doors. As an afterthought, he flushed, and there was a howling rattle in the pipes, like a banshee beating on a soup kettle. Hell. Next thing he knew, the plumbing would be gone, like the furnace and the floorboards around the old claw-foot tub.

"You want a beer?" Odell asked, headed for the kitchen.

The Boss slid a pointed glance to Odell's hands. "No, thanks," he said.

Odell made a brief stop at the sink, lathered his mitts with yellow soap, and rinsed.

After using the front of his overalls for a towel, he opened the fridge, ferreted around amid things that were starting to grow fur, and brought out a single can of brew. The Boss had had his chance; let him stay thirsty.

"Sit down if you're going to," Odell grumbled, pulling back a chair and dropping into the seat. These days, even sleeping wore him out. Maybe he had one of them fatal diseases. That would make little Miss Cindy think twice about the way she treated her old man, if he just up and died.

Boss-Man sat. 'Least he wasn't too fine for that, Odell thought bitterly.

"Where's Randy?"

"Damn if I know," Odell answered. "Could be anywhere."

Mr. Big-Man leaned forward in his chair, glaring. His whole face looked as hard as a carving on a totem pole. "He and Travis DuPres torched the Wainwright place the other night," he said. "I didn't tell them to do that." He was not a man who appreciated personal initiative, it seemed.

Odell shrugged and drained half his brew in one chug. He'd wanted to throttle those little bastards himself, when they bragged on what they'd done—after all, they might have hurt Cindy and the baby real bad—but he'd calmed down after a while, gotten the whole thing in perspective. They'd wanted to tweak J.T. a little, him being Purvis's deputy and all, but he was sure the whole thing had been intended as an innocent prank and nothing more.

"You developed a soft place in your heart for old J.T. all of the sudden?" he asked, hoping the Boss would just let the whole thing drop.

Fat chance. In the next instant, the man reached across the table and grabbed the bib of Odell's overalls, wrenching him halfway out of his chair. "You listen to me, old man," he breathed, "and listen well. If those idiots bring the law down on me, if they go flapping their lips or pull any more stupid tricks like that one, I'll see that they end up over at the county morgue, stretched out on a slab alongside Clive. The same goes for you. Is that clear?"

"It's clear," he answered grudgingly. Anybody else laid hands on him like that, Odell would have knocked out a good share of their teeth, but there were lines a man just didn't cross, dealing with this feller. Poor old

Clive had found that out the hard way. Odell comforted himself with the promise that he'd take the hide off that boy of his for leaving him open to this, and maybe peel a strip or two off the DuPres kid, too, just for good measure.

"Good." It was a growl. The Boss's grasp went slack, and Odell fell hard back into his chair. The impact of his landing rattled his vertebrae.

Boss-Man got to his feet, overturning his own chair in the process and not bothering to set it right. "One word," he warned. "One word to Purvis or Wainwright, or anybody else, and it'll get back to me. Remember that."

Odell gulped, nodded. He wished he'd never gotten messed up in this outlaw business in the first place. He'd gone into it for the money and glamour, but he didn't seem to have the knack.

The Boss left, driving away in his company car, but Odell didn't move from his chair for a long while. When he did he went to the telephone, the same heavy black rotary-dial piece of junk he'd had since 1962, when the lines finally got as far as his place, and put in a call.

Randy answered on the second ring. "Yo," he said. He always had that cell phone of his handy, no matter what he was doing. Liked to pretend he was some kind of hotshot.

"Get your ass out here to the house," Odell barked. "Now."

"I found some more papers in a trunk in the storeroom," Cindy announced, joining Maggie and Daphne in the public area of the Station, where they were sorting through some old silverware Kathleen had brought over earlier, after coming across the utensils in her attic. The handle of each fork, spoon, and knife was engraved with the letters *S.S.,* surely standing for "Springwater Station." "Shall I put them with the museum stuff?"

"Let's have a look at them," Maggie said idly, smiling when Sadie leaped into Tiffany's playpen, much to the little girl's amusement, and gave her doll's head a friendly lap with her tongue.

Tiffany laughed with glee and grabbed the dog's ears, and Sadie endured the attention with consummate patience, gazing adoringly at the child all the while.

"Silly mutt," Daphne said, with a grin, and gently hoisted the animal out of the playpen.

Cindy laid an old metal cash box on the table and lifted the lid. There were letters inside, still in their envelopes, and folded documents of various sorts and sizes.

Maggie took out one of the envelopes and smiled. On the first pass, she'd found a treasure—a letter Jacob McCaffrey had written to June-bug during a business trip to San Francisco, dated June 1883. She read it carefully, touched by the old-fashioned, formal affection Jacob had expressed to his obviously cherished wife, and longed to love and be loved in just that way.

While Daphne read that first letter, as pleased by the discovery as Maggie had been, Maggie unfolded a yellowed, crumbling document, musty with the passage of time. She was about to fold it again and set it aside in favor of another of Jacob's love letters to June-bug, when the name "Wainwright" caught her eye.

She frowned and squinted a little. As near as she could tell, the paper had been issued by an assay office, back in the 1880s. As she scanned the document, her gaze caught on Trey Hargreaves's signature. She gave a low whistle of exclamation.

"What?" Daphne asked, looking up from another letter.

"Look at this," Maggie urged, holding out the sheaf of pages.

Daphne took the offered documents and read them through quickly. "Wow," she breathed.

Cindy had made a trip to the kitchen, returning with diet colas for Maggie and Daphne and a small carton of orange juice for herself. "Did I find something important?" she asked, joining them.

"Maybe," Daphne said, sounding intrigued. "According to this, my great-great-great grandfather and J.T.'s were negotiating a business deal. Something about mineral rights on the Wainwright ranch."

Maggie invariably felt two things at any mention of J.T.: first, a distinct stir of interest, and then, a poignant, echoing resonance in the uncharted regions of her heart. This instance was no exception to the rule. "It's an interesting piece of history," she mused aloud, "but probably nothing more.

After all, we're talking about people who lived—and died—a very long time ago."

"I don't know," Daphne murmured. "It looks pretty official to me. Says here that Scully Wainwright agreed to let Trey Hargreaves and Company mine for copper on the southeastern section of the ranch." She looked up, frowning prettily while she flipped through mental files for some recollection of such an enterprise. Living most of her life in the house Trey Hargreaves had built for his bride, Rachel English, and their children, Daphne took a deep interest in Springwater history in general, and the chronicles of her own family in particular. "I don't remember ever hearing that copper was found on the Wainwright property."

"That might be precisely the point," Maggie said, spreading her hands. "They did some digging and didn't find anything."

Daphne looked unconvinced. "If Trey went to the trouble of having a document like this drawn up, and Scully agreed to sign it, then there was copper. I'd like to show this to J.T. and see what he makes of it. He's got a lot of old records out there—comes from a long line of pack rats, the same as I do. He might know what happened."

Maggie bit her upper lip, well aware that she would be the one appointed to carry out the interview, and she sighed inwardly at the prospect. She'd gone to the pound over in Maple Creek with J.T. and Quinn, it was true, but she still felt a bit awkward around J.T. because of the incendiary conversation they'd had in his kitchen a few days before. Because, she admitted to herself, she hadn't really stopped thinking about him since. More specifically, she hadn't stopped thinking about *making love* with him.

"I could take the papers out to the ranch with me," Cindy said. She'd lifted Tiffany easily out of the playpen, forgetting Maggie and Daphne's continuous lectures about heavy lifting, and was holding the little girl on her lap.

Daphne grinned meaningfully. "I'm sure Maggie wouldn't mind doing it," she said. "Would you, Maggie?"

Cindy might have dropped out of high school before graduation, but she was intelligent, and she caught on right away. "Right," she said.

Maggie waxed indignant, but she was unable to work up any sort of dudgeon, high, medium, or low. "Do you think you could be a bit more transparent, Daph?" she asked. "That way, I'd know for sure that you were trying to throw J.T. and me together on the flimsiest possible excuse?"

Daphne laughed. "All right," she teased, "I'll come right out and say what I mean: You're hot for the man. He's hot for you. Sooner or later—"

Maggie folded her arms. "That," she said, indicating Tiffany with a nod, "is no way to talk in front of a child."

Undaunted, Daphne pushed the papers across the desk. "You're opening a museum. You claim to be interested in Springwater's colorful history. Ask J.T. what he knows about this mineral rights thing."

Maggie sighed. "All right," she said, and then she felt a foolish smile steal across her mouth, and blushed with embarrassment at what she'd revealed.

Daphne and Cindy giggled like a pair of kids.

"J.T.'s over at the elementary school right now," Cindy volunteered, when she'd stopped laughing. "He was going to sign Quinn up for the summer softball league."

She glanced at the clock on the mantel. "If you hurry, you could probably catch him before he heads for home again."

"Dare you," Daphne taunted, her eyes gleaming with mischief. She'd taken on a new dimension in the short time since Tiffany had entered her life; she seemed stronger, more present, more whole.

"Stop," Maggie protested, but she took the documents and headed for the door. The walk to the school was a short one; it was just down the street, directly across from the Brimstone Saloon. The one-room log structure where Rachel English had taught was still there, long since declared an historical monument by the state of Montana, but a newer education building had been erected in the 1940s. The athletic field lay behind that.

J.T. was standing near the bleachers, arms folded, watching as a few dozen boys and girls congregated on the field were assigned to teams by their volunteer coaches. Purvis was beside him, but when he saw Maggie approaching, the marshal tipped his hat in cordial greeting, said something to J.T., and walked away.

J.T. turned toward Maggie, and one corner of his mouth tilted upward in a grin that could only be read as cocky. "I knew you wouldn't be able to resist me for long, Mc-Caffrey," he jibed, in an undertone.

She would not stoop to petty exchanges, she decided. She was bigger than that. "Here," she said, shoving the mining papers at J.T. "Cindy found these at the Station, and Daphne insisted that I be the one to ask you about them."

He unfolded the agreement and read it rapidly, then read it again, more slowly. "This is pretty old news, isn't it?" he asked. He smiled again, and his dark eyes smoldered with mischief. "If you want a date, McCaffrey, just ask."

Maggie pursed her lips, moved as if to shove her hands into the pockets of a jacket before realizing that she wasn't wearing one. "I agree." She felt her face heat up. "That it's old news, I mean. Daphne was the one who found it interesting. Maybe you should talk to her." With that, she turned on one heel and started to walk away.

J.T. took hold of her elbow and turned her around. "Hey," he said, "take a breath, will you? I was just ribbing you."

She thrust out a sigh, but before she

could think of anything to say, Quinn was running off the field toward them, his dog Winston bounding along at his side. A happy grin stretched across the boy's face, effectively softening Maggie's heart.

One of the Kildare boys was with Quinn, though Maggie wasn't sure which. At last count there had been six children in the family, according to Daphne, all of them male.

"This is Landry," Quinn said breathlessly, indicating his grinning companion. "He's six, like me."

"Seven next month," Landry clarified.

Maggie smiled and gave J.T. a sidelong glance.

"Hello, Landry," J.T. said, putting out a hand as if he were greeting the mayor.

Solemnly, the Kildare boy shook J.T.'s hand. He squinted when he looked up at him, and Maggie noticed that his front teeth were coming in crooked. Landry was seriously cute, like Quinn, and when these guys got older they would probably play fast-and-loose with more than a few feminine hearts. "My mom wants to know if Quinn can spend the night at our place," he said. "We'll bring him home tomorrow afternoon."

A slender, dark-haired woman with dancing brown eyes was coming across the grounds toward them. She waved as she approached, and Maggie remembered her name: Shannon. She was a member of Kathleen's art group.

"There she is," Landry said, resigned.

Maggie nodded in response. She wondered if the group was still getting together once a month at the high school's meeting room to paint and draw and chat about their various creative projects. Her mother hadn't mentioned the activity, but then, she'd been distracted lately.

"Hi, Shannon," Maggie said.

"Hello, Maggie," Shannon replied. "How's your mom?"

"Fine." The lie came automatically to Maggie's lips. The whole town probably knew that Reece and Kathleen McCaffrey were having marital problems, but that didn't mean she felt like talking about it.

"I've missed seeing her since the group disbanded," Shannon said, answering the question that had been lingering in Maggie's mind. "Attendance dropped off when school started last fall, and so far we haven't managed to get things going again."

Quinn and Landry, meanwhile, were turning fidgety, and Winston went with the flow by jumping around and yipping a little chorus.

"Well, Dad?" Quinn finally demanded. "Can I? Can I stay over with Landry?"

J.T. looked both pleased and reluctant to give up precious time with his son, even for such a short interval, and finally reached out to ruffle the boy's hair. "If it's really all right with Mrs. Kildare," he said, and his voice sounded a little husky to Maggie.

"Shannon," the other woman corrected him good-naturedly. "And yes, we'd be delighted to have Quinn visit. Winston, too."

J.T. chuckled. "Now that," he said, "is hospitality." He turned his gaze back to Quinn, who was all but jumping up and down by that time. "What about your PJs, bud, and a toothbrush?"

"Covered," Shannon put in. "We get a lot of company at our house."

"Thanks," J.T. said, with a slow smile. Quinn gave him a light punch on the side of one hip in masculine farewell, and then he and Landry turned and bolted back across the field, the dog barking at their heels.

Shannon and J.T. exchanged phone numbers, then she said good-bye to him and Maggie and turned to follow the crowd. Maggie and J.T. watched as she loaded Quinn, Landry, Winston, and what seemed like half a softball team into a beige minivan, got behind the wheel, and drove merrily away.

"Well," J.T. said, turning to look down at Maggie and waggling his eyebrows comically. "I guess it's just you, me, and the mineral rights agreement."

She laughed and shook her head.

He grinned. "How about dinner and a movie?"

She tilted her head to one side. "What is it with you?" she asked, and though she wasn't laughing anymore, she knew her amusement was visible in her eyes. "One minute, you're doing your best to annoy me, and the next you're talking about doing the town."

He sighed, but the grin hovered at the corners of his mouth. "Is that a 'yes'?" he countered, rocking back on his heels a little.

"No," she said.

"But it's not a 'no,' either, is it?" he persisted.

"I guess not," she said, a little sheepishly.

He leaned in close, his nose a fraction of an inch from hers. She concentrated on not crossing her eyes.

"Relax, McCaffrey," he drawled. "I'm talking about pizza and a video, not hot—wet— *slooooow* sex."

Heat surged through her system. "You are impossible," she hissed, but she was fighting a smile.

"No," he said, "I'm easy. At least where you're concerned." Again, that saucy grin. "Go ahead, McCaffrey. Have your way with me."

She rolled her eyes. "Truly amazing," she said wryly.

"Is that a step up from 'impossible'?" The tone he used was not suitable to their surroundings—it set the very marrow of her bones pulsing with heat—although he'd spoken in such a low voice that no one else could possibly have heard.

She gave him a subtle shove, but she wasn't going to be able to just walk away,

and they both knew it. Neither was she
ready to open her soul to a man who had
the power to turn her inside out, both physically and emotionally. "Pizza and a video,"
she said. "Seven o'clock, my place." *Then*
she turned and walked away.

"I'll bring the video," J.T. called after her.

Maggie didn't dare look back. Instead,
she picked up her pace.

J.T. went home, fed the dogs, and helped
Billy tend to the cattle and horses. Then,
whistling, he showered, put on clean
clothes, and drove right back to town. He
stopped at the Stagecoach Café and
placed an order for a pizza to go, then
headed for the supermarket, the only place
in town where he could rent a video.

Reluctantly he passed over steamy dra-
mas and romantic comedies and finally selected an old western. He and Maggie had
seen the movie together once, on a date at
the Maple Creek Bijoux, when they were still
in high school. He smiled, wondering if
she'd remember.

He paid the rental fee and was leaving the
supermarket when he ran into Daphne's

husband, Ben Evanston. They'd met briefly in the post office a week before, with Purvis making the introductions.

Evanston greeted him with a nod. "Hello, J.T.," he said. "I was sorry to hear about your barn."

"Thanks," J.T. answered, in a hurry to collect the pizza and get over to Maggie's place. It wasn't 7 o'clock yet, but he could always pretend he'd forgotten what time he was supposed to show up. "I suppose the thing would have fallen over if it hadn't burned."

It was a joke, but Ben didn't laugh, or even smile. "My wife tells me there might be copper on your place," he said.

J.T. recalled the papers Maggie had given him at the ball field; they were at home, on the desk in his study. He hadn't given them another thought since he'd tossed them there earlier, impatient to get back to town. Back to Maggie. "I doubt it," he said. It made sense that Evanston would be interested, he supposed. After all, the man ran the Jupiter and Zeus. "Old Scully was a businessman first and a rancher second. If he'd had a few tons of copper ore lying around the place, he'd have taken advantage of the opportunity."

Ben finally smiled. Apparently he was a stop or two behind the train. Probably had a lot on his mind. "Well," he said, "it was good to see you."

"Yeah," J.T. agreed, a bit hastily. "Take care."

He felt Evanston's eyes on his back as he walked away, and wondered about it, but not for long. His mind was on pizza, old cowboy movies, and McCaffrey, though not in that order, of course.

Purvis was waiting when Nelly came out of the library. She smiled and slipped into the passenger seat of his mother's Escort. For a moment, he thought she was going to lean over and kiss him right on the mouth, but in the end she only blushed a little and turned to fasten her seat belt.

Purvis turned the Ford around and headed toward his mother's house. It was Tillie's birthday, and he was about to introduce the two women in his life for the first time.

"Do you think she'll like me?" Nelly asked, gnawing at her lower lip.

Purvis reached over, stilled the motion by pressing the tip of an index finger to her mouth. "Mom? Sure she'll like you. Could be *you'll* be the one who wants to head for the tall timber."

She relaxed a little, settled back in the seat. "Why?"

"My mother's been waiting thirty years for a daughter-in-law and a batch of grandchildren. She's liable to produce a justice-of-the-peace's license and try to marry us herself."

Nelly's laugh was rich and soft.

"Oh, yes," Purvis went on, knowing he was on a roll. "And once she gets a look at that gold necklace you helped me pick out for her birthday present, well, who knows what will happen?" He'd been partial to a bracelet with a charm that read "#1 Mom," but Nelly had lobbied for a simple heart locket on a chain, and Purvis had deferred to her judgment.

A few minutes later Purvis drew the car to a stop in front of the small and completely ordinary house where he'd lived from birth until Uncle Sam called him up back in 1969. The lights were glowing in the living room, and Tillie Digg was out on the porch, wear-

ing her church dress and watering the red
geraniums in the hanging basket by the
steps. Her blue-rinsed hair was freshly
done, and even at that distance, Purvis
could see that she was wearing her good
pearl brooch, the one she'd inherited from
his grandmother.

Purvis smiled to himself. Tillie had been
on the lookout for them, unless she'd taken
to watering plants in her best duds.

The motor of the Escort rattled for a few
moments after he'd pulled the key from the
ignition. He turned off the headlights, got
out, and waved to his mother as he rounded
the car to open Nelly's door.

"Evening, Mom," he called. "You're looking mighty fancy tonight. Must be your
birthday or something."

The sound of Tillie's laughter reminded
Purvis of the music the bell choir made,
whenever they came over from Maple Creek
Methodist to serenade the congregation at
Springwater's one small church. "Purvis
Digg, you mind your manners and bring that
young lady of yours up here right now, so I
can get a good look at her."

Nelly, overhearing, glanced up at him
nervously.

"Relax," he told her, in a quiet voice. "Mom's not dangerous unless she misses one of her soap operas. Then, look out."

Nelly giggled.

Tillie was beaming when they reached the base of the porch steps and paused there to look up at her.

"Mom," Purvis said, with grave good manners, "this is Miss Nelly Underwood. Nelly, my mother."

"Hello, Mrs. Digg," Nelly said, putting out her hand even before she mounted the three steps to face Tillie eye-to-eye.

"Call me Tillie," said Purvis's mom, with brisk kindness. "Now come inside, both of you. I want to show you all the lovely cards I got this year. There were seven from members of my quilting club alone."

"They miss you, Mom," Purvis said, remembering a conversation with Kathleen McCaffrey, when she'd said exactly that.

"I've got to get back to my stitching, now that I'm feeling better," Tillie said. "Finish up my Drunkard's Path." She paused for effect. "Might need it for a wedding gift. You never know."

Purvis sighed as he followed Nelly and his mother into the house. The living room floor

was shiny with fresh wax, and the crocheted coverlets on the couch and the back
of Tillie's recliner were arranged neatly. The
familiar ceramic matador and bull gleamed
on top of the vintage console TV, and the
birthday cards were taped like Christmas
greetings around the arched doorway leading into the combination dining room and
kitchen.

Nelly smiled, taking the time to admire
each and every card. "You have a lot of
friends," she said.

"Yes," Tillie replied proudly. "There's one
there from Kathleen McCaffrey. She painted
it herself. See the one with the pear?"

"That's lovely," Nelly said, with sincere
admiration.

"Sometimes it just amazes me, the kind
of talent you find in a little bitty town like
this. Why, the McCracken boys are starting
a rock-and-roll band, right across the alley
there, in their garage." Her eyes sparkled
behind her glasses; Purvis remembered the
frames from before he went to Vietnam. She
just kept replacing the lenses. "Have you
heard them?"

He smiled. "I've had a few calls," he said.

"Not from their fans, though. Now let's go out and get us some supper. We've got a birthday to celebrate."

Tillie twittered like a young girl about to dance the night away. "I have a two-for-one coupon for the Stagecoach Café," she said. "It came out in Wednesday's *Gazette,* with the grocery ads."

"Good a place to eat as any, I guess," Purvis said.

"I love the food there," Nelly added, and Purvis was moved by her quiet desire to be a part of things.

The restaurant was little more than a block away, but that was too far for Tillie to travel on foot, especially in the dark. Purvis escorted her to the car, with Nelly leading the way up the walk, and when Nelly started to get into the backseat, Tillie protested.

"You sit up front with Purvis," she commanded.

Purvis cleared his throat. The backseat was hardly spacious, and Nelly would fit a lot better than Tillie. "Mom—"

"I like to be chauffeured," Tillie insisted, and scrambled into the rear of the car.

Purvis closed his eyes and held his breath until she was settled.

Nelly got in front and scooted the seat forward.

"Well, my, my," Tillie trilled, "there's a present back here, all wrapped up with shiny paper and a fancy bow. Is this for me? It doesn't look one bit like a bathrobe."

Purvis smiled at the mischief in his mother's voice. "Yes, it's for you. And maybe it's a robe after all. One of them skimpy little things, made out of space-age microfibers."

Tillie laughed lustily. "My goodness, Purvis Boyd Digg, there are ladies present."

"Mom?"

"What?"

Purvis glanced at the rearview mirror, saw her face reflected there, glowing with happiness. "I love you," he said.

She reached forward and patted his shoulder. "I love you, too, son," she replied, without hesitation.

He glanced at Nelly sidelong and noticed the soft expression on her face. Purvis recalled how she'd told him both her parents were gone. Like him, she was an only child. Unlike him, she was alone in the world. Or had been, he corrected himself, until he

came along. "Go ahead, Ma," he said, a little gruffly. "Open your present."

Tillie ripped in, and gave a gasp of delight
just as they pulled into a parking space in
front of the café. "A gold locket," she whispered. "I've wanted one of these all my life."

"Nothing but the best for you, Ma," Purvis
told her proudly.

"I think I'm going to cry," Tillie said.

"Me, too," Nelly added. And they all
laughed together. It felt good, and Purvis
was in high spirits as they entered the
Stagecoach Café. Later he'd be glad he
hadn't known it wasn't going to last.

13

Only when J.T. actually stepped into the Springwater Station carrying a large pizza box and a rented video in a vinyl case did Maggie happen to remember that her television set and VCR were in the bedroom. She felt her cheeks redden and J.T., in his damnably discerning way, narrowed his eyes at her and grinned.

"What's the matter, McCaffrey?" he teased, in a low drawl. "Did you forget how devastatingly attractive I really am?"

As if she could forget that, she thought, more than a little jangled. Her attraction to J.T. involved all five known senses and several yet to be identified. It was much bigger than the way he looked—impossibly hand-some—or sounded—all man, with no apologies offered—or felt—hard as tamarack, warm as a woolen blanket—or tasted—delicious—or smelled—like rainwater and clean denim. She closed her eyes, in a bid to gain some kind of control over her riotous feelings.

J.T. chose that moment to kiss her. He'd set aside the pizza and the video, pulled her close, and brought his mouth down on hers, ever so lightly, all in the space of one irregular heartbeat.

She moaned, instructed herself to pull away before she wound up under his spell again, and slipped her arms around his neck instead, returning his kiss without reservation.

J.T. deepened their contact, gently prodding her lips apart, teasing her tongue with his and setting all her nerves ablaze with something ancient, something fierce, something fundamentally dangerous. He held her hips in his hands, and drew her to him, as though already claiming her; she felt his erection against her belly, and longed to take him inside and keep him there, as much a part of her as her heart or her spirit.

She let her head fall back, and J.T.'s mouth strayed, hot, along the length of her neck.

"What about the pizza?" he murmured.

"Oh, hell," she whispered back, *"forget the damn pizza."*

He chuckled into the hollow beneath her ear, then lifted her easily up into his arms and started into the corridor. Sadie followed as far as the master bedroom, whimpered when J.T. closed the door in her face, then trotted away, tags jingling, into the void that was the rest of the universe.

The room was almost dark, since twilight was gathering outside, and J.T. didn't bother to turn on a lamp. He laid Maggie on the bed that had been Jacob and June-bug's and stood looking down at her.

"If you're going to change your mind, Mc-Caffrey," he said gruffly, "now is the time to say so."

She knew she ought to send him away, but she couldn't. She'd missed him too long, and too badly, and she needed him too much. Tomorrow, she would surely have regrets, but tomorrow could damn well take care of itself.

She stretched, like a cat, and then kicked

off her flat shoes and lay there in her jeans and white eyelet top, gazing up at him, letting all her desire show in her eyes.

J.T. gave a low groan and hauled his shirt off, laying it aside with a distracted motion. His gaze hadn't left Maggie's face since he'd brought her to the bed; he took off his boots, then stretched out beside her on the mattress and rested one strong arm across her middle.

"Ah, McCaffrey," he breathed, "if this turns out to be a dream, and I wake up alone, I'm not going to be able to take it."

She smiled lazily and put her arms around his neck, drawing him down for a temptress's brief kiss. "Don't talk, Wainwright," she said softly. "One of us might come to our senses if you do and spoil everything."

He laughed, kissed her again, and she was lost even before he caressed her breast through the fabric of her blouse, even before he undressed her, and somehow himself, and immediately found one of her nipples with his mouth. He sucked lightly at first, then harder, and Maggie's cry was one of jubilation, of welcome, of passion long held in check and now demanding release.

"God, McCaffrey," he rasped, nibbling his way over the rounding of her right breast, seeking the left, "I've missed you so much—"

She entwined her fingers in his hair, held him fast when he began to tease her with his tongue again, causing her nipple to harden deliciously for him. A network of sensation spread through her in a fiery flash. "J.T.," she pleaded, and then his name fell from her lips again and again, like some desperate litany.

He enjoyed her thoroughly, feasted on her breasts until she was half-wild with need, and then started tracing a path downward, over her belly, over the damp, silken junction of her thighs.

"Dear God," she gasped, when he parted her, took her full into his mouth.

The result was an exquisitely ferocious pleasure, shattering, all-consuming; she began to move in a rhythm as old as humanity, and he stayed with her, granting her no quarter, driving her further and further into sweet madness. He seemed to sense when she was about to fly apart in his arms, and in those moments he withdrew, merely breathing upon her, whispering sexy, half-coherent promises. This happened several times, and just when Maggie thought she would lose her mind for all of time and eternity if he didn't satisfy her, he lowered her to the bed and poised himself over her.

He searched her face. "McCaffrey," he ground out, "it's cold out here. Can I come in?"

She answered by grasping his flanks in her hands, digging in her nails and pulling him toward her. He gave a low, hoarse cry of his own and plunged inside her in one stroke. She arched her back to receive him and, because she had been so close to the pinnacle as it was, she immediately tumbled into the heart of a slow, elemental explosion. Over and over, her body convulsed with a savage joy she'd never experienced before, not even with J.T., and he continued to love her all the while, whispering tender words as he carried her past the rooftops, past the sky itself, past the stars. When at last she began to drift back toward earth, catching on small, velvety spikes of ecstacy as she fell, J.T. finally gave in to his own need. Flexing upon her, causing her to spasm softly around him, he surrendered at last, and filled her with warmth. Long, luscious moments passed before he fell to her, exhausted.

They clung together, arms and legs entwined, breaths mingling, for what seemed like hours. Then their strength began to return.

J.T. straightened Maggie's sprawled limbs, mounted her, and made love to her again, this time with no foreplay at all. That second session was even more powerful than the first, and when it was over, they were both utterly spent. J.T. wrapped Maggie in his arms and held her, his face buried in her hair, and they slept.

"She's wonderful," Nelly said, when Purvis returned to the car after seeing Tillie inside. She'd enjoyed her birthday dinner at the Stagecoach Café, his mother had, and she'd be on the phone to all of her friends, first thing in the morning, boasting about the gold locket he'd given her.

Purvis gazed at Nelly, marveling at all she made him feel. "You're wonderful," he countered. He would have kissed her right then and there, but he was fairly sure his mother was looking out the window.

She smiled. "Thank you," she said.

"I guess you want to head home right away," he blustered, feeling like a fool because he didn't know what to say. He was just a middle-aged, cow-town cop, and he'd had limited experience with women, even though his blood was as red as any other guy's.

"Or not," she said quietly.

Purvis stared at her, mute as a mailbox, afraid to hope he'd understood her correctly.

She laughed. "What's the matter, Lawman?" she joked. "Are you worried about your reputation?"

Purvis doubted that he had a drop of spit left in his head. When he tried to speak it came out sounding like his throat had rusted over. "I—er—"

She laid a hand lightly on his thigh. Her expression was ingenuous, tender, and yet the sassy way she smiled made him hard as a flagpole. "I want to stay with you, Purvis," she said. "All night." She glanced down at his lap. "And it looks like you want pretty much the same thing."

"Believe me," he managed to say, "I do. But—"

She touched his face with the backs of her fingers, light as the pass of a bird's wing. "But?" she urged.

"I want you to be sure," he said. He'd never meant anything he'd said in his life as much as he meant that. "No regrets."

She shook her head. "No regrets," she said. "Take me to your place, Purvis."

He put the Escort in gear, his heart rising on a swell of happiness. "All right," he told her, and pulled away from the curb.

They almost made it, too. Would have been doing what came naturally in no time at all, if they'd taken another route, instead of driving past the jailhouse.

Reece McCaffrey was standing out front on the sidewalk, looking in one direction and then the other, and Purvis knew, without giving the matter more than a passing thought, that Reece was there to see him. He might have driven on past, if it had been anyone else, but there were few people Purvis liked or respected more than this one man. If Reece wanted to talk to him, there was a good reason.

Deflating like a pool toy with the air let out of it, Purvis pulled the Escort over to the side of the road and got out of the car. "Reece?" he said. "Is something wrong?"

Reece's face looked even more rugged than usual in the shadows of evening. He glanced toward the car and probably saw Nelly sitting there in the passenger seat. "I wanted to tell you myself," he said, "before the delegation shows up."

"Tell me what?" Purvis asked.

Reece heaved a sigh and looked about as reluctant as Purvis had ever seen a man look. "There was a special meeting of the town council tonight," he said, in that resonant baritone voice that was familiar to almost everybody in Springwater. "As you probably know, most of them are members of the Cattleman's Association. They voted to serve you notice, Purvis. As of the first of August, you're out of a job."

Purvis wasn't exactly surprised, but the news knocked the wind out of him for a few moments all the same. He just stood there on the sidewalk in front of his office and the jail, trying to absorb it.

"For what it's worth," Reece went on, "I put up an argument and voted to keep you on, but the motion carried." He slapped

Purvis's shoulder with a big, work-hardened hand. "I'm sorry."

Purvis found his voice at long last. "It's all right, Reece," he said, trying to sound like he meant it. "I've been thinking it was time for a change anyhow."

Reece gazed into Purvis's face, his somber eyes missing nothing, and then nodded. "I'd better get on home," he said, and attempted a smile of his own. "That redheaded woman of mine thinks I'm chasing around town with somebody else. I'd rather not add fuel to the fire by staying gone too long."

Purvis nodded, glancing toward the Escort. He could see Nelly peering through the windshield, her face pale in the darkness. Then he turned back to Reece. "Thanks for letting me know what's going on," he said. "I appreciate it."

"I'm real sorry," Reece reiterated. Then he crossed the road, got into that big RV of his, and drove off toward home.

Purvis's feet felt almost as heavy as his heart as he made his way back to the car, back to Nelly.

"What happened?" she asked.

Purvis sighed, staring straight ahead over

the top of the steering wheel. There was no easy way to say it. "I just lost my job," he replied, after a long struggle with the taut muscles in the back of his throat.

Nelly's fingers rested lightly on his forearm, but she didn't say anything, and that was fine with Purvis. If she'd tried to comfort him, he wasn't sure how he would have reacted.

"I'll take you home to Maple Creek," he said, starting the car.

She didn't protest.

Billy set his jaw along with the emergency brake in his beat-up old truck. The old cattle trail up behind J.T.'s place was awash in mud, since the creek had overflowed with the recent rains, and he'd be lucky if he didn't get stuck there. Lucky, he thought, with a rueful smile, if he didn't get the hell beat out of him, or worse.

Travis and Randy Hough were up ahead, in Odell's old Chevy, and though they must have known somebody was following them, they hadn't tried to shake him. He watched as they got out of the car and started back toward him.

He drew a deep breath, let it out slowly.

A truck rolled in behind him, blocking him in, and he shifted uncomfortably in the seat. He had his hunting rifle along with him, a thirty-thirty his dad had left behind fifteen years ago when he hit the road, looking for greener pastures. Billy didn't reach for the gun, but simply waited, his heartbeat thundering in his ears.

Nobody got out of the truck in back of him, but Randy Hough grabbed the handle on Billy's door and gave it a yank that made the whole cab rock on its wheels. Billy pulled up the old-fashioned lock and got out to face his half-brother's friend. Out of the corner of his eye he caught sight of Travis, but he couldn't make out his expression.

He cleared his throat, but before he could speak, Randy grabbed the front of his jacket in both hands and hurled him hard against the truck.

"What the *hell* are you doing here?" Hough demanded, forcing the words through his teeth. The headlights from the other truck raised a blinding glare and turned both Travis and Randy into looming shadows. When Billy didn't find his tongue right away, Randy rammed him against the steel door again. "Well?"

"Take it easy," he heard Travis say, but he sounded scared, and Billy didn't figure he was going to rush to the rescue anytime soon.

"What are you doing here?" Randy spat. "So help me God, if J. T. Wainwright shows up, or Purvis Digg—"

"They don't know anything about this," Billy said, in all truth. He was scared shitless, but by some miracle, his voice came out steady, almost normal sounding, at least in his own ears. "I came on my own."

"Why?" Travis asked.

With no warning at all, Randy landed a punch in the middle of Billy's gut, dropping him to his knees. "Yeah," Hough snarled. "Why?"

"Let him talk," Travis said. He was almost begging, and Billy was ashamed of him, and not just for the usual reasons.

Randy dragged Billy back to his feet by the front of his jacket. "Talk!" he rasped.

Billy gasped a couple of times before he caught his breath. Hough packed a hell of a punch. "J.T. doesn't pay me spit," he said.

"I want to get my hands on some real money."

"What makes you think we can do any-thing for you?" Randy barked.

Travis shoved his hands into the pockets of his jeans and said nothing.

"Just a hunch," Billy said. And that was the truth. He squinted toward into the glare of the headlights. "Who is that?"

"Nobody you need to know anything about," growled Randy. "I ought to break your neck, right here. Thanks to you, we're all as good as dead."

Just then, a door slammed, and Billy saw the shadow of a man moving toward them, a rifle dangling from his right hand. He was wearing a long coat and a western hat pulled down low over his face, but there was something familiar in his stride.

"Shit," Travis breathed.

"What—?" Billy began, but before he could frame the rest of the sentence, the shadow man cocked the rifle, aimed it from the hip, and fired.

Randy whirled away into the darkness like a dancer moving in slow motion, arms spread, flinging an arc of blood from his chest as he went. Travis let out a schoolgirl shriek and turned to flee, and another shot flared from the rifle barrel, sending him sprawling face first into the mud.

Billy had a few moments to think about Cindy and the baby she carried, and then the bullet came, tearing into his middle, setting off black fireworks inside his head, and he went down, feeling the cold steel of the truck door, even through his clothes, as he slid. He was all but blind with pain and shock, but he kept his eyes open, staring the way he'd seen men do in the movies. He caught a brief glimpse of his assailant, bending down to make sure he was dead, before he lost consciousness.

Cindy was in the kitchen, clad in gray socks and an old bathrobe, when J.T. let himself into the house early the next morning. Leaving Maggie behind in that warm bed had not been easy, sweet and supple and ready for more, but he was a rancher with stock to look after. The chores wouldn't wait.

J.T. picked up the carafe from the coffee machine, went to the sink, and started running water into it. "Something wrong?" he asked.

"Is Billy with you?"

He felt a pang of worry, glanced toward the backdoor, half-expecting and more than half hoping to see his youthful ranch hand step over the threshold. "No," he said. "I haven't seen him since we fed the cattle last night, down by the creek."

Tears brimmed in her eyes. Her blond hair was fastened on top of her head in some kind of plastic squeeze comb and, once again, he was struck by how young she was, and how pregnant, and how vulnerable to a world that tended to play rough. "He— he didn't come home."

J.T. poured the water into the machine and added coffee to the basket. If they'd been talking about just about anyone else, he wouldn't have been so concerned, but Billy Raynor was a conscientious husband and father-to-be, and if he hadn't turned up at home on time, there was a good chance that something was very wrong. "Maybe he spent the night at his mom's place," he said. It was a lame suggestion, but all he could come up with at the moment.

She shook her head. "No," she said. "We

didn't have a fight. And he would have called me anyway."

J.T. folded his arms and leaned one hip against the counter while he waited for the coffee to brew. "I'll go out looking for him," he replied, "as soon as I've taken care of the chores."

She nodded, but she was still pale, and her eyes were wider than ever.

"If you have any theories," J.T. urged gently, "I'd like to hear them."

She opened her mouth, closed it again. Then one hand went to rest protectively on her belly, and J.T. felt a rush of sympathy for her as tears filled her eyes again. "He might have gotten tangled up with my brother Randy and that bunch he hangs out with."

"What bunch would that be?" J.T. asked calmly, though he felt a leap of instinct in the core of his gut. He also remembered the conversation he'd had with Billy a few days back. Billy suspected DuPres and Hough of setting the barn fire, and he'd made noises about doing some detective work. J.T. had warned him off, but that didn't mean the kid had listened.

"I don't know," Cindy said miserably.

Just then the telephone rang and, for a fraction of a second, J.T. was afraid to answer. Then, thinking of Quinn, away from home for the night, and Maggie, possibly suffering from self-recriminations concerning the wild night the two of them had just passed in her bed, he reached for the receiver.

"J.T.?"

Alarm shot through J.T.'s insides at the sound of Purvis's voice. It was, for all intents and purposes, the middle of the night, and the town marshal was calling him, his only deputy. That could not be good. "What is it?"

A sigh. "Something's happened, J.T. Randy Hough and Travis DuPres are dead of gunshot wounds, and Billy Raynor is on his way to the hospital in Maple Creek by ambulance. He's barely holding on."

J.T. looked at Cindy, knew she'd somehow guessed the essentials, and stretched the phone cord to its limit to catch her by the arm before her knees buckled. He pressed her into a chair and went to the sink to get her a glass of water. Although she wasn't making a sound, there was no color at all in her face, and she began to rock back and forth, her cheeks glistening.

He stood with a hand resting firmly on her shoulder. "Who called in the report?" he asked.

"Billy," Purvis said wearily. "God knows how he managed it, but he got hold of Hough's cell phone somehow and called 911. He didn't say anything, just made some noises, but they were able to run a trace. The sheriff called me, and I met him and his deputies at the scene. It's bad, J.T."

"Have you called Doris?"

Cindy looked up at J.T.'s question, and he tightened his grip because her eyes rolled back in her head and she started to pitch forward.

"That's next on my list," Purvis said. "You'll tell Cindy?"

"I think she knows," J.T. replied gruffly. "Look, we're heading for the hospital. You've got my cell number?"

"Yeah," Purvis answered. "I'll catch up to you later."

"Right," J.T. said, and hung up.

"Billy," Cindy whispered.

J.T. crouched, gripping both her hands in his, and looked into her ravaged face. Unfortunately, the bad news went further. He had to tell her that her brother was dead, as was Travis DuPres. Like everybody else in Springwater, J.T. knew that DuPres was the father of her baby. "He was shot tonight," he said, and imagined someone saying those words to Doreen, after Murphy was killed in that warehouse.

"Is he dead?" Her voice was heartbreakingly small.

J.T. shook his head. "No," he said. And then added quickly, before the spark of hope he saw in her eyes could flare up into something bigger, "But he's not in good shape, Cindy. And there's something else. Something pretty terrible."

She straightened her spine, waited.

There was no kind way to say it. "Your brother Randy was shot, too, and so was Travis DuPres. I'm sorry, Cindy."

She made a small, mewling sound, then bit her lower lip and braced herself up, drawing on an inner strength J.T. hadn't guessed she had. He felt an ache of admiration for her.

"I'll get dressed," she said. "You'll take me to the hospital, won't you? To see Billy?"

"Of course," he said, choked up.

She nodded, got to her feet, and swayed. "I'm—I'm all right," she insisted, when J.T. reached out for her again, afraid she'd fall.

Less than ten minutes later they were in J.T.'s truck on their way to the next town. Cindy stared blindly out the window and said nothing at all, while J.T. drove as fast as he dared. He was painfully conscious that Cindy could go into premature labor at any moment, from shock if not from bouncing over rutted country roads, and there was already tragedy enough in their little family, with Billy dead, or dying, years before his time.

The telephone was ringing. Maggie raised herself onto one elbow, the memory of the night just past aching in every muscle and cell, and she groaned as she groped for the receiver. Sadie bounded through the open doorway and landed on the bed, thirty pounds of exuberant beagle.

"Hello?" Maggie managed. She felt hungover, though she hadn't had anything to drink. No, indeed, she and J.T. had never even eaten the pizza he'd brought, nor had they watched the rented movie. Instead, they'd gone straight to bed, practically shedding their clothes as they went down the hall.

The answer was a soft, gasplike sob.

"Hello?" Maggie said again, sitting up straight now, every instinct on red alert.

"She's back." It was Daphne's voice.

"Who's back?" she asked, though even as the words left her mouth, she knew what her friend's answer would be.

"Tiffany's mother."

Maggie hoisted the dog to one side and kicked her way out of the tangled sheets and blankets. The fresh-air-and-musk scent of J.T. rose from the linens to taunt her. "Oh, Daph," she said.

Daphne sniffled, and Maggie knew she was trying to smile. "I know what you're thinking. It's a good thing, not a bad one. And you're right, it is—but—"

"That isn't what I was going to say at all," Maggie protested softly. "Who is this woman? Where has she been?"

Another sniffle. "She's not a woman, she's a girl, like Cindy," Daphne said. "Just seventeen. She and her boyfriend—Tiffany's father—were driving across country, hoping to find work along the way, and they got into a big fight at the rest stop, and he went off and left her and the baby there. She saw the older couple in the RV pull in and—I don't know what she was thinking— but she apparently believed Tiffany would be better off with them. So she wrote the baby's name on her little hand and hid—" Daphne's voice fell away into another sob, but it didn't matter. Maggie knew what she'd been going to say.

"I'll be right over," she said. "Is Ben there?"

"He must have gone to work early," Daphne said. "The phone woke me up—it was the Social Services people—"

"Do you want me to call him?"

"I've already done that. He wasn't in the office, so I left a message."

Maggie was already partially dressed. "Daph, we can handle this."

"Oh, Maggie, they're coming for Tiffany," Daphne said, as though she hadn't spoken, breaking down again. "They're going to take her away."

"Hold on," Maggie ordered. Less than five minutes later, after giving her teeth a quick brushing, washing her face, and finger combing her short hair, she was standing on Daphne's porch, ringing the bell.

* * *

"Another murder?" Kathleen said, horrified. She stared at her estranged husband, who stood in their kitchen, next to the counter, pouring a cup of tea for her. It was an incongruous sight, Reece performing such a delicate task, but he was actually quite graceful at it. He'd evidently come back from his morning walk while she was still in the shower and, as usual, he'd managed to garner all the night's news over coffee at the Stagecoach Café.

"Randy Hough and Travis DuPres are both dead," he said. "Shot to death. Worse, Billy Raynor was badly wounded. He may not survive."

Kathleen pressed a hand to her mouth. She didn't know Billy well, but she'd gotten acquainted with Cindy, his young wife, who worked over at the Springwater Station with Maggie. "That's dreadful," she whispered, feeling sick.

Reece drew back a chair and sank into it. "What's this world coming to?" he asked, speaking as much to himself as to Kathleen, it seemed. "Springwater used to be a safe place—"

Kathleen reached out, rather shakily, and

touched his hand. "What in God's name happened?"

"Purvis says Billy called for help on a cell phone. Nobody knows who the shooter was, but it happened on J. T. Wainwright's ranch."

"J.T. didn't hear anything? See anyone?"

Reece met her gaze squarely. "J.T. was at the Station most of the night," he said. "With Maggie."

Kathleen absorbed the implications of that. "Oh," she said. Their fingers inter-locked, probably out of old habit, and they didn't pull apart. "Then—"

They knew each other so well that she didn't have to finish the sentence, and he could answer with just one word. Reece nodded. "Yes," he said.

"How did you happen to—I mean—"

"I went looking for Purvis after the town council meeting last night, and I saw J.T.'s truck parked at the Station. When I drove past again, on my way back here, the truck was still there and all the lights were out." He paused. "I heard about the murders at the café this morning. Purvis was there, with a lot of people from the sheriff's depart-ment, and he told me what happened."

"It—it sort of puts things into perspective, doesn't it?" Kathleen said quietly, almost shyly, "when something like this happens, I mean."

Reece nodded. Then, seeing that Kathleen was crying, he drew her out of her chair and onto his lap, pressing her head against his broad shoulder. She wept noisily for a long time and got his shirt all wet, and he just sat there, patting her back.

"Did you cheat on me, Reece McCaffrey?" she demanded, after a long time.

He kissed her temple. His breath was warm in her hair. "No," he said.

She couldn't imagine life without him. Didn't even want to try. "But you've been writing to that Abigail woman. She sent you a birthday card. You didn't even try to hide it, either!"

He smiled. "That's because I had nothing to hide."

Kathleen folded her arms. "That's what Helen's husband said," she reminded him.

"I'm not Helen's husband," he replied. "Thank God." He paused, stroked her cheek with one fingertip, setting off all the old, fiery reactions. "Would you like to meet Abigail?" he asked.

"Why would I want to do that?" Kathleen snapped.

He shrugged those powerful shoulders. "Just a good deed," he said. "She's ninety-four years old and doesn't get many callers in the nursing home. I stopped in a couple of times when I was in Missoula on business."

Kathleen opened her mouth, closed it. "I thought—"

He grinned *that* grin, the one she had no real defenses against. "I know what you thought," he said. He caught her chin between a calloused thumb and forefinger and looked deep into her eyes. "I met Abigail in a travel chat room. She's a pistol, and if she were oh, say, forty years younger, she might give you a run for your money, Kathleen McCaffrey."

She sighed, sniffled. "I suppose I could blame my hormones," she said. "At least, in part."

He chuckled, kissed her lightly. "In part," he agreed. "Still, we've got some real problems, or this kind of misunderstanding couldn't have happened. It'll take time and effort to work them through."

She nodded, sniffled again. "We'll get counseling," she said.

"Yes," he agreed. "And maybe a new perspective wouldn't hurt, either."

She narrowed her eyes, stiffened a little. "You're talking about going traveling in that rolling sin-mobile," she said.

He waggled his eyebrows at her. "I am," he replied.

The idea of being alone with this man, her husband, in a bedroom on wheels, was not without a certain appeal. "We could come back to Springwater—on a regular basis?"

He kissed the tip of her nose. "Of course we will, Kathy," he said. "I love our children and this house as much as you do. We'll give life on the road a try, and if we find we don't care to be roving gypsies, we'll come back here and sell the RV. Fair enough?"

She considered the matter. "Fair enough," she said.

He kissed her again, this time on the mouth, and lingeringly. "Let's go upstairs and celebrate," he said.

A hot shiver of anticipation went through her. It had been a while since she and Reece had made love. "Celebrate?" she asked, thinking of all the tragedy that had struck Springwater, lately and long ago. "What are we celebrating?"

He smiled, smoothed her hair. "Being alive," he said. "Being together. Making a new start."

She nodded, her eyes filled with tears, and they stood. When the doorbell rang half an hour later, neither one of them heard a thing.

14

Daphne's eyes were swollen from crying, but Maggie could see that her friend was doing her best to be strong. As soon as she stepped over the threshold she put her arms around Daphne and hugged her tightly, and Sadie whimpered in sympathy, sensing that something was wrong, trying to lick Daphne's hand. Glancing down at the dog, Daphne gave a sniffly laugh.

"Come in," she said. "Both of you."

Maggie and Sadie followed as Daphne led the way into her kitchen, where Tiffany was seated in her playpen, still in her pajamas, happily engaged with a baby doll. Seeing Sadie, she gave a crow of delight, and Sadie greeted her small friend with a cheerful yip, then stood on her hind legs next to the playpen and whined to be let in.

"Down," Maggie commanded distractedly, and Sadie dropped to her belly with a sigh, whined once, and lay watching Tiffany with the beatific gaze of a saint in the throes of martyrdom.

Daphne went to the sink, washed her hands, dried them hastily, and then poured coffee for herself and Maggie. Maggie took a place at the table. Her bones and muscles still felt as though they'd been liquified by the slow heat of J.T.'s lovemaking, and it shamed her a little, feeling so good when her best friend was obviously suffering.

"I guess Ben will be here soon," she said. Under other circumstances, she would have confided in her friend that she'd spent the night with J.T., shared her doubts and misgivings, as well as her tentative hopes, but for now she was concerned only with her friend's well-being.

Daphne nodded. "Maybe not before the social worker arrives with Tiffany's mother, though," she said. Her voice caught, but she maintained her composure. "This is so hard."

Maggie cupped her hands around the mug of coffee Daphne had placed before her, glanced at the beautiful, contented child playing nearby. "Maybe they won't give Tiffany back to the mother," she said, *sotto voce.* "After all, the woman *did* abandon her at a rest stop."

Daphne sat across from Maggie, looking at the little girl intently, as though memorizing her face and form, storing the images away in her heart and mind. "We don't know the whole story yet," she said softly. "And the girl is very young—only seventeen. She can be forgiven for a lapse in judgment." She paused, dabbed at her eye with the back of one hand. "If it's at all possible, Tiffany needs to be with her mother."

Just then they heard an engine in the driveway, followed by the slamming of a door and hasty footsteps mounting the steps of the back porch. Moments later, Ben burst in, looking quietly frantic. He glanced in Tiffany's direction, nodded a greeting to Maggie.

Daphne got up and launched herself into his arms, and it seemed to Maggie that his embrace was a little stiff. His eyes, as he looked over his wife's shoulder at Maggie, held an odd expression, cool and almost detached.

"What's going on?" he asked, drawing back to look into Daphne's face.

"Tiffany's mother is back," Daphne answered.

Maggie looked away, feeling as though she were intruding, as though she should leave, but she knew Daphne wanted her there, needed her support, so she stayed.

"Oh, honey," Ben murmured, his hands cupping Daphne's face. "I'm sorry."

Daphne looked back at Tiffany, still playing, and straightened her spine. Just then, the doorbell rang. For a moment, all of time seemed to freeze; nobody moved, nobody spoke, nobody even breathed, or so it seemed from Maggie's perspective. Even little Tiffany went still at the sound.

"I'll get it," Ben said.

"We'll both go," Daphne replied.

Maggie didn't speak. It was tacitly understood that she and Tiffany and Sadie would remain where they were, in that spacious, familiar kitchen. Always a safe place, it seemed strangely isolated now, an outpost under attack by hostile forces, with walls that might or might not hold.

There were voices, more footsteps. Presently, the swinging door leading into the dining room opened, and Daphne and Ben came through, followed by a round woman with an old-fashioned pompadour, friendly eyes, and bright pink cheeks. Behind her trailed a slender young woman with a single dark braid trailing down her back, enormous blue eyes agog as she took in her surroundings.

The instant her gaze fell on Tiffany, the girl's face was alight with joy and relief. Clad in blue jeans, a worn T-shirt, and sneakers that had seen better days, the teenage mother crossed the room in a few strides. Tiffany, seeing her, clambered to her feet and cried, "Mommy!"

Maggie's eyes filled as she watched the two clinging to each other, and she couldn't quite bring herself to look at Daphne and Ben.

"This is Susan," the social worker said. "Susan Collins, Tiffany's mother. My name is Elizabeth Anderson." She produced a card, but no one took it, so she slipped it back into the pocket of her tidy blazer.

Out of the corner of her eye, Maggie saw that Daphne was leaning against Ben's side,

her expression a study in mixed emotions—
sorrow because she was about to lose the
child she had already come to love, and joy
because it was so obvious that, in spite of
everything, Susan and Tiffany belonged together.

Holding Tiffany tightly in her arms, Susan
turned to look at Daphne and Ben. "Thank
you," she whispered. "Thank you for taking
such good care of my baby."

Daphne's mouth moved, but no sound
came out. Maggie wasn't paying attention
to Ben; if he reacted, she didn't notice.

Maggie got to her feet. "Maybe I
should—"

"Stay," Daphne pleaded. "Please, Maggie."

Maggie sat down again. Ms. Anderson
assessed the situation and apparently came
to a conclusion. "I realize that this is awkward," she said. She drew back a chair at
the table. "May I?"

"Please," Daphne said.

The social worker dropped into the seat
as though she'd just climbed the stone
steps of some ancient and massive cathe-
dral, set her briefcase on the table with a
clunk, and snapped the latches. Slowly,

Daphne, Ben, and Susan all came to take places of their own. Sadie lumbered over and laid her chin on Maggie's knee with a worried little snort.

"Well," Ms. Anderson said, taking reading glasses from the briefcase and putting them on with practiced efficiency, "Springwater is certainly making a name for itself these days, and I can't say it's a good one."

Maggie assumed she was referring to the Clive Jenson murder, and felt a little defensive—it simply wasn't fair to judge the whole town by that one incident—but she kept her opinion to herself.

Ben glanced at Daphne. "I guess you haven't heard," he said.

"Heard what?" Daphne asked.

Maggie stroked Sadie's soft head, more for her own comfort than the dog's, and waited.

Ben looked rueful. "There was another killing last night," he said, lowering his voice, presumably for Tiffany's benefit, although she and Susan had eyes and ears only for each other and were oblivious to the rest of them. "Randy Hough was shot to death, along with Travis DuPres. Billy Raynor was critically injured."

Maggie felt the color drain from her face, and immediately clapped a hand over her mouth to keep from crying out. What must Cindy be going through?

"Oh, my God," Daphne breathed. "That's awful. What happened? Does anyone know why—?"

Ben shook his head. "That's all I know about it, honey. What I heard this morning when I stopped by the Stagecoach Café for coffee and a sweet roll."

"Time was, this was a peaceful town," Ms. Anderson observed.

"It's still a good place," Maggie heard herself say.

"Whatever," said the other woman in a dismissive tone, clearly ready to get on with it and move on to the next crisis.

Maggie felt her mouth tighten, but she didn't answer.

"What—what about Tiffany?" Daphne ventured.

Ms. Anderson looked at Susan, who sat stiffly in her chair now, clutching her child as though she expected someone to yank her out of her arms. "Perhaps you should explain a few things, my dear."

Susan swallowed pitifully. She was a

pretty girl, though it was easy to see that life had been a struggle for her, probably from day one. "I love Tiffany," she said, and suddenly her lovely eyes were glazed with desperate tears, "but I can't take good care of her. Dylan—that's my boyfriend—he's fed up with both of us. Says we're nothing but trouble. So I figure it will be better if—if Tiffany stays right here—"

Everyone except Ms. Anderson and, of course, the baby, looked surprised.

Susan stroked her daughter's curly hair with one hand. "I'd like to visit sometimes," she said, addressing herself to Daphne, "if you'd allow that."

If Daphne had been the selfish type, she probably would have been pleased by this development, but she was generous to the core. "What about you, Susan?" she asked. "Where will you go?"

Susan tried to smile, and the sight was heartbreaking under the circumstances. Tiffany settled against her chest, gave a shuddering little sigh, and closed her eyes. "I want to finish high school and join the air force," she said. "I could travel and even go to college—"

No one spoke for a while.

"And Tiffany?" Daphne ventured, finally.

Ben glanced at his wife, though his face revealed nothing of what he was thinking or feeling.

Ms. Anderson's expression was noncommital, perhaps a bit wary.

"I want to adopt her," Daphne insisted. If anyone besides Maggie noticed that she'd said "I" instead of "we," nobody said anything. "Legally."

"I don't know what to say," Susan murmured.

"Say yes," Daphne urged.

"Daphne—" Ben began, but she ignored him. The social worker, on the other hand, was watching him with interest.

"Maybe you'd like to know a little more about Susan before you extend an offer like that," the woman said. "Tell them why you left Tiffany at the rest area, Susan."

Crimson circles appeared in Susan's cheeks. "Dylan was real mad. I knew he'd be back, and I was afraid he'd hurt Tiffany. I saw those older people drive up in an RV and get out to stretch their legs—they were laughing and they had these two little dogs they seemed to love a lot and, well, I knew if they found Tiffany wandering around and thought she was alone, they'd see that she was kept safe. So I hid and they took her, just like I thought they would." A tear trickled down Susan's face. "I was right about Dylan, too. He came back and I told him what happened to Tiffany, and he said good riddance."

Everyone was silent. The child slept blissfully against her mother's bosom, one plump little hand still clinging to Susan's braid.

"We got as far as Missoula," Susan went on. She sounded shell-shocked, and she stared into space as though watching herself and Dylan in some mental movie. "I couldn't stand it anymore. Not knowing if Tiffany was really all right, I mean. So I told him we were through, and I hitched back to Maple Creek and asked around until I found out where the welfare office was."

"You understand," Ms. Anderson said to Susan, "that you could be charged with reckless abandonment, among other things?"

Maggie knew by Susan's expression that she and Ms. Anderson had already had this conversation.

"Yes," the girl said miserably.

"What about this Dylan person?" Daphne asked. "Is he a danger to you or Tiffany?"

Susan bit her lower lip, then shook her head. "He's glad to be shut of us. We won't see him again."

"You don't have any family to turn to?" Ben put in. His tone was gruff.

Susan shook her head again. "I grew up in foster homes, and so did Dylan. That's how we met, as a matter of fact. Tiffany and me, we're on our own." Her face contorted with emotion, and she held the baby a little closer. "I love my daughter, you've got to understand that. I love her so much, sometimes I think I'll die of it, and leaving her is going to be the hardest thing I've ever done, but I can't take good care of her, and I know it. I don't want her growing up the way I did, going from one place to another all the time. Never knowing what the next people are going to be like. I want to leave her right here, and I'll sign papers."

Maggie's heart ached for the child, for her troubled young mother, for Daphne, but half her mind was with Cindy, and poor, sweet Billy, who might be dying, or already dead. Where, she wondered, was J.T.? Did he know what had happened? Was he with Cindy, keeping a vigil in some hospital? And what about Quinn? He'd spent the night out at the Kildares'. Would he be coming home to an empty house? She frowned, feeling more anxious with every passing moment.

"You can visit whenever you want," Daphne said, addressing Susan. "And Tiffany will have a permanent home, right here in Springwater. If Ms. Anderson and the courts agree, of course."

"What about me?" Ben asked reasonably. "Don't I have to agree?"

Ms. Anderson focused all her professional attention on Ben and waited, while Daphne looked at her husband as if she'd forgotten he was there.

"Maybe we should talk about this alone," she said.

"Maybe you should," Ms. Anderson agreed, raising her eyebrows and puckering her mouth.

Maggie got to her feet, touched Daphne's shoulder as she passed. "I've got to get in touch with J.T.," she said. "Call if you need me."

Daphne patted her friend's hand. "Thanks, Mags," she said. "I will."

Five minutes later, having spoken to Purvis when she didn't get an answer at J.T.'s place, Maggie was headed for the hospital in Maple Creek.

J.T. leaned against the wall outside the intensive care unit at Maple Creek Memorial, read the Kildares' telephone number off the paper he'd scribbled it on, and punched the digits with the tip of one index finger. Shannon Kildare answered on the second ring, and J.T. briefly explained where he was and why before asking to speak with Quinn.

"Hello, Dad?"

J.T. closed his eyes, struck to the heart by the simple joy of hearing his son's voice. "Hi, bud," he managed, after a few moments of effort.

"Is everything O.K.?"

It amazed him that a little kid could be so perceptive. He smiled grimly. "I'm okay," he said, putting a slight emphasis on the first word. "Something happened to Billy, though, and Cindy and I are here at the hospital with him."

"What about Billy? Is he sick? Did he get hurt?"

J.T. shut his eyes again, and when he

opened them, Maggie was coming toward him, an angel in blue jeans and a lightweight navy sweater. She came immediately to his side and he automatically put an arm around her.

"Dad?" Quinn pressed, his voice shaky. "Tell me about Billy."

He was making an effort to be brave. It hurt J.T. to know that, even as it stirred a flicker of pride. He squeezed McCaffrey against his side, took comfort in the simple warmth and nearness of her. "Billy was shot," he said, knowing the buttons that would push in Quinn, the traumatic memories it would bring up.

"I want to see you," Quinn said.

"Bud—"

"I need to see you, Dad."

"I told you, Q., I'm all right. Can you trust me on this?"

Maggie made an inquiring gesture, and J.T. handed her the receiver. "Quinn?" The sound of her voice was reassuring to J.T., and he hoped it was having the same effect on his son. "This is Maggie. I'm here at the hospital. Yep, I'm standing right next to him. Suppose I come out to the Kildares', pick you up, and bring you here so you can see for yourself that your dad is just fine? Then you and I could go back to the Station and hang out. What do you say?" She looked up at J.T. as she listened to Quinn's reply, then smiled. "Sure," she finished. "Assuming all this is O.K. with the head office, I'll be there in forty-five minutes or so." She waited, raising her eyebrows, and J.T. nodded his assent. "Here he is," she finished, handing back the receiver.

J.T. reassured Quinn as best he could, said good-bye, and hung up.

"How bad is it with Billy?" Maggie asked. Her eyes, so bright and confident while she was speaking to his son, were wide now, and haunted.

He drew her against his chest and held her loosely for a few moments before replying. "He's hanging on. That's about all."

She slipped her arms around his waist, tilted her head back to look into his eyes. "Are they going to perform surgery?"

J.T. sighed. "Maybe tomorrow," he said, his voice a rasp. "If he makes it that far. Right now he's not strong enough to stand an operation."

"And Cindy?"

"Hanging in there. She's a tough kid, but a kid all the same."

"Has her father been called?"

"You'd have to ask Purvis about that. Odell hasn't turned up around here, but that's not surprising. He lost a son last night. Maybe that's as much as he can deal with right now."

"Maybe," McCaffrey agreed, but she was frowning, and she pulled out of his arms. "I'd like to see Cindy before I go back to Springwater to get Quinn."

He nodded. "I'm staying here as long as I can, but I'll need to go home sooner or later to feed the livestock." He thrust a hand through his hair, sighed again. "God, Mc-Caffrey, I hate this. I hate knowing that some bastard shot Billy down in cold blood, I hate that my kid is scared—"

She brushed the backs of her fingers along his jawline. J.T. was used to handling things on his own, and the tenderness of the gesture was almost more than he could bear. "Me, too," she said. "Me, too. You were telling Quinn the truth, weren't you? You really are O.K.?"

He kissed her forehead. "I was beginning

to wonder until you showed up, McCaffrey. Thanks."

She smiled sadly. It was all the acknowledgment he needed. "Where's Cindy?" she asked.

"She can only spend five minutes out of every hour in with Billy," he said. "She's probably in the waiting room."

Maggie nodded, turned, walked away.

J.T. watched until she disappeared through the doorway. Then he turned back to the telephone and dialed another number. "Purvis," he said. "Have you come up with anything yet?"

Maggie watched through the broad window framing the ICU where Billy lay, hooked up to tubes and wires. He was on a respirator, and the very slight up-and-down motion of his chest was painful to watch. Cindy bent over him, smoothed his hair, kissed him lightly, tenderly on top of the head. When she straightened, her gaze locked with Maggie's. She pressed her hands to the small of her back and stretched, her physical discomfort showing in every line of her body.

Maggie waggled her fingers in greeting

and tried hard to smile, and Cindy nodded in response, then shuffled slowly out into the hallway. She held out her arms, and Cindy came into them without hesitation. A sob wrenched itself from Cindy's throat, and she clung to Maggie, trembling in her arms.

"Oh, God, Maggie," she said. "He doesn't move. He can't breathe on his own. And his chest—"

"Shhh," Maggie whispered. "What about you, Cindy? How are you feeling—physically, I mean? You look positively worn out—"

"The baby's been kicking a lot—" Again, that fragile, fall-away attempt at a smile. "It's as if he knows something terrible has happened."

Maggie gripped the girl's shoulders. "I know you don't want to leave Billy," she said, "but you need to have something to eat and get some rest."

"There's no one else to stay with him—"

"J.T. is here," Maggie pointed out. She frowned as a thought struck her. "What about Billy's mother? Have you seen or heard from Doris yet?"

"She'll be making arrangements for Travis, I suppose," Cindy said, in a dull, disassociated voice. "I suppose my dad is busy doing the same for Randy." Her eyes grew very round, and a dry, strangled sob escaped her. "Do—do you believe in God, Maggie?"

Maggie nodded. "Yes. Yes, I do."

"Will you pray for Billy? For all of us?"

She thought of Daphne and Ben, of little Tiffany and her mother, Susan. Of Travis DuPres and Randy Hough, and those they had left behind. Of her parents, and their shaky marriage, of her brother, Wes, and sister-in-law, Franny, and the baby they were expecting. Of J.T. and Quinn, and Purvis, poor beleaguered Purvis, a lame-duck marshal with a job termination hanging over his head, still in there doing his best. There was a lot of praying to be done. "Yes," she said, squeezing Cindy's hands in her own. "If you won't go home, will you at least lie down and rest a while? For Billy's sake as well as your own and the baby's? When—" her throat caught, "when he wakes up, it's important that both of you are safe and well."

Cindy laid her hands on her stomach in a tender, protective gesture. She bit her lower lip, nodded again. "I'll ask the nurses if there's a place I can stretch out."

"I'll ask," Maggie said, taking Cindy's arm gently and ushering her in the direction of the nurses' station. "When was the last time you had anything to eat?"

"I guess last night—I can't really remember—"

"I'll send J.T. for something. Eat what you can and *rest,* Cindy. It's important—very important—that you take good care of yourself, especially now."

Cindy nodded and, after a brief conversation with a sympathetic nurse, allowed herself to be led to an empty room where she could lie down for a while. After dispatching J.T. to the cafeteria for a cup of soup and some tea for Cindy, and something for himself as well, Maggie hurried back to her car.

She ran into Wes and Franny in the parking lot.

"Looks like you're about to become an aunt again," Wes said. Franny, clinging to her husband's arm, smiled wanly.

"It won't be long," she said.

"The neighbor is watching Jodi and Loren," Wes said. "We tried to drop them off at Mom and Dad's, but nobody answered the bell."

"My mother is having a root canal," Franny explained. "She waited six weeks for the appointment." She winced as a labor pain struck her with visible force. "Mrs. Taggart is a very nice woman," she added, at no small cost, "but she's really too old to look after small children."

Maggie smiled, feeling a little dizzy, what with all that was happening. Truly, when it rained, it poured. "I'll stop by home on my way through Springwater and see if Mom and Dad are around. If not, I'll pick up Jodi and Loren myself and look after them as long as necessary. Don't worry, either of you. Just concentrate on bringing that new baby into the world."

Wes grinned a nervous, grateful grin, and urged Franny on toward the hospital entrance. "Thanks, Sis," he called back.

Maggie sprinted to the Pathfinder.

Odell stared at the body of his son, lying gray-blue on a metal table at the county morgue in the basement of Maple Creek Memorial, and felt a sick rage rising up inside him. Until this moment, when he'd actually laid eyes on what was left of his boy, he'd fooled himself into believing that there was some mistake. Now there was no denying the truth: Randy was dead.

Purvis stood beside him. "I'm sorry, Odell," he said.

Odell didn't speak. Couldn't speak. Couldn't even look away from Randy's cold, rigid face.

"The DuPres kid is dead, too. And your son-in-law is close to it. He's upstairs, in the ICU. I reckon your girl would be mighty glad to see you about now."

Odell cared about his daughter, in his way, but Randy had been his only son. His boy. A red haze blurred his vision.

"I know you're in bad shape right now," Purvis went on quietly, "and I sure don't blame you for that. We're going to nail whoever did this, Odell. But if there's any way you can help, if you know anything at all—"

He knew all right. He knew. But he would be damned if he'd let the liberal courts handle the matter, damned to hellfire forever if he'd see the son-of-a-bitch who'd done this sent to some cushy country-club prison, if he went to jail at all, where he could play tennis, write books, and earn himself an advanced degree. No, sir, Odell Hough would make sure that justice was done. He'd see to it personally. For Randy, for his lost Mary Lee, for all of them.

He wasn't fool enough to say all that to Purvis, though. He shook his head once, and Purvis let it go at that.

A woman's shriek of grief came from a nearby room.

Purvis heaved a sigh. "That'll be Doris," he said sadly. "I'd better see if she's got anything to tell me."

Odell didn't answer. He didn't give a damn, at the moment, about anybody else's sorrows. He was consumed by his own.

Purvis slapped him on the back. "If you think of something," he said, "you know where to find me."

All Odell could come up with was a hoarse grunt. Purvis could take it anyway he wanted, Odell didn't care. He stood there by Randy until they made him go away. The pain was beyond bearing; he went outside, crossed the lot, and got into his old truck. Then he headed for the nearest liquor store.

*   *   *

Billy saw the man with the rifle standing over him, and even though he felt as if he were lying crushed beneath two tons of jagged stone, he still had the strength to be afraid. He wasn't sure where he was—one moment, it seemed like he was safe in a hospital someplace, the next, he was on the ground beside his truck, bleeding to death. Either way, he was hurting more than he ever had before.

"Don't," he whispered. "Please—don't—"

He heard a sweet voice, an angel's voice. Felt a whisper-soft kiss brush his forehead. "Billy, don't leave us. Don't leave the baby and me. We need you. We love you."

He felt a flutter of recognition, but it was quickly gone. He thought the angel touched him again, just as he slipped under the surface of light, into the darkness.

Maggie and Quinn arrived with a bag of what smelled like hamburgers, a fresh set of clothes, and his shaving kit. J.T. dropped to one knee and opened his arms, and Quinn ran into his embrace, clinging. Maggie smiled over the boy's head, and J.T. thought there was a glaze of tears in her eyes. Or were they in his own?

He kissed his son on the cheek and stood, still holding the boy.

"Thanks, McCaffrey," he said.

She merely nodded. Held out the bag of burgers. He took it; he'd gone down to the cafeteria and brought back some food for Cindy, as instructed, but he'd forgotten to get anything for himself. He carried Quinn into the nearby waiting room and sat, opening the bag with one hand, taking out a burger, unwrapping it.

"How did you know I wanted pure lard?" he asked, grinning at Maggie.

She chuckled. "Just a hunch," she said. "I'm sorry about the delay—I planned to be back sooner. Franny—Wes's wife—is here, in the maternity ward."

J.T. finished one burger and reached for another. Quinn didn't slacken his hold, and his face was buried in J.T.'s neck. "Wow," he said. "Sounds like you've had your hands full."

Maggie sat down, helped herself to an artery-buster from the burger bag, and began to eat. "How's Billy?"

"No change," J.T. said.

She sighed. "Cindy?"

"Sleeping. Dr. Parrish stopped by,

checked her over, and gave her a light sedative."

"This is awful."

J.T. managed a semblance of a smile. "As burgers go—"

She shook her head. "Lame joke, Wainwright," she said.

He shrugged. "Best I could do on short notice," he replied.

Quinn began to relax. "We stopped at Maggie's mom and dad's house," he said, eyeing the bag of food with encouraging interest.

"Wes and Franny wanted them to take care of the kids," Maggie explained.

"They were with a neighbor," Quinn added importantly, rifling the grub. "But she's old and would probably let them play in the street or light matches."

J.T. raised his brows and widened his eyes at this.

Maggie smiled. "He's quoting my mother. She was a bit agitated." She paused. "And in her glory at being needed."

"We all like to be needed," J.T. observed.

Quinn took a hamburger, unwrapped it from its greasy paper, and chowed down.

Maggie studied J.T. solemnly. "Yes," she said slowly. "We do."

He was quiet after that, digesting more than the hamburgers.

～ 15 ～

That evening the reporters came back to town in a horde, drawn by the latest rash of murders. Headlines flashed across the wire services. "Small Community Erupts in Violence," one trumpeted. "Crime Rampant in Historic Frontier Town," another blared.

Maggie, standing in line at the supermarket with Quinn beside her and a cart full of groceries to feed the newly arrived lodgers, felt an almost overwhelming sadness. What, she wondered, was happening to Springwater? What was happening to America?

Quinn looked up at her. "Can we call the hospital when we get back to the Station and talk to my dad?"

Maggie ruffled his hair. "Sure," she said gently. Just then, someone called her name. She looked up and saw Daphne standing nearby, pushing Tiffany in a stroller.

"Hi," Maggie said, leaving the cart in Quinn's care to approach her friend.

"Any news about Billy?" Daphne asked quietly.

Maggie shook her head. "J.T. and Cindy are with him. They'll call if there's any change." She smiled down at Tiffany, who was trying to stuff her doll's head into her mouth. Given that the toy was nearly as big as she was, this represented a challenge.

"Tiffany will be staying on with us for a while," Daphne announced. "We're here to pick up some necessities." A smile quirked her mouth. "Like pizza."

"It's nice to be reminded that life goes on," Maggie said, with a rather wan smile. "Franny checked into the maternity ward earlier today. She's been in labor all this time, poor thing."

Daphne nodded toward Quinn and the cart he was guarding so dutifully. "That's a lot of food," she said, "and there have been cars pulling up to the Station all day. It seems safe to assume that the fourth estate has returned."

Maggie nodded. She was glad to have the business, of course, but the framework of her good fortune left a lot to be desired. "Quinn is staying with me for the time being. J.T. is spending most of his time at the hospital."

Daphne shook her head, her eyes luminous with sympathy. "Keep me posted," she said.

"You do the same," Maggie replied, deciding that Daphne's conversation with Ben regarding the new addition to their family must have gone well. No doubt she and Daphne would have a chance to catch up on things later.

Within a few minutes, Maggie and Quinn were back at the Station being greeted by an exuberant Sadie. The six reporters who had taken up residence in the various guest rooms were gathered at one table, playing cards. Waiting, just as everybody in Springwater was waiting, one way or another.

Quinn went into the office to call J.T., only to join Maggie in the kitchen a few minutes later, looking glum. She'd fed Sadie and was busy putting away groceries, but she went still when she saw the expression on the little boy's face. "I got a recording," he said. "Dad's out of range."

"Hmmm," she said. She was about to place a call herself, to the nurses' station in the ICU, when the phone rang. She answered the cordless unit resting on the end of the counter, employing a cheerful, professional tone, even though her insides seemed to be colliding with one another. The news could be so very good—or so very bad. "Springwater Station," she chimed. "This is Maggie."

"It's Wes," her brother replied, sounding weary but buoyant as well. "I'm a father again. Franny had a boy an hour ago. We're naming him Jacob Reece."

"Oh, Wes," she answered, "that's wonderful. Congratulations."

"Mother and baby are doing fine," Wes added. "Dad, however, is something the worse for wear."

She laughed, her eyes brimming with happy tears. "I'm sure you'll survive."

"I could eat everything in Mom's refrigerator and sleep for a month of Sundays."

"You'll be spending the night with Mom and Dad, then?"

"Yeah," Wes answered. "The kids are there, and the folks are spoiling them rotten." He paused. "What happened, Mags? Mom and Dad are—well—they're presenting a united front all of the sudden, if you know what I mean."

Maggie nodded, even though Wes couldn't see her. "Maybe they're finally realizing how lucky they are to have each other. It's about time."

"Let's hope you're right," Wes replied. "Listen, Sis, I'm going to let you go for now. I just wanted to let you know the baby's finally here, and everything's O.K."

"My love to the kids, and Franny, too, when you see her."

"That wasn't my dad, was it?" Quinn asked, when she'd said good-bye to her brother and hung up.

"No, sweetheart," she answered. She was just reaching for the telephone directory to look up the number for Maple Creek Memorial, when they both heard the front door open, and Sadie began to bark.

Quinn dashed into the main part of the Station, and Maggie knew by his whoop of delight and a strange, elemental quickening in her own senses that J.T. had arrived.

"These guys write for supermarket scandal sheets!" the boy piped, for all to hear, obviously repeating something he'd heard Maggie say earlier.

J.T. chuckled, and Maggie blushed. The reporters were only momentarily distracted from their poker game. No doubt they'd heard worse insults, in better places.

J.T. set his son on his feet and approached Maggie. "Hey," he said. He looked tired enough to fall over.

"Hey," she said in response. She wanted to touch him, but she didn't dare; she was afraid she might cling. So much had happened in such a short time, and she was confused by all of it. She figured J.T. was too, and there was some consolation in that. "How's Billy?"

"A little better," he said. "They're going to operate in the morning, over in Missoula."

Maggie wished the reporters weren't there, that it was just her and J.T. and Quinn. "How about some supper?"

He sighed. "Much as I love your cooking, McCaffrey," he drawled wearily, letting his gaze move over her in a way that engendered a sweet ache in some very private parts of her body, "what I need most right now is about fifteen hours of sleep. I just stopped by to give you an update on Billy and collect the rug rat."

She managed a nod, that was all, for she'd been struck mute by all that she was feeling, blindsided by it. Despite her best intentions, she realized with sudden and poignant clarity, she'd somehow fallen in love with J.T. all over again. The prospect of watching him walk out the door, even for a night, was bleak indeed, but her pride wouldn't let her give voice to what she was feeling. After all, nothing had really changed between them, except that they'd been stupid enough to have sex together, thus taking their nonrelationship to a whole new level of unsuitability.

He reached out to her, his eyes shining as though he'd been reading her thoughts, and curved his fingers under her chin. With the pad of his thumb, he caressed her mouth, setting her ablaze, not just physically, but emotionally and spiritually as well. " 'Night, McCaffrey," he said. "And thanks."

She nodded again, stupidly, not trusting herself to say a word—especially not "good-bye."

J.T. hesitated, and she thought for a moment that he might lean down and kiss her, but in the end, he didn't. With some prompting from his father, Quinn thanked her, and then the two of them were gone.

Quinn had an email message from Annie, complete with a digital photo of her and Brad standing side-by-side in front of a crumbling church in Caracas. He printed the page, with a little guidance from J.T., and tacked it to the wall over his bed. When the boy had eaten, bathed, brushed his teeth, and crawled under the covers, J.T. drew up a chair. Blackie and Winston took their places at the foot of the mattress.

"You're pretty smart, you know that?" J.T. asked, grinning at his son.

Quinn shrugged nonchalantly, though there was a gleam of pride in his eyes at his father's praise. "I'm kinda dumb about some things," he said.

J.T. made a disbelieving face. "Like what? You're six years old and you can read and use a computer. Nothing dumb about that, 'kinda' or otherwise."

Quinn cupped his hands behind his head and his brow crumpled with concentration, a sure sign that he'd moved on, into deeper mental territory. "If I have a bad dream tonight while I'm sleeping, can I get in bed with you?"

"Sure." J.T. arranged the covers under his son's chin. "You been having a lot of those?" he asked casually. "Nightmares, I mean?"

"I get them sometimes," Quinn confided. "Once, I dreamed there was a monster after me. It had a rubber face and two noses. Another time, some space guys took me to Mars and I couldn't get back home no matter what I did."

"Ah," J.T. said, rubbing his chin in a Freudly fashion and nodding. He leaned down, kissed the boy's freckled forehead, then cast a dramatic glance in one direction, then the other. "No monsters around here. No space guys from Mars, either."

Quinn sighed and settled deeper into the pillow. "I'm tired," he said.

"Me, too." It was the understatement of a lifetime, but J.T. was already wondering if he would so much as close his eyes that night, exhausted as he was. Maggie was on his mind, indeed, her image was imprinted on his very cells, as much a part of him as his

DNA. He might wind up staring at the ceiling for hours.

"Would you leave a light on in the hall?" Quinn asked.

J.T. stood, set the chair back in its place at the small desk under the window. "You bet," he said, and left the room.

The house was empty, except for himself and Quinn, as Cindy had gone to Missoula with Billy when he was flown there for surgery. J.T. locked the doors, front and back, and loaded the supper dishes into the dishwasher, finding a certain comfort in the routine. Then he got the coffeemaker ready for morning and wandered into his study to make sure he'd shut down the computer after Quinn went off-line. It was then that his gaze fell on the antique mining documents Maggie had given him at the ball field, and a spark ignited in his mind. He remembered the photograph of his parents and their friends at that long ago picnic, and the curious equipment in the background.

Upstairs, he looked in on Quinn, who was already enjoying the profound slumber of the innocent, then took a shower and crawled into bed. His mind was still on Maggie, so he reached for the mining papers and began to read, hoping to bore himself to sleep. Surely there was no connection between these papers and that old picture, he reflected. After all, a full century lay between one event and the other.

Instead of dozing off, however, he soon found himself sitting straight up, his back against the headboard, his mind clicking along like wheels on a subway track. Sleep was out of the question, and not just because of Maggie. There *was* copper on the Wainwright land, and Scully had agreed to allow Trey Hargreaves's company to do some exploratory mining, with the stipulation that no lasting damage would be done to the land. As far as J.T. knew, no one had ever dug a mine shaft anywhere on the ranch, and he was familiar with virtually every inch of the place. Apparently Scully and Evangeline had changed their mind about the agreement at some point; Hargreaves, being their friend, would undoubtedly have respected their wishes.

He stretched out on his back, trying to relax, and cupped his hands behind his head much the way Quinn had done earlier, when he'd tucked the boy in for the night. He smiled, wishing McCaffrey were there to tuck *him* in, but even with memories of a warm and willing Maggie coming alive in his body, his mind wouldn't let go of the copper. Of the structure in the picture.

It wasn't the possibility of a fortune that intrigued him, however; Billy, Travis, and Randy had been shot on his property, up in the hills, along the old cattle trail. Something stirred in his subconscious, a subliminal splash. There *was* a connection.

Wasn't there?

He switched out the light, closed his eyes, and stared at the back of his eyelids.

Copper. And copper meant money. Lots of money.

Enough to motivate someone to kill? J.T. asked himself. Suppose whoever had murdered Jack Wainwright all those years ago had known about the untapped ore just lying there under the ground waiting to be mined? Who would have profited?

Janeen? No. She'd adored her elder brother; except for J.T. himself, Jack was the only family she had. She would never have done anything to hurt either one of them. Clive, on the other hand, might have thought the place, and the attendant mineral rights, would come down to her, and indirectly to him, if Jack were removed from the equation . . .

Wild speculation on your part, Wainwright, he thought.

Then he threw back the covers, got out of bed, pulled on a pair of jeans, and headed downstairs. He flipped the switch on the coffeepot and headed for the file cabinets in his study.

When dawn came, a few hours later, he'd found nothing pertaining to any mining done on his family's land, but that didn't mean he was ready to put the matter to rest. When Quinn was up and around, and the two of them had wolfed down some breakfast, J.T. loaded the pickup and went out to feed the stock. Quinn and the dogs went along, hindering as much as they helped. When the initial work was done, they got back into the truck and J.T. shifted into four-wheel drive and headed up the old cattle trail.

"Where are we going?" Quinn asked.

"I want to check something out," J.T. answered. After a lot of puzzling, he'd pinpointed the area in the photograph of his parents as kids somewhere near the head of the overgrown track that crossed the northern section of his property. He was nervous about bringing Quinn along, and he'd almost taken him to town to hang out with Maggie for a while, but in the end he'd decided against the idea because he didn't want to communicate his own paranoia to his son. If he started babying Quinn all the time, the kid would respond accordingly—by being helpless and afraid. Not a good idea.

The truck jostled and strained, but it pulled the incline without a problem, and soon they'd reached the place J.T. had in mind, a high meadow framed on three sides by snow-white birches and cottonwoods with leaves that seemed to shimmer in the breeze.

Quinn gazed out over the valley below. The house was visible, as were the remains of the barn and the wreckage that had once been Cindy and Billy's trailer. "Look," he said, pointing. "I can see all the way to town."

Sure enough, Springwater was in plain sight, a collection of tiny houses tucked in among folds of greenery. The view made

J.T. exquisitely aware of his own roots, reaching deep into the Montana soil, holding on. No matter where he'd traveled, no matter what he'd gone through, as a boy and as a man, he'd always belonged right here, in this place, and he always would. The land, the town, and the people were all as much a part of him as the veins channeling blood through his body, and he wanted his son to feel the same powerful connection, to understand and appreciate his heritage.

"Can I have a pony?" Quinn asked. "Landry has one."

J.T. smiled. "That's one I'll have to discuss with your mother," he said. "In the meantime, you can ride with me. Just till you get used to being on horseback."

"You mean sit up on the saddle with you, like a little kid?"

"Yeah," J.T. said. "That's what I mean."

Quinn heaved a sigh. "I guess that's okay."

"Good," J.T. answered, beginning to look around for signs of the structure he'd seen in that old photograph, "because the topic isn't open for debate."

"What's that?" Quinn asked, pointing at something J.T. hadn't noticed before. It resembled a pyramid, standing about waist-high, constructed of field stones.

"Let's have a look," J.T. said, starting off in that direction.

Quinn scampered to keep up.

The rock pile had been undisturbed for a long time, but it was plainly a marker of some kind. Searching the deep grass that surrounded it, they found bits of rotten wood and a few rusty nails. A prickle at the back of J.T.'s neck, familiar from his days as a cop, told him they'd found something. The question was, what?

He pulled the photo from his shirt pocket and studied it, scanned the horizons, and knew the place to be the one where his mother and father and their friends had held that long ago picnic.

"I don't like it here," Quinn said, startling J.T. "I feel like somebody's watching us."

J.T. secretly agreed with that assessment, but he was damned if he'd let himself be spooked on his own land. Still, on instinct, he drew his son against his side. "Let's go," he said, fully intending to come back alone and have a better look around. He couldn't

shake the feeling that he was missing
something. Something important.

Saturday morning brought virtually the
entire community to J.T.'s ranch, along with
truckloads of lumber and almost that much
food. While the younger men immediately
set to work on the new barn, the older ones
laid boards in the grass to make a dance
floor, and then set up folding chairs around
the perimeter. Portable picnic tables
sprouted like mushrooms beneath the trees,
their bright cotton cloths flapping in the
summer wind.

Maggie, arriving with Sadie and a basket
full of fried chicken, surveyed the scene
with pleasure. One side of the barn had
gone up already, and she knew that by
nightfall J.T.'s horses would once again be
sheltered in stalls of their own. Ed Allen, the
neighbor who'd been keeping the animals
since the fire, drove up just after she did,
pulling a horse trailer behind his truck.

J.T., working shirtless in the summer sun,
was a sight to see. Maggie stood by the
Pathfinder for a long moment, Sadie fussing
at her side, just admiring him. Although his
side was scarred where he'd been shot, he

moved without self-consciousness, confident and strong.

"He's definitely hot," Daphne observed, from right beside Maggie, causing her to jump. She hadn't known anyone was close by, but there was her dearest friend, grinning broadly and holding Tiffany in one arm.

"Who?" Maggie asked, blushing.

"You *know* who," Daphne replied. "Your eyes were practically bouncing on springs, you were staring so hard at J.T."

Maggie gave a sheepish smile, glanced around. "Where's Ben?"

It seemed that Daphne's spirits dipped a little when Maggie asked that question, but the impression was so fleeting that she decided she'd only been imagining things. "He had to work," Daphne said.

"He'll be here for supper and the dance, though, right?" Maggie asked, and then wished she'd just left the subject alone.

Daphne looked away, looked back, and shrugged.

Maggie took a step closer. "Daph, is something—?"

Before she could complete the sentence, a horn blared, and she looked up to see her father and mother drive up in the RV. Reece got out on the driver's side, went around and opened the door for Kathleen, who spilled into his arms, laughing like a young girl. She wore an apple green scarf in her hair, and she was soon followed by her dog, Ethel, who was barking with wild happiness.

Daphne watched, shading her eyes and smiling. "Well, now," she said. "It looks like there's a reconciliation afoot."

Maggie laughed, more from joy than humor. "Yes," she agreed. Her father placed some steps on the ground and reached up to help another passenger alight.

"Who in the world is that?" Daphne asked, when an old woman alighted.

"No idea," Maggie said, starting toward the RV.

"This is Abigail," Kathleen told her. "Your father's girlfriend."

Abigail cackled with delight and waved one hand. She was tiny, fragile as a bird, with white hair and age-spotted skin. "I've tried to steal him from you time and again, Kathleen," she said, "but he won't let himself be stolen."

"This is—?" Maggie began.

"Abigail," Kathleen said. "The woman your father has been emailing."

Maggie glanced at her father, then took a step toward Abigail, one hand extended. "I'm glad to meet you," she said, and she certainly meant it.

After that, the day seemed to rush by. Children and dogs chased all over the property, making equal amounts of noise, while the men worked on the barn and the women cooked and served food.

At sunset the band arrived and set up in the back of an old hay wagon, running cords into the house to power their keyboard and electric guitars. Ben appeared at last, driving a company car, and he and Daphne had words, although Maggie didn't hear what they were. Nor did she ask.

When the last board had been nailed into place, everyone took a tour of the new barn. Although the building was only roughed in and would require considerable finishing, it was usable, and J.T.'s horses were led in with fanfare and installed in their proper places.

Maggie was standing with her back to a cottonwood tree, admiring the new structure as the moon rose over its sturdy roof, when J.T. walked over to her. He'd had a shower and put on clean jeans and a crisply pressed white shirt. He smelled of rainwater and sweet grass.

"Every dance is mine," he said.

She was thrilled, though she made an effort to be coy. "Oh, really? Every dance with whom?"

He laughed, caught her chin in his hand, and bent to place a cool, teasing kiss on her mouth. "With you, McCaffrey."

She trembled in spite of herself. "You're awfully confident," she said.

He smiled, but offered no comment. He'd spotted Purvis and Nelly at a nearby table, filling their plates and chatting with other picnickers. Maggie followed his gaze.

"They make a nice couple, don't they?" she asked.

"Yeah," he answered. "Like us."

She didn't know what to say to that.

He ran a fingertip from her chin, along the length of her neck, to the base of her throat. Her breasts, though untouched, responded as if they'd been caressed, and another shiver went through her, a visible one that betrayed her to him. "Going to the Founder's Day parade day after tomorrow?" he asked.

She was relieved at the change of sub-

ject, even though her body was still reacting
to his nearness, his touch, even the timbre
of his voice. "I wouldn't miss it," she said.
"My dad is grand marshal. He's dressing up
as Jacob McCaffrey and driving Al Fen-
wick's covered wagon down Main Street."

J.T. grinned. "Speaking of your dad,
who's the little old lady he's been squiring
around? She's the toast of the pie table, not
to mention the horseshoe tournament."

"Her name is Abigail Tintall," Maggie said.
"She's his Internet buddy."

The band was tuning up, the sun was setting, and kerosene lanterns were winking
on, here and there, gleaming in the dusk.
J.T. drew Maggie into his arms, and began
a slow waltz beneath the branches of the
cottonwood tree. She was excruciatingly
conscious of the heat, hardness, and
strength of his body, a perfect counterpoint
to her own softness. "Ummm," he said
musingly.

"Why are we dancing?" Maggie asked.

J.T. laughed. "Because we're in public,"
he answered.

She smiled, shook her head. Out of the
corner of one eye she saw Quinn running
toward them, trailed by Sadie, who was off

her leash for the evening, as well as Blackie and Winston.

"Hi, Maggie," the boy crowed.

She ruffled his hair. "Hi, Quinn," she answered.

Quinn's attention turned to J.T. "Can Landry spend the night?"

J.T. glanced at Maggie, and a look of rueful mirth lighted his eyes. "Sure," he said, "if it's all right with his parents."

Quinn gave a whoop and rushed off to tell his friend the good news, and then couples began to step out onto the improvised dance floor, swaying in each other's arms, while the band played a cheerful accompaniment. Others lined up at the food tables, talking and piling their paper plates high. Over it all loomed the new barn, sturdy enough to withstand the next hundred years.

J.T. took Maggie's hand, led her through the grass and onto the board platform, and they continued the waltz they'd begun beneath the sparkling cottonwood tree.

The next day, Springwater, Montana, made the national news.

It wasn't because J.T.'s barn had been

torched and then rebuilt, or because Clive Jenson, his throat already slit, had been thrown from the top of the water tower out at the Jupiter and Zeus in a classic case of overkill. It wasn't even because Travis DuPres and Randy Hough were dead of gunshot wounds, and Billy Raynor had been injured so badly that he'd had to be airlifted to Missoula for chest surgery. No, Springwater was the top story on CNN and all the other major networks because Odell Hough, after drinking for more than twenty-four hours straight, loaded his shotgun, climbed into his pickup truck, and set out to avenge the murder of his son.

Both Purvis and J.T. happened to be at the Jupiter and Zeus when he showed up; J.T. wanted to look at the company records going back into the last century, and Purvis had come along out of curiosity. Ben Evanston was explaining that the precomputer-era stuff was stored on microfilm, when the plate-glass window at the front of the office shattered.

Evanston's secretary shrieked in fright, and J.T. tackled her, forcing her to the floor. Ben and Purvis took shelter behind another desk, just a few feet away.

"Son-of-a-bitch," Purvis breathed, in the throbbing silence that followed that first blast. "I left my service revolver in the car."

The secretary began to cry.

"Put down your gun!" J.T. yelled to whoever was outside. It was an automatic response; though he'd been formally deputized, he wasn't armed. He blinked; for a moment, he was back in the warehouse in New York, and Murphy still had a chance.

"You killed my boy!" bellowed an anguished, whiskey-sodden voice, and another round of shotgun fire splintered the back wall of the office. "You dirty—murdering—piece of crap—"

J.T. urged the middle-aged secretary under her desk, held a finger to his lips when he thought she would scream again, and raised his head far enough to catch Purvis's eye. Ben Evanston lay between them, both hands over his head, but J.T. didn't see any blood, so he didn't figure the man had been hit.

"Odell!" Purvis yelled. "What the hell are you doing? Put down that goddamned gun before you hurt somebody!"

J.T. thought about the workers outside,

and hoped they had the good sense to lay low.

Odell's voice was a ragged bellow of grief, and he was reloading. J.T. heard him cock the shotgun. "I got no beef with you, Purvis," he shouted back. "You can come on out, and I won't hurt you, long as you don't try to interfere!"

"You out of your mind, Odell?" Purvis demanded. "You can't just go around shooting up public buildings, endangering life and property. And I'm sure as hell not going to waltz out of here and leave you with that gun in your hands. You're all drunked up. You put the gun down, and we can talk. There's still a chance, Odell. But if you keep up that shooting, I'm going to have to throw you in jail. My reckoning is, you won't get out for a long, long time, if you let things go any further than they already have."

Odell made a sound reminiscent of a wounded bull. "You think I care what happens to me? *My boy's dead!*"

"I know that, Odell," Purvis called reasonably, "and I'm sorry. But your breaking the law like this, maybe hurting somebody, won't bring Randy back. Besides, you've still got your daughter, and a grandbaby on the way—"

"You come out of there!" Odell raged. "I don't want to hurt anybody but Jenson. That's who I came to get, and I ain't leaving until he's as dead as my boy!"

"Jenson?" Purvis echoed. "There's nobody named Jenson here. It's just me and J. T. Wainwright, a lady who works in the office, and Mr. Evanston."

" 'Evanston?' " The name echoed with scorn, with hatred, with unbearable despair. "That ain't Ben Evanston in there."

J.T. stared at Daphne's husband, and in that instant, he knew. The blurry mug shot boiled up from his subconscious mind, crystal clear. Steve Jenson, Clive's son. The convict who had escaped from Washington State Penitentiary over in Walla Walla.

Jenson lifted his head, moved toward one of the desks.

J.T. was on him in a heartbeat, had both the man's arms wrenched behind him before he realized that he didn't have cuffs.

"J.T., what the—?" Purvis began.

"You're right, Odell," J.T. called, struggling with the prisoner. "Damned if you aren't right as rain." He subdued Evanston a second time, but not easily. "Purvis," he rasped, "give me your cuffs."

Purvis unhooked the bracelets from his belt and slid them across the floor to J.T. Within a few seconds, "Ben Evanston" was properly restrained.

"We got him, Odell," Purvis called. "We'll get to the bottom of this—you've got my word on that. Now, damn it, put down that shotgun and let the law take things from here." With that, to J.T.'s furious amazement, the marshal stood, Gary Cooper–style, his hands out from his sides in the time-honored manner of a peacemaker on a mission. "You and me, Odell, we go way back. We've had our problems, I won't pretend we haven't. But until the first of August, I'm still The Man, and I can't let you do this."

"Jesus, Purvis," J.T. spat, *get down!*"

"Odell isn't going to shoot me. Are you, Odell? He's just upset about his boy. Has a right to be, too." Purvis moved slowly toward the front of the office, shattered glass crunching under his feet as he went. "This isn't an easy thing," the marshal went on, without so much as a quaver in his voice. "I won't lie and say you're going to walk away from this without getting into some trouble. But I promise you, Odell, nothing you're facing now will be as bad as doing a lifetime stretch for murder."

J.T. closed his eyes, sure that Purvis was a dead man. The secretary whimpered, crouched beneath her desk, both hands clasped over her ears. "Evanston" was momentarily still, which was not surprising, considering that he was shackled, not just by the handcuffs, but by J.T.'s grip on the back of his collar.

Suddenly, Odell began to sob, and the shotgun clattered to the ground and discharged again. Purvis vaulted through the broken office window with the agility of a man half his age and recovered the gun. "Take it easy," J.T. heard him say gently. "Just take it easy, old buddy. It's all over, and you did the right thing when the chips were down."

J.T. wasn't sure if he agreed that Odell Hough had ever done anything right in his life, but one blessed fact was indisputable. It *was* over. He got to his feet and wrenched Steve Jenson along with him.

*   *   *

Maggie stared at J.T., hardly able to credit what he was saying. Daphne's husband, Ben Evanston, wasn't Ben Evanston at all. He was Steve Jenson. He'd skipped out on his parole after leaving prison, encountered the real Ben somewhere in his travels, killed him, and taken over his identity. He'd married Daphne and taken the job at the Jupiter and Zeus, all under false pretenses. He'd killed Travis and Randy when he thought they were going to sell him out to Billy Raynor, and thus to J.T. and Purvis, and he'd murdered Clive, his own father, for pretty much the same reason. Clive, in on the con game from the first, evidently had started getting greedy at some point, and when Steve had refused to give him a bigger piece of the pie, the older man had threatened to go public. To prevent that, Steve had cut his throat in a cold rage, and then thrown the body off the water tower as a lesson to anyone else who might be thinking about blowing his cover. Charlie, the bartender over at the Brimstone Saloon, had fled right after Jenson's arrest, and the state police were looking for him. According

to Odell, Charlie had been a minor player in
the game, but a player all the same.

"What about the fire? And Billy?" Her
knees gave out; she sank onto a bench at
one of the trestle tables. "I don't understand—"

"It's complicated," J.T. admitted, sitting
astraddle the same bench, facing her and
taking both her hands in his. "Apparently,
Travis and Randy set the fire for the hell of
it. Billy was suspicious and thought he'd
play hero and solve the crime. Instead, he
got himself shot." He paused, reflected for a
long moment. "The rest of it goes way back.
Clive found out there was copper on the
ranch, and at some point he must have
started digging, because I came across the
crude beginnings of a mining operation a
couple of days ago, up in the high meadow.
No doubt old Clive expected to get rich. My
dad would have refused—he didn't want
the land torn up for any amount of money,
anymore than Scully and Evangeline did—
and Clive killed him one day after an argument, probably thinking the land would
come to Janeen. Instead, I inherited everything. He backed off for a while, but when I
came back—"

Maggie swayed slightly, caught herself. "My God. They were going to kill you?"

"At some point, yes," he answered.

She took a while to get past that. "The rustling—Pete Doubletree's poisoned cattle—?"

"All part of the show," J.T. said grimly. "Mostly meant to confuse the issue, though they made some money changing brands on the cattle they'd stolen and selling them to a couple of less than aboveboard meatpackers who, by the way, are chatting with the feds even as we speak."

"Daphne," Maggie whispered, and started to rise again.

J.T. pressed her gently back onto the bench. "Purvis is over there right now, explaining things. Give him a few minutes."

She nodded, feeling numb. "Daphne's life—her marriage—everything was a lie?"

J.T. sighed. "Her marriage, anyway."

"Oh, God."

Just then, J.T.'s cell phone rang. He pulled it out of his pocket and snapped it open. "Wainwright," he said. Then he began to smile. "That is great news. Yes, I'll spread the word. Thanks."

Maggie waited, still in something of a daze.

"Billy came through the operation without a hitch," J.T. told her. "The doctors say he's gaining ground by the minute. They figure he's going to make it."

A sob of relief escaped Maggie's throat; she clasped a hand over her mouth.

J.T. put his arms around her, held her close. "McCaffrey," he said into her hair. "I love you."

She felt as though he'd just touched her with a cattle prod, and leaned back to stare into his face. *"What?"*

"I love you. Not only that, I need you."

She blinked, not trusting her ears.

"Is this the part where you tell me to take a hike?" J.T. asked. The grin lingered in his eyes, and he looked tired to the bone, even a little gaunt. "God, I hope not, McCaffrey. I'm a slow study—it took me a long time to work this out—but I mean it. I love you. I always have."

Her vision blurred, and she sobbed again. Then she flung her arms around his neck and wept in earnest. He held her until the storm of emotion had passed, and then kissed her wet, salty mouth.

"When things calm down around here, McCaffrey—and I know it might be a while before that happens—will you marry me? Will you live on the ranch with me and have our babies?"

"I—"

"I know you'll want to keep the Station open, and we can work that out. Please, McCaffrey? Marry me?"

She started to laugh, even as tears burned her eyes. "Yes," she blurted finally. "Oh, yes."

"And?"

"And I love you, J. T. Wainwright."

He smiled, evidently satisfied, and kissed her again, this time at his leisure.

～ *16* ～

Reece McCaffrey led the Founder's Day parade, which had been put off for a week so that things could simmer down a little, at the reins of an antique covered wagon drawn by two black horses. He looked magnificent in his old-time clothes and black, round-brimmed hat, and Kathleen, perched on the hard wooden seat beside him, made a very good June-bug. Maggie's heart filled as she watched them roll by the Station, waving and smiling to a cheering crowd of townspeople lining either side of the street. In just a few days, they would be loading up the RV and taking to the road.

The high school band followed, playing

"You Are My Sunshine" with enthusiasm, if not grace, and behind them was the marshal, ensconced in the back of a borrowed convertible. Banners hung on either side of the car proclaiming, "Purvis Digg for Sheriff." Nelly, his lady, sat beside him, smiling shyly.

"Think he'll win?" Wes asked, standing beside Maggie. Franny was at Reece and Kathleen's with the kids, taking it easy.

"Yes," Maggie said, and smiled. "I do."

"How's Daphne?"

Maggie looked over at the familiar house across the street. "She's in shock over what happened with Ben," she said. She'd spent much of the past week with her friend, listening when Daphne wanted to talk, but mostly just being there for her. "But she's a strong lady, and she has Tiffany. It'll take time, but she'll be okay."

"The adoption's still in the works, then?"

Maggie nodded. J.T. was riding past, mounted on that glorious paint gelding of his, with Quinn in front of him, waving and beaming. As her gaze connected with J.T.'s, a jolt went through her, and it must have been palpable, because Wes picked up on it right away.

"Something going on between you and J.T.?" he asked, with a smile in his voice.

Maggie didn't look at him. She didn't want to look away from J.T. "What makes you ask that?" she countered.

Wes laughed. "Oh, I don't know," he teased. "Maybe it's the blue sparks in the air, or the way the ground shakes when you look at each other."

She smiled. "We're engaged," she said, in a low voice, "but keep it under your hat. We're not ready to make the announcement."

The amusement lingered in Wes's voice. "Right," he said.

Again, Maggie smiled. J.T. winked at her, and she felt a happy blush climb her cheeks. *Later,* the look in his eyes said, as clearly as if he'd shouted it. When the surrounding crowd cheered and applauded, she realized that the word was out, and the whole town knew she and J.T. were back together, this time for good.

Three months later . . .

"You didn't think I'd miss a chance to be a bridesmaid, did you?" Daphne asked, when

Maggie turned around, clad in the newly altered heirloom wedding dress they'd found
in the storeroom. Outside the sturdy log
walls of the Springwater Station the air was
crisp with the coming of autumn, and the
green wooded hillsides were dappled here
and there with splashes of crimson, rust,
yellow, and gold.

Kathleen, who'd come back from her
travels, along with Reece, to oversee her
only daughter's wedding and spend some
time dandling Wes and Franny's new baby
on her lap, was kneeling on the floor, Maggie's hem in hand, her mouth full of pins.
Cindy had been helping.

Maggie hadn't seen much of Daphne
since Steve Jenson's arrest. It wasn't that
Daphne had withdrawn, because she
hadn't. But she'd had to cooperate with the
authorities seeking to get to the bottom of
the real Ben Evanston's death—not much
progress had been made on that score—
and she'd been besieged by reporters for
weeks. Then there had been endless ses-
sions with lawyers and accountants, ironing
out various legal and financial complica-
tions. Daphne had, of course, never been
married at all, and "Ben" had spent a siz-

able chunk of her money, too, though she was far from destitute. She hadn't closed the mine, since so many people depended on it for their employment, though Maggie knew she'd been sorely tempted.

Now, here she was, thinner, the shadows in her eyes reflecting a season of intense suffering, but tanned and wholly herself. Smiling. She opened her arms, and Maggie embraced her.

"I've missed you so much, Daph."

"And I've missed you." Daphne stepped back to look her friend over again. "Mags, you look merely sensational in that dress."

Maggie admired Daphne's Armani pantsuit, Italian leather boots and bag, and exquisitely crafted gold jewelry. "You don't look so bad yourself," she said.

Daphne smiled. "Thanks, Maggie," she said. A smile lit her eyes. "I just got word. The adoption is going through."

"That's wonderful," Kathleen put in gently. She'd gotten to her feet and put the pins neatly back in their red cushion, and now she approached Daphne and claimed a hug of her own. "You'll make the best mother ever."

"What about you?" Daphne asked. "Are you and Reece staying in town, or hitting the road again?"

"We'll be here until after the holidays," Kathleen said briskly, her green eyes twinkling with well-being and happiness. She'd branched out into painting landscapes in her travels, and seemed to be blooming like a young bride. "There's so much to do, what with Maggie and J.T. getting married tomorrow, and Purvis Digg—he's got this election won already, you know—is tying the knot with Nelly Underwood at Thanksgiving."

Since disarming Odell Hough that day at the Jupiter and Zeus, and thus preventing further carnage, Purvis had been a hero in Springwater and the surrounding county. Although there were still three weeks to go until the actual voting, Purvis was indeed the projected winner. The town council had tried to draft J.T. for the marshal's job, but he'd refused. He was a rancher, he declared, not a cop. A headhunting firm had been hired to find a replacement for Purvis, and they were having a hard time.

"So," Daphne said, "everybody got a happy ending." She paused, blinked.

"Some were just happier than others, that's all."

"Oh, Daph," Maggie whispered.

"It's all right," Daphne insisted. "Together, Tiffany and I make a family. If a knight in shining armor happens to come along someday, even better. But I can be happy on my own, Mags. I *am* happy, because I've got my daughter, and you, and all my beloved friends."

"You've got the whole town of Springwater," Kathleen added. And then they all hugged, and laughed, and cried together.

"You look real spiffy there, Purvis," J.T. remarked, taking in his friend's new black western suit, white shirt, and string tie. He even sported a white boutonniere on his lapel.

Purvis gave J.T.'s rented tux a once-over and smiled. "You don't look half bad yourself," he remarked. The strains of organ music poured in from the sanctuary and, according to Reece McCaffrey, who'd sneaked in earlier to reassure J.T. that Maggie was indeed on the premises, dressed for the occasion in a white dress and veil worn by a great many Springwater brides before her, they were playing to a sold-out house.

"Thanks," J.T. said, straightening his cuffs. Quinn burst in just then, wearing a miniature penguin suit himself, his hair slicked down and his eyes bright. He'd made the choice to stay on in Springwater for the school year, rather than join Annie and Brad in Caracas, and though he missed his mother, the arrangement seemed to be working out.

"You look nervous, Dad," Quinn said. "Are you scared?"

J.T. grinned. "No," he said. "I'm not scared. I've got you to lean on and my old buddy Purvis, here, soon to be sheriff."

"Grandma's out there, too," Quinn announced. "Your mom," he elaborated, at J.T.'s blank expression. "She's got a guy with her. His name is Buck."

J.T. sighed, shook his head. "Great," he said. He hadn't been sure Becky would show up at all, or bring her main squeeze, but it was nice to know she cared enough to make the trip. No doubt McCaffrey was right—again—and he ought to try—yet again—to mend some fences in that quarter.

The minister appeared in the doorway leading into the small sanctuary. "Time to take our places," he said. He was an older man, cheerful and apparently fond of his job.

J.T. followed the reverend out into the church and Quinn, his best man, came to stand beside him. Purvis slipped into a pew beside Nelly, who'd been saving him a place.

The organist cranked up, and Daphne came down the aisle, wearing a simple blue suit and carrying a bouquet of daisies. She winked at J.T. and waited while Cindy Raynor made the same progress, from the back of the church to the front. Her earnest young husband looked on proudly, their baby boy, Sam, bundled in his arms. Billy had made a good recovery, though he was still working only part time, and he and his little family were happy in the small house J.T. had built for them on the ranch. He was the official foreman, and people called him "Mr. Raynor."

Before J.T. was quite prepared, Maggie was there in the doorway, wearing that amazing dress, with Reece standing at her

side. She held her father's arm, drew a deep
breath, visible in the nearly imperceptible
rise of her bodice. The organ played more
loudly, with jubilant good cheer, and then
she was coming toward him, toward their
life together.

Standing there, waiting to make Maggie
his wife, J.T. couldn't help recalling another
wedding ten years before, in the McCaffreys' back yard. He'd thought his life was
over for good that day, that he'd never be
happy again, but here he was. He had a
ranch, a wonderful son, a town full of
friends, and he was about to marry the
woman he loved. *It doesn't get any better
than this,* he thought, but in the next instant,
he knew he was wrong.

Everything would get better, in the hours,
days, weeks, months, and years to come,
and then better still.

He smiled, his heart warm in his chest, as
Maggie reached his side, looked up at him.
"Hey, Wainwright," she whispered, from be-
hind the delicate, gossamer veil.

"Hey, McCaffrey," he whispered back.

"Dearly beloved," began the preacher,
"We are gathered here—"

*   *   *

"We are gathered here—"

The lovely old words echoed in Maggie's heart. Indeed, they were gathered, herself and J.T., their families and friends, and probably a few people who had invited themselves. Everyone was welcome.

Maggie gave her vows when prompted, and J.T. responded with his own. They exchanged rings, and the minister pronounced them man and wife. Then J.T. took Maggie in his arms and kissed her soundly, and the members of the congregation laughed warmly and cheered. Kathleen was crying and beaming, both at once, and Reece looked proud and solemn. Maggie's brothers, Simon and Wes, stood at the back with the other ushers, wearing wide grins.

Arm in arm, J.T. and Maggie, now Mr. and Mrs. Wainwright, came back down the aisle and, outside in the crisp fall afternoon their wedding guests showered them with birdseed and good wishes.

The reception was to be held at the Station, and as the wedding party headed in that direction, in one festive, joyous mass, Maggie marveled that it was possible to be so happy and still live. Surely, she thought, her heart would burst at any moment.

Kathleen, Daphne, Nelly, and Cindy, among others, had decorated the Station with balloons, flowers, and streamers, and a beautiful cake awaited cutting. Gifts were stacked on every surface.

Photos were taken, and the tables had been moved back against the walls so that everyone could dance. It was a dream come true for Maggie, and as she whirled in J.T.'s arms, tears of joy filled her eyes.

"What's this?" J.T. whispered against her temple. "Crying? On our wedding day?"

"I can't help it," Maggie sniffed. "I'm so happy. Everything is so perfect."

He kissed her forehead. "Especially the bride."

"Flatterer."

He laughed, and they went on dancing. "You think I'm trying to seduce you?"

She smiled up at him. "You don't *have* to try, and you know it," she said saucily. "I'm all yours."

"Just wait," he teased, and bent her over in a graceful dip, much to the delight of the onlookers, and kissed her thoroughly before letting her up again.

She was flushed with happiness, grateful to be with that man, in that place, among these dear people. So many had loved and laughed, danced and married, celebrated and mourned in that lovely old landmark of a building, and Maggie was sure they were all there with them now, June-bug and Jacob, Olivia and Will, Scully and Evangeline, and all the rest, sharing in the celebration.

~& Epilogue &~

Maggie clung to J.T.'s hand.

"Breathe," he told her. "Come on, McCaffrey. You can do this."

Maggie had been in labor for several hours, and she'd already given birth to the first of their twins, a boy they planned to call Jack, after J.T.'s father. The other baby was apparently reluctant to make his or her appearance. "That's easy for you to say, Wainwright," she gasped, and then gave a long, anguished cry as her uterus contracted. "You're doing the easy part!"

He chuckled, kissed her forehead, touched her mouth with a cool cloth. "We're going to need another name," he said, to distract her.

Fat chance. She felt as if someone was opening her pelvis with the jaws of life. "This is it, J.T.," she groaned, arching her back. "We stop right here. Three kids is enough for anybody." The fact that they were having twins had come as a surprise, since only one baby had shown up on the sonogram taken weeks before, and the doctors had picked up a single heartbeat.

"Whatever you say, darling," he crooned, and his eyes, warm with love, were dancing. He exchanged a look with the obstetrician standing at the business end of the delivery table, who nodded. "Okay, McCaffrey, one more push."

Maggie pushed, raising her shoulders up off the table and making an animal noise as she strained. She felt the child slip out of her body, heard a tremulous cry, and saw tears of happiness glittering in J.T.'s eyes.

"We have a daughter," he said.

A sound escaped Maggie, part sob, part shout of triumph. She was through, she was empty. She was a mother.

J.T. let his forehead rest on hers. "You did good, McCaffrey," he said.

She slipped her arms around his neck. "Thanks, handsome," she replied, and kissed him.

Nurses, approaching from either side, laid the freshly washed and bundled babies in Maggie's arms, and she looked from one to the other, and then at their father. "They look like you," she said.

He laughed. "Darn good thing," he teased. "What are we going to call our daughter?"

"You're really hung up on that, aren't you?" Maggie asked, grinning. She felt as though she could sleep for a month, and she was still in pain, but she was also gloriously happy. "How about Olivia?"

"I like it," J.T. said. He kissed Olivia's tiny, tender head, and then Jack's, and then looked into Maggie's eyes, not even trying to hide the fact that he was crying. "How soon can we start another one?"

Maggie gave a long-suffering sigh, then glanced pointedly at the clock on the delivery room wall and screwed up her face, calculating.

J.T. laughed. "I love you," he said.

Maggie smiled up at him. "Kiss me, Cowboy."